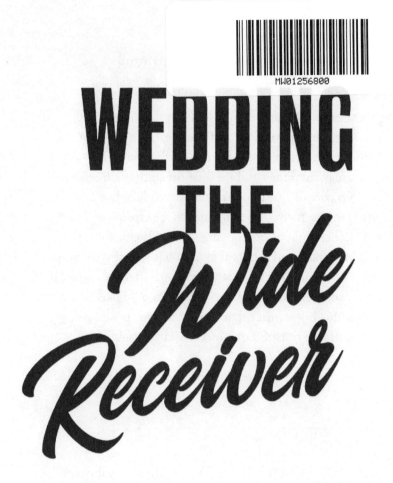

WEDDING
THE
Wide
Receiver

LISA SUZANNE

WEDDING THE WIDE RECEIVER
© LISA SUZANNE 2024

Published in the United States of America by Books by LS, LLC.

ISBN: 978-1-963772-11-1

This book is a work of fiction. Any similarities to real people, living or dead, is purely coincidental. All characters and events in this work are figments of the author's imagination.

Books by Lisa Suzanne

THE NASH BROTHERS
Dating the Defensive Back
Wedding the Wide Receiver

VEGAS ACES
Home Game (Book One)
Long Game (Book Two)
Fair Game (Book Three)
Waiting Game (Book Four)
End Game (Book Five)

VEGAS ACES: THE QUARTERBACK
Traded (Book One)
Tackled (Book Two)
Timeout (Book Three)
Turnover (Book Four)
Touchdown (Book Five)

VEGAS ACES: THE TIGHT END
Tight Spot (Book One)
Tight Hold (Book Two)
Tight Fit (Book Three)
Tight Laced (Book Four)
Tight End (Book Five)

Visit Lisa on Amazon for more titles

Dedication

To the three people I love to build Lego sets with.

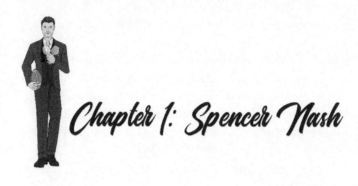

Chapter 1: Spencer Nash

What the Fuck Happened Last Night?

As consciousness plows into me, I'm reminded why I don't drink tequila anymore.

My entire body aches as I try to remember how the hell I even got here, and...nope.

The night is a complete and total blank.

The last thing I remember is tequila. An allergic reaction. Benadryl. Mixing tequila and Benadryl is *never* a good idea.

Never.

I try to remember the last time I got black-out drunk, and just as a vague, faded memory starts to spark in my foggy brain, a voice beside me startles the hell out of me.

Apparently, I'm not alone.

"Oh shit!" the voice says, and the woman darts out of bed and runs for the bathroom, slamming the door.

What the fuck?

Where am I right now?

I open my eyes slowly and glance around. I'm in a hotel room. My hotel room in Las Vegas. I've been staying at the Aria for the last few days.

Why am I here?

My three brothers and my father live here. I'm a frequent visitor. This time I came for my brother's weeklong bachelor party, and apparently last night, the liquor was flowing.

And was that woman running to the bathroom…my ex-fiancée?

I'm honestly not entirely sure, but I don't think it was. Amelia has blonde hair. It's dark in here despite the light trying to get in on each side of the drawn drapes, but I don't think that was blonde hair swirling around the woman who bolted.

And just as I think of Amelia, another realization plows into me.

As far as I know, Amelia's not here in Vegas.

Her sister, however, is.

I freeze as I wonder if that was Gracie Newman running to the bathroom just now.

Oh shit. Did I hook up with my ex's sister last night?

Is that Gracie Newman retching in the bathroom right now?

Should I go help her? Hold her hair back? Do…something?

Wait. Gracie was here to tell me about something. It was a warning. My memory is starting to come back, but the thunder clapping in my head isn't helping me make much sense of anything.

I can't make myself move with the way my head is pounding and my stomach is rolling.

I suck in a deep breath. Did I sleep with her last night?

Fuck. If I did, and I don't remember it—

There's no way the commander-in-briefs could've worked after a night of tequila that resulted in a morning of complete memory loss, but I suppose anything is possible where Grace is concerned.

I raise my hands to rub my face as I sit up against the headboard, and that's when I feel it.

Something hard and metal against my cheek as I rub the haze from my face.

Oh no. Oh God, no.

I slowly pull my hands away from my face, and I practically jump out of bed as I stare at the new golden band encircling my left ring finger.

As my feet plant on the ground, they don't hit the floor. They stop on top of some fabric. It feels...scratchy.

I slowly angle my head down as I spot the billowing layers of white silk and that weird netting shit that turns a regular dress into one of those puffy princess ballgowns.

Jesus Christ.

What the fuck happened last night?

I hear the toilet flush, and a moment later, the bathroom door opens.

I glance up, and my eyes meet those of Grace Newman. She looks even worse than I feel, and she freezes as she sees me standing in...

I glance down.

I'm standing in my birthday suit.

I'm as naked as the day I was born.

Seriously, and I cannot stress this enough: What the fuck happened last night?

I glance around, but no clothes that belong to me are within my reach, though she's wearing one of my T-shirts. I take a step back and bend down to pick up the dress off the floor. I hold it up to cover my entire...*area.*

"Um," she croaks. She clears her throat. "This may be a dumb question, but is that a wedding dress?" She gestures toward the garment I'm holding.

I glance down at the dress. "I, uh—" I clear my throat, too, since it also seems not to be working at the moment. "I think it is." The words come out in a rush as my stomach churns.

"Oh, okay. That may explain the wedding ring on my finger, then," she says. Her voice is a pitch higher than usual as she twists the ring.

"Um, I'm wearing one, too." I shuffle on my feet and draw in a deep breath as I try to remain calm. This has to be a joke. Right?

"Yeah. Uh...this is kind of embarrassing to admit, but I can't remember a thing from last night." She shakes her head as if she's trying to will it back, but it's as blank for me as it appears to be for her. She rolls her shoulders a little. "Can you fill me in on what happened? Did we get married?"

I'm still standing with the dress in my hands, shifting back and forth on my feet as the need to pace takes over, but I'm not wearing any fucking clothes, and what the hell happened last night? Panic rises in my chest, but I'm trying to stay calm. For her. "I'll be honest, Newman," I say, calling her by her last name. "I have absolutely no idea."

"Right," she says, and she twists her lips. She looks like she might cry, and that's just making that rising panic feel even worse as it combines with the hangover.

"Can you, uh…can you turn around for a second?" If we really did get married, it's a dumb request, but last I checked, Grace Newman is nothing more than my friend…and the sister of my ex-fiancée. Or, the last time I was sober, that's all she was, anyway.

"Sure." She turns and puts her hands over her eyes even though it's sort of redundant to turn around *and* cover her eyes.

I rush over to the drawer I set my clothes in when I got to this hotel, and I grab a pair of shorts that I pull on in a hurry. "Okay. I have shorts on."

She turns back around, and her jaw slackens a little. She clears her throat again. "Maybe a shirt, too?"

I glance down, and when I look back up at her, I can't help but ask, "A shirt?"

"Yeah. Those are making me…" She pauses, and she indicates my abdomen. "Uncomfortable."

"Uncomfortable?" I repeat. "We're both wearing wedding rings, and there's a wedding dress on the floor, and *my abs* are making you uncomfortable?" My voice is rising as the panic starts to edge its way in.

She clears her throat. "Don't forget the tuxedo on the bathroom floor."

There's a tuxedo on the bathroom floor?

Oh, Jesus.

I scratch the back of my neck and glance at the top of the dresser, where I see a piece of paper. "Oh, fuck," I mutter as I scan the words on the top of the page. I pick up the paper and realize my hands are trembling.

State of Nevada Marriage Certificate.

Spencer Thomas Nash. Grace Marie Newman.

"What is it?" she asks, and she walks over toward me. I hand her the certificate, and she stares at it for a few beats before her eyes move up to mine. "Is this real?"

I toss my hands up. "I have no idea. It looks like it."

"How did this happen? And why can't either of us remember?" Her voice is louder on the second question.

None of this is helping the hangover. I rub my temples. I can't seem to think straight with the thundering in my head. "I don't know."

She walks over to the bed, sits, and sucks in a few deep breaths. "Okay. Let's go get some coffee, and then we can try to figure it out."

Coffee? I don't know if I can drink coffee at a time like this, but my head is aching for a cup to try to clear the fog of last night. I suck in another deep breath as I try to keep it together.

"Okay, wife," I say. She looks like she might throw again. If we can't laugh, well…I might give in to the panic clawing at me. "Too soon?"

"*Way* too soon. Let's just go get that coffee."

Chapter 2: Grace Newman

Backspace Backspace Backspace

Three and a Half Months Before the Wedding

It's weird, right? Too weird. I can't text Spencer Nash lamenting his team's loss today. I don't even know what to say, but I want to say *something*.

I stare at the text I drafted anyway.

Me: *You'll get them next season. That catch in the middle of the second quarter was unreal. You deserved it. [heart emoji]*

I backspace on the heart emoji.

[smiley face emoji]

Backspace.

[poop emoji]

Definitely not.

[sunshine emoji]

What, like *the sun will come out tomorrow?* No.

I sigh, and then I delete the whole text. This is my sister's boyfriend—fiancé—whatever—and I shouldn't be texting him.

It doesn't matter if my sister and I don't get along, and it doesn't matter that she treats him like shit. He's in a relationship with her.

Still, we're friends. I'm going to be his sister-in-law someday. It's okay for us to communicate without my sister being in the middle of it, and we've gotten to know each other pretty well over the last year or so.

With that in mind, I draft another text.

Me: *You doing okay today?*

I send it before I change my mind again.

I stare at my phone as I will a reply. I wonder what he's doing. Is he with Amelia? She's not here, though it's Sunday, and she's never here on Sundays since she's usually watching Spencer play.

We all watch. The televisions at the bar in the restaurant are all tuned into the channel he's on.

Do I stop and stare at him in his uniform? Of course I do. I have for years—long before he got together with my sister.

Do I play it off like I'm looking at someone else? You're damn right I do.

I slip my phone back into my pocket as I swing by the tasting room at the vineyard where I work. The game is over, but I'm still proudly wearing one of my Vikings tees in support of our local team despite the tough loss. Nana is in here working the room like she always does, and Delilah, our longtime tasting room manager, is here, too.

My phone vibrates in my pocket as I'm saying goodbye to the last guest in the tasting room before we close for the evening, and I nervously fish it out as I hope it's a reply from Spencer.

I can't get this worked up about texting him. He's off-limits. The nerves racing up and down my spine are ridiculous, really, and I probably shouldn't have texted him when Amelia is most certainly still there, but obviously I wasn't really thinking when I sent it. I was too busy focusing on the content to worry about the timing.

I glance at the screen and see it's just Drew, the head of our cellar workers, letting me know the schedule for the week. He's asked me out several times. He's cute, and he's nice, but I'm not really the kind of girl who mixes business with pleasure.

As I'm replying to him, a new text comes through.

This one's from Spencer. I navigate immediately to his text to read it, abandoning my drafted reply to Drew.

Spencer: *I'm okay. It's nice of you to check in on me. It was a tough loss, but we had a great season.*

It sort of leaves the door closed for me to ask anything else, and I stare at it in disappointment as I try to come up with something, *anything*, to say in reply.

But then another one comes through from him.

Spencer: *What about you? Sometimes it's as tough on fans as it is on players.*

Me: *I'm good. Just thinking about you.*

Backspace backspace backspace.

Me: *I'm good. Just wondering what you're up to.*

Backspace backspace backspace.

Me: *I'm fine. Are you coming up to the winery soon? Because I'd love to see you.*

Backspace backspace backspace.

Sigh.

Me: *I'm fine. I've got a tall glass of malbec waiting for you.*

Send.

Spencer: *I will take you up on that.*

I'm smiling at my phone when Amelia walks through the door, and the smile immediately leaves my face as I'm pushed back into reality.

As she passes by me, she smacks my phone out of my hand, and it clatters to the ground. I bend down and snatch it up, glaring at her as I slide it into my pocket and wondering if she really is thirty-one or if she's still eight and pushing me over as I learn to walk.

Same sentiment twenty-three years later, I guess.

"How was your weekend?" I ask, trying as ever to be nice to the girl who seems to hate me for no reason that I can fathom.

"Well, my fiancé's team lost, so how do you think it was?"

He didn't seem to be in the same terrible spirits she's in.

"Tough loss. How did Spencer take it?" I ask.

She sets a hand on her hip and raises a brow at me. "You're awfully interested in him. But he asked *me* to marry him. Just remember that."

I remember, and she wastes exactly zero opportunities when it comes to reminding me of that fact. "Just making sure my future brother-in-law is okay. It wasn't a personal attack on you."

She purses her lips. "He's fine." She sweeps out of the room without another word, and when I look at my phone, I see I have another text from him.

Spencer: *I'll be there Friday. I have a few loose ends to tie up this week, but I'm looking forward to sharing a bottle. [glasses toasting emoji]*

Me: *Can't wait!*

Backspace.

Me: *Looking forward to it, too. [smile emoji]*

Chapter 3: Spencer Nash

Don't Call Me Spencie

Three and a Half Months Before the Wedding

"Wedding's off, and I don't even know if I'm staying in Minnesota." I say the words with zero emotion behind them as I state the facts.

"Wait...what?" my brother asks.

"You heard me. I've got more calls to make." I hang up and get ready to click on the next contact in my family listed alphabetically after Grayson, but Amelia's hand on my arm stops me.

"Please don't do this, Spencer."

I stare at her for a few beats. It feels like I don't even know her anymore. Maybe I never did. I just blindly stayed with her because it became easier to stay than to go. I fell for her, I proposed to her, and I instantly regretted it.

She's been trying to set a date while I keep pushing it further down the road, but this feels like the final straw.

"I have to do this, Amelia."

"Why?" she challenges, setting her hand on her hip.

"Because you tried to set me up and catch me cheating on you when, if you knew me at all, you'd know I'd never do that. I can't be with someone who A, doesn't trust me, and B, would lie to me like that. It's manipulative and cruel."

"I'm sorry, Spencie. You just keep pushing back the wedding, and I hardly ever see you. I had to know that if given the chance, you'd be faithful to me."

She really doesn't see the manipulation in her own actions, and *that* is the real reason why I want to end things with her.

That and the fact that she calls me *Spencie*.

And the fact that we're too different to ever really make this work.

"Look, I trust you. I do. I just got scared when you said you wanted to push the wedding back."

"You know why I said that," I say, my tone incredibly exasperated because I know that somehow she's going to figure out how to cling onto me when I'm just ready to be done.

"I know, baby." She takes a step toward me, but I don't move. We're in her office, and I'm perched at the edge of her desk. She awkwardly stands there waiting for me to pull her into my arms, but I won't do it.

She sighs. "Because you got the feeling you're getting released from your contract, and the future is unknown. And all of that is an emotional and mental drain for us both. Don't act out of a place of fear when it comes to us."

And there it is.

She's right. I think.

We would have made the playoffs if we'd won our last game of the season. Instead, we lost.

I can feel it coming. I'm on the chopping block, and I might be on the next flight out of Minnesota.

And if I am, I have no idea where I might land.

It's sending everything in my life into a complete tailspin, and I'm honestly not sure if breaking up with Amelia is part of that tailspin or if I'm acting out because I'm scared I'm about to lose my career and everything I've worked for over the last seven years.

I get it. This is a business. I'm nothing more than a commodity.

But if my hunch is accurate, it's still a hefty blow to my self-esteem.

I have three years left on my contract, and I haven't decided when I'm hanging it up just yet. By the time my contract expires, I'll be thirty-three. At least ten percent of players in the league have had their thirty-third birthday at this point, and it's not an impossible age to play through.

I turn thirty soon, and I'll admit that's giving me some pause. It's pulsing these feelings in me like *it's time*. I'm not sure what it's time *for*, exactly, though. Getting married? Maybe. It's not a small part of why I proposed to Amelia.

We've had a lot of fun together. She's so different from me in every way. She's impulsive—obviously—and she acts first and apologizes later. She's quirky and wild, and she makes me laugh.

And up until now, I thought I could trust her.

But she has made it clear that I cannot.

There's more to it than that. She's been pressuring me, asking me what I'm waiting for, and I guess there are times I want to be less logical. There are times I want to be impulsive like she is.

So as soon as the idea entered my mind that she was my future, I gave her a ring.

I figured we'd have a long, long, *long* engagement. I thought maybe we'd get married sometime after those three years.

She had different ideas. I'm not sure what the rush is, but it sounds stupid to say that I was hoping for a longer engagement when I gave her a ring. A ring is a promise, one I only plan to make once in my life despite the example set for me by my own parents, and since I made the promise, I intend to keep it.

Or I did, anyway. Until she lied to me.

"Then maybe we're better off just ending things," I say quietly.

She starts to cry, and she *knows* the way to get to me.

It's another reason why I asked her to marry me. Not the crying thing—but the fact that she knows me well, and very few people can say that.

But when she uses it to her advantage, it feels less like knowing me well and more like another manipulation.

"What's better about ending things?" she wails. "I love you, Spencer."

I reach over and put my arm around her in some attempt to console her. "I know, Amelia. But this is a huge betrayal, and it's not one I can just sweep under the rug."

She sniffles, and I force myself to hold strong. She did this to herself, and throwing out the *I love you* in some attempt to smooth things over makes the words feel meaningless to me.

"I'm sorry. I promise I'll never do anything like this again."

I'm quiet while I process how to handle this. I can't be with someone who would stoop so low...but maybe I'm overreacting.

This is a woman who loves me. This is the woman I proposed marriage to. This is the woman I planned to spend the rest of my life loving.

I'm so goddamn confused right now.

"I just need a little time to process all this." With those words, I push to a stand and walk toward the door. I need to get out of this office. I need a little time with my thoughts. I need...exercise.

Exercise always helps me clear my mind.

With my hand on the knob, I say, "I hope you can understand that."

And then I open the door and practically plow right into Amelia's little sister.

Chapter 4: Grace Newman

That Bottle of Malbec

Three and a Half Months Before the Wedding

I'm walking out of my office when the office door next to me opens, and Spencer very nearly mows me down.

"Sorry," he says to my *oof* sound as he walks right by me…just like he always does.

Just like he did the night he met my sister when it was supposed to be me.

Drew's cousin, Blake, is on the offensive line for the same team Spencer plays for, and he was having a party the night we were introduced to Spencer. Blake told him he had a friend he wanted Spencer to meet, and it was me.

But Spencer saw Amelia first.

Everyone *always* sees Amelia first.

We're opposites in almost every way. She's fun and wild and spontaneous. She has platinum blonde hair and bright blue eyes. She wears a lot of makeup and acts with her heart. Her catchphrase is *apologize later*.

As for me? I'm not wild or spontaneous. I'm serious, and I'm a hard worker. I have dark hair and dark eyes, and I don't stand out in a crowd the way she does, and if I had a catchphrase, it would likely be *take responsibility*.

Of course he saw her first.

But he was supposed to see me.

As soon as his eyes landed on her, they never left. And now they're engaged.

Or…they were. Maybe they aren't anymore. There was definitely some arguing, and the walls here aren't that thick. I heard him yelling about how she manipulated him.

I've kept my mouth shut, but the truth is that I've been pushing away my feelings for him since the night he asked Amelia out. We've never dated the same guy. We go for completely different types.

She loves him for his connections, money, and social status.

But he's become my friend over the last year and a half, and I've learned what a truly great guy he is. I've seen the way he gives back to the community. He spent his entire offseason here at my family's winery last summer, and now that another season is coming to a close, I've been looking forward to seeing him here more often than just Mondays and Tuesdays.

Only…I'm not sure if he will be. Not if he and Amelia are done.

I think about following him outside, but I stay put. He seemed like he could use some alone time after their fight.

I know the truth about my sister, but most people are too blinded by her beauty to see it. They chalk up her poor decision-making skills as impulsiveness. They say her wild streak is endearing.

I'm all for spontaneity. A spur-of-the-moment picnic under the stars? That sounds lovely and sweet.

But being reckless and wild isn't always endearing—like the time she found a random group of strangers at the gas station and decided to take a road trip with them, or the time she quit her stable job as a fourth-grade teacher midyear so she could take over the marketing department at our family's winery when she has exactly zero marketing experience but claims she's an expert in graphic design.

We don't get along. We never have. When she was seven, along came a little surprise named Gracie to ruin her whole life.

And if you think that's a joke…it's not. It's a direct quote from seven-year-old Amelia caught on video for posterity.

She hated me from the moment I was born because I took some of the attention from her. She worked hard to get the focus back on her any way she could, negative or not, and that has carried into adulthood. For my part, I try to ignore her. I try to take the high road. Sometimes that's hard.

Our family is close—so close that my dad's best friend is his brother. They both live at the same estate here at the vineyard with my grandmother. Both men are in their sixties as they work together to run this place. All the pieces are in place for Amelia and me to be close like that.

But we're not.

I mostly stay away from her. Or I did, anyway, when she decided she didn't want to work at the family winery. It was perfect when I only had to see her once a week on Sunday evenings for our weekly family dinner.

The winery is a business that has been in the Newman family for three generations. My great-grandfather bought the farm as a wedding gift for my great-grandmother, and since they were just married combined with the fact that their last name is Newman, they named it Newlywed Vineyard and Winery.

My great-grandmother willed it to my grandmother, and she's willing it to either my father or my uncle, though with the name *Newlywed*, I'm not entirely sure.

Neither man has been a newlywed for a long time. Uncle Jimmy never got married. My parents have been divorced since I was ten. My mom and dad are still on good terms, but she's remarried. She comes around on weekends to help out since she fell in love with the winery when they were married.

Dad is quiet and reserved, and he has put his all into the winery. But he's not getting any younger, and I'm not sure how much longer he wants to run this place.

Enter Gracie.

I have the know-how and the drive to take over Newlywed Vineyard and Winery, and it has been my lifelong dream to run this place. I think back my childhood, of hours sitting in the tire swing out behind the original estate dreaming of anything I

could dare to dream about, and that's when it started. I'd watch
Nana sit on the back porch overlooking the fields after a long
day, and I'd see Pop Pop press a glass of wine into her palm.

I couldn't help but think that was what I wanted out of life,
too. To relax on the back porch overlooking our family vineyard
with pride as the man who loves me more than anything in the
world brings me a glass of wine after a long day.

But my current prospects are sort of limited to the people
who work here at the vineyard. I'm the hospitality manager of
Newlywed Vineyard, which means my job includes tasting room
and venue operations. It keeps me busy, and I'm nothing if not
dedicated. When it's a family business and you literally live on
the land, it sort of becomes a lifestyle, and maybe one of my
family members is hurting right now and could use a
sympathetic ear.

That thought is what pushes my feet into motion. I knock on
the door to Amelia's office.

"You okay?" I ask quietly when I see her pacing in front of
the door.

"Get out!" she yells at me, and she slams the door in my face.
Apparently, she's *not* okay. I'm not sure why I bother.

I head down the stairs, through the tasting room, and out the
front door, and I spot Spencer as he rounds the estate toward
the backyard. The firepits aren't going yet, but they'll be on once
it gets dark. People will stand around in the freezing cold with
glasses of wine by the fire. It's romantic even if it's cold, and
then they'll warm up at the restaurant and maybe at whatever
hotel they go to afterward.

I swing by the tasting room to grab a bottle of malbec along
with two glasses. I pop the cork and head out back, and right
now, it's deserted. I set my supplies on the table beside me and
rub my hands together as I wish I would've grabbed my coat.

"You okay?" I ask.

He glances up at the sound of my voice, and when his blue
eyes meet my brown ones, suddenly I don't feel the cold any
longer.

Even though he looks angry and upset, and even though his
eyes are stormy, I still see a warmth in the way he looks at me.

It's comforting. It's kind. It's nothing my sister is, and for the millionth time, I wonder why the hell he's with her.

"What are you doing out here?" he asks. His voice is sullen.

"Checking on you," I admit. "I tried Amelia first, but she yelled at me and slammed the door in my face."

He exhales sharply as he drops into one of the Adirondack chairs by the firepit. "Yeah. We're kind of...fighting."

"Is it okay to admit the walls are thin and I overheard everything?" I ask, clicking a button so the fire roars to life and sliding into the chair beside him.

"Yeah," he mutters.

I hold my hands up toward the fire to grab some heat, and I shiver.

He's not wearing a coat, either, but he's the kind of guy who would offer it if he were. And just as I have the thought, he says, "Do you want my sweater?"

I can't help a small chuckle. "No. I'm okay." I clear my throat. "I'm sorry she did what she did." I pour us each a glass and hand one to him.

He offers a tight smile without looking at me as he accepts the glass. "Thanks."

"Would you like to be alone?"

He lifts a shoulder. "It's nice having you out here." He clinks his glass to mine, and we each take a sip.

Why are you with her?

I want to ask him, but I can't make myself form the words. Maybe I'm afraid of the answer.

He stares at the flames as they crackle and snap in the pit. "She's just...stubborn and persistent, and I thought we sort of balanced each other out. I thought some of my own traits of responsibility and accountability were starting to rub off on her. I guess I was wrong."

I get the sense for the first time that maybe he's with her to give her that balance. He seems like he's the kind of guy who takes care of those around him, who takes on projects to help others. Maybe he's got that white knight syndrome where he thinks he can save her from herself. But what he doesn't realize is he's sacrificing his own emotional well-being by trying to fix hers.

"She's thirty-one now, Spence. You can't teach an old dog new tricks." I push as much sympathy as I can as I deliver those words, but I'm not sure they soften the blow.

"Yeah," he murmurs.

"Do you want to marry her?" I finally ask. I keep my eyes on the fire.

He's quiet a few beats, and I feel him glance at my profile. "I'm not sure."

I exhale the breath I was holding.

He sucks in a breath and changes the subject. "What's new around here?"

I fill him in on the latest news. We finish our first glass, and I pour another while we chat about everything except Amelia.

I've just split what's left in the bottle between our glasses when I say, "Talk to me, Spence. How are you *really* doing?"

He sighs as he takes a sip of his wine. "I'm hanging in there." His eyes are focused on the fire as he takes a beat to think about something, and then he says, "When we lost, I sat down on the bench and looked around the stadium, and I got the strangest feeling like it was going to be the last time I did that."

My brows dip at his admission. "Are you leaving?"

He shakes his head. "I'm not planning to. But the offseason, especially the first two months, is always a wild time where anything can happen. We fell short this year, so Coach is surely going to be mixing things up to try something new next year."

"And you think that falls on you?"

He shakes his head. "Not at all. I've always been of the mindset that players aren't really people in the game. They're commodities. I know my worth, and I know what my team could get for me. I wouldn't be surprised if the front office decided to use that to their advantage, especially since we ended up with a decent draft position."

"And you have no say in that?" I ask.

He takes another sip of wine. "No. I didn't work a no-trade clause into my contract, so they're free to move me how they see fit. I know I'm the highest paid wide receiver on the Vikings.

I know we're receiver heavy, and I know that our offense is turning more to the running game than the passing game. It makes some of us superfluous, and the team is going to want my high salary back in their salary cap."

Fear flitters through me. "You might...you might not play for Minnesota anymore?"

He lifts a shoulder. "I might not play for anybody anymore. I doubt that would happen, but every moment I step out onto that field, I realize there is not a single guarantee that I'll get to do it again."

"But...but...I can't cheer for another team. I just can't do it."

He chuckles. "And you shouldn't. You were raised bleeding purple, and for now, I'm not going anywhere."

"Good," I murmur. I chug a little of my wine as I realize how heavy things just got between us.

"I should go," he says quietly, and he lifts to a stand. "Have a good night."

He heads for my sister's bungalow, and I keep my eyes on the fire as I try to categorize my feelings. I'd only be sad if he left because he's my friend. My hot friend, yes, but still just a friend.

He can't be anything more than that.

Chapter 5: Grace Newman

It's Not, and It Can't Be, But It Feels Like It Is

Three and a Half Months Before the Wedding

The week drags, but Nana mentioned a symposium coming up in Vegas for hospitality in the beverage and restaurant industry. My uncle was going to attend, but they decided to send me instead.

And as it happens, Spencer is in Vegas visiting his brothers since the Vegas Aces—the team two of his brothers play for and the other is the head coach of—have Wild Card weekend off.

Spencer mentioned maybe we could get together while we're in town at the same time, and I know it was just him being friendly since he's going to marry my sister, but that chat we had the other day makes me think maybe he's *not* actually going to marry my sister.

I've spent the last few days making sure everything is lined up so I can attend this symposium. That means I have Heidi, my part-time assistant, on double duty.

Heidi attends a small college not far from here. She's a senior studying communications, and she's organized and smart. She started working with us when she was looking for an internship last year, but she was such an asset that I offered her a position helping on the weekends with weddings. And at this point, she's done so many of them with me that I have full confidence she can easily run one without me there. Between Nana and my dad, they'll be fine.

It does feel good to know that three people are necessary to fill the role I've taken on at the winery. I have a lot of pride in what I do, and I'm working hard to prove to my grandmother that I'm the one who deserves to run this place once my dad retires. He's sixty-three, and I get the feeling he's getting closer and closer to wanting to just enjoy life without the responsibilities here tying him down.

I head toward the airport Thursday morning for my late morning flight, and I land in Vegas three and a half hours later. I take an Uber to my hotel, and on the way there, I text Spencer.

Me: *Just got into town. Waving!*

His reply comes quickly.

Spencer: *Waving back. Do you have dinner plans?*

Me: *No, I don't. I'm on my way to the MGM to check in and get settled and have no plans beyond that.*

Spencer: *Then consider yourself booked. How does Mediterranean sound? There's a place at MGM I want to try.*

I have no idea what Mediterranean is. But if he wants to try a place, and he's asking me, then yes. I am all in…because he's my *friend*. He didn't just ask me on a date, even if it sort of feels like he did.

He didn't.

Me: *Sounds great!*

I don't feel like I packed enough clothes for this.

I check in and get to my room, and I pick through the meager clothes I brought with me. I settle on a pair of black pants and a cute white top with my sneakers since it's a long walk through this hotel. It'll have to do for my not-a-date-sort-of-feels-like-a-date dinner with Spencer.

I head down to the restaurant a little early, and I wander through the casino as I make my way there. The symposium starts early tomorrow morning, but it feels like I could waste a little bit of time having some fun here tonight ahead of the business that starts tomorrow.

28

He's already standing out front when I show up five minutes early. He's ridiculously hot in his black button-down shirt with the long sleeves pushed up a little, and my eyes fall to his forearms. What is it about a man's forearms with the sleeves pushed up that's just…hot?

His arms are strong and powerful since he uses them to catch footballs and lead his team to victory.

He paired his black shirt with dark gray pants, and somehow the effect is casual and sexy at the same time.

I mean…not sexy. I'm not thinking my sister's fiancé is sexy.

His blue eyes flick up to mine, and when he spots me, a small smile plays at his lips. I feel awkward as I approach him. Do we hug? We just saw each other a few days ago, and we're just friends, and when the hell did I get so awkward around him?

"Newman," he greets me as I get a little closer, calling me by just my last name.

"Hey, Nash," I say softly.

He takes a step toward the restaurant just as I take a step closer to give him the hug I want to give him, and I lose the moment. Thankfully he doesn't see me nearly make a fool of myself as I start to reach for him, and I clear my throat and battle away the embarrassment as I follow him toward the host stand. The guy standing by the doorway saw, though, and he's laughing at me.

I shoot him a glare as Spencer gives his name to the hostess. He holds out a hand for me to go first, and I feel his hand on my lower back to guide me into position as the line leader just behind our hostess.

His hand. My back.

I know it's nothing. It means nothing. It's just a gentlemanly thing some guys do, and he was just offering to let me walk first.

If he's engaged to my sister, then there's no way he'd ever have any sort of interest in me. And not just because he's a stand-up kind of guy who would never cheat on a woman—but because if she's the type of woman he proposed to, then I'm the type of woman he could never fall for. We're just too different.

I remind myself of that fact. I force myself to acknowledge it. He's just being kind. I'm the girl who didn't have any dinner plans, and he's the guy who stepped in to make sure I wouldn't have to eat alone in my hotel room.

We both peruse the menu, and even though it's quiet at our table, it doesn't feel awkward.

"Want to split a bottle of the red?" he asks.

I nod. "What are you ordering?" I'm not really a charred octopus kind of person, but I've also never tried it.

"The salmon, I think. You?"

"I was looking at the chicken kebabs."

"Can I try yours?" he asks.

"Only if I can try yours."

He chuckles. "Of course."

We place our orders, and after we hand our menus over, I ask, "So where do you stay when you come to town?"

"Usually with my brother Lincoln, and sometimes with my brother Grayson. Sometimes I get a hotel. It depends what everyone has going on," he says.

"Not your dad?" I ask.

He shakes his head. "Dad and my youngest brother, Asher, are in a two-bedroom place, and I'd have to sleep on the couch. And Dad and Asher can be…a lot sometimes."

"Are you with Lincoln this trip?" I ask.

He shakes his head. "I'm staying at the Aria."

Our server brings our bottle of wine and pours us each a glass, and we clink glasses without a toast.

"Do you gamble?" I ask after I take a sip.

"Sometimes. I like blackjack. It's one of the few games there's an actual strategy to. Have you ever been to Vegas?" he asks. I shake my head, and his brows rise. "You haven't?"

"Nope. How many times have you been here?" I ask.

"Oh, I have no idea. Dozens. Between playing here against the Aces and visiting family now that they're here, plus the occasional trip for fun before they moved here." He shrugs.

"What is there to do in Vegas? I always hear how great it is, but I've never gotten to experience it for myself." I'm not sure why I ask. It's not like he's going to take me on a tour of the town.

"Depends what you're into. Nightlife, shows, food, gambling." He shrugs. "I can take you on a mini tour while you're here, if you want."

"Are you a nightlife kind of guy?" I ask—mostly teasingly.

"I can bust a move on the dance floor if that's what you're asking. After a few drinks, anyway."

I laugh and hold up my glass of wine. "Then get to drinking, my friend."

He chuckles, but he does take a sip of his wine, and is he really going to take me to a Vegas nightclub tonight?

Apparently, the answer to that is yes.

We finish our meals—and our bottle—and as the bottle empties, the laughter and conversation at our table gets louder and more boisterous. The awkwardness feels like it's stripped away as I let go of all the inner turmoil and just enjoy a meal with the man sitting across from me.

And once we've paid and the bottle is empty, he leads me through the casino and stops at a blackjack table.

"I thought you were taking me to a nightclub," I say, narrowing my eyes at him as he pulls out a chair and motions for me to sit.

He laughs. "It's only nine. The club doesn't even open for another ninety minutes." He takes the chair beside me and tosses some money onto the table, and I follow suit.

The dealer pushes some chips toward us, and Spencer stacks four and puts them on a little spot in front of him.

I do the same as I lean in toward him. "How much is each chip?"

"Five bucks. So you're betting twenty on this hand."

I nod, and I wait for the dealer to shell out our cards as I try not to think about what I could spend twenty dollars on. I'm not hurting for money, exactly, but I'm also not used to blowing it like this. I get what I need when I need it, and I don't have a ton of expenses since I live at the vineyard.

I'm dealt a seven, and Spencer gets a queen. My next card is a ten, and Spencer gets a nine.

The dealer busts with a twenty-three, so we both win.

I rake in my winnings, feeling pretty damn good but also thinking I should cash in and keep my extra twenty dollars.

We both win some then lose some, and the next hour flies by as a server brings us wine, and I find myself passing the threshold of tipsy land.

I cash in when I'm back to even, and I stand behind Spencer and watch him as he starts to win. He high-fives me with each win, and when he triples his original investment, he calls it quits. We head toward the cashier to trade in our chips for cash, and then we head toward the nightclub.

"That was fun," I say as we walk, and then, because I'm me, I trip on absolutely nothing at all, and Spencer moves quickly to catch me.

I find myself holding onto his arms, my chest heaving as he clutches me. Our eyes meet, and a heated moment passes between us.

"You okay?" he asks.

I nod as I straighten and step back out of his arms despite every single urge telling me to stay right there, to move in closer, to cling to him. "I'm fine. Just a klutz." I offer an embarrassed smile as we keep walking.

"No, you aren't," he says softly, his tone slightly defensive of me for insulting myself.

We arrive outside the nightclub, which has a line of people waiting to get in wrapped around the corner, and I start walking toward the back of the line.

"Where are you going?" Spencer asks me.

"To get in line." I say it almost like a question, and he chuckles.

"No need for that." He walks up to the bouncer and says something, and the bouncer nods and pulls aside a rope for the two of us to walk right in.

"Who even are you?" I wonder as we head into the loud club.

"Spencer Nash. NFL superstar. Nightclubber extraordinaire." He grins, and he detours toward the bar. Once the bartender hands over his beer and my vodka soda, I let go of my own self-consciousness as Spencer leans in closer to me. "Want to dance?"

I nod, and he leads me to the dance floor, where bodies all around us are grinding. We stand out as we sway to the music, bouncing together with a respectable distance between us since we're just friends, but there's a lot of people out here. Someone bumps into me, sending me directly into Spencer's chest.

His hard, solid chest.

Lucky for me, Spencer is recognized as the person who bumped me turns around to apologize, and thus begins the frenzy of people wanting selfies with the popular football player.

I'm sort of edged out of the way all together, and I step back awkwardly to let him have his moment. I'll just stand back here and drink my vodka as I wait for the crowd to disperse.

Maybe he's more like Amelia than I thought. Maybe he likes this attention.

And as soon as I have the thought, I hear a voice close to my ear. "Have you had enough?"

I glance over at him, and he's looking at me in earnest, like he's ready to get the hell out of here.

"Let's go."

He grins, grabs my hand, and navigates through the crushing crowd of people. He drops my hand once we're out of the club, and I push away the thought that I sort of wanted him to hold onto mine for another minute.

I also push away the feelings of guilt that slide right in beside it.

Chapter 6: Spencer Nash

The Only Constant in the Turbulence

Three and a Half Months Before the Wedding

I sit in my car and stare out the windshield at the practice facility.

Or, I guess…my *former* practice facility.

The place that's been home for the last seven years.

Seven seasons.

The *only* home I've had during my tenure as a professional football player.

The news hasn't quite sunk in yet, but that feeling I got at the end of our last game of the season was right on the money.

It was my last home game at that stadium.

Coach just said the dreaded words nobody in the prime of their career on a team they love wants to hear. "We've decided to release you."

Coach was everything he needed to be. Supportive, sympathetic, sorry.

But the three *S* words don't keep me on the team.

He told me they wouldn't make the information public for another few weeks. It'll give me time to digest it before it's public.

A mix of emotions plows into me, but disbelief seems to grab hold of the reins the tightest.

It'll sink in later. Tomorrow, or the next day, or…

In April, when voluntary minicamp starts, and I have to report to work on a new team—if anybody picks me up since I'm a free agent now.

Fuck. Fuck!

It feels like my carefully planned life is falling apart. Like I can't control anything at all anymore.

I thought I could. I thought I had my path all figured out. I'd play three more years an hour away from the woman I planned to marry. I'd retire to the vineyard.

Everything feels like it's been thrown into a tailspin lately, and not just because of this news. The feelings for my fiancée have shifted to be less than positive. The little voice in the back of my head keeps asking me why I'm with her at all.

Because it was part of the fucking plan, and it feels like it's the only part of the plan I can still safely hold onto. We're so different, and that just seems to become more and more evident to me the longer I'm with her. But as soon as I'm convinced I should just end it, she manages to put it off or find a way to convince me to stay with her.

And now…she feels like the only constant in all this turbulence.

So do I end it with her and start completely fresh when I find my new team? Or do I hold onto the one constant that I've had over the last two years?

I'm very much a creature of routine, and this is throwing it all out of whack for me. But maybe that's what I needed. I got stuck, and this change that's being forced upon me is forcing me out of my comfort zone toward something different.

I've never been a big believer in the fate of everything happening for a reason. My logical brain strives to find the cause-and-effect relationship in every aspect of life, and I get it. Getting rid of me opens up a hell of a lot of money to pay someone else. But maybe fate is at work here, too.

And right now, fate is telling me to let Amelia go and to move on with my life.

I'm not looking forward to the conversation, but it needs to happen.

Now.

I shift my sleek black Audi into drive and head toward my soon-to-be ex-fiancée's house. I pull onto the street leading there, but the vineyard is a huge complex comprised of over eighty acres. There's the mansion with the offices, tasting room, restaurant, and gift shop. There's the wedding venue, the production facility, the barn, the original estate where Amelia's grandmother, dad, and uncle— Maggie, Steve, and Jimmy—live, and five three-bedroom bungalows near the office, one of which Amelia lives in.

Even though it's January, it's still busy at the vineyard. The close proximity a little over an hour southwest of Minneapolis means lots of tourists during football season, and the production staff is hard at work aging wines in barrels while the winery hosts various events and prepares for the upcoming busy season.

Aside from the wine, though, what really made this place famous is the wedding venue, the Grand Hall and Gardens. Brides find the name to be good luck, and the old wives' tale that couples married at this venue have never gotten divorced seems to have spread far and wide.

And it's true, by the way.

Maggie and Steve Senior were married here, and they were married until Amelia's grandfather passed away eleven years ago. Maggie's parents were together until death, too.

Amelia and Grace's parents were not married here, and now they're divorced.

Amelia wants to have the wedding here sometime this year despite my wishes to wait a few years. Grace said the venue is booked solid—thankfully. Amelia reserved the first opening, which isn't until November of next year—nearly two full years away.

I think we can go ahead and cancel that.

Or, that's my plan anyway. Until I park behind her bungalow, get out of the car, knock on the door, and find my would-be future bride wearing a white bridal gown as she opens the door.

LISA SUZANNE

A sharp puff of air escapes my mouth.

She looks beautiful—there's no denying that.

I can't let this throw me off course.

"Oh, Spencer! I didn't know you were coming!" She rushes out of the room and returns a beat later with a blanket wrapped around her. "It's bad luck to see the bride in the dress!"

"Is, uh…is that the dress?" I ask.

She nods as her eyes move up to mine. "It's one I'm thinking about. But now you've seen it, so I'll have to pick another one."

I press my lips together. Why is she wearing a bridal gown at five o'clock on a Friday? This is one of the busiest times at the tasting room. Shouldn't she be working?

I don't ask.

"I'll, uh…give you a minute to change."

I walk around Amelia's place and across the road toward the tasting room.

The first person I see is Grace. She's leaning over the counter as she talks to Maggie, who's serving the samples from behind the counter this evening on one side while Delilah serves the other side. She's laughing at something Maggie just said along with the customer Maggie is serving, and that's not unusual. The woman is always saying *something* totally inappropriate, and it's part of her charm. Hell, it's part of the charm of this entire place. She's really built an empire here, and I know what it means to her entire family.

But none of us know what her intentions are with this place once she can no longer run it. She *hasn't* been running it for years. From what I understand, she's not ready to give it up even though Steve is the president and has been the head winemaker for at least a dozen years.

Amelia has expressed her interest in wanting to be the next president, and I think it was part of her motivation in quitting her teaching job. She wanted to prove she belonged here.

But from everything I've witnessed over the course of our relationship, I can't help but feel like the only reason she's interested in it at all is because her sister is.

I've never once seen Amelia interacting in the tasting room with customers the way Grace is. I've never seen Amelia hop in

38

to help at the restaurant when someone called in sick. I've never seen Amelia fire up a tractor. I don't even think she knows where they keep the keys, to be honest. But I've seen Grace do all those things.

She glances over at me as if she can feel my eyes on her, and her smile broadens as she straightens to a stand and walks over to me. She gives me a hug that feels warm and welcoming.

"Hey," she says softly.

I clear my throat as I take a step back, pulling out of the hug early. "Hey."

"Glass of malbec?" she asks.

I glance over at the customer, who's looking curiously at me. He definitely recognizes me, so I offer a smile and a nod of my head.

"I'd love it—maybe after seven."

She chuckles as I name the time the doors close in just a half hour from now. "I'll be here. And I can snag us a flatbread from Pete."

"Deal." I grin at her. She knows I can't resist Pete's flatbread.

"Get over here, boy," Maggie says, and I round the corner of the counter to give her a hug.

"I missed you, Maggie."

"Right back at you, Spencer." She slaps my ass in a way only a woman in her eighties would be able to get away with, and I chuckle.

The customer snaps his fingers. "I knew it. Spencer Nash. Helluva loss." He shakes his head as he laments what could have been had we not lost our last game of the season.

"Don't I know it," I mutter.

"Next year," he says, and he's friendly enough. You never really know what you're going to get with football fans who recognize you. I'm glad this one isn't the harassing kind.

But his words plow into me.

If it *is* next year for me, it won't be here in Minnesota.

Coach's words still haven't quite hit me.

"And he'll sign any bottle you buy," Maggie promises.

I narrow my eyes at her. "She does this to me every time I come in."

"He's going to be my grandson-in-law," she says proudly.

"Oh? You two?" the woman with the fan asks, and she points between Grace and me.

"Oh, no! No, no," Grace says, and she flushes as if she's flustered by the insinuation. "He's engaged to my sister."

I chuckle as I watch her stammer. I haven't told Amelia. I haven't told Grace.

I've thought a lot about retirement and what comes next after the game. I've always wanted to have the next phase of my life planned when I finally do hang it up, and now that I'm a free agent, something that still hasn't quite settled in, maybe I should hang it up *now*.

But what's waiting for me?

A woman I don't want to marry wearing my engagement ring?

Statistical analysis was the first thing that came to mind. It would keep me connected to the game beyond playing.

But I'm starting to feel like I don't *want* to be connected to the game beyond playing. And that feeling first started the moment I stepped foot on the grounds of Newlywed Vineyard and Winery.

This place feels like home, and home is hard to come by these days. I grew up in New York, and that always felt like home. The college years took me to Indiana, where I attended Notre Dame, and then I was drafted by the Vikings in the first round. I've only played here, and while this has become my home over the last seven years, the apartment I've rented the entire time I've been here has never really felt all that homey. I've thought about buying a place, but the fear of being traded or released kept me from settling into permanence.

As I fell in love with Amelia, I also fell in love with the charm of Maggie's estate, with the walking paths around the winery, with quiet serenity behind the Grand Hall overlooking the lake...hell, even with the process of winemaking, not to mention the fantastic wines made here.

I glance at the counter where Grace is already sitting waiting for me, and I slide onto the stool beside her.

"Cheers to the offseason," Grace says, lifting her glass in the air.

I clink my glass against hers. "Cheers."

We each take a healthy sip, and I set my glass down, gesturing to the flatbread for her to take the first piece. She digs in.

"What are your plans for your time off?" she asks.

"Well, your dad asked me for my opinion on the business reports here at the winery, so I'll work on that a bit." I think it's his way of involving his future son-in-law in the family business, which is fine. I like Steve, and I'm happy to help with an area where I have some knowledge. "I'm heading to New York to see my mom on her goat farm tomorrow. My brother's getting married in a couple months and having a huge blowout weeklong party there, so I'll be in Vegas for that. Otherwise…" I shrug as I trail off.

"Goat farm?" she asks, backtracking a bit.

I chuckle. "She always had this dream of owning a farm with goats, and she makes soaps and lotions and stuff out of their milk."

"That sounds fun."

I nod. "It is. And seeing my mom is always great. How have things been here?"

She shrugs. "The usual. What about you? What's new?" It's like she has this sixth sense that something's up with me despite my best efforts to hide it.

I blow out a breath.

"Whoa. That sounds serious."

My phone starts to ring, and I glance at my watch. It's my agent.

I send him to voicemail. He wants to talk about the release, but I don't want to talk about it with him in front of Grace.

"It is," I admit.

"Is everything okay?"

I glance up at her, and her eyes are wide with concern for me. She's being a good friend. A good future sister-in-law.

"I'm being released from the Vikings."

She gasps, and she reaches a hand over to cover mine with hers. "Oh, God, Spencer."

"Don't say anything to anyone yet, okay? I just found out today, and I haven't told Amelia yet."

"Of course," she murmurs. "Why, though? I'm sorry. Is that insensitive to ask? You had amazing stats this season. You're the strongest receiver on the team."

I nod and press my lips together. "Doesn't matter when we ended up with a losing record. I'm the highest-paid receiver, so they got rid of me to clear that money for the salary cap. They're restructuring, and I'm not part of that."

"You say it so…matter of fact. But how are you feeling about it?" she asks.

I lift a shoulder, and I can't ignore the fact that not only is this woman asking me about how I'm feeling about this news, she actually cares. She's making it about *me*. And that's precisely the reason why I haven't told Amelia about it yet. She'll make it about *her* when it's just not about her.

"I'm disappointed. I'm nervous about what's next. You know me. I like my routine, and the unknown is a little scary." Not to mention, I'm the first in my family to be *released* from a contract. The fucking embarrassment and hit to my ego aside, I can't wait to face my father's disappointment in me.

"A little?" she presses.

"Terrifying," I admit.

She sighs. "I'm so, so sorry. What can I do?"

"Nothing." I glance at the bottle, and she takes the hint of my unsaid request.

She pours more into my glass. "What are *you* going to do?"

"I have no idea. I'm a little overwhelmed at the moment," I admit.

"You want my honest opinion?" she asks.

"I wouldn't have brought it up if I didn't."

She sucks in a breath, and before she gets the chance to speak her mind, we both hear the door open.

Amelia prances into the room. "There you are! I have a new crime documentary all queued up for us. Are you almost done in here?"

I take another bite of flatbread. "Not quite."

"Okay. I can wait." She offers a smile and plops down on the stool on the other side of me, effectively ending my conversation with my soon-to-be ex-fiancée's sister.

Chapter 7: Grace Newman

Did They Do It On My Desk

Three and a Half Months Before the Wedding

It's another Saturday at the winery, which is our busiest day of the week, so I head to the Grand Hall first thing in the morning. The cleaning crew and Heidi are there making sure everything is in tip-top shape for today's wedding.

When I head toward the office, Amelia is in the tasting room chatting with Nana, and she seems to be in fine spirits, which makes me think Spencer didn't make his confession to her yet.

I unlock my office door, and something in here feels...off. It's a weird vibe or something.

And my laptop isn't where I left it. I always keep it in the exact same spot on my desk, but it's a few inches to the right. I notice it when I sit down to start typing and my fingers are on all the wrong keys.

I'm sure I just shifted it a little bit when I left yesterday, though I'm pretty careful not to do that.

I also notice a few other strange things. They're small things nobody else would ever notice, but this is my office. It's my home, really. And when things are off, I know.

My pencil cup is missing a pencil. The pad of paper I keep at exactly the right place to take notes is on the left side of my desk. I'm right-handed.

Someone was in here, and I intend to find out who...and why.

I have records in here for the employees who work in the tasting room and the Grand Hall, and while I keep them locked up, if someone wanted to get in badly enough, they'd be able to.

But why would someone want to see the employee records? Why would someone come in here at all?

It doesn't make any sense.

My dad installed a security system a few years ago, and he trained me on how to navigate through the footage. I left last night after wine and flatbread with Spencer a little after eight o'clock.

I pull up the footage from just outside my office to see who might've come in after eight.

There's nothing.

I fast forward to nine.

Ten.

Still nothing.

But just after midnight, I see it.

Amelia with her arm hooked through Drew's as she walks toward my office. He stops her partway to my office and pushes her up against the wall. His mouth crashes down to hers.

Amelia and *Drew?*

What in the *hell* am I looking at right now?

I gasp as I keep watching. They share a steamy, passionate kiss against the wall, and then he pushes her into my door.

Oh, God.

Did they come in here and *do it* on my desk?

Amelia uses her keys to unlock my door, and sure enough, they come in here. I don't have a camera in here. She doesn't have one in her office, either.

But she was in here, maybe having sex right here.

I reach into my bottom desk drawer and pull out the Clorox wipes. It's all I can think to do in the moment as my chest aches.

Why would she do this to Spencer?

He's such a good, kind person. He's smart and sensitive. He's strong and athletic. He's logical and responsible. He deserves better.

If I run to him with this news, it'll be a betrayal to my family.

Why is she with Spencer if she'd rather be with Drew? What am I supposed to do with this information?

Drew is…well, he's Drew. He lives here at the vineyard in the second bungalow—next door to Amelia in the first—while I'm down in number five. He's good at his job, and he's cute enough, I guess, but he isn't personable the way Spencer is. He doesn't go out of his way to chat with our guests in the tasting room even though he's well-versed in everything that happens here at the vineyard.

And now he's sleeping with my sister. Or, at the very least, he's kissing her and humping her against my office door.

My stomach turns over.

I have to deal with today's wedding. I don't have time to confront my sister with this information, and I'm not entirely sure I want to. I'm not sure I want to know *why* she's doing this.

What will she think when Spencer admits to her that he was released?

He's still got money. He has a business degree, and from what I know about him, he's incredibly smart with money.

He needs to know what she's doing, but I intend to figure out why she's doing it first.

With that in mind, I take care of my tasks at the Grand Hall, and then I head toward the production facility where I know I'll find my dad.

I walk into his office and close the door.

"Closing the door? Must be serious," he says.

"I think we should tighten up security around here a bit. I think we need cameras in each of the offices in the mansion."

His brows crinkle. "May I ask why?"

"I just feel like it's an added measure of security to have some cameras around."

47

He nods. "You got it, kiddo. I'll have them installed Monday, say…five a.m.? Nobody should be around yet, so nobody will have to know."

"You know when I say you're the best, I mean it, right?"

"Hey, Gracie. If you ask me for something, I trust that you have all the right intentions in mind."

"I love you, Daddy." I walk around the desk, and he stands to give me a hug.

"I love you, too, Gigi," he says, using the nickname he gave me when I was just a kid as he pulls me into his arms. It started as G since that's the first letter of my first name and evolved into Gigi, and it's even sometimes Gigi-bear or Gigi-bug.

And Gigi-bear is ready to figure out what the hell is going on.

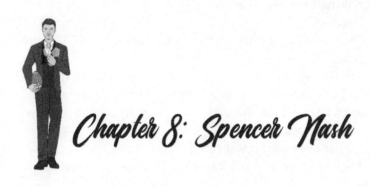

Chapter 8: Spencer Nash

We Need to Talk

Three Months Before the Wedding

I head up to the offices, and Amelia isn't in hers. But Grace is in the one next door.

"Goat soap," I say, plopping a small tote bag onto her desk before I take a seat in the chair opposite her. "My mom makes it, and I helped her with everything you've got in there while I was in New York, so enjoy my hard labor."

"Thanks," she says, giggling as she peeks inside the bag. "It's nice to see you back here."

"You, too. What did I miss?" I ask.

She shakes her head as she sets the bag aside and leans back in her desk chair. She clears her throat. "We've been bracing for the cold weather to end so we can head into our busy season. How was New York, aside from the goat work?"

I chuckle. "It was good. I haven't spent that much time with my mom in…" I trail off then shrug. "Years. I caught up with some old buddies still in town, and being on the farm was more relaxing than I was expecting." And long talks with my mom where I figured out a few things about what I really want out of life were pretty damn good, too.

Before I left, I told Amelia I needed some space. She left me alone, and not hearing from her for ten whole days told me everything I needed to know.

I'm done.

"Any word yet on what's next for you?" she asks, lowering her voice.

I shake my head. "I've had a few people reach out. I've been invited to tour some facilities. I'm letting my agent field the calls, and he told me the Vikings are making it official by the end of this week."

"Where would you want to go?"

I twist my lips as I think it over. "I've always loved San Diego."

"The Storm?" she guesses, naming the pro football team there.

I nod. "I've heard great things about the organization. They're rebuilding, and they need a new WR."

"Like Spencer Nash?" she guesses.

I shrug. "We'll see."

"Ugh! There you are!" A voice at the doorway interrupts us, and I blow out a breath as the tornado otherwise known as my fiancée steps foot into Grace's office. "You just got back, and you're already in here?"

"You weren't in your office, and I brought some gifts," I say calmly to the whirlwind at the door as I hold up the bag of soaps I brought for her, too.

She folds her arms as she glares at me. "Well, I'm here now if you'd like to talk."

"Sure," I say, and I raise my brows at Grace before I follow her out to her office. I hope Grace caught the secret message I was trying to toss her direction that I'm here to end things with Amelia.

Ten days with my mom were enough for me to realize the truth.

Marrying Amelia isn't the right thing for me.

As much as I want a future at the vineyard, it can't be at the expense of my own happiness.

Figuring out where I'm playing next season is the next step.

There's really nothing like ten days with Mom to help put shit into perspective, and petting goats while we talked seemed to be exactly what I needed.

I follow Amelia into her office and shut the door behind me.

"Ooh, baby. Are you closing the door because you want to get frisky after so much time apart?" she asks, and she slides her hands up my chest to my shoulders as she moves in close.

I shake my head. "No, Amelia." I take a step back and walk over to the ugly green couch in her office. I sit, and nod for her to come sit beside me. "We need to talk."

"Ten days away, and you barely talked to me, but *now* you're ready?" She sighs and folds her arms across her chest. "What is it now?"

"Can you please come sit?" I ask.

She purses her lips and stands firmly where she is.

"The Vikings released me from my contract," I say quietly.

She gasps. "They *what?*"

"They released me."

"When?" she asks through a clenched jaw.

"Before I went to New York."

"And you didn't bother to tell me?" she demands.

"I needed to deal with the reality of it myself first."

"You didn't think to share that with the woman you're going to marry?" she asks.

I shake my head. "No. Because I can't marry you, Amelia." My chest thunders as the words fall from my lips.

"Excuse me? Then what is this?" she asks, holding up her left hand and pointing to the ring I gave her.

A mistake?

I don't say that.

"I fell in love with you, and it was a whirlwind. But things changed when I gave you that ring, and I realized we rushed into things."

She turned into someone else. She went from the girl courting the football player to being very comfortable in our relationship, and I think *this* is the woman I'm set to marry—not the one who worked so hard to pursue me.

And I don't like this version of her. I can't spend forever with this woman—with someone who lies and manipulates.

Some guys in the league have reputations. But that's not me. It's *never* been me. I'm not really into long-term relationships, either. Amelia has been my longest. Instead, I just put the focus on football and kind of left it there.

"Rushed into things? We dated for a year before you asked me to marry you!" she protests.

"Right. Six months of which I was focused on the season rather than on our relationship. I'm sorry. I made a mistake when I asked you to marry me." I realize I'm not being clear enough. I don't want to be with her at all anymore. "I'm ending this relationship."

She gasps as her hands fly to her mouth, and then she rushes over to sit beside me on the couch like I asked her to do a few minutes ago. She takes my hand between hers. "Spencer, no! You can't do that to me! To us! I love you!"

"I know, Amelia. But this isn't working for me anymore."

"You're just overwhelmed because of the release. Your future is unsure, and I get it. Don't do this. Don't rush into this kind of decision," she begs.

"I'm so sorry. I'm not rushing into it. It's been over a long time, and I'm ready to make a clean break so I can move on," I say.

She starts to cry, and I knew that would happen. I braced for it.

It's not going to work this time.

"But we have our whole future planned out. You can't do this to me," she wails.

"Sometimes plans change."

She starts to sob, and I'm not sure what else I can do. "Please, Spencie. Please don't do this."

"It's over." I stick firmly to my words just as my mom advised me to do when the waterworks started.

Her lip quivers even as she sort of bares her teeth at me. "Fine, then. Get out."

"Excuse me?"

"I said get out," she hisses.

Gladly. "I'll just…I'll go sit by the firepit for a bit if you want to come talk." I stand and head out of the office, and even though I'm leaving a woman I care about crying behind me, I can't help but feel a huge burden lifted as I walk toward the mansion, around back, and toward the firepits.

I spot Gracie sitting there, staring into the fire.

"This seat taken?" I ask quietly.

She startles a bit at my voice, but she turns and glances up at me. "No. Are you okay?"

I sigh as I take the chair beside her. "Yeah. I'm okay."

"Remember when you two were fighting last time, and I said the walls are thin and I heard everything?"

I huff out a little chuckle. "Yeah."

"I came out here to give you two some privacy."

"It's over," I say quietly. "I did it."

"I know." She reaches over and pats my knee. "How are you feeling?"

I shrug. "I'm not sure yet. On the one hand, it's the end of a relationship, which is always difficult and sad. On the other…it was time. We ran our course. And then she told me to get out."

She twists her lips as she draws her hand back toward her own lap.

I look at the Grand Hall off in the distance from where we sit. I hate the idea of leaving this place behind, but it's time.

She's quiet a few beats, and then she sighs. "You're a good, kind man, Spencer, and you always deserved better than how Amelia treated you."

I need to get out of here. I know I promised Steve I'd take a look at his books and his procedures to ensure the vineyard is being run efficiently, but maybe that's not such a good idea anymore.

The idea of leaving this place behind—of leaving my friendship with Grace behind—is overwhelming.

But *everything* in my life is overwhelming right now, and this is something within my control.

"I need to go," I finally say to Grace.

She nods, and she stands. I stand, too, and I give her a quick hug.

"Thanks for…well, you know," I say. I offer a half smile before I turn to walk away to leave her and Amelia and this entire vineyard behind.

I don't know when I'll be back, and for some reason, that pulses an aching feeling of loneliness in my chest.

But the loneliness is replaced by anger as I turn the corner and spot my ex as of five minutes ago in a passionate embrace with Drew, the head of the cellar workers, out behind his bungalow.

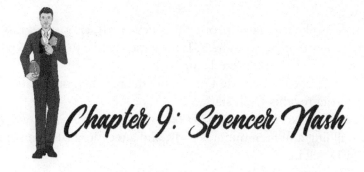

Chapter 9: Spencer Nash

No Better Way to Get to Know a Guy

A Month and a Half Before the Wedding

I draw in a deep breath as I look at the building in front of me.

I haven't been back to the winery in a month. I haven't heard from Amelia. Our last conversation was an accusation that she'd been waiting for me to break up with her so she could green light her relationship with Drew, and she informed me that she actually hadn't waited at all, and they'd been together for quite some time.

So learning my ex-fiancée was cheating on me for who knows how long was a fantastic punch to the gut I didn't see coming.

I should have.

Over the last month, I've been biding my time waiting for the legal tampering period when teams can start talking to free agents.

Though I've not heard from Amelia, I *have* heard from Grace. Mostly because she's my primary contact with the business analysis I'm doing for Steve, but it's not all business. She occasionally texts me funny cat memes or wine memes, and I text back with something ridiculous Asher sent me.

It's been a whirlwind of a month. I spent a good chunk of it in Vegas with my brothers, and now I'm staring at this building that might become my new home. Or, my new *second* home, anyway.

It feels like the start of something new, and I almost get this strange sense of freedom here. It took me a while to pin down the word for it, but it's like I can breathe again.

And maybe it's because I'm leaving the past behind me in Minnesota for this fresh start.

I finally gear myself up to get out of the car and walk toward the building a full ten minutes early, and a receptionist greets me when I walk in.

"Good morning. Who are you here to see?"

"I have an appointment with Mr. Dell, Mr. Hall, and Mr. Elliott," I say.

"You must be Spencer Nash," she says with a bright smile.

"That's me." I offer a smile back, and she nods.

"Okay, Mr. Nash. Take a seat, and Coach Dell will be right down." She nods over toward a deserted row of chairs, and I thank her as I head toward them.

Not two minutes later, the elevator doors open, and the head coach of the San Diego Storm, Brian Dell, steps out. He beelines right toward me, walking quickly as if he has somewhere to be.

And he does. Right here. With me.

He's on the younger side at just forty-three, and he's smart, a little quirky, and an incredible play caller. He's single with no kids, and his entire life is dedicated to football—much like mine has been since I started playing as a kid. Much like everyone in my family *was*, now that I think about it. But that can't be said anymore for Lincoln, who's married now with a kid and a step-kid, or Grayson, who's getting married in a month and a half.

Coach Dell holds out a hand as I stand.

"Spencer Nash. What an incredible honor it is to meet you," he says as we shake hands.

"And you, Coach Dell," I say respectfully.

"Please. It's Brian. Or just Coach."

I chuckle. "Okay, then, Coach."

He nods with a smile. "Come with me, and we'll start with a tour around our training facility."

I nod, and we get started. He shows me the weight room and locker room. We go through the training room, rehab center, and hydrotherapy rooms. We stop in a player lounge with a VR system for game simulations and other video-game-type consoles that will help us prepare for games. He takes me to a nutrition center and cafeteria, and he points out the practice fields—two outdoor fields and a smaller indoor field that only gets used on rainy days. And then he takes me through the meeting rooms, classrooms, and, lastly, the offices.

It's a state-of-the-art facility with all sorts of advanced technology to help us analyze our performances as we turn into faster, stronger, and better players, and honestly, the excitement of being in a new place starts to take root in the pit of my stomach.

I loved my time in Minnesota, but that doesn't mean I can't love my time somewhere else, too. It's been long enough now that I can focus on a new mindset that will allow me to feel this sense of anticipation rather than the dread that lanced through me when I first heard the news that I was being released.

The tour ends in the team owner's office, and the man behind the desk lifts to a stand as he walks around to greet me. "William Hall," he says as he reaches out a hand to shake mine.

"Spencer Nash," I say in return. "It's an honor to meet you, sir."

He offers a smile. "Welcome to our facility. Coach has shown you around?"

"Yes, sir. What an extraordinary and progressive facility," I say.

"We look forward to the opportunity to have you train here."

A knock at the door pulls our attention in that direction, and another man walks into the office. "Spencer Nash," he says. "Great to meet you. I'm John Elliott, the general manager here."

"It's a pleasure, Mr. Elliott," I say, shaking his hand.

"Please, it's John. Hey, are you available for the next few hours? I was able to secure a tee time in twenty minutes at the course across the street, and I tell you what, there's no better way to get to know a guy than on the golf course, you know what I'm saying?" he asks.

I nod. "I can make that work if you've got a set of clubs that isn't from when Bobby Jones played."

He laughs at my request. "I keep a spare set in my trunk at all times just for such an occasion. Graphite shafts, not wood like ol' Bobby used."

I chuckle as I nod. "Then I'm in."

"Brian?" John asks the head coach.

"You know it," Coach says, agreeing to this seemingly impromptu tee time that was likely planned all along.

"Mr. Hall?" John asks, turning to the team owner.

"Rain check."

John nods. "I also have Clayton Mack joining us," John says, naming a wide receiver on the Storm. I've met him twice post-game on the field, and he's young at just twenty-five, but he's definitely someone I've kept my eye on.

We exchange a few more pleasantries before we head down to John's Escalade to head over to the course. I jump in back to allow Coach in the front seat while John drives.

"Let us know if you need some recommendations for housing or activities nearby," John says.

"I do, actually," I say.

They launch into what's nearby, and I take mental notes as I stare out the window at the terrain that's much, much different from Minnesota.

Four hours later, I'm feeling good with a few beers in me and a decent score as I walk off the eighteenth green.

John was right—the relaxed atmosphere of the long game of golf combined with the camaraderie of being with men who enjoy the same activities I do has given me a chance to get to know them a bit. I shared a golf cart with Clay, and I got to know him the best as we searched for our balls together and complained about slices and the landscape of the course when it was really just our terrible shots causing the issues.

We laughed a lot. We drank some. We golfed hard.

I learned that Clay is a San Diego native. He's single, and from the way he spoke on the course, I get the feeling he's reveling in the single life as he uses his status as a professional football player to his advantage.

I can see him becoming a good friend of mine even if our lifestyles aren't the same, and at one point during our golf outing, he leaned over and said quietly to me that since he's a native, he can recommend better places than what the staff at the Storm will.

It feels like I made my first friend here, and I hope it's just the start of this brand-new life.

I hang around a few days solo as I get to know this new town and wait for the official offer to come through, and it's Friday morning when my phone rings with a call from my agent, Jake Barlow.

"Hey, Jake," I answer.

"Mr. Nash, good morning. I just fielded an offer from the San Diego Storm and wanted to present it to you."

"That's great news," I say, excitement shooting up my spine at this new opportunity.

"Before I tell you, though, I want you to be aware that I've heard rumors that some other teams are also getting ready to make an offer to you."

"But they haven't yet. So what's this one?"

He clears his throat. "Forty-eight over three years with twenty guaranteed and a twelve-point-seven-five signing bonus."

"So sixteen million a year?" I ask.

"That's right. Thoughts?"

"What do you think?" I don't want to share my thoughts before I hear his.

"I think it's an incredible offer."

I feel like he's leaving something out. It's an incredible offer *for a player like you.* I'm aging, but it hasn't affected my performance.

It's more than I would've made on what was left on my contract in Minnesota, and the signing bonus will be an immediate paycheck.

But still, it's hard not to feel a certain way after everything that's happened over the last two months. Maybe I'm San

Diego's first choice, or maybe I'm not. Maybe I'm never anybody's first choice.

And there it is. The effect of Amelia's cheating as it hits me right in the face.

It took a minute for me to get to this point—for me to see some of the lasting effects of it. But there it is, making me feel like I'm not good enough in a moment when I should be celebrating an offer from a new team.

My entire life, I've strived to be perfect for everyone around me because everyone always expected me to be a certain way. I had straight As. I worked hard. I made it all the way to the NFL. But none of those successes have given me an ounce of victory when it comes to my personal life.

I chose wrong, and breaking up with Amelia was admitting I'd made a mistake. I think that's part of what took me so damn long to do it—something my mother pointed out to me when I was with her in New York.

Is accepting the first offer another mistake?

There's no way of knowing. It's one of the risks that comes with this profession. But putting them off is a different risk entirely since they could pull the offer if I make them wait.

I stare out the window of the hotel I've stayed in for the last five days. I'm looking out over the water, palm trees swaying gently in the breeze, and for the first time, it feels like home.

Maybe it'll be a mistake, but it's only a mistake for the next three years.

"Take it," I say.

"You sure?" he asks.

"I'm sure."

"You got it, Nash," he says. "I'll be in touch with the details."

"Thanks, Jake." We cut the call, and I stare out the window as a feeling of excitement washes over me.

A new team. A new town. A new home.

I think this is exactly the fresh start I needed.

Chapter 10: Grace Newman

Two Years, Seventy-Five Acres, and Complete Confusion

The Week Before the Wedding

I watch the footage again just to be certain I heard what I thought I heard.

My new routine each morning is fast-forwarding through any footage taken the previous night on the new cameras to see whether Amelia and Drew showed up again, and so far…nada. Apparently they're more comfortable doing it at her place—or his—since Spencer isn't around to catch them.

I watch as Drew walks into my office, but this time he's by himself.

I watch as he rifles through the papers on top of my desk.

I watch as he tries the drawers, but they're all locked.

"Did you find anything?" I hear Amelia's voice before I see her on the screen.

"All the drawers are locked. Do you have a key?"

Amelia shakes her head as she walks into my office.

"Dammit. How will we find out if she knows?" Amelia asks.

Drew shrugs. "No idea. But if you marry *me*, then you'll get the vineyard."

"I guess that's our only option at this point." She sighs as she folds her arms across her chest.

"Don't forget that special clause in there about great-grandchildren," Drew says.

"I know, I know. An additional seventy-five acres near Temecula. I don't know if I even *want* kids, but for seventy-five acres…that's some prime real estate right there."

Seventy-five acres in Temecula? What the hell is she talking about?

"Look, I know I don't have the kind of money you would've gotten after two years of being married to that jock, but we have something better, Amelia. We have love," Drew says.

She snorts. "Right. Love. Speaking of which, want to go back to your place and have sex?"

"We could just do it in here again," he suggests.

"Ew, no. It smells like Gracie." She turns so she's facing the camera she doesn't know is capturing her every word—not to mention every facial expression—and she wrinkles her nose. "No thanks."

Drew follows her out, and the light turns off. I feel like I have some detective work to do, but I don't want anyone to know I'm digging. And I don't know *where* to dig. Or how. Or who to question.

Still…she mentioned seventy-five acres in Temecula, great-grandchildren, and marriage—possibly for at least two years. And a plan to be married to *that jock* for two years.

Is there some secret clause of Nana's that says whoever gets married first gets the vineyard?

This place *is* called Newlywed Vineyard, and I feel like Nana is just eccentric enough to come up with some sort of test to decide who she'll will the family vineyard to.

How about the responsible one? How about the one who has dreamed of running it since she was a child? How about the one who loves wine instead of the one who won't take a single sip because she hates the taste and opts for rum instead?

Just a thought.

And if there *is* a clause like that…how did Amelia find out about it? And not just that, but was she only with Spencer for his money?

God, if that's true…what a horrible, awful, evil person she is.

These are all things I intend to find out, but considering it's been three months since I discovered Amelia was cheating on Spencer and I still haven't figured out why, I'm not banking on my detective skills.

In my defense, I've been busy doing my job. It's April now, and spring break was madness as the vineyard was busier than it's been in ages. Spencer and I touch base often, and I offered him a bottle of celebratory malbec the next time he's in town after hearing the news that he signed with the San Diego Storm.

But truth be told…I'm sad.

I'm sad he won't be with the Vikings anymore.

I'm sad he isn't coming around here like he used to.

I'm sad we've drifted apart over the last few months.

He dumped Amelia, and I don't blame him for staying away from here, especially given how things ended.

But I feel like I lost my only friend.

Everyone around here is either a colleague or a relative. I live on a vineyard in the middle of nowhere, which isn't exactly conducive to forming friendships. I'm good at being personable with whoever's visiting the tasting room, but it's not like visitors turn into friends. They come, taste some wine, buy a few bottles, and leave.

Several Minneapolis stores carry our label now, too, so patrons don't even have to come back here to snag a bottle of their favorite merlot or rosé. It makes for fewer repeat visitors even though it makes for a nicer figure on the bottom line.

Maybe I need to get out of here for a while. I could even get an apartment in Minneapolis and commute to work.

But this is home. It's *been* home my entire life. And I'm not going to allow Amelia to snatch it out from under my nose because she found out about some unwritten technicality.

I need to learn more about this. It seems like what she knows is hazy at best.

It takes me a few days to gear up for this conversation, in part because I'm extra busy over the weekend with the biggest wedding we've hosted.

But I know I have to ask the only person at the vineyard I can trust with anything I say.

It's Tuesday morning when I take a walk from the mansion over to the production facility.

I knock tentatively on my dad's office door.

"Hey, Gigi," he says absently, glancing up from some paperwork on his desk as he pulls his glasses off. He sets them on his desk and rubs his eyes. "What's up?"

"Can we talk?"

He nods. "Always."

I close his office door and plop into the chair across from him. "What are Nana's plans with this place once she decides to let it go?"

He shrugs and offers one of those secret smiles that tells me he at least has an idea about her plans.

"What aren't you telling me?" I demand.

"She mentioned an idea, but I've never actually seen it in writing. And I was sworn to absolute secrecy."

"If I guess the plan, can you confirm it?" I ask.

He thinks about that for a beat, and then he seems to come to a decision. "I suppose that wouldn't be breaking my promise to Mom."

"Is she handing the vineyard down to whichever of her grandchildren stays married for two years?"

He looks surprised that I know. He neither confirms nor denies my hunch, instead asking, "How'd you find out?"

"Is there a secondary clause that if a great-grandchild is produced in that marriage, there's a bonus vineyard in Temecula?"

His brows knit together. "You know about Newman Vineyard?"

"I didn't until you just confirmed it." I fold my arms across my chest. "Do you really think Amelia should be getting it? You really weren't going to tell me?"

"Gracie-bug, you know I couldn't tell you. Nana just wanted it to be fair, and since neither Jimmy nor I was married when she decided she was ready to pass it down, she chose to give it to whichever one of you gets married first. But it's not two years, it's only one. She'll sign over the deed to you on your one-year anniversary. Now can you tell me how you found out?"

"That camera you installed in my office. Drew and Amelia were in there talking, and somehow she knows," I say flatly.

"She knows?" he asks.

"Drew said something about her only marrying Spencer for his money. She was going to divorce him after two years and keep his money. Win-win for her. She gets the vineyard *and* Spencer's money."

He closes his eyes and shakes his head. "But that wedding is off, right? So there's nothing to worry about. You know now, so maybe we just…I don't know, be *honest* with Mom that you both know so she can come up with another way."

"Is the great-grandchild thing true, too?" I ask.

He shrugs. "Sort of. I haven't read her will. I can't bring myself to do it, but there are a number of secondary conditions, one being if one of you produces a great-grandchild, I think. But she didn't want either of you to know. She wanted the wedding and children to happen naturally."

An idea forms in my head.

It's crazy.

It's a complete longshot.

It's wild and impulsive.

It's all the things I'm not.

And somehow…I immediately know I have to give it a try. I'll spend the rest of my life regretting it if I don't.

"I have to go," I say. "Don't tell Nana I know." I dart out of the office and over to my bungalow to set this plan into action.

Chapter 11: Grace Newman

Additional Security Needed by the Pool

The Day of the Wedding

I land in Vegas with literally no plan. I don't really know what I'm thinking or why in my right mind I thought this was a good idea. Maybe I'm *not* in my right mind, but I'm here now, and there's no turning back.

Well, except… I mean, there is technically a way to turn back. I could always just buy a ticket and go back home.

But I don't think I can do that without taking my shot here.

And speaking of shots, the two I took on the plane did little to calm my nerves, so once we get off the plane, I stop at the first bar and order myself another one.

And then…I'm not quite sure what happens next, so I send a text.

Except *drafting* said text is a bit of a challenge.

Me: *I'm in Vegas and I'd love to see you!* *[red heart emoji]*
Backspace.
[smiley face emoji]
Backspace backspace backspace.
Me: *Where did you say Grayson's bachelor party is taking place?*
It sounds too weird to ask that out of the blue.

LISA SUZANNE

I pull up a browser and search for some cat memes, but I think I've sent him all the good ones.

I sigh. I need to figure this out quick so I can get the heck out of this airport.

Backspace backspace backspace.

Me: *Hope you're having fun at your brother's big bachelor party week.*

I wait a beat, wondering if he's going to respond and what the hell I was thinking when I decided to fly here without telling him—or anybody, for that matter.

His reply comes a minute later.

Spencer: *It's been...something. Lol. It's good to hear from you.*

Me: *Where did you say the party is?*

I'm not sure if he ever *did* say, but this is my chance to go find him and clue him in on what I know.

Spencer: *At the Palms. I guess it has some meaning for Grayson and Ava. Right now, I'm at a pool party.*

I don't reply as I pull up the Uber app to find a car that'll take me to the Palms.

This is bananas. It's *so* not me to fly across the country with some ridiculous plan that's never going to work...except maybe it *will* work.

The only way failure is guaranteed is if I never take the shot.

It feels like centuries pass by the time my car pulls up in front of the hotel. I was too nervous to reply to Spencer, and besides, what would I even say? *I flew here to come see you* sounds desperate, even if it's the truth. So...I guess I'll just show up and tell him that in person since that's not desperate at all.

He said he's at the pool, so I stop at guest services to check my suitcase then wander through the casino as I follow the signs out toward the pool. I didn't pack a swimsuit for this impromptu trip, so I'm stuck in the jeans and t-shirt I wore here.

When I walk through the double doors leading out to the pool, I find a rather large man standing in front of a gate holding a clipboard. Beside him is a sandwich board letting outsiders know what's inside of that gate is a private party, and music blares from the pool. There are a bunch of people in there, both male and female, and they all seem to be having a good time.

"Name?" the large man asks.

"Grace Newman, but I'm probably not on your list," I say. "I'm here to see Spencer Nash."

"Yeah, you and twenty other women," he grunts. He's not very nice. "Get in line."

Tears burn behind my eyes, but thankfully I'm wearing sunglasses so he can't see. "Excuse me?"

"If you're not on the list, I can't let you in." He's firm as he taps the clipboard with his pen.

"But I need to talk to Spencer! I flew all this way just to see—"

He interrupts me. "No name, no entry."

I glance around him toward the pool area to see if I can spot Spencer to somehow get his attention, but instead, I see Lincoln Nash, Spencer's oldest brother.

"Lincoln Nash!" I yell from where I stand.

"What the hell are you doing?" the large, mean man with the clipboard asks.

"Getting in to see Spencer, like I said," I say calmly to him, and then I yell again. "Lincoln! Over here!"

"You need to get out," he says, pointing toward the doors back into the building.

"Lincoln!" I scream one more time.

The mean man grabs a walky-talky and presses a button. "Additional security needed by the pool."

Lincoln must've heard my last attempt because he glances up and spots me. There's no recognition there, but why would there be? I've never met him.

He walks over toward the gate. As soon as he gets close enough, I start to yell even though the large man tries to block my view of him.

"Lincoln! I'm Grace Newman, a friend of Spencer's. Is he here? I need to talk to him."

Just as Lincoln opens his mouth to reply, I hear a voice behind me. "Newman?"

I whip around at the sound of my last name.

Only one person calls me that.

My jaw drops as I spot Spencer Nash wearing just a pair of navy blue swim trunks, slides on his feet, sunglasses on his face, a backward hat, and what almost reminds me of one of those shirts with fake abs painted on them because there is no way in hell that body is *real.*

"Nash! Thank God," I say, forcing my eyes off his abs. I rush over and throw my arms around his neck. "I'm not on the list, and this man was about to kick me out, but—"

"What are you doing here?" he interrupts, sliding his hand around my waist for a quick hug.

I ignore the heat of his skin as I back away. "I need to talk to you." My eyes flick to his abs again.

Focus, Gracie.

Focus.

Abs.

Focus.

"Okay," he says. "Come on in."

The mean man opens the gate for Spencer.

"She's with me," he says to the mean guy, who glares deeply at me as he lets us through the gate. I force myself not to smirk at him, though I'm tempted to.

Lincoln is still standing there, and he introduces himself. "I'm Lincoln, but I'm pretty sure you already knew that."

"It's nice to meet you. I'm so sorry to crash your party, but I need a word with Spencer," I say, and I hear the desperation in my own voice.

"Must be serious if you flew all the way here to talk to him," Lincoln says.

"It is," I confirm.

"Well, it's nice to meet you, and I hope we'll see more of you." Lincoln smiles, and he heads back toward a row of lounge chairs.

Spencer leads me over toward his lounge chair. He grabs a white T-shirt and pulls it over his head.

"You don't have to do that on my account," I say. The dumb words are out of my mouth before I can stop them.

He chuckles. "What did you have to tell me?"

I glance around. The music is loud here, and he's in a swimsuit, and somehow…this doesn't seem like the right place to have this conversation. "Can we, uh, go somewhere more private to talk?"

He nods and stands. "Come with me."

And then I follow him past the mean guy, through the casino, and toward a bank of elevators. He takes me up to his room, and when he opens the door, I spot three garment bags hanging in the open closet—a white one and two black ones.

"You brought your fancy clothes, I see," I say, trying to make light of things. I glance down at the bottom of the closet where I see at least five pairs of shoes. "And your entire closet of shoes."

He laughs. "Only one of those garment bags is mine. Grayson trusts me the most out of the three other Nash brothers, so I'm storing the bride's and groom's clothes until the wedding."

"Why here and not at their house?" I ask. It's a dumb question, but I can't just cut right to the reason why I'm here.

"The bride just picked them up today and came straight here rather than stopping home. She didn't want to leave them in the car, so she asked me."

I raise my brows. "That's nice of you." I'm tempted to peek inside the bag, but I refrain.

He grabs some clothes. "Give me a minute, okay?" he asks, and he disappears to the restroom.

I wander over toward the windows. I stop and look out at the view of the Strip from here. When he emerges, he's wearing a pair of shorts and a nicer shirt.

"So, I don't mean to be rude, but you've got me curious. What's going on?" he asks.

I shift my gaze back out the window. "I found out some things about Amelia and the vineyard that might explain why she was cheating on you."

He sucks in a breath—his only response to my words.

I turn around and face him. "I've been trying to dig into why she'd do that to you, and I found some video footage of her and Drew in my office after hours. They were looking for something, trying to figure out if I knew something they knew, and Drew said something about if she marries him, she gets the vineyard."

His brows furrow. "How does that affect me?"

I clear my throat. "Drew mentioned that he doesn't have the kind of money to give her that being married to you would've given her."

"Oh," he says. And then the truth hits him. "*Ohh*. So she was planning to marry me to get the vineyard and then...divorce me and take me for all I'm worth?"

"Something like that," I say softly. "I'm so, so sorry to be the one to tell you this. But I felt like you had to know, and I felt like it warranted an in-person discussion."

"Yeah," he mutters. "Wait a minute. Why would she get the vineyard if she married me?"

"I guess Nana decided she was willing it to whichever grandchild got married first—and *stayed* married for at least a year. And if they produce a great-grandchild, they get a bonus plot of land in Temecula."

"Jesus," he curses, running a hand through his hair.

"I have the recording if you'd like to see it." I hold up my phone, and he stares at it with a look of disgust on his face.

"No." He shakes his head. "No, I don't need to see it. But I do need to get the fuck out of here. Excuse me." With those words, he bolts out of the room, leaving me standing by the windows, wondering if I should take off after him or just stay put until he returns.

Chapter 12: Spencer Nash

That Damn Mustard Allergy

The Day of the Wedding

Fuck it.

I'm getting blasted.

It's bad enough to know I was being cheated on, but to learn that the woman I loved—the woman I asked to spend her life with me—was just using me the whole time for my money?

On a different level.

What a horrible, awful, terrible person.

I'm not sure what else to do besides numb myself to all of it, so I beeline for the bar the second the elevator doors open.

The bachelor party is still in full swing out by the pool. My three brothers are out there, none of them any the wiser about the inner turmoil Gracie Newman just brought upon me.

What the fuck is wrong with Amelia?

No shit she didn't give me the ring back. Of course she didn't. She probably already pawned it off for cash.

Fuck her. Fuck Drew. Fuck the vineyard and the will and all of it—except for Gracie.

She's the only one who was honest with me. I wonder how she feels about all of this. I wonder why she felt like she had to fly out to tell me this. She said it warranted an in-person discussion, but she could've done it over the phone. Instead, she cared enough to show up for me.

I've been nursing beer all day, but I go straight for what's going to get me drunkest the fastest. "Double shot of tequila," I say to the bartender. He drops it by a minute later.

I suck it back. Fuck, that tastes like shit.

"More," I say, holding up the empty glass. "Or better yet, a glass of it, neat, and start me a tab."

"Yes, sir," he says, and he pours me a nice, steep tumbler with tequila.

I sit back and sip.

As if it didn't hurt enough to find out she was sleeping with someone else when I put my trust in her, now this.

How long was it going on? I hadn't had sex with her in nearly a month by the time I finally ended things with her, so ever since I found out about the infidelity, I allowed myself to believe it was just for that month. The alternative is thinking I was somehow inadequate in bed, but I don't really believe that.

I think she met me, scammed me, and was planning to take me for some money—as if I ever would've been stupid enough to enter into a marriage with her without an air-fucking-tight prenup.

But despite wanting to believe it was just for that month, something tells me she was sleeping with Drew long before she ever even met me.

She was lying to me our entire relationship. How will I ever trust another woman again?

I don't know the answer to that. Right now...it seems pretty bleak. I've embraced the belief that people will only disappoint me in the long run. I've started to feel like I'm better off alone.

I've spent most of my time over the last six weeks in San Diego getting to know the town and my teammates as I avoid women completely, and that seems like the right path to continue down. It's just safer that way.

"There you are," a voice beside me says.

I glance over and spot Grace. She's the bearer of bad news today, but she's been a good friend over the time I've known her.

"Are you okay?" she asks.

"No. Want to drink with me?"

She chuckles and nods.

I wave the bartender over. "Add whatever she wants to my tab."

He raises his brows at Grace, and she says, "Paloma."

My brows dip as the bartender nods and walks away. "What's a paloma?"

"Tequila, lime juice, and grapefruit soda. What's that?" she asks, nodding to my glass.

I hand it over for her to try, and she makes a face. I can't help but chuckle.

"Why are you down here drinking tequila by your lonesome?" she asks.

"Trying to numb the ridiculousness," I admit.

She scrunches up her nose. "I'm sorry I came. I'm sorry I interrupted your party."

"It's nice sitting here with you, despite the news you brought."

"I'm glad you said that," she says, bumping into my shoulder with hers. "Because I was thinking about heading back home."

"May as well stay a night or two," I suggest. "Hell, stay for the wedding if you want. Are you hungry?"

She nods. "I haven't eaten since early this morning."

"There's a happy hour menu," I say, nodding toward the little stand with our options.

"I'm down for anything."

The bartender comes back with her drink, and I order a few appetizers for us to split. He walks away, and I glance over at Grace as I let out a long sigh.

She holds up her glass, and I hold mine up, too.

"What should we toast to?" I ask.

"To new beginnings," she suggests.

I touch my glass to hers, and we each drink. She makes a face of approval at her first sip.

We each drink quietly for a few beats before I break the silence with a question. "So, what do I do?"

"About what?" She takes another sip of her drink, and it's going down quickly. So is my tequila.

"About your sister. About…all of it."

"Oh. Uh, I had an idea, but it's sort of out there." She chugs a little more of her paloma, and I get the sense she's gearing up with liquid courage for whatever it is she came here to say to me.

"What is it?" I ask, narrowing my eyes at her.

"You get revenge," she says.

"I'm not really the revenge-seeking type," I admit. I take another sip, and curiosity gets me. "But what are you thinking?"

She draws in a deep breath, and then she says, "Marry me."

Tequila sprays out of my mouth and all over the bar at her words. "What?"

She picks up a napkin to wipe her cheek. I guess I sprayed more than just the bar.

"Fuck, I'm sorry. But…*what?*"

She offers a small, awkward laugh. "Marry me. Stay married to me for a year, and then I get the vineyard. She's out. You get revenge, she gets karma, we all win."

"We all win?" I repeat. How, exactly, is this proposal of hers winning for *me*? I mop up the mess on the bar I just made with some tiny napkins. "I suppose next you're going to tell me you want to have a kid with me for the Temecula land, too."

She blows out a breath and stares at her drink. "No. I would never do that. These rules Nana made up were meant to be kept secret. It all was supposed to happen naturally."

"How did Amelia find out?" I ask.

She shrugs. "No idea. But she found out, and then I found out, and now I'm going to take what's rightfully mine. You know…if you're up for my revenge plan."

"This is ridiculous, Gracie. I can't *marry* you."

The bartender walks over with some plates filled with food, glancing up at me as he catches my words. "Drunken shrimp and nachos," he says as he sets the plates in front of us.

He stays out of it, thankfully, but we probably shouldn't be having this conversation publicly.

"It's fine," she says quietly. "I knew it was a longshot. I just…don't want her to get the vineyard. She doesn't even like wine. It's a money machine for her, and that's all, but it's been my dream to run it since I was a kid. I just need a year. If you want a part in running the vineyard, you're welcome to it. If you don't, you can walk away from it and never hear from me again."

The thought leaves me feeling hollow and alone.

I don't *want* to never hear from her again. I reach for a shrimp and bite into it, chewing thoughtfully.

Could I really do that? Could I really *marry* Grace to help her get her vineyard?

Grace grabs a shrimp, too, and we both chew quietly. She takes another one, and I do, too.

And then my mouth starts to feel a little funny…tingly, like it's almost itchy. "Oh shit," I mutter at the same time Grace starts scratching her arm.

"Does this sauce have mustard in it?" she asks, glancing at what's already becoming a rash on her arm.

"Wait, are you allergic to mustard?" I ask as panic starts to rise.

She nods.

"Holy shit. So am I." What a weird coincidence. "My mouth is getting itchy and tingly."

"Shit," she mutters. She starts to dig through her purse, pausing to scratch her arm. "I keep Benadryl in here just in case. Want one?"

"Two, please."

She locates the pills and hands me two, and I swallow them down with tequila as she takes two, too.

I call the bartender over. "More drinks. And take the shrimp."

He eyes us both for a beat. "Are you okay?"

I nod. "We're both allergic to mustard."

"Oh, the barbecue sauce has a mustard base. Can I get you anything?"

"We both took Benadryl," Grace says.

"Are you sure you want another drink, then?" the bartender asks.

I glance at the woman who just proposed to me over mustard shrimp at a bar in Vegas. "Yeah, I'm sure."

And by the time the next drink is gone, the Benadryl has started to kick in, and my mouth is tingling for another reason entirely—well, two reasons.

One, because of the tequila.

And two, because I'm suddenly itching to kiss Gracie Newman.

Chapter 13: Grace Newman

Is Five the Afternoon or Evening

Two Hours Before the Wedding

My third paloma slides right down, and I attacked those nachos with gusto after the allergic reaction. I don't know why I didn't think to ask if the barbecue shrimp had a mustard-based sauce. I always ask, but I guess being here in Vegas around Spencer and offering my solution to the Amelia problem distracted me.

I'm fine now. The Benadryl did the trick, though you're not supposed to mix Benadryl with alcohol. I have a feeling whatever happens tonight will be a hazy memory in the morning, so at some point, I'll cut myself off from palomas.

But they're so good. And the more you have, the better they taste.

Spencer hasn't slowed down on the tequila, though he orders us some cheeseburger sliders next.

"Well, now what?" I ask once our burgers are gone and our drinks are empty.

He shrugs. "I want to get out of here. Go somewhere. Do something." He's slurring.

"Let's go up to your room and change clothes and find a club or something." Am I slurring, too? I think I might be slurring.

"It's five in the afternoon. Clubs aren't open yet." He signals to the bartender to cash out our tab as I giggle.

"Is five the afternoon?" I ask. "Or is it technically evening?"

"I think evening starts at six."

I laugh and plant my feet on the floor to stand, and the whole room feels like it's moving around me. I shake my head to clear it, and I follow Spencer over toward the elevators.

"Oh, my luggage," I say as we stand there waiting for the doors to open.

"Where is it?"

"I checked it at guest services. I don't have a room."

"It's fine. Stay with me. I've got plenty of space."

"'K," I say.

"We can just call down there and ask them to bring up your bag."

"Sounds good," I say. We step onto the elevator, and he stares at the keypad. I can't quite discern if he's trying to focus or if he can't recall his room number, but then he makes a decision and pushes a button.

We stumble down the hall together, the tequila hitting me harder than I realized, and he fumbles with a door for a full minute before it opens. I'm standing behind him, giggling the entire time, but once the door opens, I remember something important.

There's only one bed in his room.

He invited me to stay here with him.

Are we going to share a bed?

The door closes behind me, and I step back so I'm leaning against the door. My balance feels compromised after all that tequila, and he spins to look at me.

"You okay?" he asks.

I nod, and he takes a step toward me. He takes another, and another, and then there are no more steps to take as he stands mere inches from me.

He rests one of his arms on the door beside me as his gaze burns heatedly into mine.

"Wha—what are you doing?" I ask softly.

His other arm shifts as his fingertips locate my hip. He moves his body in so he's flush against me. "I was going to kiss you. Is that okay?"

My breath catches in my throat. I nod, my eyes never leaving his.

And then his mouth drops down to mine. His lips are as soft as they look as they press to mine, and all the thoughts fly directly out of my mind as I can only focus on one thing: Spencer Nash is kissing me.

Holy. Shit.

Spencer Nash is kissing me.

And then his mouth, which has formed to mine, opens, and his tongue moves against my bottom lip. He sucks on that bottom lip, and then he offers just the slightest edge of his teeth as he bites down a little. He opens his mouth a little more, and his tongue brushes mine.

I feel weak in the knees as he kisses me. I finally come to my senses enough to wrap my arms around his waist, mostly because I have to do it in order to keep from falling flat to the floor since it feels like my legs will give out at any second.

That's how much this man is currently knocking every bit of wind out of me. Well, that and the tequila.

His tongue starts to move a little faster, a little more urgently, and his hips push against mine as I feel his length hardening between us. The thought pulses a deep, needy ache between my legs. I have no idea if this is leading somewhere, or if this kiss is *just* a kiss, which is fine if it is. We're probably both too drunk for it to be more than that.

He pulls back abruptly, and his eyes are full of heat as they burn into mine. "Let's do it. Let's get married."

"*What?*" I shriek. I mean…I came all this way for this to happen, but never did I actually believe he'd agree to it.

"Let's do it."

"But…but…I don't have a gown. You don't have a tux. We don't have a license."

"There are places here that have all that. Or, wait—" He backs away from me and walks over to the closet. "Voila. Wedding attire."

I stare at the gown and tuxedo in the closet meant for another bride and groom.

"We'll just wear it for an hour. Long enough to tie the knot. Nobody will see," he says. "Nobody will know."

That...

That seems...

That seems like...

That seems like an *excellent* idea.

"Let's do it," I say with a grin.

He hands me the white garment bag and grabs one of the black ones. He reads the tag. "This says *groom*. Looks like that's me. You can change in the bathroom. Meet me out here, and I'll look up chapels nearby."

Oh my God. Are we really doing this?

We're really doing this.

I feel positively giddy, though that could be the alcohol talking. Who the fuck cares? I'm marrying Spencer, and I'm getting my freaking vineyard.

I fix up my makeup quickly, though my movements seem like they're a bit sluggish, and I pull just part of my hair back, leaving the rest of it loose and flowing.

I unzip the garment bag, and oh, the dress is so, so lovely. It's a satin A-line gown with an empire waist, and there's a veil hanging behind it in another bag.

I strip down to my underwear and pull the dress over my head. It fits like a glove—like it was waiting in the closet specifically for me. I stare at myself in the mirror.

Am I really doing this?

I'm really doing this.

I slip the veil into place, and I stare at myself in the mirror.

It's like it was all meant to be. The wedding garments are even here in the room just waiting to be used.

I draw in a deep breath.

This is it.

I'm about to marry my sister's ex.

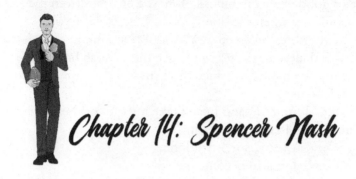

Chapter 14: Spencer Nash

It's Now or Never

The Wedding

"Right now is perfect," I confirm, and I hang up. I went with the Elvis package—the one that sends a limousine directly to the hotel to pick us up. Why the hell not?

I fill out the form online, leaving questions I can't answer about Grace blank—for now. The chapel I chose has a service where they'll take couples in a limo to the marriage bureau so we can get our license and make it official first.

I have to close one eye to focus on what I'm typing, and I have to type two or three times, but I get my end of things filled out.

I don't have time to second-guess this decision. I'm not even sure why I stopped kissing her to tell her I'd marry her. It's wild, impulsive, and all the things I'm not.

It's nuts.

And it feels like it's the right thing to do. Filling out the digital paperwork hasn't scared me from doing it anyway. Choosing between the Elvis package and the standard one didn't, either.

She wants the vineyard. I'm dedicating my life to football for the next few years anyway. Win-win.

It's a good twenty minutes before she emerges from the bathroom, and when she does...

"Wow," I breathe quietly. "You look...stunning."

"It's bad luck for the groom to see the bride in her dress before the ceremony, but since this is more of a business deal, I think it'll be okay."

"Yeah," I murmur, and I can't take my eyes off her.

I'm staring. I know I'm staring.

But she's just so...so...so stunning.

And she's about to become my *wife*.

Whoa.

The word pulses a bead of anxiety in the pit of my stomach.

We'll worry about that later. A little more tequila should fix the issue. On that note, I grab the bottle from the minibar and take a healthy swig. I pass the bottle over, and she takes a swig, too.

"Ready?"

She nods. "Ready."

"Oh! Wait. I have some questions." I read off simple things I should know about the woman I'm marrying, like her *middle name* and *birthdate*, and then we're all set.

I get a text that the limo has arrived, so we stumble back downstairs and out the front door to the waiting limousine.

Never once do we stop and think maybe this is a bad idea. It only seems like a *good* idea. A great plan.

We're taken directly to the bureau, where we get our certificate. I stare at the paper in the back of the limo—with one eye closed, naturally—and yep...it's real.

We pull up in front of a white building with hot pink lettering, and we're ushered to the lobby, where a receptionist dressed like Lisa Marie Presley asks us a few questions, including whether we have rings to exchange.

We do not.

She sells us some, and she also sells us on an upgraded photo and video package, and then we're taken to a chapel.

In no time flat, Elvis is making it official.

"It's 'Now or Never.' We 'Can't Help Falling in Love,' and that's what brought you, Spencer, and you, Grace, here today. We'll begin with the vows. 'Don't be Cruel,' and don't be a 'Hound Dog.' Don't have 'Suspicious Minds,' or you'll end up in 'Heartbreak Hotel.' Got it?"

He looks at me first, and I can't help my chuckle as my eyes meet Grace's. "I do."

"'It's 'Now or Never,' Grace. Do you?" Elvis asks her.

She nods resolutely. "I do."

"The rings?" Elvis asks.

The witness, who happens to be Lisa Marie, hands over the two bands we just purchased a few minutes ago.

"These are a symbol of your 'Burning Love.' Repeat after me as you place the ring on your bride's finger. With this ring, I thee wed."

I repeat the words as my eyes meet hers again. I slide the plain gold band onto her finger.

She says the words back to me as she slips the gold band on my finger, too.

"You both have got me 'All Shook Up.' I now pronounce you husband and wife. You may kiss the bride," Elvis says.

"Viva Las Vegas" starts playing at full blast, and I look into her eyes before I lean forward and press my lips to hers, sealing in the commitment we just made.

It's just for the next year.

Why does a small voice in the back of my mind want it to be longer than that?

We take several photos before we walk down the aisle arm-in-arm.

"The photos will be in your email by morning, video by next week," Lisa Marie tells us, and then we get into the limo.

"Where to?" the driver asks.

I glance at my bride. "Back to the hotel, or out to dinner?"

"Dinner. And more drinks," she says with a gleam in her eye.

I nod. "You got it." I glance up at the driver. "Take us to the closest restaurant with the best food."

"Yes, sir," he says, and he takes off. We stop in front of a quaint little brick building with the name Chicago Joe's perched on top.

Chicago Joe's for our wedding feast. Sounds magical.

We each order tequila as soon as we sit, and my wife orders spaghetti and meatballs.

Neither of us stops to think that ordering a meal with red sauce when we're wearing someone else's clothes is a bad idea.

Our server points that one out. "You sure you want spaghetti in that dress?"

"Oh, right," Grace says. "Yeah, don't want all that pasta making the dress too tight."

"No...I meant the sauce."

She giggles. "Oh! Right. Okay...how about just a Caesar salad then?"

The server nods, and I order the lasagna since my tux—or *Grayson's* tux—is black.

The food is delicious, though it does nothing to quell the buzzing in my head. Probably because I'm adding more tequila on top of the tequila.

It's my first meal as a husband.

I'm married now.

Reality hasn't hit me yet. I don't know whether it'll hit me at all—at least not until morning, when the buzzing is replaced by a headache.

We laugh all through dinner as we reminisce about the wedding that literally happened twenty minutes ago. Patrons of the restaurant congratulate us constantly, and someone at some point recognizes me. I sign autographs, and Grace does, too. She signs *Grace Nash*.

Grace Nash.

That's my wife.

Holy shit.

We somehow make it back to the hotel, but don't ask me how, and we arrive back in my room. Again, don't ask me how. I'm drunk and horny, and the loopiness of the Benadryl has started to dissipate, though the tequila is keeping my buzz fresh.

And now that the loopiness has subsided…I want to fuck my wife.

It's been a long time since I've had sex.

Too long.

Maybe it's the tequila talking, but it's been talking all night, and it's been doing a damn fine job making decisions for me.

"I should hang this dress back up," she says softly.

"Let me help you out of it."

She turns around, and I tug on the zipper, every centimeter exposing more of the smooth skin of her back.

I have the urge to taste it, and I do. I bend down and drag my lips along the path of the zipper, and she shivers.

The dress falls in a pool around her feet, and she spins around. She's not wearing a bra, just a pair of lacy white panties, and her breasts are exposed to me.

My dick is immediately hard.

Holy hell, this woman is gorgeous. I don't know how I never really acknowledged that before.

And, for the next year…she's my wife.

She presses her chest to my still tuxedo-clad body, and I wrap my arms around her as my mouth crashes to hers. I kiss her like my life depends on it, and how have we only done this once before? It's like our mouths were made for each other. I can only imagine our bodies will feel that way, too.

She pulls back. "Give me one sec, okay?"

I nod, and she rushes toward the bathroom. She emerges a beat later, the veil that was in her hair no longer there.

"I'll take a second in there, too," I say, and she nods as I head toward the bathroom.

I strip out of the tux and my boxers down to nothing, and when I return to the bedroom, the lights are off and my bride is wearing one of my San Diego Storm T-shirts…and she's fast asleep. Or passed out. Either way, sex is off the table.

I climb into bed beside her, not discounting the possibility of morning sex with my wife, and pass out beside her.

Chapter 15: Grace Nash

My Already Misfiring Brain Completely Malfunctions

The Morning After the Wedding

I open my eyes and feel my stomach as it rolls.

I'm definitely going to throw up.

"Oh shit!" I say, and I jump out of bed and run to the bathroom. I make it just in time before I heave up whatever I ate last night.

Where the hell am I right now?

I can't seem to think clearly as the heaving stops and the loud thundering of a headache steps into its place.

I spot clothes on the floor. Black pants, a black jacket, a white shirt…

Is that…a tuxedo?

I'm wearing a T-shirt that's about four sizes too big, and when I glance in the mirror, I see makeup smudged all over my face.

I can't remember the last time I got so drunk that I didn't wash my face before bed. I don't know if I *ever* have, and I live at a freaking winery.

I wash my hands, and as I'm scrubbing them under the water, I freeze as I spot a shiny gold band on my left ring finger.

I also see what looks like a veil on the counter, and I can't quite put the pieces together in a way that makes them make sense.

Is this a joke?

I don't even see my toothbrush. Is this my room?

I walk out of the bathroom and find Spencer Nash standing next to the bed.

Naked.

He's naked.

He's not wearing any clothes at all, and my already misfiring brain completely malfunctions.

My eyes meet his, and he reaches down and pulls whatever's on the floor beneath him up to cover himself.

"Um," I say, and my voice is hoarse after losing last night's dinner a moment ago. I clear my throat as I try to understand what's happening, but I drank *way* too much last night for any of this to make sense. "This may be a dumb question, but is that a wedding dress?"

He looks down at the dress in his hands. "I, uh—" He clears his throat, too. "I think it is."

"Oh, okay," I say as I try to keep calm. My head continues to thunder. Exactly how much tequila did I drink last night? "That may explain the wedding ring on my finger, then."

His eyes meet mine. "Um, I'm wearing one, too." He shifts and draws in a deep breath.

"Yeah. Uh…this is kind of embarrassing to admit, but I can't remember a thing from last night," I say. "Can you fill me in on what happened? Did we get married?" I vaguely remember coming here to ask him to marry me, and I definitely remember him telling me he couldn't marry me.

But now…it sort of seems like we're married.

"I'll be honest, Newman. I have absolutely no idea."

"Right." I twist my lips. So I might've married the guy my sister was supposed to marry…and I don't remember it?

"Can you, uh…can you turn around for a second?" he asks.

"Sure." I turn toward the bathroom and put my hands over my eyes.

"Okay. I have shorts on," he says a second later.

I turn back around, and my jaw drops. It's those damn abs. I remember those abs from yesterday when I first arrived here in Vegas.

I clear my throat one more time. "Maybe a shirt, too?"

He glances at his abs and back up at me. "A shirt?"

"Yeah. Those are making me…" I try to find the word as I gesture to his stomach. "Uncomfortable."

"Uncomfortable? We're both wearing wedding rings, and there's a wedding dress on the floor, and *the abs* are making you uncomfortable?" he asks.

"Don't forget the tuxedo on the bathroom floor."

He must not know about that one yet. He walks over toward the dresser and murmurs, "Oh, fuck."

"What is it?" I ask, walking over toward him.

He hands me a piece of paper, and even in the darkness of the room with the curtains still drawn, it's light enough to see what it says.

State of Nevada Marriage Certificate.

Spencer Thomas Nash. Grace Marie Newman.

"Is this real?" I ask.

"I have no idea. It looks like it."

Oh my God. We actually did it? We're *married?* "How did this happen? And why can't either of us remember?" I'm starting to panic that I missed out on my own wedding.

"I don't know."

I need to sit. I walk over to the bed and collapse for a beat, sucking in a few deep breaths. "Okay. Let's go get some coffee, and then we can try to figure it out."

"Okay, wife," he says.

I glance up at him…nearly with a glare.

He looks at me innocently. "Too soon?" he asks.

Considering we don't even know for sure if this is real, and even if it *is* real, it's nothing more than a business deal between friends…yes. "*Way* too soon. Let's just go get that coffee."

I realize too late that I don't have any clothes up here except what I arrived in yesterday and apparently a wedding dress, so I put my clothes from yesterday back on. I spot my purse and grab a hair tie, and it's just as I'm twisting back my hair that I hear Spencer's curse.

"Oh, shit."

"What is it?" I ask.

He's staring into his closet where two empty garment bags are hanging.

"The dress that's currently crumpled in a ball in the middle of the floor? Yeah...that's Ava's."

All the blood drains from my face. "Your brother's future bride?" I whisper.

"Future as in three days from now. And the tux in the bathroom is the groom's."

"Oh my God, Spencer. What the hell did we do?"

"I remembered something," he says, turning to look at me. "Drunken shrimp."

"Drunken shrimp?" I repeat. What the fuck is he talking about? Were *we* the drunken shrimp? "We were pretty drunk, but we weren't shrimp."

He shakes his head. "No. We had an appetizer. Drunken shrimp. It had mustard in it."

"Oh! Right! We're both allergic to mustard!" My words are riddled with way too much pride as the memory seeps through the haze. "Oh! So we took Benadryl! Two each."

"Yeah...chased down with tequila." He squints a little as he thinks back. "Evidently not a smart plan given that neither of us is clear on what came next."

"I guess mixing Benadryl with tequila equals complete memory loss."

"And making choices that are, uh..." He pauses as he searches for the right word. "Out of character."

I'm pretty sure he was going to say stupid, and I'm not entirely sure he'd be wrong about that.

He pulls out his phone and scans something for a beat. "Fuck," he mutters.

"What?"

He jerks his head to indicate that I should come over and look at his phone with him, and once I'm standing beside him, he opens the email from the Now or Never Vegas Chapel.

There's an attachment to a website, and when he clicks it, we see the first photo.

It's Spencer kissing me in front of Elvis.

I'm wearing Ava's dress. He's wearing Grayson's tuxedo.

Okay, yes. It was a wild, crazy plan that I *never* thought he'd really agree to.

He did, and we're married…but we did it in *someone else's wedding attire*. In our defense, I'm not sure we knew what we were doing.

But that's not much of a defense.

I feel terrible—not that I'm married to Spencer, but that we used Ava's gown and Grayson's tux when they trusted Spencer to keep them safe.

I must gasp or sigh or something because he glances over at me, and he turns off the phone before we look at any more of the photos.

I rush over to where the dress is in a ball on the floor, and I pick it up. It has a few wrinkles, but it doesn't look worn. I didn't spill anything on it, at least.

Still, we have photographic evidence that I wore it last night, and photos are meant to be shared. There's no way in hell the Now or Never Vegas Chapel is going to keep those photos private given that Spencer is an actual celebrity.

Wait…did we sign a prenup? Did we even think about that?

My guess is absolutely not.

We weren't thinking clearly about much of anything.

Spencer is panicking a little, but the panic that was starting to rise in me has gone south now as I realize my big plan actually happened. I might actually get my vineyard.

He hangs up the tuxedo, and we each zip the garments we wore into their bags before we head downstairs.

The walk does me some good. The elevator is empty save for the two of us, and he glances over at me. "Let's come up with a plan over breakfast, okay? How to make this up to Ava and Grayson, what we're going to do next…all of it."

I nod. "Okay."

By the time we get to a café, I even feel like I might even be able to put down some sausage links and eggs. Or maybe whole wheat toast, plain.

We follow the hostess through the restaurant, and we both hear it. "Spencer! Over here!"

He turns and spots his brother, Grayson, sitting in a booth on the same side as a woman I assume is his bride—you know, the woman whose dress I got married in last night.

Well, I guess breakfast isn't going to be the time we figure out what comes next.

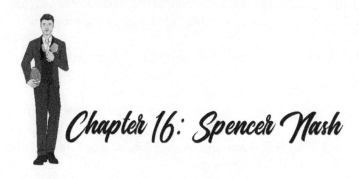

Chapter 16: Spencer Nash

Prove It, Prove It, Prove It

The Morning After the Wedding

*F*uck.

What the fuck are Grayson and Ava doing here at the café at—I glance at my watch, and oh, Jesus—at ten-fucking-thirty in the morning?

It's not as early as I thought it was, but then I spent my night in a drug-induced haze of Benadryl and tequila.

"Good morning," Grayson says as his eyes fall to Grace. "Who have we here?"

I glance at Grace. "This is Grace Newman." Is she still Newman? Or is she a Nash now? According to the certificate upstairs and the photos in my email…I think she might be a Nash if she chooses to change her name.

I blow out a breath. What the fuck have we done?

"Well, hello, Grace Newman," Grayson says. "I'm Grayson Nash, and this is Ava Maxwell, soon to be Nash."

"Nice to meet you," Grace says softly.

"Join us," Ava says, nodding toward the empty side of the booth since the two of them are sharing a side—and likely doing inappropriate things under the table since they're in a corner.

"Love to," I mutter, though nothing could be further from the truth when Grace and I need to clear our heads and figure out a plan of attack. Like, for example, whether or not we plan to tell these two what we did last night and the clothes in which we did it.

I still don't know if I had sex with her. I can't remember. What a goddamn shame if we did and the memory is just—*poof*—gone. She deserves more than that.

Grace scoots into the booth first so she'll be across from the woman whose wedding dress she stole, and I slide in beside her.

"Can I, uh, ask a dumb question?" Ava says before we even get a chance to look at the menu.

I glance up at her to give her the go-ahead.

"Why are you wearing a ring on your left hand?" Her eyes fall to the ring, and *fuck*, why didn't I think to take the goddamn thing off? Her eyes fall to Grace's hand next, and I'm sure the question on her mind is why Grace is wearing a matching one.

"Because we got married last night," I say, and Grace gasps before I lean in and bump my shoulder to hers as I offer a hearty laugh like I'm joking.

Come on, Spence. You might be hungover, but you can be quicker than this on your feet. Use your sharp-cut wide receiver skills.

"We're just wearing them so people leave us alone," I say.

Grayson narrows his eyes at me. "How, uh, did you two meet?"

"Gracie's family owns a vineyard, and the cousin of Blake Townsend works there, too. He introduced us," I say, keeping it simple.

"Well, he introduced you and Amelia," she clarifies. "That's my sister," she says to Ava and Grayson. "They dated a while, broke up, and now…" She trails off since she seems not to be certain whether we're sharing the news that we got married during the week leading up to their wedding.

In their wedding clothes.

This feels messy, and I don't do well with messy.

"And now?" Ava prompts.

"We're seeing each other," I finish. It's not a lie, exactly. She's sitting right beside me, and I can see her. It's also not the full truth, but I don't think we *can* tell the full truth right at this particular moment. How do you tell someone you got so blasted that you wore their wedding attire to your own impromptu wedding?

It sounds absolutely and completely ridiculous.

And at the same time, I feel like they should know. It feels wrong to keep that from them.

The server comes by to take our order, and I honestly didn't even look at the menu. I order a coffee, water, orange juice, and the first thing I see when I glance at the menu—the breakfast special, whatever the fuck that is.

I watch as everyone else at the table places their orders, too, and I realize I can't sit here lying to my brother. Maybe we don't need to tell him *all* the details about what went down last night—like, for example, the wedding dress topic—but I do feel like he needs to know that last night I married the woman sitting beside me.

It still seems surreal. It still seems like it's not true.

I don't know how one thing led to another, and this is where we ended up, but I do remember her proposing marriage to me yesterday as a means to an end. I'm not sure the bride and groom sitting in front of me would quite understand that since they're getting married for love.

And I do have feelings of friendship for Grace, and I think she's gorgeous, but it's not like this is going to turn into a real marriage.

I'm still very burned and hurt by the fact that her sister cheated on me. I apparently agreed to the next year, but I don't know what might come next. It's not like I can just stay married to her and eventually create a future at the vineyard where the scene of the crime occurred.

It's probably safer for me to extract myself altogether from the Newman family.

But I'm tied up in it now, that's for damn sure. For a year, anyway, since it seems that might be what I agreed to last night.

When the server ducks away to get our order started, I can't help it when the words tumble out of my mouth. "We actually did get married last night."

LISA SUZANNE

Ava gasps at the same time my blushing bride does, and Grayson's eyes widen.

Nobody says a word for a few agonizingly long seconds.

"You...you what?" Grayson finally asks.

"We, uh...we got drunk on tequila, we both had an allergic reaction to mustard, and then somehow we woke up with no memory of last night, these rings on our fingers, and a marriage certificate on the dresser," I say.

Grayson stares at me as if I've grown two heads.

"Uh...what?"

I shrug, and I glance at Grace. "Feels good to get that off my chest."

"Are you serious right now?" Ava asks. She sounds...incredulous.

"Serious as a W2," I confirm. I glance over at Grace. "Right, wife?"

She sighs and covers her eyes with her hands for a beat.

"Yep. That's right, hubby."

"Jesus Christ, Spencer. I expected this out of Asher, but you?" my brother berates.

"It's...a lot. I know," I say. "And I'm sorry. But I promise you here and now, this takes nothing away from your wedding weekend, okay? Nobody else has to know. Nobody will find out. This is your time, and we're here celebrating you."

"Oh, come on, Spence. It's a pretty great story," Ava says, and I love that she's lighthearted and sweet and can poke fun at this. She's definitely a great match for my brother in that regard.

"If you really feel that way, then A, take your rings off, and B, you might want to make sure nobody else knows," Grayson suggests.

"Who else would know?" I ask.

He shrugs. "I have no idea, but if you can't even remember getting married last night, then you probably also can't remember what you did after that and who might've taken pictures of you."

Fuck. He's right. I didn't think about that.

I think about pulling my phone out to check. Did I take any photos? What about receipts showing where we might've gone?

98

"Where did you get married?" Ava asks, and she seems to be coming around to the idea.

I, however, am not quite there just yet. I'm still trying to make it make sense in my brain, but it just…doesn't.

"Now or Never Vegas Chapel," I say, finally equipped with the answer to at least one question.

Grayson narrows his eyes at me. "How do you know that?"

"Because they sent me an email with the photos," I blurt, honesty prevailing yet again. What the fuck is with that? Keep your goddamn mouth shut, Spencer. Because we all know what's coming…

"I wanna see!" Ava practically yells as she claps her hands together.

Oh, fuck.

"No. It's…no," I say flatly.

"Oh, come on. You did it, and it's funny, and now you have this amazing story to tell," she says. "Photographic evidence, or it didn't happen."

"Oh, it happened," I say.

"Prove it," she says.

"Prove it, prove it, prove it," Grayson starts chanting as he bangs his palms on the table, drawing glances from other restaurant customers nearby, and his future wife joins him as they both laugh.

"I'm way too hungover for this," Grace says.

"So am I."

The server comes by with four cups of coffee, thankfully distracting these idiots from their chanting, but I have a feeling they're not going to let us off the hook.

And I have no idea how they're going to react when they see what we wore to our wedding.

Chapter 17: Grace Nash

Look At Us Now

The Morning After the Wedding

I feel guilty. I feel like we need to confess what happened last night even though neither of us knows exactly *how* it happened. All I know is that I got married in a dress meant for somebody else, somebody who's getting married in a few days, somebody who is expecting to wear a dress that's brand new, not one worn by another bride.

And if we show them the pictures, Grayson will see the dress before the wedding, which, as we all know, is bad luck.

I'm torn, but the chanting starts up again as I'm pouring cream into my coffee.

"Prove it, prove it, prove it." It's the banging on the table that convinces me. My pounding head can't take it, and there's only one way to get them to stop.

I sigh as I glance over at Spencer. His eyes meet mine, and he looks as annoyed as I feel.

"Show them," I say softly. They're chanting too loudly to hear me say that to him.

He raises a brow. "Are you sure?"

"I feel like it'll be worse if we hide it."

"Yeah. You're probably right." He sighs, and he pulls out his phone. He holds up a hand to get them to pipe down before he shows them the photo. "We need to tell you something before you see these photos."

Grayson narrows his eyes at his brother. "Are you both naked? Because that would be the icing on this shit cake for you, broski."

He glances at his brother. "You know, I sort of *wish* we'd have gotten married naked because it would save us from this...awkward conversation."

"Awkward?" Ava asks.

Spencer pulls open the photo.

I snag my bottom lip between my teeth. "Can I just, um...remind you that we were wasted and high on Benadryl and neither of us can remember exactly *how* this happened?"

Ava's arched brows knit together, and then Spencer slides the phone over to the two of them.

Ava recognizes it first with a shocked gasp.

"Aw, look at you two lovebirds," Grayson says. Of course he doesn't recognize his future wife's wedding dress. He's never seen it.

Ava's eyes are wide when they move up to mine. "Is that—" she begins.

She freezes when I nod.

"I'm so, so sorry," I whisper.

"What?" Grayson asks. "What's going on?"

"And is he—" Ava begins again, and I close my eyes and nod when she looks over at me.

"I don't know what to say," I begin.

"What is it?" Grayson asks, looking incredibly confused.

"They wore our stuff," Ava says flatly.

"They wore our..." Grayson trails off as he looks at the photo again. "Ohhhhh," he says, exaggerating the sound of the word. "Oh, fuck." He looks up at his brother. "Are you serious, dude?"

"I'm sorry," Spencer says quietly. "We didn't mean—"

"We gave you that shit to keep safe! We trusted you!" Grayson roars at his brother, and it's really not so funny right now.

"It is safe," Spencer protests a little weakly. "It's up in the closet, and nobody will ever know."

"I can't wear that dress!" Ava wails. "Grayson's *seen* it now!"

"I will pay to replace it with any dress you want," Spencer says calmly. "We'll fix this. We will make this right."

"How? That was *the dress!*" Ava says, wiping a tear away from her cheek. "The wedding is in *three days!*"

Oh, God. I feel horrible.

The server chooses that moment to deliver our food, and this certainly isn't the impression I wanted to make with my in-laws.

"I can't eat," Ava says, pushing her plate away. "I can't sit here. Grayson, let's go."

Grayson gives his brother a look of disgust, and then the two of them slide out of the booth without looking at me.

Spencer leans his elbow on the table and rubs his forehead then leans on his palm. "Fuck," he mutters.

Well, that went worse than I expected.

He looks at the biscuits and gravy on his plate and trades it for Grayson's plate across the table. When I give him a look that plainly says *what the hell are you doing*, he says, "I didn't look at what the special was when I ordered it. I wore his tux...might as well eat his breakfast, too."

I reach for his biscuits and gravy and eat one along with everything on my own plate.

Good thing we got married last night. That dress wouldn't fit me any longer after this breakfast.

We head upstairs, both of us feeling like shit and not really sure what to do to make this right.

I lay down and close my eyes, but I can't sleep—especially not with the man pacing back and forth at the foot of the bed. "What are you doing?" I ask.

"Pacing," he says.

"Well...can you stop?"

He shoots me a glare.

"Don't be mad at *me*," I say.

"Why not? This was all your idea!" he yells.

"My idea was to protect the vineyard. You know Amelia. She'd sell the damn place off for parts, and I wanted to keep it in the family, and this was my best shot at doing that. I never thought we'd get blackout drunk, and I wouldn't even remember my own goddamn wedding."

"Neither did I," he mutters.

"Look, Spencer, we're in this together. Let's not turn on each other. Let's figure out how to fix this."

"You're right," he says. He sits on the edge of the bed. "So…how?"

I try to think it through, but my brain is still foggy. "I have no idea." A shower might help clear my mind, but I don't have any clothes with me.

Obviously.

I got married in someone else's dress, not that I brought a wedding dress along with me.

On that note, I pick up the phone on the nightstand and call guest services to have my suitcase sent up.

"I'm going to shower," he announces as he stands and steals my idea before I get a chance to.

I lean back against the headboard as I wait for my bag, and it arrives shortly after.

I grab my phone and pull up a browser.

How to make it up to someone when you wore her wedding dress.

That particular search doesn't quite yield the results I'm looking for.

I don't know what will ever yield the results I'm looking for, but this is a real problem.

I got him to marry me, I guess. But this isn't really what I was picturing when I came up with this plan.

Guilt racks me, and I know we have to figure out some way to make this right. I can't have Spencer's brother mad at him, and his bride mad at me, and a division splitting the family apart. What sort of way is that to start a marriage?

And I'm not referring to Grayson and Ava, though starting a marriage based on a contract rather than based on love isn't really rooted in reality either.

Not that we have a contract.

Spencer's phone starts to ring, and I glance at the screen.

It's his mother calling.

Oh, God. Does she know?

I hear the shower turn off, and I yell from where I am. "Spencer, your mom is calling!"

He rushes out with a towel tied around his waist, and water beads run down his chest.

Dear. Lord.

That guy right there? That's my *husband.*

For as much as this morning has brought pain—physically, given my hangover, as well as emotionally, given how we betrayed his brother's trust—I'm also met with the realization that *I'm married to Spencer Nash.*

And that's one hell of an interesting realization. I'm a wife. I have a husband. Thirty seconds ago—or last night, at any rate—I wasn't even dating anybody.

Look at us now.

I watch his retreating back as he walks into the bathroom again, this time with his phone. "Hey, Mom." He leaves the door open, and I can hear his end of the conversation. "He told you already? Jesus Christ. Give a guy a second to figure things out." A pause as his mother most likely yells at him for what we've done, and my chest feels like a heavy weight is set on top of it.

We'll figure this out…right?

Chapter 18: Spencer Nash

A Big Enough Screw Up to Warrant It

The Morning After the Wedding

The shower helped, but getting yelled at by my mother is sending me right back into hangover territory.

I grab the clothes I left on the floor and walk out of the bathroom so Grace can use it while I listen to my mother. I nod at Grace to go ahead to the bathroom as I perch on the edge of the bed.

"This is just so unlike you, Spencer! What were you thinking?"

"I wasn't thinking," I admit. "I was on a mix of tequila and Benadryl, and I guess it makes you do things you wouldn't normally do."

"So, what are you going to do?"

I clear my throat and go for the truth. "Gracie flew to Vegas to tell me that she figured out why Amelia had been cheating on me but was still pushing for a wedding. Apparently, whichever of Maggie's grandchildren gets married first and stays married for a year will inherit the vineyard. Amelia figured she could con me into marriage and take me for all I'm worth after a year."

"Oh, Spencer. I'm so sorry," she says quietly.

"I guess I agreed to marry Grace so she would get the vineyard instead of her sister. And we were so messed up that we didn't even realize what we were doing. You know I *never* would've thought to wear their wedding clothes if I was in my right mind, but she needed a dress, and there was one in the closet." I shrug even though she can't see me over the phone. It's a horribly weak defense, but I can't really change what's already been done.

"So you just…took it?" she asks.

"Like I said, we were hopped up on a strange cocktail. She's allergic to mustard, too."

"Oh, honey," she says, sympathy in her tone. "All that aside, are you going to stay married to her for a year?"

"I haven't thought any of this through. I'm still too hungover to even believe this really happened, let alone figuring out how the hell I'm going to make it up to Grayson and Ava."

"Yeah, that's a tough one," she agrees.

"Thanks," I say dryly. "Now hit me with it. I know you have ideas."

She laughs. "You know me well. It's too late to get new attire for the bride and groom since they're getting married in three days, but I'd start by getting them dry cleaned. You foot the bill, obviously. I'd also get something special for Ava to make the dress unique. A belt or something like that, maybe with a matching veil. And, of course, treat them to something special on the honeymoon. An excursion on you, dinner, or heck, pay for the whole thing. You got any connections to anyone famous you could get to their wedding last minute?"

An idea sparks in the back of my mind. "Actually, I met the guitarist for a band when I was in San Diego, and I think I remember Ava saying she's a fan."

"Get them there."

"I'll see what I can do. It's a new connection, and I hate to pull strings when I just met somebody, but…"

"But this was a big enough screw up to warrant it?" she guesses.

"Yeah," I mutter.

"Look, my sweet boy. I know it's hard right now, but someday down the road, you'll all look back on this and laugh," she says.

"God, I hope so." I just can't imagine a day when any of this will be funny...especially not if the *marriage* is only going to last a year.

Jesus. I really fucked things up.

I draw in a deep breath. I need to get this done while Grace is in the shower, so I call my new friend and hope for the best.

"Spencer?" he answers.

"Hey, Adam. I hope you don't mind me calling you with a favor after we just met."

He laughs. "As long as there's a pair of tickets to a game in it for me, you know I'm down."

"I think we can make that happen."

"Sweet. So what's the favor?"

"I, uh...it's a long story, but I sort of got married last night. We were blasted out of our minds. We're in Vegas for my brother's bachelor party week, culminating with the wedding on Saturday, and my bride and I, uh...we stole the bride and groom's wedding attire, and now we need to make it up to them."

"And you're wondering if MFB happens to be free to perform a song or two at the reception?" he guesses, finishing my thoughts for me.

"I was thinking maybe like four or five songs, but if you're down for one or two..."

He chuckles. "It's a lot to coordinate, to be honest. Especially last minute. But we'll be in Vegas for an event Saturday night, so we might be able to time it right. I'll check with Dax and the guys and see if we can swing it."

Holy shit.

I never thought I'd even *ask* for something like this...let alone actually get it. "Are you sure? Because if you can make it happen, I'd owe you a huge one."

"Like I said, man. Tickets to a game, and we're square. Honestly...I was actually where you are now once upon a time."

"You were?" I ask.

"Yeah. Waking up married was a shock, but now I'm waking up every day next to her." *Waking up every day next to her.* Before I can process what that would be like, he says, "We'll probably need six tickets so we can all go. Twelve would be ideal so we could each bring our girls."

There are only five members of My Favorite Band, better known as MFB, but I'm guessing the sixth ticket is for the former member who left years ago but is still tight with his former band.

I laugh. "You got it. I'll get you all tickets to every damn home game if you can make this work."

"I'll hold you to that. I'll get back to you."

I thank him, and we end the call.

Well, hopefully that's one way to make up for my horrible lack of judgment.

Bachelor party week is still in full swing, and according to the itinerary Ava printed out for guests, today we're having another pool party followed by dinner later tonight.

When Grace comes out of the bathroom, I can't help but stare at this woman who somehow overnight went from my ex-girlfriend's sister to my *wife*.

I always just saw her as a friend. I never noticed the way she always smells like vanilla or how she has this quiet beauty about her. Or maybe I noticed, but I didn't allow myself to acknowledge it. I couldn't—not when I was with her sister.

But that's been over nearly three months now, and now I'm married to this woman who is going to get to run her vineyard someday.

Maybe it's okay to acknowledge those things.

Chapter 19: Grace Nash

You've Done Enough

The Day After the Wedding

I feel slightly less terrible once I'm done with my shower, and I find Spencer sitting on the bed staring at me when I walk out of the bathroom.

"You okay?" I ask softly.

"I'm okay," he grunts.

I'm not sure what I'm supposed to do next. Do I go home? I got what I came here for, but it feels somehow wrong to leave now.

Grayson and Ava deserve an apology from us, at the very least.

"I was thinking—" I begin at the same time he says, "I had some ideas—"

We both pause, and he nods at me to go ahead.

"I was just thinking I'd like to apologize to Grayson and Ava," I say softly.

"Yes. We need to. And I have a few ideas regarding how we can attempt to make this up to them."

I nod. "And?"

"My mom had some ideas, actually. I'll get their clothes cleaned, and she suggested something special for Ava to wear to make the dress different. I thought maybe champagne each night in their room on their honeymoon. And there's one other thing, but I'm waiting to hear back from a friend."

I sit down beside him. "Okay, yes. Those are all good things. What can I do to help?"

He presses his lips together and shakes his head a little. "Nothing. You've done enough."

His words rip through me. He blames me for this, and while yes, I'm the one who came here with this crazy idea, he's the one who agreed to it. Maybe we were wasted out of our minds, but that doesn't change the fact that he was a willing participant in what occurred last night, and I refuse to sit here and take the full blame for it.

Even though it was my Benadryl.

It was his tequila.

And now I'm getting defensive and snippy even in my own head. This is ridiculous.

Before I get a chance to put a voice to any of those thoughts, he says, "I'm sorry. That came out wrong."

"Thank you for acknowledging that." It's a good step toward better communication, anyway, and isn't communication the base of every successful marriage?

That's what Nana says, anyway. And she would know. She's one of the few who I can look to for what success means in a marriage.

I should call her. I should tell her what I did last night.

Oh, God. I'm going to have to tell *my dad* that I got married.

And Amelia, but somehow that doesn't feel quite so daunting.

No…all that can wait.

I rushed to Vegas without a backward glance, and I'll be returning to the vineyard with a husband.

"So, uh…do you want to be my date to my brother's wedding?" he asks.

"Oh," I say, a little taken off guard by the question. "Sure, though I'm not sure they'd want me there."

"They'll be fine. And thank God my wife agreed to be my date."

I can't help but laugh.

He stands and walks over to the dresser, and he picks up a piece of paper. He scans it and reads off the events as he goes. "Looks like I missed today's tee time, but there's a dinner scheduled tonight for both sides of the bridal party with a burlesque show to follow." He glances up at me. "You're invited to all of the events, obviously."

Am I, though?

Would Ava really want me there after what happened last night?

"Thanks," I mumble instead. "Should we find a dry cleaner for the gown and the tux?"

"Already on it. I talked to the front desk, and they had a recommendation. Why don't we drop that stuff now and go shopping for bridal belts?"

I press my lips together and nod, and we each grab a garment back and head downstairs to catch a ride to the dry cleaner. The driver waits out front for us while we tend to our errands, and the cleaner happens to be in the same strip mall as a bridal store, so we head in there next.

"What a lovely couple," the woman behind the desk says when we walk in. "I'm Gina. What can I help you with?"

I open my mouth to launch into the whole story, but Spencer beats me to it, keeping things simple.

"We're looking for a crystal belt and matching veil to make a bridal gown look unique."

"Of course." She leads us toward a rack of accessories and shows us a few options, and Spencer chooses three different belts since he has no idea which one Ava will prefer.

"What do you think?" he asks me, holding two of them out while I hold the third in my hand.

I have no idea what Ave prefers, either.

"They're all beautiful," I say softly. I wish I was picking this out for myself. I wish I'd chosen my own wedding gown.

I wish a lot of things, but mostly I wish we could have a do-over.

"Then we'll take all three," he says.

Gina's eyes light up as she considers the commission on three crystal belts plus their three matching veils, and she practically runs to the register to take payment before we change our minds.

We do a little more shopping—mostly for me since I only brought two days' worth of clothes, and I'll need something nice to wear to the dinners the bride and groom have planned.

We head back to our hotel with our supplies that will hopefully be a start to making things up to Ava, and when we get back to our room, Spencer's phone starts to ring.

I catch his end of the conversation, curiosity clawing at me as I listen to his words.

"Damn...Holy shit, you can? I knew it was a longshot, but yeah, that would totally work...Yes, of course...I'll text you the details...I did...Actually, I looked into a suite and just booked one for the whole season, so you're welcome to any of the home games..."

He booked a suite for the whole season? Where? Why? What?

I wait for him to hang up, and before I plow forward with questions, he glances up at me. His eyes are brighter than they've been all day, and I can tell he's excited before he even opens his mouth to start answering the questions on the tip of my tongue.

"That was Adam Wilson," he says proudly.

Adam Wilson...Adam Wilson...Adam Wilson.

The name rings a foggy bell, but I have no idea why.

"Is he a football player?" I ask stupidly.

He laughs. "No. He's the lead guitarist for MFB."

"MFB?" I ask. "As in My Favorite Band?"

"I don't know if they're *your* favorite band, but I'm pretty sure they're Ava's, and they just agreed to play a set at the rehearsal on Friday." He tips his chin up at the end, and wait a hot second...

"Are you serious?"

He nods. "Serious as a W2," he says.

I giggle, and I'm not sure if it's a nervous giggle that MFB is going to be in the same room as me or if it's a giggle at his silly turn of phrase that sounds much nicer than when people say *serious as a heart attack*.

"Holy shit, Spence!" I practically yell, and I rush toward him and link my arms around his neck. "You really did that?"

"I did," he says, and he grabs me around the waist and twirls me around. "All for the low, low cost of season tickets to a suite so any member of the band can come to a Storm game any time they want during the season. And families, I guess." He sets me back down, and his eyes meet mine. "Or, you know…my wife."

My chest wavers with emotion, and I let go of my grip around his neck and back up a step. "You…you want me at your games?"

His lips tip up in a smile. "I'm not sure there's anything I'd like more than seeing you up in my suite wearing a jersey with number seventeen on it."

Seventeen.

That's his number.

Nash-seventeen.

That's my last name now.

Grace Nash.

And my husband wants me at his games.

In the same suite as MFB.

What is this life? It can't be real, can it?

I draw in a deep breath as I pinch myself.

We may have some obstacles ahead of us, but for now, yep…it feels pretty damn real.

Chapter 20: Grace Nash

Spencer in a Suit

The Day After the Wedding

I smooth down the silver sequins on the cocktail minidress I bought for tonight's dinner. Spencer read me the dress code from the itinerary, and this was what I went with. I'm nervous to walk out of the bathroom to see his reaction, though I'm not sure why I'm nervous.

I feel pretty in this dress. I feel sexy and sensual.

But I'm not sure if sexy and sensual is appropriate. It's a bit lower cut in the boob area than I'm used to, and it's a bit higher cut up the thigh area than I'm used to.

So it's a short, tight, lowcut dress when I'm usually more of a cover-it-all-up kind of gal—and I'll be meeting his family in this dress.

I've already met Lincoln, but that was before the wedding when I was screaming like a banshee around a security guard.

I've already met Grayson, and he walked out in utter disappointment at both of us when he learned the truth.

I haven't met Asher yet, and I haven't met Spencer's parents, who may or may not be in attendance tonight. I haven't met Spencer's sister-in-law, a former sports reporter married to the head coach of the Vegas Aces.

It's a family of celebrities, and I'm just a nerdy girl hoping to inherit her family's winery as I walk into a situation I probably have no business walking into. Spencer's barely been broken up with Amelia for five seconds—or three months, anyway—and now he's married to me when there were no signs whatsoever that we were even dating.

So...yeah. The nerves are in full force, and after dissecting all of that in my mind, I think they have every right to be.

But there's no turning back. Eventually, I'm going to have to face my husband's family...or I'll have to meet them anyway.

I draw in a deep breath and slowly let it deflate through my mouth, and then I open the door.

On the other side of it stands Spencer Nash in a suit.

Spencer. Nash. In a suit.

My brain malfunctions. My mouth malfunctions.

I gasp.

"Holy shit, Spence."

He looks *good* all day, every day, but something about seeing him in a suit as he gets ready to attend a fancy dinner followed by a Vegas show is out of this world. His hair is slicked back, which highlights the blue of his eyes, and he looks as if he hasn't shaved in a few days, which somehow makes him look tough and rugged even though his personality comes off more on the golden retriever side. His eyes connect with mine, and his heat as they sweep down my frame before moving back up again.

"Wow," he grunts. "That dress...you look great, Gracie."

Hearing him turn my name into two syllables with a bit of a rasp in his tone does things to me.

Crazy things.

Intense things.

A deep, dark ache pulses between my thighs.

I want to rush at him, to take him in my arms and kiss him and let him do whatever he wants to my body. His eyes dip to my cleavage again, and then they flick to my lips before they move to my eyes once again.

He feels it too. I know he does.

I clear my throat. "Thank you," I say softly. "And you in a suit...wow, Spence. Impressive."

One side of his mouth tips up into a smile, and then he reaches for my hand. "Ready?"

"Ready," I confirm. I grab the handbag I bought that matches the dress, and we head downstairs to get into the limo provided by the hotel to take us to another hotel for dinner. We end up at a fine dining steakhouse at the Aria, and we're led through the restaurant toward a private room in the back.

And that's where we find the party just getting underway.

I recognize Lincoln right away, and his arm is around a woman who's holding a baby. By her side is a young boy of maybe nine or ten, and they're talking to a woman who has to be Spencer's mom—a woman who looks quite a bit like the man she's currently chatting with. She's wearing a dusky rose-colored ruffled dress, and her hair is pinned up, and I can't help but wonder if she's also going to the burlesque show.

Won't that be weird to go to a sexy Vegas show with your *mom*? I wouldn't want to go with mine.

My relationship with my mom isn't very complicated. She's my mom, and I'm an adult who no longer lives with her. We text and talk a few times a week, but she's busy living her best life while I'm busy living mine—best or otherwise.

She's a free spirit, and I'm more conventional like my dad. Nana really took on the role of raising me, but she sort of took on the role of raising Amelia, too—which is why it's such a mystery that we ended up so completely opposite of one another. You know, that whole good versus evil thing.

Though I suppose I'm giving my evil sister a run for her money by marrying her ex-boyfriend five minutes after their relationship death certificate was signed. Maybe I'm giving my free-spirited mother a run for hers, too.

The woman talking to Lincoln glances toward the doorway as we enter, like she has some sixth sense that one of her sons just arrived, and she excuses herself from her conversation with Lincoln as she ambles over toward us, her ruffled dress sashaying all the way over.

"Spencer Thomas, introduce me to your bride immediately," she demands, and even though she's yelling at her son, there's an air of cheer about her that tells us both she's joking around.

"Mother, meet Grace, your new daughter-in-law," he says dryly, and he holds a sweeping hand out toward me.

"Nice to meet you, Mrs. Nash," I say softly.

"Oh, stop all that formality, my dear," she says, and she moves in for a hug. She squeezes me tightly. "Call me Missy or Mom, but never Mrs. Nash." She pulls back and holds me at arm's length as she studies me. "You're a gorgeous girl that I wish I could've seen as a bride. In your own clothes, of course."

My cheeks burn red in total and complete mortification.

"She's teasing you," Spencer says. "She does that to the people she loves most. You'll see."

She can't love me yet. She doesn't even know me. But at least her teasing me seems like a good sign that maybe eventually I'll win her over.

"See? It's funny already," she says, letting go of me and elbowing Spencer in the ribs.

He grunts a little.

"Tell me all about yourself, and leave not a single detail out," she says to me, and she slings an arm around my shoulders and starts to guide me toward the bar.

Yes. The bar. A glass of wine is needed promptly if I'm going to make it to the other side of this evening alive.

"There's my ex, also known as your new father-in-law," she says, nodding toward a man talking to a slightly younger, slightly shorter and leaner version of Spencer wearing a purple velvet tracksuit when everyone else here is dressed to the nines. "And Asher, my youngest, in the velour." We approach the bar, and Missy yells to the bartender. "Take care of this one, okay? She's a newlywed."

Oh, God. My face burns again, and I know she's just being sweet, but she's really talented at embarrassing me.

"Oh, is this the girl Spence drunk-married last night?" Asher asks, turning away from his conversation with his father and beelining toward Missy and me.

"The very one," Missy confirms.

I feel like this is going to be a very long night.

Chapter 21: Spencer Nash

Velour Tracksuits and Matching Drinks

The Day After the Wedding

I'm cornered by Lincoln the moment Mom leads Grace toward the bar, and he's berating me about what I've done.

Just what I wanted.

As if I haven't berated myself enough over this whole thing.

Grayson isn't here yet, and I'm sort of dreading the moment he walks in and sees me here with my date. My wife.

Except somehow, I think the surprise I have planned for the two of them will help them get over their anger. I hope.

At least my mother can see the humor in the whole thing, though it may take some time for Ava and Grayson to get there.

I glance up and see a velour-clad Asher talking to my mother and Grace, and that feels like trouble.

It's not jealousy that pinches at my nerves, exactly, but it's something a little darker than I was expecting to feel. Grace is a full five years younger than me, closer in age to Asher than to me. I can't help but worry that one day she'll wake up and think...man, this guy's old.

Especially since Asher can snag any woman he wants. It's his superpower, I guess.

He can wear stupid clothes like velour tracksuits and get away with it because of his charm. He has an easy way with people. He's outgoing like my other brothers, where I'm the quiet, reserved one.

I do okay for myself, too—obviously. Both Newman sisters wanted to marry me, even if it wasn't for love.

Okay, fine. Bad example. But sometimes the way Grace looks at me makes me think we could get there someday.

I'm sure it's my imagination.

But sometimes I look at her and think we could get there someday, too, which is absolutely insane since we're nothing more than good friends.

Only…she proposed marriage to me to get revenge on her sister and to inherit her family vineyard, and that thought will forever be cemented at the forefront of my interactions with her.

Something peeks through, though. A memory. Her lips beneath mine, soft and pillowy. It's a fever dream, maybe. If I really kissed her, I'd remember it, wouldn't I?

"Excuse me," I say to Lincoln, and then I stride across the room to slip my arm around her waist.

It feels like the natural, right thing to do, just as it feels natural and right when she leans into me a little at the feel of me beside her. The sweet scent of vanilla wafts up from her hair.

"I'm just meeting your wife," Asher says, nodding to Grace.

"Yes, Grace," I say to him.

She glances up at me, likely at my clipped tone, and then she reaches out a hand for Asher to shake. "Lovely to meet you."

"Asher," he says with a nod. "The youngest and best of the four Nash boys."

Mom elbows him in the ribs with an eye roll. "Definitely the one with the strangest fashion sense."

He glances down at his tracksuit. "It's an inside joke between Grayson and me," he admits, and thank God it's something like that rather than a genuine attempt at looking good—though I wouldn't put that past him, either.

The bartender is pouring a glass of red.

"Can you pour a second one of those?" I ask.

He nods and grabs another glass, and then he hands them over the bar. Naturally, Grace picks up one, and I pick up the other.

"Matching drinks already. How sweet," Asher says, teasing in his tone.

But between the hangover and the strangeness of today, I'm not in the mood for it.

"Fuck off," I snap at him, and Mom rolls her eyes while Grace stiffens at my side.

"Here comes the bride," Asher says, nodding toward the door.

This time, I stiffen. And then my dad starts making his way over toward us.

Jesus.

It's one hit after another.

"Eddie Nash," he says to Grace. "And you are?"

"Grace," she says softly.

"Your new daughter-in-law," Mom says pointedly.

I blow out a breath. "Can we save all that for another time? This is Grayson's weekend."

"Should've thought of that before you got drunk and took a car to a chapel," Dad points out.

So that's how it's gonna go.

Instead of responding, I turn, my arm still wrapped around Grace, and choose to walk away. I'm just not sure exactly where I'm heading. Lincoln is in one corner shooting me wary glances. Grayson is in the doorway, avoiding eye contact with me altogether while he greets his guests. And Mom, Dad, and Asher are at the bar with their quips and jokes at the ready.

I chug down the wine, suddenly sure there's not enough wine in this bar for me to get through this night unscathed.

But I guess I made my bed, and now I have to lie in it.

I empty my glass, which does nothing in terms of helping me feel any differently, but at least it's taking the edge off.

"You okay?" her voice asks beside me, small and sweet.

I blow out a breath. "Would you be?"

She looks offended, like I took a shot—which I did. It's not fair to her, and she's going to have to face her family with what we've done, too. But it's different for her. She didn't betray her brother by wearing his wedding attire and taking attention from what's supposed to be his week.

"Sorry," I mutter. "You don't deserve that."

She pulls my arm from around her waist, and for a second, I feel a little lost.

But then she grabs my hand and drags me out of the room. We keep walking through the restaurant until we're out in front of it, and she pulls me a few paces away from the door. She stops and stands in front of me, and she takes my jaw between her palms so I'm forced to look into her eyes.

"Listen to me, Spencer Nash. This is you and me now, okay? I know you're struggling, but I'm putting a stop right here, right now, to you taking it out on me. I'm struggling, too, and maybe instead of being snippy with each other, we can try facing this thing head-on. Maybe you blame me, or maybe you're mad at me, but this is your family's first impression of me, and they all hate me. If you could just, I don't know…maybe *try* not to be such a dick to them, then maybe they can find something about me they don't hate so we can get through the next year without completely avoiding them."

I stare down into her eyes. Hers are flashing with anger and frustration, and I feel bad that I put her in that position.

"They don't hate you," I say quietly. The fact that she thinks they do tears at my chest.

"Huh?" She drops her hands from my jaw, and I grab onto her waist and haul her into me.

I'm met with an *oof* of surprise.

"They don't hate you," I repeat. "I told you, my mom only teases the people she likes. My dad, well, he's my dad. He doesn't know you yet, but soon enough he'll find a way to try to get something out of you. Free wine for life or something. And my brothers, they just think this is so far out of left field for me that they're being protective. Gray might be a little angry, but he'll get over it, and once Linc and Ash get to know you, they'll love you. Ash might love you too much, which is why I ran across the room the second I saw him go near you."

"Too much?" she repeats. "Why would you care if it's too much?"

My chest tightens as the urge to kiss her pulses over me. What the hell is that?

I've never felt that urge with her before, though I snuck a look at the wedding photos, and we definitely shared a kiss there.

And now…I can't help but want to know what it's like to kiss her again.

"Because I care. Okay?" I lower my head and brush my nose along hers, and then I drop my lips to hers for the briefest brush of a kiss.

Her eyes are wide when I pull back and look at her. "Oh, uh…okay, then," she stutters.

I can't help when my lips tip up in a small smile.

I sort of like taking her off guard. And I sort of like being taken off guard by her, too—something she did the second she took my hand and pulled me out here to confront me with my behavior and set the tone for maybe the entire basis of this marriage, sham or not.

"Should we go back in?" she asks quietly.

"Do we have to?"

She chuckles, and she pulls out of my grasp, taking my hand in hers again. "Yes, we have to."

I twist my lips in disappointment but follow her through the restaurant toward the party.

When we return, Asher's standing by the door. He wiggles his eyebrows at me, and he looks ridiculous with the wiggling eyebrows and the purple velour thing he has going on. "You feeling all relaxed after your little boink sesh?"

"Fuck off, Asher," I say to him for the second time this evening.

His response is to burst into laughter, and I just roll my eyes at him as I head toward my mom, who feels like a safe space for Grace, and take a seat to get this dinner under way.

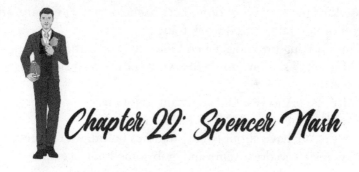

Chapter 22: Spencer Nash

Your Husband Was Released

Two Days After the Wedding

The alarm wakes me up at six, and Grace doesn't move. It's the second time we've shared a bed, but the first time, we were blackout drunk, and the second time, we were both exhausted after a full day that started with a hangover.

We made it through dinner, and we had fun at the burlesque show afterward—which my parents opted *not* to attend, thankfully. But it was late by the time we got back, and I'm pretty sure Grace fell asleep on my shoulder for a few minutes in the car on the way back to the Palms.

All in all, it was a nice night, though not what I would've expected for my first day as a married man.

Since all my brothers know, and everyone who's here attending Grayson's bachelor week knows, I have a feeling word will get out to the media soon that we tied the knot—if it hasn't already.

I haven't spent much time on my phone looking, but I wouldn't put it past a wedding chapel in Vegas wanting the free publicity of letting the world know a pro athlete used their facilities for his wedding.

And if the media gets hold of the news, it won't be long before Grace's family finds out.

These are the thoughts swirling around my brain as I get dressed for the first event on today's bachelor party itinerary, an early morning hike at Red Rock Canyon.

I'm just tying my shoes when Grace rolls over then sits up.

"Morning," she says softly, her voice raspy from sleep. "Is it time for the hike already?"

"Morning. And yes. Did you want to join us?"

She clears her throat. "Do I have time?"

I nod. "We have about twenty minutes before we're meeting. I was going to go downstairs and grab something to eat."

"Order me whatever you're having. I'll be right down."

I nod, and she heads to the bathroom. Day two of being married feels somehow different from day one. Day one was hangovers and confusion. Day two is starting our new normal, which apparently means early morning hikes and yogurt parfaits with coffee for breakfast.

She joins me ten minutes later, her hair pulled back into a ponytail as she wears sweatpants and a Vikings T-shirt.

I chuckle when I see her shirt. "You do know your husband was released, right?"

She lifts a shoulder. "Skol for life, babe."

I laugh at her reference to the war chant cried by our fans.

"Get me a Storm shirt, then," she says. "I'll wear it."

"Deal."

I nod toward the untouched yogurt parfait waiting for her, and she sits beside me and digs in. I finish mine and chug my coffee, and then we head toward the front of the hotel to meet with everyone else who will be going on the hike.

I'm met with a bunch of quiet, tired people.

"Who thought six-thirty in the morning was a good idea after staying out so late last night?" Asher whines when we walk up.

I chuckle. "The groom, who isn't even here yet."

"As opposed to the one who *is*?" Lincoln guesses, sidling up behind me.

I roll my eyes at Asher before I turn around. "And a top of the morning to you, too, asshole."

Lincoln laughs. "I feel like I was in a much better mood than you are when I was a newlywed." He glances at Jolene. "Wasn't I?"

Jolene holds up both hands as if she's going to sit this one out.

"To be fair, I was getting laid, like *a lot*. I don't know your situation, though." Lincoln offers a shrug.

I glare at him before I turn away from him and back to Asher. I'm not sure which option is worse, to be honest, and I'm starting to think we should've just slept in rather than joining in on this particular adventure.

I'm debating when to tell Grayson about the surprise I have planned for tomorrow night—or if I should tell him at all. Maybe I'll just leave it as a surprise.

"Oh, the thunder stealers are here," Grayson says, announcing his arrival. His arm is around his soon-to-be bride's shoulders, and she rolls her eyes a little, which makes me think even *she* is getting tired of his antics. Or maybe I'm totally off, and she's rolling her eyes at *us*.

"Dude, let it go," I say. "The only reason anybody even knows is because you keep bringing it up."

"He's right, Gray," Ava says softly. "All we can do at this point is let it go."

"Can I talk to you two?" I ask. "Privately?"

Grayson purses his lips at me, and Ava steers him away from the group.

I follow behind them, holding Grace's hand and pulling her along behind me. Once we're a safe distance from the rest of the group, I look between Grayson and Ava. "Look, I want to make this up to you, so I did a few things. First, I took your clothes to be dry cleaned, and they'll be delivered to your house this afternoon. Ava, I got a few different accessories for you to make the dress unique and different. We can't apologize enough for what we did. And there's one other thing, but I'm not sure if I should tell you or just surprise you with it."

"I think we've had enough surprises out of you," Grayson snips at me.

I blow out a breath. "I arranged for some live music at the rehearsal tomorrow night. I hope that's okay."

"Live music?" Ava repeats, narrowing her eyes at me.

I nod. "A band you like. I promise."

"Who is it?"

I glance back at Grace, who nods a little. "Well, I sort of got friendly with the guitarist, and he's a big Storm fan. I called in a favor, and, well, MFB will be playing a short set tomorrow night at your house."

"M...M...MF...MFB?" Ava says, stuttering the letters.

I chuckle. "Yes. MFB."

"As in My Favorite Band?" she asks.

"In both meanings of that phrase, yes." I raise my brows hopefully, and both Ava and Grayson are frozen for a beat that feels like a fucking hour.

Then, finally, Ava glances at Grayson before her mouth breaks into a wide smile. "Holy shit! Are you serious?"

I nod. "Serious as a W2."

She flings her arm around my neck. "Okay, okay. You're officially not my least favorite future brother-in-law anymore."

"Who is?"

She twists her lips. "I'll have to think about that one."

I laugh, and she laughs, and even Grayson laughs, and relief fills me that even though we fucked up big time, maybe we didn't ruin this weekend the way we first thought we did.

Ava hugs Grace next, and I blow out a breath.

We head out for the hike, and Ava and Grace chat excitedly about the band they both love. Ava asks more questions about our surprise nuptials, and I listen quietly as the two women are at the precipice of becoming actual friends.

They bond some more at the pool party, and again at dinner—the last dinner before the rehearsal dinner.

I can't help but think that maybe someday down the line, they won't just be sisters-in-law in name only. I can't help but imagine big Nash family gatherings where the two run off to a corner to talk about whatever it is women who walk into a family like this one talk about.

And the thought of that for the future is hopeful and bright.

It's so bright, in fact, that I forget about the possibility that it could very likely still crash and burn. But that's sort of the problem with turning a blind eye.

Harsh reality always somehow sneaks its way in.

Chapter 23: Grace Nash

Head in the Hole

Three Days After the Wedding

"The itinerary did say it was a couple's massage," Spencer says. He shrugs, and he looks nearly as uncomfortable as I feel.

We're standing in a room at the spa staring at each other. Two massage therapists just told us to take off our clothes and slip under the blanket on the table. Even though we were nearly naked when we drunkenly slept in the same bed after the wedding, and even though we're *married*…I don't think we're there yet.

How ridiculous does that even sound?

I'm not ready to get naked with my husband.

One of them did tell us we could leave our underwear on. We can get as naked as we're comfortable with.

Well, I gotta say, I'd likely feel most comfortable with perhaps a turtleneck beneath overalls.

I sigh. "I guess I didn't realize that meant we'd be getting naked in the same room together."

"We don't have to—"

"No," I say, holding up a hand. "It's all right. Just…turn around or something. No peeking."

"If you want, I can go first and stick my head in the hole so I don't see anything."

I nod. "Okay. Let's do that."

"Turn around," he says, as if I didn't see him wearing nothing more than a towel two days ago.

I turn around, but there's a mirror beside me, and I can't help when my eyes dart over to it.

He's already out of his shirt, and good God, those abs are something else. Are they even real? How exactly does one chisel muscles quite like that?

He leaves his boxer briefs on, and that's when his eyes move to the mirror.

He catches me looking.

My eyes dart away immediately.

His only reaction to catching me is a soft chuckle as he finishes up. "Okay, my head is in the hole."

"No peeking," I warn.

He outright laughs this time. "Oh, so it's okay for you, but not for me?"

My cheeks burn. "I was just checking if you were on the table."

"Right," he says, drawing out the word sarcastically as if he doesn't believe that for a second.

I undress quickly down to just my panties and practically leap for the table, pulling the blanket up over my body as I try to settle my face into a comfortable position on the cradle.

"Are you naked?" he asks.

I laugh. "Wouldn't you like to know?"

"Turnabout is fair play, my wife."

"I took off everything except my undies."

"The black silky ones?" he asks.

My head darts up from the cradle as I glare at Spencer, who's still face down. "Excuse me, Mr. Nash, but how in the hell do you know that if you didn't peek?"

"I didn't peek in here! I swear. At breakfast, when you got out of the booth next to me, your shirt was riding up a little, and, well…I peeked then."

My cheeks burn again, but you know what? I kind of like the fact that he peeked.

It makes me feel like maybe, just maybe, this drunken mistake could take us from good friends to something else entirely.

The massage therapists return to the room before I get the chance to respond to that, but it's in my mind the entire time the therapist works my back.

After the couple's massage that feels like it upped the ante between us a bit, the two of us head for couple's pedicures, where we find Lincoln and Jolene as they're about halfway through their own pedicures.

"It's the groom and his new bride," Lincoln teases us, and at least the teasing is getting slightly less awkward.

Slightly.

It's still pretty awkward.

"Oh Linc, knock it off," his wife scolds him, and she pats the seat beside her. "Let's chat, Grace."

I offer a small smile, but I know this woman. She's a former sports reporter who now runs a popular podcast with her head coach husband, and she's not afraid to ask the hard questions.

It makes me just a little fearful about what's coming next, but I take the seat beside her anyway. Spencer sits on the other side of Lincoln, and part of me wishes he would've sat beside me. This *is* supposed to be a couple's pedicure, after all.

But I suppose my husband and I aren't really a couple. Yet.

"Tell me about yourself," she begins, and she grabs the remote and makes some adjustments to the back massager on her chair.

I do the same as I stick my feet into the warm water. "Well, I'm twenty-four, and I'm the hospitality manager at my family's vineyard."

"What's it like having a family vineyard?" she asks. "It sounds so magical."

I launch into the history and my dream of running the place.

"That sounds really special," Jolene says quietly. "Heck, it sort of sounds like a dream I'd like, too. Life is just so crazy right now with Josephine and Jonah. I can't imagine having a calm, quiet place to relax at the end of each day when life is full of chaos right now."

"It's a different kind of dream having kids, though," I point out.

"It is. It's the best, most wonderful, most frustrating job in the world."

I laugh.

"Do you want kids someday?" she asks.

I nod. "I always pictured at least two who are close in age. I always wondered what it would be like to have a sister who was my best friend instead of one who hates me."

"You think she hates you?"

"Well, if she didn't before, she probably will now that I married her ex," I point out.

She laughs. "So this wedding was all just a business deal?"

"I don't know. It all just feels so natural and right with him, and sometimes I think maybe…" I trail off, not sure I should be confessing this to her with him a mere ten feet away.

"Maybe?" she prompts me.

I lift a shoulder and glance over at her. I press my lips together.

She nods a little encouragingly as if she knows exactly what I was about to say, and somehow, I picture sitting with her again, the two of us chatting like this as she gives me sage advice from her life experiences. "I could see it," she says softly. "You two, I mean. You seem like a good fit."

I look around her at Spencer, and he looks around Lincoln at me.

He smiles, and I get the feeling deep in my chest like maybe we are a better fit than I ever realized.

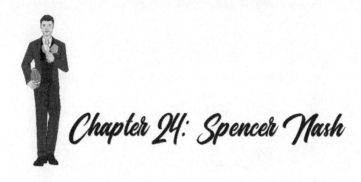

Chapter 24: Spencer Nash

All Systems Go

Three Days After the Wedding

The day was relaxing, just as the bride intended, and now we're heading toward Grayson's house for the rehearsal this evening. When I RSVP'd to this wedding, I had no idea I'd be attending with my *wife*.

And I certainly never thought my *wife* would be *Grace*.

I'm used to seeing Grace Newman in jeans, sneakers, and a sweater as she runs around the vineyard.

But this is Grace Nash, a sophisticated woman in a black cocktail dress and heels that make her legs look fine.

Damn fine.

The urge to kiss her again is *strong* this evening, and I'm not quite sure how I'm supposed to keep myself together when I can't stop looking at her.

I know this was just her big plan to get revenge on Amelia. This isn't a genuine marriage. And somehow, my drunk ass agreed to it.

But the more time I spend with her, the more compatible I feel like we are. And the more I lean into that, the more I can see this switching from an arrangement into something more.

What the fuck is there to lose by giving it a try?

She needs me for a year.

So what if we spend that year as a truly married couple and conclude that we actually like it? What if it doesn't have to end in a year?

That's a whole lot of what-ifs for someone who enjoys being firmly planted in reality, and all that does is tell me that if she can make me think these thoughts, she's someone different.

Someone who might be worth exploring.

I reach over and take her hand in mine. It's pure instinct, and she glances up at me, those brown eyes landing sweetly on my blue ones. "You ready for this?" I ask.

She nods. "The more time I spend with your family, the less I feel like they hate me."

"Not a single one of them hates you," I say softly. "How could they?"

Her cheeks turn a little pink at the compliment, though she doesn't answer.

We pull up in front of Grayson's mansion. The happy couple decided to keep things simple and do this thing at their home because of his celebrity status. They're hopeful that means there won't be helicopters circling while they exchange vows, but the guest list is a virtual who's who of Vegas superstars—and apparently MFB, who's set to arrive toward the conclusion of the rehearsal.

We walk into the house and find a wedding wonderland, though most of the fresh flowers won't be delivered until morning. It's been transformed from the house I've visited many times into a beautiful wedding venue fit for my brother and his bride.

"Oh, good, you're here," Ava says to me, a flurry of activity in a navy dress with swinging hair as she rushes over to give me a quick hug. She hugs Grace next before she turns back to me. "We need you standing at the back row outside. Grace, you can sit with Jolene, okay?"

Grace nods, and I may have neglected to mention to her that I'm an usher at this shindig along with Asher. We head out to the backyard that's now covered in white—the turf is covered in white rugs, and a white aisle runner runs toward an altar with a floral arch under which Ava and Grayson will be married tomorrow.

Lincoln walks by once I take my place, and I nod at him. "What do I call you now? Officiant? Minister? Preacher? Asshole?"

He laughs and punches me in the arm. "*Sir* would be fine."

"Good luck with that."

He heads toward the altar since he's officiating, and I stand with Asher while Ava leads Grace toward Mom.

I can't help but watch as she walks away. Somehow, she fits into the picture in a way I never really expected. Better than Amelia ever would have, that's for damn sure.

We go through the motions of the rehearsal with some event planner Ava nailed down, and my phone buzzes in my pocket toward the end of the practice run.

Adam: *We're out front. Where do you want us to set up?*

I guess I hadn't really thought that through. "Excuse me," I say to Asher, and then I head toward the driveway and find the five members of MFB: Dax, the lead singer; Brody, the drummer; Will, the keyboardist; Gage, the bassist; and Adam, the lead guitarist. Two other guys hang toward the back, and I assume they're the roadies who will assist with setting this thing up, and a woman stands beside Dax. I think she's his wife and the band's manager.

"Holy shit," I breathe. "Thank you so, so much for being here."

"Thanks for the season suite," Adam says, reaching out to shake my hand as I come to a stop in front of him.

I chuckle. "Hope your schedule isn't too booked so you can make it to some games."

"We'll be there," Dax says.

"Come on in," I say. They follow me inside, and Dax surveys the area.

"Maybe in the yard?" he suggests.

I nod. "There's a huge side yard so you can set up undetected. The rehearsal is almost over, so you can get set up while everyone comes inside for dinner. How long will it take?"

"Thirty minutes or so," he says.

"Perfect. I'll keep everyone in here. You can use the side gate to get back there, and I'll bring some plates out so you can eat, too."

They all nod in agreement, and they head out front to start dragging their gear around to the side of the house.

Meanwhile, the rehearsal portion of the night ends, and everyone else comes in for dinner. Grayson gives me a strange look as he walks by me, and I grab his arm and pull him aside.

"All systems go for that surprise I told you about."

His brows rise. "They're here?"

I nod. "Setting up in your side yard now."

"Ava!" he yells without turning away from me. She moves to his side. "Come with me."

They head outside, presumably to meet the band, and Grace walks tentatively over toward me. "What's going on?"

I lean in toward her. "The band is here," I murmur quietly toward her ear since I'm trying to keep a secret, but I guess it comes out more intimate than I intend for it to since she shivers a little.

"Oh my God, are you serious?" she whisper-yells at me.

"Serious as a—"

"W2," she finishes for me. "Can I meet them?"

I chuckle. "They're around the side of the house in the yard."

She tugs on my hand. "Come introduce me."

I nod, and I glance around. Everyone is busy talking and getting drinks as they find seats so the servers waiting in the kitchen can start delivering the plates of food. "Help me bring plates out to them."

"Deal."

We tell the servers we need seven plates for some extra guests, and they set four on one tray and three on another with silverware. We take them outside, and I find Ava gushing over her favorite band, My Favorite Band. It's just fun to say.

Grace's hands are shaking, and I spot a table and set one tray on it before I take the tray from her hands. She follows me toward the band, where we find four of them setting up and the fifth talking with Ava.

"What songs do you want to hear?" Dax asks her.

"Oh my God, all of them!" Ava squeals. "For sure 'What Did We Just Do.' That's my all-time favorite. And 'Love out of Nowhere.' Basically everything on *No Room for Regrets.*"

I chuckle as she names their most popular album.

Dax nods. "We have time for six songs before our roadies need to clean up, so we'll do a mash-up. But we might be able to hang out awhile afterward."

"You're the best!" Ava's still squealing when we walk up behind her.

"I'd like to introduce you to Grace," I say, nodding at the woman standing beside me. "Grace, this is Dax."

"Is this your wife?" Dax asks.

"Of three whole days, yes," I admit.

He chuckles and leans in toward Grace. "Adam confessed the real reason Spencer asked us to show up."

She giggles as her cheeks turn pink. "I'm such a huge fan!" She tosses her arms around his neck.

"And you're married now," I say dryly.

"And so am I," Dax admits.

Dax and I both laugh, but Grace looks, well, starstruck. Like she's in a complete daze.

It's comical, actually.

"Let me introduce you to the rest of the guys," Dax says to Grace, and he slings an arm around her shoulders and takes her to their small stage so she can meet everyone.

I hang back with Grayson.

"This is great, man. I can't believe you made it happen," he says.

"I wanted you to know how truly sorry I am for what happened." I give him my words in my most genuine tone.

"I know you are. And this more than makes up for it."

"You sure?" I ask.

"Don't question it, man," he says, slugging me in the arm.

I decide to take his advice on that.

We head inside to eat after I physically pull Grace away from the band so they have time to finish setting up, and by the time we're done eating, I get a text from Adam letting me know they're ready.

"We have one final surprise," Grayson says to the friends and family gathered here after I give him the green light. "Can you all join us out in the yard?"

I text Adam to let him know we're on our way out, and the forty-or-so guests inside make their way outside to the sound of MFB's opening song, one of their biggest hits.

A good chunk of Grayson's guests scream and yell as they make their way toward the band, and they sound fucking incredible as they play on a makeshift stage, the sound of their music filling the air around us.

I glance over at Ava, and she's singing along with every word.

So is Grace.

Warmth fills my chest that I was able to make this happen.

My arm slides around Grace, and she glances up at me, her big, brown eyes full of happiness, and I get this feeling of hope.

Hope that someday I can be the one making her eyes look that happy.

Chapter 25: Spencer Nash

She's My Wife

Three Days After the Wedding

What's better than getting your soon to be sister-in-law's favorite band to play at her wedding rehearsal?

Getting that same band to join us at our after-party.

We're heading to Honey's, the world-renowned strip club not too far from the center of all things Vegas. Grayson said his teammates frequent the joint. Ava thought a strip club sounded fun since she'd never been to one, and it's part of the time-honored, clichéd history of bachelor parties.

Even though the four Nash brothers would all be respectful without dates since that's how our mother raised us, having our women here with us will keep us in check. There's something kind of hot about sitting with my *wife* while we watch half—or fully—naked women dancing for our enjoyment.

And then there's Asher, who's here solo and will more than likely go home with a stripper.

You know that old saying about how strippers only like men for their money?

That's true—for the average guy.

Asher Nash is not your average guy. He's young, he's single, he's apparently good-looking, even though to me he's just my brother with an odd sense of fashion, and he's the wild card of the Nash family. Women flock to him, and I'm certain tonight will be no different, stripper or otherwise.

But we're here with MFB, and while the four Nash brothers have a certain celebrity status because of our professions, the band's international popularity leaves the four of us quite literally in their dust.

All five members of the band are married, but only Dax's wife is here with him tonight. I can't help but wonder whether the other wives approve of their adventure out with the Nash brothers or if they even know. Something tells me they know, though. If Dax's wife is here with him, I can't really imagine her keeping that secret from the others.

We're taken to three different VIP booths toward the front since our group is so large, and I move to pull my credit card out of my pocket to treat the whole group when the server stops me. "Dax took care of it."

I glance over at Dax. He did?

Man, these guys are really pretty damn awesome.

Grayson is on my left, and Grace is on my right. The band is scattered between my brothers, our dates, and Grayson's friends.

We drink. We order appetizers. We drink some more. We watch the dancers. We tip generously. We eat chicken wings like it's normal to chew on chicken bones while tits bounce in our faces mere feet away.

We laugh. I avoid tequila, opting instead for a lighter beer tonight, but Grace is by my side, her cheeks flushed as she seems to move fractionally closer to me after every sip of her glass of wine.

I have to admit...I like it.

A lot.

I would've thought she'd be moving closer and closer to Adam. He's the guitarist in her favorite band, after all. But she's moving closer to *me* while we're here at this place that's filled with sensuality and sex, and it's making me want sex. With her. Immediately.

It wouldn't be right to do that after yet another night of drinking. But the more time I spend with her, the more I seem to want her.

The feelings are growing instead of diminishing, and I'm not sure I can keep fighting that. Hell, I'm not sure I need to keep fighting it. She's my wife now. Even if it's just for the next year, why not have some fun with it?

It's not like I was planning to meet a woman and get married my first year in San Diego anyway. It's not like this is setting me back on some invisible timeline.

It shouldn't feel as right as it does.

She excuses herself to the restroom, and I feel the loss of her warmth when she gets up. Usually girls go in groups to the bathroom, but she's a strong, independent woman who heads there alone.

She's been gone a while, and at first, I assume it's because the ladies' room had a line.

But when a full ten minutes have passed and she hasn't returned, I start to get worried.

I excuse myself to head that direction, thinking maybe I'll see her along the way. It's not like I'm going to bust into the women's bathroom to check on her, but maybe a woman outside the bathroom can check on her for me.

It's as I approach the small hallway leading into the restrooms that I spot her.

A big, burly guy has her cornered near the bar, and she looks...scared. He's just talking to her. His hands aren't on her, but I get the very real sense that she's in some sort of danger, and the immediate thought is that she needs my help.

The immediate thought is that I need to save her, and I will stop at nothing to get that look of fear off her face. I will stop at nothing to make sure she knows she's safe with me.

I stride in her direction, butting my way in to end their conversation. "There you are," I say, glaring at the big dude.

"You're with her?" he asks me.

"She's my wife," I say thickly.

"I was just telling her how pretty her titties would look up on that stage." He grins lewdly at me.

I feel sick at his words, and if I feel sick, I can't even imagine how she feels.

My instinct is to punch this asshole right in the mouth, but a stronger instinct to get her out of this situation takes precedence.

"She's not here to dance." I take her hand in mine and pull her away from the guy, and I walk right past the group gathered across the three VIP tables that's here to party tonight in celebration of my brother and his bride.

I lead Grace straight out the front doors, and she sucks in a breath of fresh air as soon as we're outside.

"Gracie," I say softly, and I pull her into me.

"Oh, God," she whimpers, and she bursts into tears.

I wrap my arms around her, and she rests her head on my chest. "Did he hurt you?"

She shakes her head. "He didn't touch me," she sobs.

I rub my hand around her back in a soothing circle.

"It was how he looked at me. The things he said to me. It made me feel…gross."

"You're not," I say fiercely. "You're beautiful, and that's all he could see. That's all he cared about. He didn't care that you're one of the most organized people I've ever met, or how intuitive you are when it comes to people, or how kind you are even when someone treats you like shit. He didn't care about the way you schedule the staff at the vineyard or how you can identify every note in a bottle of wine. He wasn't looking at how you would drop anything to help someone out or how you never take time for yourself because you're so dedicated to giving your family and the vineyard everything you have."

She pulls back, her teary eyes lifting up to meet mine. She raises her hand to my jaw, her fingertips gliding softly along the scruff there. "Is that really what you think of me?" she whispers.

I look down tenderly into her eyes, shocked she even has to ask that question. "Of course it is, Gracie."

Her eyes flick down toward my lips, and then she closes her eyes and leans in to press her mouth to mine.

I hold her close, careful not to deepen this kiss, careful not to take the lead. Careful not to spook her after she's already full of fear from the encounter inside.

She pulls back and looks up at me in wonder. "Nobody has ever said those kinds of things to me. Nobody has ever *noticed*."

"I have." And I find it hard to believe nobody else ever has, but then I think of the night we met.

Maybe the reason nobody has ever noticed has less to do with Grace and more to do with her sister, who excels at taking center stage and stealing the light from Grace.

Not anymore. I won't let anyone steal anything from her ever again.

Not now that she's my wife.

Chapter 26: Grace Nash

What the Hell is a Postnup

Four Days After the Wedding

I thought for a split second that maybe he'd kiss me some more, but he didn't. I didn't want to go back inside and run into that asshole again, so Spencer took me back to the Palms. We settled into bed and flipped on a movie to distract my thoughts, and it helped.

I fell asleep snuggled onto his chest, his arms wrapped around me.

I'm not sure I ever want to fall asleep another way ever again.

The problem is that morning always comes quickly, and that's no different today—especially since Spencer has a tee time with the boys ahead of the wedding.

And that also means I have nothing to do until he gets back.

Once he's out the door, I take a quick shower then head down to the diner for a solo breakfast, and I think it might be time to call my dad and confess what's going on.

I've been married for four days now, and he, my mom, and Nana don't even know.

Or maybe they do.

Maybe we've made the news by now. Part of me thinks we'd have to given Spencer's status in the media, but it's his brother's wedding weekend, so maybe the paparazzi is focused on the wrong brother—which would be pure luck for us since I haven't found the right moment to call my family.

Maybe I don't want them to know. Maybe I don't want *Amelia* to know.

I could tell my dad and not risk Amelia finding out. Nana might be a different story, though.

It's as I'm sitting at my solo breakfast that I finally dial Dad's number.

"Hey, pumpkin," he answers. "When are you coming home? This place is falling apart without you."

I chuckle. "Hey, Dad. I have a flight back tomorrow night." Sadness fills me that I'm going back to Minnesota, and my husband is not.

"Thank God. How's it going out there? Did you do what you needed to do?"

I clear my throat. "In fact, I did."

"And are you ever going to clue in your clueless old man about what that was?"

"I got married," I whisper.

I'm met with silence. Stunned silence, to be exact.

"You...you what?" he asks.

"I got married."

"Oh, Gracie," he mutters. "Because of the vineyard?"

"Well...I mean, yeah. That was my motivation in coming here to present the idea. But I realized how ridiculous of a plan it was, and I knew he'd never say yes."

"He?" he asks carefully.

"Spencer."

"Jesus, Gracie. But he did say yes if you're married now," he points out.

"Well, that's where it gets a little crazy."

"*That's* where?" he claps in.

I clear my throat. "We were drinking tequila, and we ordered some appetizers. As it turns out, he has an allergy to mustard, too, and the sauce we ate had mustard in it. We both reacted, and we took some Benadryl, and I guess Benadryl plus tequila equals—"

"Blackout," he supplies, interrupting me.

"Yeah. The rest of the night is a total blur. But a wedding certificate in our room tells me it happened."

"Please, please, *please* tell me you two were lucid enough to draft up a prenup." He's begging me, and for the first time, I realize I'm heir to an asset Spencer could take from me if he was so inclined.

After the kiss we shared last night, right after he gave me the tenderest look anyone has ever looked upon me with, I can't really believe he'd have it in him to do that.

But maybe.

"No. We weren't."

He sighs heavily. "I'll get Farnsworth on a postnup, then. For both your sakes."

A postnup? What the hell is a postnup? "What's a postnup?" I ask more politely than my brain drums up the question.

"Same thing as a prenup, except it takes place after the vows. It protects you both in the event of a divorce, which I assume is imminent after a year's time, right?"

"I, uh…actually I have no idea." Initially, yes. That was the plan.

But now…it sort of feels like maybe there's a chance for us to make it beyond that.

We're compatible. I like him. I feel like maybe he likes me, too.

I take an Uber toward the Strip and do a little shopping at Caesar's Palace, and then I return to the Palms and start getting ready for the wedding.

I've just slipped my shoes on when Spencer walks through the door, and he stops short when he sees me.

"Wow," he says quietly.

He's wearing gray pants, a navy Nike polo shirt, and a visor, and he just looks so…*athletic*. And hot.

"How was golf?" I ask, my mouth suddenly dry. I'm nervous. I've never been nervous around him, but somehow, something changed between us last night when he knew exactly what I needed. He took care of me. He made sure I felt safe.

No one has ever made sure I felt safe before—not like that, anyway.

He held me all night, and I know it was because he was worried about me.

It was sweet. It was caring.

One might even call it *loving.*

His eyes are still moving up and down my length, his jaw a little slackened. "Nothing compared to coming back here and seeing you."

My cheeks burn with heat at his words.

"I, uh...I need to take a quick shower and get dressed for the wedding," he says. "How was your day?"

"Fine. I told my dad about us," I mention casually.

"Oh, shit. Will he tell Amelia?"

I shake my head. "He'll let me have those honors. He mentioned a prenup, to which I told him we hadn't been coherent enough for one. So he said something about a postnup, which I've never heard of, but he's having his lawyer draft something up."

"It's a good idea to protect us both," he says. "Your dad's just looking out for you and the family vineyard, but I swear, I won't touch it. Unless you want me to, of course. Once it's yours, it's yours."

"I feel the same way about your assets, but you're right. It's a good idea."

He sighs. "Okay. Well, I guess I'll go get in the shower now."

I twist my lips and nod as I wish I had something to say to break the sudden tension between us, but I've got nothing.

I'm tempted to peek in on him, but I don't.

We've shared a few kisses now, but I can't tell if they're the hot kind that'll take us to the next level or if they've leaned more on the friendly side. My gut tells me it's the friendly side, but my heart is starting to hope it's more than that.

He emerges from the shower and walks out in a towel, padding across the room to grab his garment bag with the tux. I'm carefully perched on the bed so as not to wrinkle anything.

I got ready way too quickly, I think, but that's par for the course for me.

He shaves and gets dressed, and when he emerges, my jaw drops as a sharp ache throbs squarely between my legs.

Good Lord, he's hot in a tux.

He's tall and lean, strong and athletic.

And somehow…he's my husband.

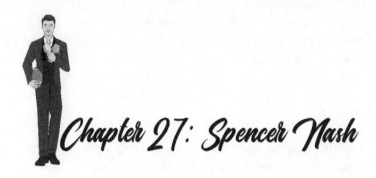

Chapter 27: Spencer Nash

Gray's Day

Four Days After the Wedding

It's only been four days, but I'm starting to think I married right despite the circumstances in which they happened.

Maybe I wasn't at my most coherent at the time, and it wasn't logic or responsibility speaking for me in the moment, but in hindsight, it might've been the right thing anyway.

I'm not sure yet, but the more time we spend as husband and wife, the more I want to see where it can go.

"Are you ready?" I ask.

"You clean up nice," she says as she swings her legs over the side of the bed and lifts to a stand. She stops short of me, and I find myself wanting to reach out for her hand.

I don't.

"I just need two seconds in the bathroom," she says.

I nod, and I wander over toward the window to wait for her.

I haven't slipped off my ring.

Neither has she.

I'm not sure what that means.

As she emerges from the bathroom with shiny gloss on her lips, I can't help but stare at them as the overwhelming feeling to kiss her washes over me.

I've kissed her a couple times now, and each time it's been because a rush of emotions crashed over one or the other of us. And maybe we kissed the night we got married—something neither of us can remember, but somewhere in the deep recesses of my mind, I can imagine a kiss that was molten lava between the two of us.

I want to take her there again.

I want to explore these feelings that keep plowing into me.

I want to take her to bed and make her moan.

I've been doing my best to maintain proper, respectful etiquette, but a man can only take so much of those stunning eyes as they fall on me with something like desire.

Maybe tonight will be our night.

I blow out a breath.

"Ready," she says, and I nod as I try to shake off those thoughts.

It's becoming harder and harder, though. We ride in the back of a car together toward my brother's house. His neighborhood is gated, but that doesn't keep out the media, so he has tents set up along his driveway to allow guests to exit their vehicles in privacy.

I'm thankful for that, at least. I know we need to break the news to Amelia in person, and I'd really rather not have her find out ahead of time, if that's at all possible.

The fact that she *doesn't* know by now seems less and less likely, but she hasn't called me out on it, and as far as I know, Grace hasn't heard from her either.

We're escorted toward the front door, and Grace's hand slips naturally into mine. It's so natural that I almost don't even notice it except for the fact that her hands are ice cold. I glance down at her, and her eyes are looking at me. I squeeze her hand, and her lips tip up a little as something passes between us. It's that feeling you get when you're distinctly a couple—that understanding that we can talk without words at all.

Each moment I spend with her seems to be pushing me closer to her as I feel myself starting to fall.

There's just one problem.

Even though my brain tells me Gracie would never, ever cheat on me, the last woman I was with did.

And Amelia's not the only one.

Athletes have reputations as dogs, and a lot of them are. But it's just as easy for the women left behind managing their day-to-day existence to step outside of a relationship as it is for the men who are in different cities every night playing a sport that's a part of their DNA.

I'm scared to give all of myself to someone only to be blindsided again.

Gracie is different, and I know that. My heart doesn't truly believe she'd ever be capable of cheating. But my brain likes to intrude on that conversation and remind me that I didn't think Amelia was capable of it either.

We're taken into the office on the first floor, where I find my parents, Lincoln, Jolene, their kids, and Asher.

"Hey, family," I say, waving as I walk into the room.

"My handsome boy," my mom says, walking over to adjust my tie before she pulls me into her arms.

I squeeze her tightly, and I do a little bro-shake with both Linc and Ash while Grace and my mom hug.

As my dad claps me on the shoulder, I ask, "Where's Grayson?"

My mom fields that one. "He's up in one of the guest rooms getting photos taken with Beckett," my mom says, referring to Grayson's best man, his best friend from high school.

"How's he doing?" I ask.

"Calm as a cucumber," Mom says. "He's ready, and Ava is an absolute vision. The dress is perfection, and that belt you picked out is stunning, Spence."

"It was all Gracie," I say honestly, nodding at her.

She sets a modest hand on her chest. "I'm still mortified that we even had to consider figuring out how to make that up to her."

"That reminds me," Mom says. "I never saw the picture of you two at your wedding." She raises her brows pointedly.

I laugh and hold up both hands defensively. "This is Gray's day."

"That's true, but he's not here. Show me," she goads, and I glance at Grace, who lifts a shoulder as if to say, *go for it.*

I pull my phone out of my pocket, and I pull up the email from the chapel since I haven't downloaded the photos to my phone just yet.

I flash the phone at my mother, and she grabs onto it and stares. "Oh, Spencer," she says softly. "And Grace. What a gorgeous bride. A beautiful couple." She sniffles a little and wipes her eyes, and I toss an arm around her shoulder and pull her in for a side hug.

Lincoln chuckles and rolls his eyes good-naturedly. "The first of many tears she'll shed today, believe me."

"I'm just sad I missed it," she moans.

"It's not like it was real," Asher pipes in, and I'm not sure why his words poke at me.

He's right. It was never supposed to be real.

Yet as I spot the look of pain in Grace's eyes that matches the one pressing on my chest...I think it's becoming real faster than either of us ever imagined it might.

I have the strangest urge to do anything I can to wipe that look off her face.

I don't dare make a move—not in here. Not in front of Asher and Lincoln and everyone who's watching my every move.

But that doesn't mean I won't make my move later tonight.

We chill in the office a while before Grayson joins us, and he's his usual outgoing and gregarious self.

"The Nash family is looking good," he announces from the doorway, and we all turn toward him. "Ready for photos out by the altar?"

We head outside for family photos, and Grayson takes photos with Mom and Dad first. Despite the rough way their marriage ended, they're civil enough with each other that they can be in the same room to celebrate this joyous occasion.

The brothers are called up to the altar, and I squeeze Grace's hand as I leave her behind with Jolene to smile for the camera.

I spot her eyes on me.

I spot something in those eyes that I'm not sure was there before—or maybe it was, and I just chose not to see it.

I see it now, though, and there's nothing I want more than to act on it.

I don't think it's just me feeling these new things.

Is it scary? Yes.

But might it be worth it anyway?

I think it might be.

It almost feels like the last four days have been leading us here, like they've been foreplay for the main event.

As her eyes heat when they meet mine, my cock responds.

I want her.

Holy shit, I want my wife.

The feeling is fierce as it rolls over me. I want her *now*. I want her any way I can get her. I want to jump off this altar and carry her to one of the guest rooms where I can kiss her the way she deserves to be kissed.

I want to strip her down to nothing and taste every inch of her body.

I want to drive into her as I watch her give into the pleasure.

I want all of her.

"The brothers' wives may join their husbands," the photographer says, interrupting my thoughts.

Jesus.

I can't wait to see what the fuck I must look like when these family photos come back.

Grace hangs back as Jolene makes her way toward Lincoln.

"That's you, too, dear," my mom says to Grace.

"Oh," she says, a little flustered as she makes her way across the white aisle runner to take her place beside me.

She slides into the little slot open for her, and I wrap my hand around her hip, pulling her toward me.

I know she feels my erection on her ass. It would be impossible to miss it.

She doesn't respond, though. She doesn't twitch or move away.

And then, just as the photographer tells us to smile, she shifts. It's infinitesimally, but it's in my direction, and it's enough for me to know she's acknowledging what's digging into her ass...enough for me to know she wants it, too.

The wedding's about to start, though. I can't duck out on my usher duties any more than she can duck out on sitting beside my mother as we're dismissed from the photos. I shoot her a longing gaze as I watch her settle into the row where my mom will join her in twenty minutes or so, and when I find her eyes on mine, and I see the same look of need in them that's reflected back from me...

I know tonight's going to be our night.

Chapter 28: Grace Nash

This Group Means Business When It Comes to Partying

Four Days After the Wedding

I t's hot in here.

Only...

In here is actually outside, and it's early May, but it's Vegas, which means hot temps. I'm wearing a dress, which is comfortable in the heat, and there are coolers strategically placed around the yard to ensure guests are comfortable. So it's not so much that it's hot out here versus Spencer's hot, and I'm...*needy*.

Okay, that's my nice way of saying I'm horny as hell, and something changed for Spencer because he's looking at me like *he's* horny, too, and I get the very strong inclination that he's going to act on it.

God, I hope he acts on it.

I need him to take care of the ache that's been steadily pulsing between my legs for days—the one that's only intensified in strength every second I spend with this man.

Maybe it's me in a dress, or maybe it's him in a tux. Maybe it's because he swooped in like some superhero to save me last night from that creepy dude who cornered me, and he made me feel safe and protected.

Maybe it's the fact that we're married now.

The bonus side of Spencer being an usher is that once he seats the last guest, he takes his seat—beside me.

He slides into his seat just a smidgen closer to me than he needs to sit. Maybe he's putting on the act for the guests gathered here, but something tells me it's more than that. This is the first interaction we've had with each other since that searing gaze he gave me when he was up on the altar and I was hanging back near the rows of chairs, and he takes my hand in his.

The connection is somehow endearing and sexy at the same time. My hand tingles where it meets his, and this simple act of hand holding suddenly feels like it means a lot more.

Grayson walks with his mom down the aisle, and he drops her off at our row, which from the far end of the row includes me, Spencer, Asher, Eddie, and Missy.

Grayson and Ava wanted to keep the wedding simple, so it's a small wedding party. Beckett walks Kelly down the aisle, and then the music changes and the guests gathered stand to welcome the bride.

The doors open, and Missy was right.

The belt is a nice touch.

Ava looks gorgeous in the dress I never should've touched. It was clearly made for her.

She has tunnel vision on her soon-to-be husband as she walks down the aisle.

I glance at Grayson as he sees his bride, and he wipes his eyes.

There's honestly nothing sweeter to me than a man getting emotional over the woman he's about to marry.

I wonder what Spencer thought as he watched me walk down the aisle.

I wonder if I even walked down the aisle. If I did, I'm sure I stumbled.

A wave of guilt darts through me. How did I do that without my dad there?

Oh, right. Because it didn't mean anything.

Except I think it's starting to.

Come to think of it, in the few days since our wedding, we really haven't studied the photos as much as we should have. Maybe it would jog our memory of the night, and I think Spencer had mentioned a video at some point, something I definitely haven't seen yet.

I make a mental note to ask him about that later.

I swipe at a tear as I watch the bride, and Spencer turns to glance at me. His lips tip up into a half smile when he sees I'm getting emotional over a bride I hardly know, and he lets go of my hand and instead slips his arm around my shoulders, squeezing me in tightly beside him.

A shudder runs through me at his proximity. At his scent— clean and soapy and sexy. At his warmth.

At the knowledge that something *definitely* changed, and the more time we spend together, the more this thing between us continues to transition and shift into a brand-new shape.

A shape that I can't wait to explore.

And just as I have the thought, he leans down and presses a soft kiss to my temple. It's sweet, and somehow it's also exactly what I need from him in the moment.

My heart latches on just a little more tightly to him.

Lincoln begins the ceremony with a few words about what marriage means and how he's had the pleasure to watch Grayson and Ava navigate their love story from the sidelines. He tosses in a few football puns and even more puns about the bakery Grayson and Ava opened a couple months ago, and he has the small group gathered laughing and tearing up in equal parts.

By the time Grayson and Ava recite their vows, I feel like I've been on a total emotional roller coaster, and the man beside me has taken every opportunity possible to remind me he's right here with me. His hand is linked with mine or on my thigh when we're sitting. His arm is around my shoulders when we're standing. He's attentive and sweet while he watches one brother pronounce another now a husband with his wife, and he only lets go of me when he has to since the crowd is clapping and cheering wildly as Grayson dips Ava with a nearly indecent kiss.

The party starts immediately after Lincoln ends the ceremony, as if the deejay was listening for the words.

"Ladies and gentlemen, your newlyweds, Mr. and Mrs. Nash!" he yells into the microphone, and he starts playing Whitney Houston's "I Wanna Dance with Somebody."

Grayson and Ava shimmy down the aisle and right over toward the makeshift dance floor as we continue to cheer for the newlyweds, and we all exit our rows to join them.

Servers walk around with hors d'oeuvres, and after the first song, the deejay lets us know the bars are now open. There are maybe a hundred guests here in total, but there are four bars, which just lets me know that this group means business when it comes to partying.

And I am down for it.

I go with vodka instead of my usual glass of wine, and Spencer raises his brows in surprise.

"Hey, at least it's not tequila," I point out, and he laughs.

"Good point." He orders himself some whiskey, and we take our drinks back to the dance floor as Lizzo sings about how "It's About Damn Time." We're moving and grooving, and then the deejay slows it down with one of MFB's most popular ballads.

Rather than asking me if I'd like to dance, Spencer takes my nearly empty drink from my hand and sets it beside his on a table, and then he wraps his arms around me and holds me close as we start to sway to the song.

Being this close to him…it's electrifying. It's a little terrifying, too, if I'm being honest. Every part of me wants to learn every part of him.

He's holding me close, his arm snug around my waist, and I shift to glance up at him. He's gazing down at me, his eyes fire on mine, and as he shifts his hips fractionally closer to me, I know what that look means.

It's more than just lust and desire, though that's certainly present too. There's a need in his eyes the likes of which I've never seen in any man's eyes before.

And what makes it so different is that I feel it too.

Before I even register what's happening, he leans down and drops his lips to mine. It's a soft kiss, sweet and tender and appropriate on the dance floor, where members of his family are dancing nearby.

He pulls back, and my chest tightens as I see the certainty there in his eyes.

He wants this.

I want this.

I sort of want to go find a room in which to do this.

Stat.

Chapter 29: Spencer Nash

My Brothers Enjoy Seeing Me Suffer

Four Days After the Wedding

When I see the same look reflected back at me, I know I can't waste another second without feeling her from the inside.

There's just one problem.

I don't have any condoms with me.

I didn't exactly pack them for this trip. I'm less of a one-night stand sort of guy than, say, Asher might be, and I wasn't expecting the girl I've fallen for to show up, propose marriage, and actually want to have sex.

But I know that look in her eye, and she wants it. I want it.

Now we just have to figure out the logistics.

And by logistics, I mean a private space and a condom. That's literally all I need right now. It's all I can think about right now.

My mind is a haze of lust, and so after I give into temptation and kiss her right in the middle of the dance floor, I grab her hand and lead her over toward the bar.

I don't say a word. I don't have to.

We each grab another drink, and then I spot Asher.

If I had to wager a guess, Lincoln likely doesn't use condoms with his wife—an assumption supported by the fact that they have a kid.

Gray might have some to spare upstairs, but since it's his wedding day, I can't exactly run up to the groom and ask to borrow a condom.

Asher might be my best bet. He's probably got a stash in his pocket, and while I could run out to a store somewhere…I'm not sure I can take another second of waiting.

"Be right back," I say low into her ear, and she nods as she turns to coo over Jolene's baby. I glance at her for just a beat, freezing in my tracks as I see Jolene hand the baby over to her.

Does Grace want kids?

I told my ex I wanted to wait until the end of my contract before I made decisions about kids.

But as I see *my wife* holding *a baby*…

I feel a shift in my priorities.

What the fuck?

I beeline for my brother, and I catch him just as he's turning from a conversation with my dad.

"Hey, do you have a condom?" I whisper so only he can hear me.

Asher turns and looks at me, his brows knit together. "Aren't you married? Don't you, like, not need them now? Isn't that sort of the point of marriage?"

I tilt my head and stare at him like he's lost his damn mind. "Are you seriously questioning my intentions right now? Do you have one or not?"

"Yes and no."

"Yes to what? No to what?" I'm too goddamn horny for this conversation.

"Yes, I'm questioning your intentions, and no, I don't have a condom."

"You don't have a condom? You're like the poster boy of random sexual encounters."

"I'm not sure if that's an insult or a compliment," he says, tilting his head at me. "But regardless, I'm not really so much a condom kind of guy."

My eyes might bug out of my head a little at his words. "You don't use condoms? But what about STDs?"

"Are we really going to get into this right now? I'm not saying I don't use them. I'm careful, and I certainly don't want to knock anybody up. I use them when it's necessary. But if I don't have one on me, then I guess that means I can't use it. So I don't carry them around, and I hope for the best." He shrugs.

How the fuck are we related?

I blink a few times as I stare at him. I really didn't think I was about to get into a whole condom discussion with my brother when I walked over to approach him, but I give him the *older brother* spiel anyway. "You need to use one every time to protect yourself and your partner," I scold.

"Right. Are you going to stand here lecturing me, or are you going to move onto someone else who might actually carry condoms in their pocket so you can get laid?"

I blow out a breath and keep my *fuck you* in my head as I spin around and look for Grayson. He may be my final hope here.

I see him talking to some buddies, and I make my way in that direction. They're all laughing about something, and I wait to ask my question.

Grayson acknowledges my presence with a quick nod, and I lean in toward him. "Can I ask you a question? Privately?"

He glances at Beckett then turns toward me. "What?"

"Do you have any condoms?"

His brows rise. "I do, but they're probably expired by now since I haven't used one in months with Ava. Why?"

"Why the fuck do you think?"

He laughs. Clearly, my brothers enjoy seeing me suffer. "Master bathroom, third cabinet door from the left under the counter. Take the whole box if you want. Just stay off my bed."

"Got anywhere else I can go?"

"You're that desperate?" he asks.

"You have no idea." I'm definitely that desperate, and I hear the desperation in my own tone.

"Nobody is staying in the third-floor guest room where you usually stay. Enjoy. Be safe. And for God's sake, make sure she gets hers."

LISA SUZANNE

I make a face of disgust at the insult. "Who do I look like, Asher?"

He laughs. "To be honest, man, I'd expect shit like this out of Asher. Vegas Spencer is just full of surprises."

He's not wrong. But I don't have time to chat about it.

"Thanks, brochacho." I rush away from him back toward my wife, wait until she finishes her sentence, and then I lead her toward the house so we can go find that third-floor guest room that will henceforth be known as the room where I first fucked my wife.

170

Chapter 30: Grace Nash

I'm Married to Those Abs

Four Days After the Wedding

Wherever he's going, he's in a rush.

At first, I think he's planning some surprise for Grayson, particularly when he tells me to wait a second as he walks into his brother's bedroom.

But he emerges a moment later holding a box of condoms, and...*ohhhh.*

I don't bother telling him I've been on birth control for years. We haven't really spoken specifics about our histories, and if he wants to play this game prepared, I'm all for that.

He grabs my hand and pulls me up another set of stairs to a door on the third floor, which he opens.

I step in and find a guest room complete with furniture...but no guests.

He steps into the room and kicks the door shut behind him. He tosses the box onto the bed, and before I have even a moment to realize what's going on, his mouth crashes down to mine.

This is a different Spencer than the one I've come to know. This one is hot and hard and absolutely *crazed* with lust.

Now *this*…this is the kiss I've been waiting for. His body moves in toward me, backing me up against the door, and I hear the quiet click of the lock, signaling privacy for whatever we want to do next.

And I guess if we got married in his brother's clothes, it only makes sense to have sex in his brother's guest bedroom.

Or something like that.

His kiss is fierce and demanding as his fingertips move toward my hip. The fire that's been building between us is a raging inferno now—like the ones we've stared into so many times side by side in the firepits behind the tasting room back home, but this one is all because of the heat that's been building between us for the last four days.

Our tongues tangle together as I wrap my arms around his neck, and all I can do is hang on for the ride that's been a few days or maybe two years in the making.

He somehow intensifies the kiss, the urgency fervent between us as we plow forward into this new, uncharted territory. This kiss doesn't follow any sort of sensible pattern—it's messy and beautiful as those fingertips dig into my hip as if he's doing everything he can to hold himself back from the rush of need he feels.

I don't want him to hold himself back. I want him to give it *all* to me.

His intention is clear with that entire box of condoms, and I'm here for it. The whole box.

I tangle my fingers in his neat, slicked-back hair, mussing up his trim, tidy appearance a bit. He likes it, and I know that because his tongue changes course as he seems to lose control. He's falling apart, and it's because of me.

I'm not sure I've experienced anything hotter than that in my entire life.

He groans as he thrusts his hips against me. It's as if he's trying to get inside me even though there are far too many clothes separating us, but this wild lust that's been building has to be satisfied. Now.

His tongue moves from tangling to thrashing, and then he closes his mouth and trails his lips from mine down my neck. I lean my head on the door, arching my back into him and lengthening my neck to give him more space to work with. I can't help a soft moan and a shiver as he kisses his way down my neck toward my collarbone, and then he moves back up toward my neck, leaving soft, wet kisses as he drags his lips along my skin.

"I'm so fucking hard for you," he murmurs, his tone full of desperation as his words heat my skin. He thrusts his hips against mine again as if he's proving his words true.

I trail one hand down to feel him, palming his length over his slacks as he drives his hips into my hand with a grunt. "Oh, God, yes," I moan as I feel how hard he really is.

"You're going to be moaning that again in a minute when I'm inside you," he warns.

I can't help a small chuckle. "Prove it." My words are all hoarse and throaty, need evident in them as he moves his lips back to mine.

He reaches under my dress, shoves it up, and yanks my panties to the side all in the span of a heartbeat—well, a normal heartbeat, anyway, since my current one is quite a bit accelerated.

I have no idea what sort of lover he is. Gentle, fast, selfish, selfless, or something else. But I know in this moment, I want to give him all of me.

He slides a finger right into me, and I whimper some incoherent throaty noise at the feel.

"Jesus, that's a hot, wet cunt," he breathes.

"Wet for you," I murmur. He thrusts his finger, pushing up harder into me, and I moan. This man is about to get me off standing upright against the door when honestly, achieving an orgasm in the past for me was like aligning all the stars in the sky for one perfect, magical moment.

It's been a while since I've been with a man, and the others were boys compared to Spencer.

To be fair, my experience is limited. There was Patrick, and before him, my high school boyfriend, whom I lost my virginity to.

Apart from a few kisses here and there, nobody else really even hit the radar.

Until Spencer.

And now it feels like he's the *only* one who ever really deserved to be on the radar.

I claw onto his shoulder as he fingers me, the edges of pleasure folding in on me, and then it all stops. He pulls his finger out, and he reaches down for the bottom of my dress. He pulls it over my head in a quick swoop until I'm standing in front of him wearing just my black panties and bra set, and he backs up a pace and stares at me.

He shakes his head a little as his eyes move to mine. "Jesus Christ, I'm the luckiest man alive."

I can't help it. The needy ache pounding at my core prompts me into action, and I leap at him.

His words are everything, and while my previous relationships were fine, nobody has ever given me the sort of reassurance and encouragement Spencer Nash does.

He catches me with a grunt, and my legs hook around his waist as I cradle his jaw between my palms and lower my mouth to his. He thrusts his rather hard cock up at me, and I'm in a frenzy to get to the part where we're both naked and he's sliding into me.

We don't have a ton of time—later we will, sure, but right now, we're at a wedding. We need to get back downstairs before anyone realizes we've gone missing, before his family starts making assumptions about our whereabouts, even though they all still believe this is a business deal more than anything.

Somehow it's become more to both of us, and as I kiss him and move my hands from his jaw to wrap my arms around his shoulders, it feels like the kind of thing that could last forever.

He shifts us, walks across the room, and leans down until I feel the cool comforter under my back. He backs off me as I bend my knees and set my feet right at the edge of the bed to watch his every move.

He shakes off his tux jacket and tosses it on the floor, and next comes the tie and the cufflinks. He works the buttons on his shirt next, and he tosses that on the floor, too, along with the undershirt he wore.

He stands in front of me in just his black slacks as he kicks off his shoes, and my eyes zero in on those abs.

Good Lord.

I'm married to those abs.

I'm about to get banged into oblivion by those abs.

I think I'm in love with those abs.

Scratch that.

I'm *definitely* in love with those abs. And the man who owns them.

He unbuckles his belt and drops his slacks next, and then he stands in just a pair of black boxer briefs with a giant bulge in the center.

I draw in a shaky breath as I wait for him to return, and when he does, he slides his palms from my ankles up my calves, along my knees, and down my thighs until he hooks his thumbs into my panties. He drags them slowly down my legs, tossing them on top of his pile of clothes, and he pushes my knees apart to give himself a bird's-eye view of my pussy.

A groan rises up from his chest, and I swear I've never felt a throb quite like the one that pulses at his needy sounds.

I watch him carefully, not sure what his next move is going to be as I clutch the sheets between my fists.

"Fuck, you look so hot right now."

He leans down and pulls me up a little to unhook my bra, and once it's on the floor with the rest of our clothes, he buries his face between my breasts. I let go of my grip on the bedding to pull his face into my chest, and he moves over a little to suck one of my hard nipples into his mouth.

"Yes, Spencer. Yes," I murmur.

He runs his tongue back and forth over the tight bud while he makes a similar movement with his thumb on the other one, and I thrust my hips up as I try to find some relief from the pressure between my thighs, some friction, something, anything to alleviate the pain there.

He shifts his hips back out of my reach, continuing the teasing on my nipples, and I make some sound of desperation that's enough to spur him into action.

He pulls away from me completely, and I'm desperate as I reach my fingers down between my legs to rub some relief onto my clit. He catches me as he grabs the box of condoms, and he stops, shifting back to take my hand away from what I'm doing.

He raises a brow at me, his grip firm on my wrist. "That's my job."

"Hurry," I sob, even more desperate than I realized.

He wastes no time fishing a condom out of the box, pulling off his briefs, tearing the packet, and rolling it on.

I take the time to appreciate the full naked body of Spencer Nash for the very first time.

His cock is pointed straight up, and it's huge. Way bigger than the other two I was with, but not so big that I'm intimidated by it.

Okay, well…maybe a little.

He's packing some heat there, that's for sure, but I'm so lost in lust that I can't quite comprehend much of anything at the moment other than I need to know exactly what that feels like inside of me.

His gaze meets my eyes, and he runs a fingertip along my jawline before his finger moves up to my lips. He pushes the finger into my mouth, and I wrap both my hands around his one hand as I suck on his finger.

"Fuck, Grace. Someday, I'm going to fuck your mouth. Maybe tonight, maybe tomorrow. But right now, it's your cunt I'm after."

With those words, he pushes my shoulder back and pulls his finger from my mouth. I settle back onto the bed, and he remains standing as I wrap my legs around his waist. He grips onto his dick and strokes it a few times, and then he slides it through my slit. His eyes meet mine as he lines himself up and pushes into me for the very first time, and I close my eyes as my head rolls back.

Holy hell.

"Fuuuuck," he groans as he seats himself in as deeply as he can go.

It's pure, unadulterated perfection as my body adjusts to his size and he starts to move.

"Jesus, that's so tight," he curses, and it's true. I'm so wet for him that he glides easily in and out, and I keep my legs wrapped around his waist as he drives into me. I grip the sheets again, my body tightening everywhere, and he leans forward and grips onto my breasts, massaging them as he thrusts into me over and over.

It feels so good. *He* feels so good.

I open my eyes to see him staring at me, wonder and a bit of awe in his eyes amid tenderness, even though he's pounding into me like he can't fuck me hard enough or fast enough. It's somehow gentle and rough at the same time, and the answer to my earlier question about how he fucks?

Perfection.

Complete and total perfection, as if our two bodies were put on this planet solely to find each other and do this.

The connection between us is strong enough that I can feel my orgasm looming closer and closer.

"Oh, God, Spencer," I yell. He keeps going. "You feel so good," I moan.

He leans down, and I feel the heat of his body over me as his lips find my neck. I dig my feet into his ass to urge him to keep going, and he's panting when his voice moves toward my ear. "I love hearing the sounds you make while I'm fucking you."

His thrusts somehow pick up speed and intensity, and I start to scream. "Oh God, oh God, oh God!" He slaps a hand over my mouth at the third *oh God*, and he leans forward as he continues his drives into me.

"Shh," he warns, his voice breathless close to my ear. "They'll hear us."

It's only then that I notice the music that was pounding outside has come to a stop. Someone is saying something—the best man's speech, maybe, or the maid of honor's. Or maybe it's a prayer, and I'm up here praying, too, as I just screamed, "*OhGodOhGodOhGod*," over and over.

"This pussy is fucking addicting. *You* are fucking addicting."
His lips land on my neck again.

The thought that what we're doing up here in private during
a party going on downstairs collides with Spencer hitting that
spot inside me that's pure magic. His hand is still over my
mouth, and something about that is really hot.

Like...*insanely* hot.

So hot that I start to come. I thrash wildly as my body takes
control, and he wrings every last drop of pleasure out of me,
pounding into me over and over with the force of his hand on
my mouth not allowing me to scream through the pleasure the
way I need to.

"Fuck, Grace," he mutters, letting up his grip on my mouth.
He shakes out his hand. "That was the sexiest thing I've ever
seen. You're going to make me come so fucking hard." He
growls out the last part of his words, and then he shoves up a
little harder into me as I feel him start to let go. His mouth finds
mine again as he releases into me with a series of grunts, and he
shoves hard and stays seated there a few beats as his release
draws to an epic and sensual end.

He wraps his arms around me and holds me as he stays
inside me, and I get the sudden feeling like I don't want him to
pull out. He feels like a part of me now.

In the past, when the sex was over—which usually ended
with the man's climax first followed by getting me off with his
fingers—I was ready for it to be over.

But with Spencer, I want to stay here forever basking in his
warmth, his scent, his sex, his love.

All good things must come to an end, though, of course.
That's how life works. He slips out of me, and I have the
immediate sensation that as beautiful and magical as that was, I
don't want it to be over. I don't want to be apart from him. I
don't want to lose the beautiful connection we just made.

Not because I wasn't totally satisfied by it.

I was. And then some.

But I already want it again.

After one time, I'm addicted—just as he said he's addicted to
me.

And I'm not quite sure how I'm going to let him go after our year together is up.

Maybe you don't have to.

A tiny voice intrudes on my thoughts, and hope fills me.

We have a lot of obstacles ahead of us…but I'm going to hold onto the hope that tiny voice gives me for as long as I can. Maybe forever.

He keeps kissing me for a bit even after he slips out, and eventually he pulls back. He's leaning over me, his face close to mine, when he says, "Wow, Grace. That was even better than I imagined it would be."

"You imagined it?" I tease, raising a brow.

He chuckles as he nips one more kiss to my lips then straightens to a stand, and I drop my legs to the floor, relief flooding me after the workout they just got.

"You have no idea," he murmurs, and he disappears to the en suite bathroom for a few beats before he returns and starts to pull his clothes back on. I force myself up from the bed, and I use the restroom next.

When I emerge, he's tucking his button-down shirt back into his slacks.

"I liked your other outfit better," I tease.

He strides across the room and takes me into his arms. "And I like this one you've got on."

I giggle, and then he lets me go.

"I guess we should get back downstairs," he says.

I reluctantly head toward my clothes to start getting dressed. "Before anyone notices we're gone, anyway."

He smirks. "Probably too late for that."

"You think they know?"

"Well, Asher does since I asked him for a condom, but he didn't have any, so I hit up Grayson, who came through in the clutch."

I set my hand over my eyes. "Oh my God. They know what we were going to go do?"

He laughs. "I needed a condom. If you saw the way you were looking at me all day, you'd understand."

"If it's anything like the way you were looking at me, I do."

He shrugs. "It was building for a while, I think."

I pull on my panties first, and then my bra. "How long for you?"

He shrugs. "Honestly? Probably since the night I met you."

I gasp. "What?"

"That night I met you, I was drawn to you first. But you didn't seem interested, and your sister took the reins, and I buried whatever I thought I felt for you. The rest is history. Or it was, anyway, until she cheated on me, which I get the feeling may have been happening the entire time we were together."

I slip my dress back over my head and smooth it out. "I didn't seem interested that night?"

"Not as interested as she was."

"I was. The moment I met you, I felt like we were a better match. But you left with her because she was louder."

He takes a step toward me and wraps an arm around my waist, pulling me against him. "It was your quiet beauty that always intrigued me, Gracie."

I don't know why, but hearing him call me that feels intimate and precious. "It was *everything* about you that always intrigued me," I admit. I glance up into his eyes, and I see it there.

We're both at the precipice of this…this…this *thing*. It's big and lovely at the same time that it's terrifying. We could dive into it headfirst and see where it takes us, but neither of us is used to taking those sorts of risks.

Especially not when I need him for the next year. I can't go all in only to lose both him *and* the winery before our year together is up.

And I especially can't lose to Amelia. Not again.

Not ever again.

He presses a quick kiss to my lips before things get too much heavier in here. "Let's head back down, okay?"

I nod, and slipping my hand into his feels so natural. So right.

I just hope I can hold onto that feeling for longer than a year.

Forever seems like a decent amount of time to me.

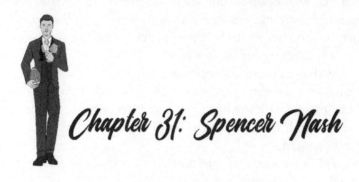

Chapter 31: Spencer Nash

Heard You Praying Earlier

Four Days After the Wedding

"I can't believe I go home tomorrow," she says quietly as we sway to the voice of John Legend. "I'm not ready to leave you."

I get the very real sense that this is the longest number of days she's been away from the vineyard, and I'm sure she's missing it—especially since she wants to take it over. She must feel the need to be there now more than ever.

But I feel her words harder than I was expecting to. "I'm not ready, either," I admit.

And maybe we don't *have* to part just yet.

"What if I came with you?" I ask softly.

She pulls back and glances up at me. "What?"

"We can tell Maggie and Amelia together." I shrug. It's the first time I've had that thought, and I sort of think it's a *good* thought. It's not right to send her into the lion's den alone.

Her jaw slackens. "You'd do that?"

I tighten my arms around her. Does she really have to ask after what we just shared upstairs?

When we came back down, the party was back in full swing. Grayson and Asher both gave me knowing, wolfish smiles, but apart from that, I don't think anybody knows where we disappeared to. I don't even think anybody noticed.

But that little disappearing act has me fully in love with the woman currently swaying in my arms. It wasn't just the sex— though hearing her moan how good I felt inside her was certainly something for the books.

It was the emotional connection I felt when I was inside her. The way my chest felt open and exposed for her to take it—as if she'd be careful with my heart in a way I never trusted any other woman to be. It was unique and beautiful, raw and real. It was simply everything.

So yeah, to answer her question...I'd do that. At this point, I think I'd do pretty much anything for her.

"Of course I would," I say, giving her the short answer instead of the longer one.

"How'd I get so lucky?" she wonders softly, her eyes meeting mine.

I drop a soft kiss to her lips, and then I give her my answer. "You waited for the right time."

We've eaten dinner and cake, and we're at the dancing the night away phase of the night. Lincoln and Jolene are dancing nearby, and Lincoln leans over toward us.

"Heard you praying earlier," he says to Grace. "Hope everything's okay."

Jolene smacks him in the arm and rolls her eyes.

Grace shoots him a curious look, her brows knit together as if she has no idea what he's talking about. "Praying?"

Lincoln nods. "Something about *oh God*."

"You heard us?" Grace asks, gasping as her eyes grow wide.

"No!" Jolene interrupts as Lincoln is about to answer that question. "Nobody heard a thing." She tries to sound reassuring, but the damage is done.

Grace buries her face between my collarbone and shoulder. "I'm so embarrassed."

If I'm being honest, I'm not. I've never been prouder. That might be the competitive brother in me speaking—the sibling rivalry. Did any of my brothers make a woman scream like that today?

There's only one right answer: not loud enough for the other three brothers to hear it.

"Don't be," I murmur softly, trying to hide the quaking pride in my voice and also trying—but failing—to sound sympathetic. "Lincoln's just an asshole making a guess."

I raise my brows at my brother as Grace continues to hide her face in my chest, and he wiggles his eyebrows at me.

That only indicates one thing. He *definitely* heard.

And maybe everyone out here did. I can see why Grace might be embarrassed by that, but I'm sure as hell not. All I did was bang my wife, and there aren't any laws against that—at least not that I'm aware of. This whole being married thing is still pretty new to me, though, so I can't be sure.

Nobody else says a word to us about it. We sit with my mom for a bit, but Grace has grown quiet since Lincoln's words to her.

Guests start to leave, and Grayson pulls me over to talk with a few of his teammates—guys I've met on the field plenty of times. I glance at Grace, who nods that she's content with my mom, and head over to talk to the guys for a while. By the time I walk back over, my mom has Grace in stitches—probably regarding something embarrassing to me, but I'm glad to see she has snapped out of the mini-funk she fell into.

"Excuse me for just a minute. I'm going to run to the ladies' room," Grace says when I sit back down, and I squeeze her hand and grab her for a quick kiss before she goes.

"That's really something, Spence," Mom says.

"What is?"

"That girl you found," she says, nodding toward Grace's retreating figure. "Don't mess it up."

"I'm not Asher," I say petulantly.

"I know, honey," she says, and she reaches over to squeeze my arm. "And I know how this thing started for the two of you, but I can also see that you two genuinely care for one another. Just think hard before you lead her into something you can't come back from. Are you over Amelia? Are you biding time for the next year?" She shrugs. "Grace deserves all of you, and I just think you need to be honest with both her and yourself. She's incredible, and she deserves the world. Give it to her."

"What about what I deserve?" I ask quietly.

"You know I hope all the best things for all four of my boys," she says softly. She glances over at the dance floor. "Linc and Gray are there. Ash…I don't know about that boy. And you, you're my special one. You're so smart and thoughtful, and you're kind and sensible. I know you'll always do the right thing."

"Barring marrying someone during an allergic reaction," I say dryly.

She chuckles. "Perhaps. Or maybe it *was* the right thing. Time will tell, but she's in deep with you already. Don't take that for granted."

"I won't." I appreciate the advice, but I also have to take what she says with a grain of salt. She spent forty years married to my father, so she has the life experience on me. But ultimately, their road wasn't one of success.

Maybe Grace and I rushed into this thing, but that doesn't mean we can't take a different path where we do end up finding a way to make it work.

My mother has given me some good food for thought this evening, though, and I know she's right about one thing.

Grace deserves the world.

In this moment, I hope I'm the person who can give it to her.

But deep down, I'll always wonder whether I'm good enough.

Chapter 32: Grace Nash

My Inner Nerd is Coming Out

Five Days After the Wedding

As the plane races down the runway before it lifts into the air, Spencer grabs my hand. Together we look out the tiny airplane window up here in first class as we rush past the famed skyline of hotels, and I can't believe I flew in here single and desperate five days ago, and I'm flying back to Minnesota holding my husband's hand.

I can't even *think* it without choking a bit.

"You okay?" he asks, and I nod as I pull myself together.

We made it through the five hard days with his family—days that didn't turn out to be so hard after all. I *feel* like I have a new family. I exchanged numbers with both Jolene and Ava, and even Ava laughed about the dress fiasco before we left brunch with the family this morning.

It's weird leaving a place and feeling like I'm leaving family behind. I've never had that. My entire family has always lived at the vineyard—my mom until she divorced my dad, my dad, my uncle, my sister, Nana, and Pop Pop. That's it. That's the whole family.

My mom was an only child who lost both of her parents when she was in her twenties before I was born. My dad's only sibling is my uncle, and he never had kids.

It's so strange feeling like I'm part of a family like the Nashes. Only the four brothers plus the parents were in attendance since Grayson and Ava wanted to keep it small, intimate, and a secret from the press, but there's more extended family out there—an uncle who also played in the league plus cousins.

The core family is all so close, and they're all so scattered. Well, sort of. Spencer and Missy are scattered compared to the rest who call Vegas home.

Could I call Vegas home?

It sure *feels* like Spencer's and my place now, but it's not—not really.

Not when I'm firmly based in Minnesota with the vineyard calling me to my future. Not when Spencer will firmly be planted in San Diego until further notice.

He hasn't specified when he plans to stop playing, but we had some chats about his career. He didn't see himself playing past thirty-five, and his thirtieth birthday looms ahead of us in less than two weeks.

Should I do something for his thirtieth? As his wife, does that fall on me now?

I know *when* it is because I remember once, long ago, we had a discussion about birthdays. He's turning thirty-three days before I turn twenty-five.

He's a full five years and three days older than me, and if we were teenagers, that would matter. We're not, and it doesn't, though he's spoken more than once about how he often feels older than thirty given the beating his body takes on a weekly basis during the season.

There was no evidence of that beating on Saturday evening, that's for damn sure.

We haven't had the chance at round two just yet, but I have a feeling it's going to be even more powerful than round one was.

We arrived back at our hotel late the night of the wedding, and it was an early morning getting packed up and making it over to the restaurant for brunch with the Nashes. Our flight was at three, which means we land at eight, and then it's getting our baggage and the hourlong trip back home.

I'm guessing everyone will be retired to their bungalows and estates by the time we roll back into town, and that's fine. I'm not ready to face everyone with the news of our marriage just yet—and paradoxically, at the same time, I can't wait to share the news.

"You know I've never seen the inside of your bungalow?" he asks suddenly after the fasten seatbelt sign is turned off.

I think back to all the times he's been to the vineyard. He always stayed with Amelia, or we'd hang out together by the firepits or in the tasting room, but I realize he's right.

I've never seen his apartment, either—not that he has it anymore.

But I wonder what a space lived in by Spencer Nash is like.

What hangs on his walls? Is he neat or messy? Based on what I know of him and spending a few days sharing a hotel room…I'm certain he isn't messy.

Just like I'm not.

Everything has a place, and things are returned to their proper places after they're used. It's easy enough since I live alone…and even as I have the thought, I realize I will *still* be living alone even now that I'm married.

It's not like I can leave the vineyard and work remotely from San Diego so I can be with my husband.

It's not like this is a real marriage, either.

Though last night it felt like one.

Today it has, too.

Everything will change once my family knows the truth, though. Nobody at Newlywed will believe Spencer married me out of love when he and my sister broke up a few months ago.

But things are growing. They're progressing. I'm struck with a whole lot of hope.

"I hadn't realized," I murmur.

"What's it like?" he asks.

"My house?" I ask, and when he nods, I lift a shoulder. "A lot like Amelia's. Same floor plan, anyway. All five bungalows have the same plan. But mine is tidier."

"Yeah, she wasn't the neatest." He chuckles a little, and it has to be my imagination when I swear I hear a bit of wistfulness in his tone.

Wistful that they aren't together?

It's the first time the thought crosses my mind, and I don't like it.

It's just jealousy rearing its ugly head.

He's not sad they're apart. That is a fact. But what we haven't really gotten into is whether he's still hurt by the way things came to an end between them.

And I'm the one who told him about the cheating. I told him the *why*. How can he look at me and not be reminded of those things?

It's the first time I've had that thought, and it pulses a bit of hopelessness in the pit of my stomach.

I push it away. His fingers are tangled in mine. He's here with me so I don't have to face my family alone. That means something.

"What about your place?" I ask.

He lifts a shoulder. "I'm tidy, too. I'm renting an apartment near the stadium in San Diego. I have no idea how long I'll be there, so it doesn't make sense to buy."

"Weren't you renting here, too?"

He nods. "I lived in the same place a long time, but look how easy it was to get out when I was released. Apart from packing up all my Lego sets, of course."

My brows shoot up in surprise. "Lego sets?"

"I've been obsessed since I was a kid. Back then, I just had a few sets, but now I have…" He trails off, and I stare at him curiously. "Sorry. My inner nerd is coming out."

"I think it's cute," I admit.

"Well, I have a lot of sets."

"Which is your favorite?" I ask.

"Millennium Falcon, hands down. Seven thousand, five hundred forty-one bricks of pure joy."

I giggle as I nod. "Interesting. How long does it take you to build those seven thousand bricks?"

"In the offseason, I can do it over two days."

"Do you build when you're in season?" I ask.

"Absolutely. Yes. It's the calm before the storm each week, but my time is limited, so I usually go with smaller sets. There's just something so satisfying about creating something out of a bunch of interlocking plastic pieces." He shrugs. "It takes me out of whatever's going on in the real world and lets me focus on something else for a while."

"I get that," I murmur. More than he even realizes. "What do you need to escape from in the real world?" My voice is soft as I ask the hard question.

He twists his lips a little, but he doesn't remove his hand from where it's nestled in mine. "Getting cheated on and losing my job in the same month." He sighs. "I took apart and rebuilt the Millennium Falcon set four times when I moved to San Diego."

I squeeze his hand. I wish I could've been there with him through all that turmoil.

"But look at you now. New job in San Diego, and you're married." I glance down at the simple gold band encircling the ring finger on my left hand. I haven't removed it since I put it on, and I don't intend to.

He leans his head on my shoulder, and there's something so sweet about it. I turn and press a kiss to the top of his head, and I lean my cheek where I planted the kiss.

We stay like that for a bit, and something about sitting on a plane as he confesses secrets to me makes me feel even closer to him than we were before.

Eventually, we land. We get our luggage, and we head to my car in the long-term parking lot. I was on target when I said it'd be after nine by the time we got back to the vineyard. It's nine thirty-seven when I pull into the little space where I leave my car behind my bungalow.

Lights are on in Amelia's bungalow but not in Drew's. The estate is dark, though, and I'm certain Nana and Dad are already asleep.

I lead the way to my front door, and I flick on the light as I let Spencer in. He sets his suitcase and mine by the door as he glances around the place, taking in the simple tan couch, the brown recliner I fall asleep in most nights, and the white furniture. Bookcases line the walls around my television, and they're filled with all sorts of books—mostly spicy romance, some women's fiction, with a few self-help books and marketing titles sprinkled in, and, of course, a handful of thrillers just for fun.

But the centerpiece taking up one of the center sections of my bookshelves is what Spencer first zeroes in on. He walks over toward it to make sure his eyes aren't playing tricks on him, and they aren't.

"Holy shit, Gracie. The Millennium Falcon?" His jaw is practically dropped to the floor as he turns toward me.

I can't help my smile. "It took me more than two days, but it's a staple in every avid Lego Master's arsenal, don't you think?"

He's frozen to his place for a beat, but then he strides over toward me. He hooks an arm around my waist and pulls me into him. "Every new discovery I make about you has me falling deeper, Newman. You know that?"

My eyes widen at his admission. I knew we were having feelings for each other, but his words are so much more than just feelings.

Still, my sassy pants are on. "It's Nash now," I correct him, and I move to my tiptoes to press a kiss to his lips.

Damn if I'm not falling in deeper every second myself.

Chapter 33: Spencer Nash

Give It to Me

Five Days After the Wedding

The words are out of my mouth before I can stop them, and in typical Gracie fashion, she eases the tension with humor.

There's just something about this woman that has me tied up in knots. I think back to when I was falling for Amelia, and it wasn't like this.

Looking back, there was badgering—from her end. There was convincing. There were irritations.

But I brushed them aside because that felt different, too. But it never felt like *this*.

With Grace, everything feels so damn easy and natural and *right*.

She means to just press a soft kiss to my lips after my verbal slip, but I grab her into my arms and hold on tightly.

Yesterday, we were pressed for time, and we were both horny as fuck after fighting it for days, weeks, months…years.

Tonight, though…we have nowhere to be.

It's still early. We have all night.

And this time, I plan to take my time with her. I plan to worship her in the way she deserves.

Most of all, I plan to make her come.

And come.

And come some more.

I want us both coming until neither of us can see straight any longer, until we're both so worn out and sated that we have no choice but to pass out naked in each other's arms.

I want to see my come splattered on her tits, on her ass, on her chin.

And in time, that'll all happen.

But right now, I want to take my time. I want her to feel my emotions as I pour them into our connection.

And so it begins with the kiss. I deepen it first, pulling her body close against me as I open my mouth to hers. My tongue caresses hers as I keep the pace tender and slow, setting the tone for what's about to happen between the two of us.

I run my hands down her back and over the sweet curve of her ass, pulling her toward me as I move my hands toward her hips and up her torso before they go around her back and tangle into her hair. She moans into me at the feel of my hands all over her body, and I repeat the process as her fingertips move up and down my spine.

She pulls back first, and her eyes are hooded with lust as she looks up at me. She doesn't say a word, instead reaching down to take my hand in hers. I follow her through the house toward her bedroom, and once we're standing in the room with white furniture and white bedding, we pick up the kiss from where we left it in the other room.

I sweep her up into my arms, and I set her on the bed, moving over the top of her and kissing her as I hover over her. She reaches for my ass, pulling me down on top of her, and instead of moving down to cover her with my weight, I drive my hips against hers.

"Oh," she murmurs into my mouth when she feels how fucking hard she makes me.

I move my lips from hers to kiss her neck, and she leans back, her neck corded and lengthened for me as I slam my cock against her pussy again.

"Yes, oh God, Spencer. Give it to me," she murmurs, and hearing the begging in her tone is everything I need in this moment.

I promised myself I'd take my time since we *have* time for once. But hearing her beg me to give it to her is enough for me to break my promise to myself.

I slam my body to hers again, and I feel like a wild man out of control when I'm with her like this. I just want to be inside her, to feel her again, to pump into that sweet, tight little pussy until I watch her face screw up in pleasure.

I've never seen a more beautiful sight.

But first, tonight...I need to taste her.

I move off her and stand, and I reach down to flick the button of her jeans and peel them off her legs. She sits up and pulls her shirt and bra off, and in mere seconds, the gorgeous woman is naked and waiting.

I tear my clothes off in record time, too, and I move back over her, hovering with my cock bobbing between us. I tease her with it as I settle it between her thighs, and she looks up at me with so much trust in her eyes that it's damn near overwhelming.

I kiss her for a minute or an hour, who knows, and I'm about to blow it right here if I don't get started on the action. I pull back off her, settle onto my knees on the floor, and yank her until her ass is right at the edge of the bed. She links her legs around my shoulders, and I glance up at her.

"I need to taste you," I murmur.

She nods as my needy eyes meet hers, and I lick my fingertips before I push one into her.

Jesus. She didn't need me to lick my fingertips with how fucking wet that pussy is.

A growl of need rises up out of me, some incomprehensible sound that flows right out of me as my cock grows painfully hard. I need to be inside her.

I stroke myself a few times just to feel some measure of relief, but it's not enough. It'll never be enough unless it's her.

"Oh God," she yells as her eyes close. Her head rolls back, and I keep that finger moving in and out of her wet cunt as I lean forward and suck her clit between my lips.

She thrashes and moans, and I keep the pace as I finger her and lick my way through the most delicious pussy I've ever tasted in my life, growls and moans coming involuntarily out of me, the likes of which I've never made before.

I stop sucking on her clit to flatten my tongue and lick my way through her, and I pull my finger out to dip my tongue inside her.

Holy fuck.

She's sweet and tangy, and she smells incredible, as if her very essence was made by design with my preferences.

She grabs onto the sheets as I dip my tongue in and out of her, and her opening contracts around my tongue just as she lets out a moan of approval. Fuck, she likes that, so I do it over and over before shoving my finger back in and focusing on her perfect clit once again.

"Fuck, Grace," I rasp. "Your pussy is fucking heaven."

She moans in response, and then she whimpers, "I'm going to come."

"Do it, baby. Come all over my tongue, and then I'll make you come again."

"Oh my God," she yells, and she starts to really ride my face, her hips moving up and down as I suck on her clit harder and harder, flicking my tongue over the bundle of nerves as I finger her tight pussy.

She loses control, her legs shaking as her body quakes around me to a symphony of gorgeous groans and gasped breaths. I ride along with her through the wave of pleasure, enjoying giving it to her every bit as much as I'll enjoy taking my own, too.

And when she collapses back, her body wrung out and sated, I wipe my mouth with the back of my hand. I climb over her again to kiss her some more. She takes my jaw between her palms, and I *love* when she does that. I love when she touches my face sweetly, especially after the way I just ate her pussy.

Once I give her a minute to recover, I'm going to wreck that pussy. With my cock. All damn night.

Except I already know I won't last all damn night. Not when I'm about to lose it. Why is it so fucking hot to kiss her so she can taste herself on my tongue?

The mere thought has more come leaking out of me.

Fuck, I need to get inside her. I need to fuck her.

I need *her*. It's all I can think or do or see.

She pushes back on my shoulders a little. "My turn to taste you," she murmurs.

I raise a brow. "Are you ready?"

She nods a little lazily, and she's somehow both adorable and the sexiest goddamn woman I've ever seen all at the same time. "But I don't think I can move right now, so just fuck my mouth, okay?"

Um…okay. I think I can make that work.

I don't need to be told twice.

I scramble to move so my cock is aligned with her mouth, and she grabs me between her fists, lining me up as I push in.

"Mmm," she hums around me, the vibration fucking killing me as I try to hold back from coming in her mouth the second I feel her warm lips wrap around me.

She keeps her fists at the base of my cock, stroking them up and down in rhythm with me as I start to move in and out of her mouth, balancing carefully so as not to choke her while still allowing myself to give into the vast land of pleasure that is her warm, wet mouth.

She sucks hard on me, and fuck if it isn't the greatest head of my life. I move in and out slowly as I fuck that sweet mouth, and she groans, the hums spurring me closer and closer to release.

I love it all—her fists, her grip, her tongue at the slit of my cock, her mouth, her sounds.

It's too good. Way too good.

I'm going to lose it.

"Oh fuck, I'm gonna come, baby, I'm gonna come so fucking hard," I grunt.

I shift my hips back since we never discussed whether she's comfortable with me coming in her mouth, and she finishes me with her hand as my come jets out all over her tits. She moans as I grunt through each pulse of hot come that hits her soft skin, and as the shudders through my body start to calm, she takes my dick and runs it through the mess I just made on her gorgeous tits.

"Mmm," she murmurs, as if she's getting still more pleasure from rubbing my cock through the jizz I marked on her body.

Jesus Christ.

I'm never letting this woman go.

Chapter 34: Grace Nash

Hands on the Headboard

Five Days After the Wedding

He gently wipes the mess from my chest with a warm washcloth, and even *that* somehow feels good. He takes care of me, and my heart sinks deeper into him. We lay tangled together for a while, neither of us talking as we just breathe the other in and relax in the quiet afterglow.

I'm ready to go again.

I've never been ready to go again so soon after an orgasm, but Spencer Nash just does it for me.

In all the ways.

He's amazing, and he's mine. Somehow.

For now, anyway. For the next year.

And I plan to take advantage of the next year in every way I possibly can.

Starting with now.

"I want you," I murmur.

He leans up on his elbow and peers down at me. "Huh?"

I giggle as I realize he was almost asleep when my voice woke him up. "I want you to fuck me," I say, my cheeks burning with embarrassment at the admission.

"Oh, I plan to. Just give me five more minutes."

I giggle as he gets up off the bed and pads naked around my room. He walks out, and he reappears a minute later with both our suitcases. "Condoms to the rescue."

He fumbles around in his suitcase before he produces the box swiped from his brother's house, and he pulls one out. He sets the packet between his teeth as he closes the box and tosses it back on top of his clothes in his suitcase, and why is staring at a naked Spencer as he grips a condom between his teeth one of the hottest damn things I've ever witnessed in my twenty-four years?

He pulls the condom out from between his teeth. "Can I take my time with you, or are you tired?" he asks as he rips it open.

"Take your time."

His eyes flash with something—fire, maybe—and he asks, "How do you want it?"

My brows push together as I don't quite grasp his meaning.

"Do you like doggie, cowgirl, reverse cowgirl…"

My cheeks burn.

"Missionary? There's something to be said for missionary."

"Um…I'm—I, uh, I don't have a preference."

His brows dip together. "You don't have a preference?" He wiggles his eyebrows playfully. "Cowgirl it is, then."

"I'm sorry. I have no idea what all the positions are called. Exactly how many women have you been with?" I ask, and it totally ruins the moment, but the words come out of my mouth before I can stop them.

He freezes, and he glances up at the ceiling as presumably he counts them off…but now Amelia has to be in his head, and I don't love that for us.

"Including you, fourteen." He ducks his head with a touch of embarrassment as he wrinkles his nose. "What about you?"

"Including you?" I ask.

He lifts a shoulder. "Sure."

"Three."

"Three?"

"Three. Bear in mind, I'm half a decade younger than you."

He chuckles. "Knock off that *half-a-decade* nonsense."

"I better be your best."

He rolls the condom onto his cock and strokes it a few times until he's fully hard again. He walks over and stands in front of me. "No one else even holds a candle to you, Grace. No one has ever turned me on so much just by being in the same room as me—and certainly not enough that I could go twice in an hour."

Not even Amelia?

Her wild boldness *has* to translate to the bedroom, but I suppose that's not exactly a detail I want to know.

"No one," he repeats as if he can read my mind.

I reach for him and pull his neck down until he's closer to me, and I press a kiss to his lips. "Let's try again just to be sure."

He chuckles, and then he shifts so he's hovering over me. His mouth is on mine when he aligns himself and pushes into me, and I grip around his neck as I wrap my legs around his waist. He drives into me slowly, luxuriously, tenderly, as if we have all night.

We kiss, and we hold each other. Sweet caresses drag along soft skin as names are whispered in vigilant devotion.

First, he fucked me.

Now he's making love to me.

And I feel it. I feel the love transferring from his heart to mine. I feel the intimacy of this connection between us. I feel closer to him as his fingertips glide sensually up my torso. I feel bonded to him in all the ways that matter, and every time he plunges inside, that closeness only feels stronger. The marriage only feels more real.

The love growing between us only intensifies.

He's lasting longer this time since he just came, and I'm reveling in every thrust.

After a while, he shifts us with barely any effort at all, and suddenly I find myself on top of him. He still manages to control our movement from the bottom, and this is the benefit of being with a strong and fit athlete like him.

"Hands on the headboard," he commands, and I set my palms flat on the wooden surface. He holds on around my ass, and then he stares up at my breasts as they hang over his face.

"Fuck, Gracie. Yes. Just like that." The way he rasps my name and adds an additional syllable to it while he's inside me is nearly my undoing.

And then he really starts to move.

"I love fucking this tight cunt," he says.

He's always so pulled together. Cool as a cucumber.

Hearing dirty talk fall from his lips while he thrusts into me is so out of character for him—and so damn hot.

He holds on tightly to my ass, and he slides in and out of me, the friction driving me to a place I'm not sure I've ever visited. It's beautiful and thrilling, magical and satisfying.

"Oh, God, yes!" I yell, throwing my head back as I keep my hands planted on the headboard. "Fuck me harder, Spencer!"

He does, and it throws me headfirst into a brutal, intense, jarring climax.

I screech my way through it, yelling out his name and praying once again as *Oh God* comes out of my mouth, clearly my go-to phrase when I start to come, and my reaction must spur him into his reaction, too, because he growls out a *fuck, Gracie,* before he picks up speed and thrusts up hard into me a few times before he freezes and lets out a mighty roar followed by a few more pumps that are just enough to take me to the end of my own release.

I drop my hands from the headboard and collapse on top of him. His hands are still on my ass, and he's still inside me, and I'm struck with the thought that I could stay right here for the rest of my life.

I *want* to stay right here for the rest of my life.

I know that's not realistic, but goddamn, this man is really something else.

If I could just figure out how to hold onto him longer than a year, I'd really have the dream.

But there's someone else involved in all this who has other plans, and she'll stop at nothing to get what she thinks she deserves.

Chapter 35: Grace Nash

What Time on Tuesday

Six Days After the Wedding

He looks so sweet when he's sleeping. I haven't really taken the time to observe that, but as I wake up a little before seven, I allow myself the time to study him for a few beats.

We're both naked, tangled together after the night where we finally had the time to express how we're both feeling, and I don't ever want to move.

I know I have to. I need to get to my office. I've been gone nearly a week now, and I'm sure there's a mountain of things to do.

But right now, I just want to stare at the way his forehead smooths in his sleep, at the little freckles I never noticed before peppering across the top of his straight nose, at the short hairs of his eyebrows, and at the scruff covering his strong jawline. At the hair that's always so neat now mussed from sleep, and the full lips that worshiped my body last night.

And speaking of his lips, that dirty mouth of his…my God. It's going to be the end of me.

His eyes slowly start to open, and I close mine before he catches me staring. I shift in his arms to let him know I'm awake, and when I open my eyes, I see him peering at me with those blue ones of his. My privacy shades keep it fairly dark in here, but his eyes are still bright from the little bit of light peeking its way in around the sides.

And it's as our eyes meet that I know for sure.

I'm in love with him.

It's not just from the sex, though holy hell, that's been top-notch. It's from the strong foundation we built first as friends.

I can picture this love carrying us into a future where he's the one pressing that glass of wine into my palm after a long day.

He leans forward and presses his lips to my forehead. "Morning," he murmurs.

"Morning." I duck my face so my morning dragon breath doesn't scare him away. "As much as I don't want to move out of your arms, I need to get to work."

Instead of words, he responds by turning into me and tightening his arms around me. "I don't want to face reality. I just want to keep living in this dream with you."

An overwhelming sensation tightens my chest as I snuggle a little more closely into him. "Same."

We don't move for a few sweet moments, just holding onto one another in this perfection, but then my alarm starts to ring, letting me know I need to get into the shower or I'm going to be late.

We both sigh, and I turn out of his arms to click my alarm off before I get up and pad over to the bathroom to shower.

When I get out, he's not in bed anymore. I get dressed, pull my wet hair into a bun since I'm already running short on time, put on some makeup, and meet him in the kitchen.

To my surprise, he made me breakfast.

"You didn't have much, but I found the coffee and your stash of breakfast burritos in the freezer. I hope you don't mind that I made you one."

"You…you—" I cut myself off as I try to figure out whether this man is actually real or just a dream. "You hope I don't mind? This is amazing, Spencer." I sit down, pour salsa on the side of my plate, and dig into the burrito. "Make yourself one, too. These are the best."

He chuckles. "I already ate mine, and you're right. I'm going to take a quick shower while you eat, and then we can go over and tell Maggie our news together."

He knows she'll be in the tasting room making sure we're ready for the day. It's always where she starts the day, usually an hour before anyone else is even awake. It's her favorite place to be…and I need to go tell her that Spencer and I are married now.

I am beyond grateful that Spencer is the kind of guy who wasn't about to let me do this on my own. I don't think Nana will have a negative reaction. After all, I did confess my feelings to her regarding Spencer once upon a time, so I don't think it'll come as a complete shock to her that *I* went through with this. However, it might come as a shock to her that Spencer did, and all of this will shock Amelia, who we will more than likely have to tell next.

Now *that* is a conversation I'm not ready for. I'm going to need some backup with that one.

Once I'm done eating and he's out of the shower, we regroup in the kitchen.

"Did you want to practice how you're going to tell Maggie on me first?" he asks.

I chuckle. "It's probably a good idea, but I think we should just head in and get it done."

"Whatever you want," he says with a nod.

When I walk out the front door, I glance over toward Amelia's bungalow out of habit. I think I probably always glance over at her bungalow when I leave mine, thinking maybe I'll get the chance to see Spencer.

I think back over the many times I *did* get to—when his car was parked behind her place, and I was looking for him, hoping I'd get to run into him, pining away for my sister's fiancé when I shouldn't have been.

But look at us now. I guess things work out how they are supposed to.

She's not out of her bungalow yet, unsurprising since it's only eight o'clock and she usually doesn't roll into her office until closer to nine.

I glance up at Spencer as he shuts the door behind him, and I type the code into the keypad next to it to lock it.

"Oh-five-two-oh? Isn't that your birthday?" he asks.

"Shit, now you know my secret. Don't break into my house."

"I'm your husband. Shouldn't I have the code?"

He makes a good point.

We make our way over toward the tasting room, and as predicted, Nana is sitting at the counter with today's newspaper. She flips it down onto the countertop when we walk in together.

She's alone, which means Delilah is either not in yet or in the inventory room, and Nana's eyes move slowly between us as she studies the couple in front of her. She's quiet as she squints and tilts her head, trying to piece together what's going on.

And then, finally, she speaks. "You two? Together? Happy glows all about you…is there something you need to tell me?"

I giggle a little nervously. I nod, and I glance over at Spencer as if to tell him to go ahead.

He shakes his head a little. "It needs to come from you."

He's right, and so I look back at Nana as I allow the truth to tumble out of my mouth. "I flew to Vegas to meet Spencer, and while I was there, we eloped."

I leave out the part about being raging drunk and hopped up on allergy drugs that caused us to blackout and completely forget the night when we tied the knot.

All that matters is that we have a certificate proving my words to be true.

"Well, I'll be…" she says, surprise evident in her tone. "Of all the things I thought you might come in here saying this morning when I saw your car behind your bungalow, I don't think it would've been that, but congratulations."

She stands and walks over toward us. She pulls me into a tight hug.

"I'm happy for you, sweetheart," she says to me. She hugs Spencer next. "And you, my boy. You have become like another grandchild to me, and I was devastated when you and Amelia ended things. But now…I'm thrilled. I'm thrilled to welcome you into the family, even if it's under circumstances I wasn't expecting."

He opens his mouth to respond, but we all hear the voice of complete and utter disbelief before he gets a chance to utter his words.

"Welcome to the family? What the fuck is going on here?"

I whip around at the sound of Amelia's voice, and so does Spencer as Nana's eyes focus on her other granddaughter.

"Oh, hey, Amelia," I say, going for casual even though my voice is shaking as I face my sister. "We were going to find a better time to tell you…" I suck in a breath as I say the words she already heard Nana say anyway. "Spencer and I got married."

Her face reddens with anger. "You?" she asks, pointing at me. "And…and…*you?*" she asks, pointing at Spencer. "You two? When?" She doesn't give us time to answer. "Wait. You told me you wanted to wait until your contract was up." She turns her accusatory gaze onto Spencer.

"I did," he says simply. "And my contract with the Vikings ended." He says it so easily even though we all know that's not what he meant when he told her he wanted to wait.

"So, you just…marry the first girl you see?" she asks snidely, jabbing a thumb toward me.

"It's not like that, Amelia," he says quietly.

"Then what the fuck is it like?" she demands.

"Amelia!" Nana scolds. "I know you're emotional over this shocking announcement, but I will not allow you to use that kind of language in my tasting room."

Amelia doesn't bat an eyelash at the scolding as she continues, staring the two of us down as Spencer leans in toward me, draping a defensive arm around my shoulders.

"And you," she says, turning to me with a hiss. "How could you do this to me? You know how much I loved him."

"Did you?" I ask. "Because the last time I checked, you were sleeping with Drew behind Spencer's back *on my desk.*"

She glares at me. "When?"

"Months ago," I admit, assuming she means not when we got married but when I caught her and Drew doing it on my desk.

Her face blanches. "You've been married for months?"

"No," Spencer clarifies. "I was in Vegas. Gracie came to see me, and while we were there, we knew we couldn't wait another minute."

Now he's just lying to her, which I'm fine with if it helps this look as believable as it's starting to become.

"So, you swoop in on my man five minutes after we broke up?" she asks, turning toward me.

I shake my head. "It wasn't like that. He was hurt over getting cheated on by the woman he was planning to marry, and he confided in a friend. We grew close."

"Oh, come off it," she spits at me. She glances at Spencer. "You were always close, and I was always competing with her for your attention."

"I won't deny that we shared a special friendship," Spencer says. "But we didn't cross any lines."

"No?" she demands. "You don't think getting married to your sister's ex is crossing some sort of line?"

"Not when it was something we both agreed to," I say with a shrug. It doesn't matter at this point that neither of us remembers it. We *had* to have agreed to it. The state of Nevada wouldn't have granted us a marriage license if we didn't both agree to it, never mind the question about being of sound mind. Maybe we were, maybe we weren't, but we're nearly a week into this already, and things are going pretty damn good—barring Amelia's reaction, anyway.

"How long have you been married?" she asks again, and it's kind of an odd piece of the puzzle for her to be suddenly obsessed with. "How many days?"

"Tuesday," Spencer says.

"Shit," she mutters under her breath, and she glances at Nana. "Sorry." She looks back at us. "What time on Tuesday?"

"What the hell difference does that make?" I ask.

"I just need to know," she says.

To be honest, I have no idea what time we got married. But I'm not sure why she would care. Just then, the door to the tasting room opens, and Drew struts in.

I feel Spencer stiffen beside me at the entrance of the guy his ex-girlfriend was cheating on him with.

"Oh, there you are, sweetheart," Amelia says, really laying it on thick.

"Here I am," Drew confirms as she rushes into his arms. "Why did you text me to come over here?"

Amelia clearly didn't want him to say that, but he did anyway. She huffs out a sigh as she points an accusatory finger at the two of us. "I saw them walking over here from Grace's bungalow, and guess what?"

He looks at her a little dumbly. "What?"

"These two got married in Vegas on Tuesday."

His brows shoot up. "On Tuesday? Er…what time?"

"What do you two care about Tuesday for?" I demand.

"Well, as it turns out," Amelia begins. "We have some news of our own."

"You do?" Nana asks.

"We do," Amelia confirms. "Drew and I also got married on Tuesday."

"On Tuesday," I echo.

There's only one reason she would have gotten married on Tuesday.

Somehow, she figured out my plan.

Somehow she knew I was going to Vegas, and she had to get ahead of me and get married before I did. There's no other explanation for why she would've married Drew so quickly. Especially not given her reaction to that footage I found when he told her they had love.

They don't have love.

They have sex.

"I didn't realize you were *there*," I say as I try to keep the accusations out of my tone.

"Well, that's a hell of a statement coming out of you," she retorts, looking between Spencer and me.

"Oh, so it's okay for you to marry someone when you were trying to make us all believe that you were in love with Spencer, but it's not okay for Spencer to marry someone he actually does have real feelings for?" I ask.

"You're saying that he was in love with you the whole time he was with me," she says flatly.

"You're the one who said that. But you can make whatever assumptions you want out of the fact that he wanted to wait three years to marry you, but he married me a few months after he got out of the trap you set him in."

"You bitch," Amelia screams at me, and she raises a hand into the air like she's going to come over and slap me across the face.

Maybe under other circumstances, I'd have it coming after the things I just said, but this is Amelia. She was cheating on this wonderful man and using him for his money. There's no part of me that thinks she doesn't have all of the worst things coming to her.

"What's going on in here?" another voice demands, and this time it's Uncle Jimmy with my dad sauntering in behind him.

"Oh, Daddy, thank God you're here!" Amelia cries dramatically.

She only pulls out the daddy card when she's being dramatic, though I'm sure Drew would say differently.

"What's going on?" Dad asks, repeating Uncle Jimmy's question as he glances around at the scene in front of him. What a complicated web.

"You want to know what's going on?" I ask, my hackles fully risen at this point. "Amelia found out about Nana's plan for the future of this winery, and she tried to get married before I did to steal it out from under me. Turns out we got married on the same day." I turn toward Nana, but before I can continue, Dad jumps in.

"Wait...what? You're married?" he asks Amelia.

"I'm so sorry, Daddy. Drew and I went to City Hall last week to make it official."

Uncle Jimmy sighs. "And you?" he asks, turning toward me. "Wait, let me guess. You and Spencer?"

I press my lips together, and Spencer fields this awkward one.

"I fell for Grace over the last couple months. We eloped in Vegas." The way he says it makes me believe it's the truth.

I *want* it to be the truth.

With everything in me, I want it to be true.

"On the same day as Amelia and Drew," he says flatly.

Spencer nods. "Apparently so."

"Well, Mom, I guess...ball's in your court," Dad says to Nana.

"I'm older. I deserve it," Amelia snarls.

"Age doesn't matter! What about the person who practically runs this place now as it is?" I ask, and I do my best to keep the whining out of my argument.

"Seems like everyone got by just fine for the last week in your absence," Amelia says thickly.

God, I could slug her. "Well, I'm back now, and I'll be stepping back into whatever I need to do to fix whatever you messed up while I was away," I snarl right back at her.

"Girls, girls, that's enough," Nana says. "It sounds like you all discovered my plan for the future of the vineyard, something I was trying to keep secret so things would happen naturally. I don't know if either of these marriages are real, but I suspect foul play. Regardless, I want to see out the next year. I will figure something out in the event both of these couples are still married one year from last Tuesday. I'll also take into consideration how involved you both are in the vineyard as well as your spouses. Drew has been around a long, long time here, but we've come to love Spencer, too." She shrugs. "I'm sorry, but I don't have an answer for any of you beyond that. Now, if you'll excuse me," she says, and she bolts from the tasting room.

A heavy silence falls over the six of us still in here.

It's Amelia who breaks the silence—I know, big shocker there.

"We'll see if you're still married a year from now." She smirks at me, and I get the sinking feeling she's got some tricks up her sleeve to make sure that doesn't happen.

Chapter 36: Grace Nash

It Started as a Blackout

Six Days After the Wedding

Uncle Jimmy and my dad glance at each other, and Jimmy walks out next, presumably to follow after Nana.

Drew takes the reins as he practically drags Amelia out of the tasting room.

My dad sighs when it's just the three of us left in here. "You do realize how messed up this entire thing is, don't you?"

I glance up at the camera he installed in here, and I shrug. "It's not messed up."

"Come with me," he says. We both follow him out of the tasting room, past the firepits, and down the path toward the chapel. "I'll ask again now that there are no cameras recording our conversation. What is this?"

I'm not sure how detailed to be here.

On the one hand, Amelia is also his daughter. But on the other, this is my dad. I want to be honest with him.

"As I told you, it started as a blackout," I say. I'm not sure where to go next after that. I don't actually know what it is. It's not like either of us has defined it yet, at least not to each other, though knowing him and the way he categorizes everything in his life, surely he's put me into some sort of category in his own mind with feelings attached to it labeled *wife*...sort of like I have in my own mind with the *husband* label.

Spencer breaks the brief moment of silence. "Can I be honest with you, Steve?"

"I'd expect nothing less," my dad says.

"It started as a blackout, and we were both stunned when we woke up on Wednesday morning with rings on our fingers. But the more time I spend with your daughter, the more I can see this lasting longer than the year I initially agreed to."

My chest tightens at his words, and a soft gasp falls from my lips as I rush into his arms. "I feel the same way."

My dad nods. "Were there feelings between the two of you prior to this?"

"Not that we acted on," Spencer says carefully.

My dad stops and looks between the two of us. He sighs. "I'm glad it's more than just a drunken mistake, but there are things we need to discuss. I mentioned a prenup on the phone Saturday to you. Any chance you magically found one that you wrote when you were blacked out?"

We both shake our heads.

"My lawyer, Glen Farnsworth, drafted up a postnup. It's very simple but protects both your assets. It's in my office if you're both willing to sign it," he says.

"I'll do whatever it takes to ensure the vineyard is safe." Spencer grabs my hand and links his fingers through mine. "And for the record, that includes making sure Grace is the one standing at the end of whatever tests Maggie crafts for us."

My dad presses his lips together and shakes his head a little as if he doesn't really believe what he's hearing. "Okay, then."

We change our direction to walk over toward my dad's office to sign off on the postnup.

And as I sign my name with a flourish, I can't help but think there's a better chance than ever that we'll never have to execute it.

Amelia, however, has other plans.

Starting later in the afternoon, after I've caught up with Heidi via Zoom and I head into the tasting room and see Amelia *talking to customers.*

She's *never* in the tasting room, but she's clearly trying to throw her all into this new challenge as if history means nothing to any of us. Nana's there, too, and they're all laughing together. Drew is obviously back to work, and Spencer stayed with my dad to talk about some of the financials and best practices.

While Drew is essential to this vineyard as the head of the cellar workers, it's not like he's irreplaceable. Does he have a big role scheduling tasks and monitoring our product development? Of course he does. But could someone else be trained to take care of those tasks just as well as he does? Absolutely.

By the same token, I suppose that Spencer is also replaceable, especially considering he isn't actually employed here. Anyone can analyze the business to see what's working successfully and what can be changed, though it's hard to find trustworthy people invested in the winery who can take care of those tasks.

And me? I'd like to think I'm not replaceable, but I was just gone for nearly an entire week, and everybody seems to get by just fine without me.

As for my sister, well, I was essentially doing her job before she quit teaching to come work here. But since she's been here, I've been given other responsibilities, ones that I deem more important than the ones that she's taking care of.

I'm sure she'd have words to say about that.

So what it comes down to is that all of us are replaceable, but which one of us is most likely to give this place the sort of future it deserves?

I want it to be me because I love this place. It's my childhood, which Amelia could also say, but this place is my heart and soul. I can't help but constantly remember that she left. She went off to be a teacher, and when that didn't work out, she came back, begging for a position here. It's something that has always rubbed me the wrong way because one of us always knew our future was here while the other of us chose to walk away and only returned when it benefited her.

Nana has to see that I'm the right choice.

To Amelia, it's only about money and what she could get out of it.

To me…it's a love of the product and the land and pride in what we create literally from the ground up.

Maybe Nana sees something I'm not seeing. Maybe there's some promise she made to Pop Pop that I don't know about.

"I was hoping for something a little sweeter," the customer Amelia is talking to says. Amelia looks helplessly at Nana, and this is where I step in.

"Our pinot grigio is pretty dry," I say. "How about this one?" I pour a glass of our moscato, one of our most popular sweet wines.

She takes a sip, and her brows rise—the signal that I'm about to close a sale. "Oh my word, that's delicious."

I pour one for the man with her, too, and he also likes it.

"That's exactly what I was looking for," she says to him.

"For the party?" he asks.

She nods, and it feels like such a win to me since Amelia never would've known to give her that one next. She's in here trying to prove Nana should give this place to her, but it feels more and more like Amelia knows nothing about it at all.

"Are you looking for a few bottles or a case?" I ask.

"What's the price?" the man asks.

I glance at Amelia to allow her to field a question—maybe a slight manipulation since I know she has no idea—and when she looks lost, I answer the question. "Twenty-six for a bottle, two-eighty for a case of twelve."

The woman glances at the man. "Case?"

He nods.

I smile at them both. "I'll be right back." I head back to our inventory room behind our gift shop, and I grab an already packed case off the shelf. When I turn around, Amelia stands there scowling at me.

"You think you can just come in and steal the clients from me?"

I blow out of breath. "A, they're not clients, they're customers, and B, it's not stealing because we don't work on commission here. I closed the sale that you never would've been able to because you don't know our products the way I do."

She doesn't have a snappy retort for that because she knows it's the truth. She huffs out some sound of annoyance and stalks off. She's not in the tasting room when I return, and Nana is taking payment from the customers.

Once they leave, she turns to me. "Well done with the moscato, my dear."

I'm thrilled at the acknowledgement. And I hope it's a start for her to see that even if somehow Amelia manages to hold onto Drew for the next year, only one of us deserves this vineyard, and the other one is named Amelia.

I head back to my office to catch up on some of the things I missed while I was gone, and I realize maybe this place really didn't run so well without me since there's a lot of work to catch up on.

Spencer walks in just before the end of the day. He closes my office door and sits in the chair across from my desk.

"Where have you been all day?" I ask.

"With your dad. Trying to justify Drew's role here without making it seem like I'm trying to cut him out of the picture."

My brows dip together. "What do you mean?"

"He's getting paid a lot, and no matter what formula I tried, he kept coming up at the top of the list of which employees to cut. But if we get rid of him, Amelia will think we're doing it to purposely hurt her chances of inheriting this place. So it's a kind of lose-lose situation where it'll look like your dad's trying to give you an advantage."

I blow out a breath. "Seems like it just keeps getting more and more complicated, doesn't it?"

"It does, and I know it'll just cause more problems than it's worth, so it's not an option right now." He shrugs.

"Or maybe even after…" I trail off, but we both get the gist of what I'm trying to say.

After I'm the one who gets control of the vineyard at the end of all this, I can't exactly fire Drew as my first order of business.

"What did my dad say?" I ask.

"He agreed with me that it's more or less the wrong thing to do, no matter how much the bottom line tells us it's the right thing to do."

"Okay, then we take a harder look at things and try to figure out where else we can trim things down." I click a few buttons to wrap up what I'm working on then lock my screen so nobody can come in and touch anything while I'm away.

Spencer and I head down to the restaurant, where we put in an order, and we drink wine while we wait. Once the food is ready, we take it out back to the firepits. And as I take the first bite of my favorite flatbread, I feel a wonderful sense of the future.

And then another thought hits me.

What if Nana can't decide, so she chooses to split the responsibilities in half, sort of like she did with my dad and Uncle Jimmy?

I can't be stuck here running this place with Amelia. I can't work that closely with her.

But now that the very real threat has crossed my mind, I need to figure out the best way to show Nana that I'm the most deserving of this place.

The alternative is far too heartbreaking.

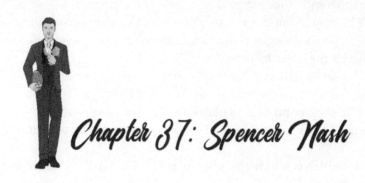

Chapter 37: Spencer Nash

We Were So Wasted

A Week After the Wedding

I click on the email as we make breakfast the next morning. "Our video is in."

"Ahh!" she squeals. "Have you watched it?" she asks from where she's making scrambled eggs by the stove.

"No," I say, shaking my head. "I just got the email."

"Show me!" She turns off the burner on the eggs and moves in beside me so we can both see the video on my phone.

I love when she moves in close to me. I love when I can smell the vanilla in her hair, the sweet scent that is starting to feel more and more like home to me.

I click the link, enter my password, and we see the video pop up. It's only three minutes long.

"Go ahead," I tell her, and she presses the play button.

Elvis's "Can't Help Falling in Love" begins, and we watch as the two of us get out of the limo, already dressed in our wedding attire.

The video cuts to me standing in Grayson's tuxedo at the altar next to Elvis as I wait for my bride to walk down the aisle, and the music lowers to the background as I'm shown raising a glass in the air and yelling, "Here comes my bride!"

I'm clearly very drunk—at least to myself, I look like I am, and by the way, I didn't know drinks were allowed in chapels, but apparently they are.

The camera moves to catch Grace as she walks down the aisle in Ava's dress, and she giggles nervously on the screen. "There's my soon-to-be hubby!"

She sets a hand on her forehead with a murmured, "Oh my God, we were so wasted," as we keep watching.

The song continues to play lower in the background so we can hear Elvis's words as well as each of us agreeing with an *I do*.

When Elvis tells me to kiss the bride, I dip her and plant a good one on her.

A little thrill bursts along my spine over that kiss, if I'm being honest.

It's beautiful and poetic, and then we walk with our hands clasped between us down the aisle toward the camera, both of our hands on the outside raised in the air with happiness and celebration.

The video lasts as long as the song, and then it fades out with a congratulatory message for a long and happy marriage.

I raise my brows and turn to look at her to get her reaction first. "Well?"

She shakes her head. "Apart from being totally drunk, it was nice."

"Nice?" I repeat, and I chuckle.

She giggles. "Okay, wrong word. It's a great video, and now we have proof it actually happened."

I clear my throat. "And a time stamp…if we need it."

She tilts her head. "I don't think Nana cares about the timing."

"But don't you think it's a little strange that Amelia got married the exact same day we did? Don't you think there's a chance she somehow found out about us and rushed to the altar to make sure she had a shot at this place?" I ask.

"I wouldn't put anything past her," she admits. "And I had a horrible thought yesterday, by the way, and I couldn't sleep last night thinking about it."

It's my turn to tilt my head as I wait for her to tell me what it was.

"What if Nana can't decide so she gives us each fifty percent?"

I twist my lips. The thought hadn't occurred to me, but then this has all been such a whirlwind that I haven't had much time to think rationally about much of anything. "Do you think she'd do that?"

Her brows knit together. "She's kind of doing it with my dad and uncle," she points out.

"But they don't *own* fifty percent each. Maggie still retains ownership, and she's just having them *run it* at fifty percent each."

"Fair point. But still…I can't work every day for the rest of my life with Amelia in charge here." She sighs. "I don't know what I can do to prove it should be me."

I press my lips together, and I set my phone down as I take her into my arms. "Just be you, Gracie. Keep doing what you've always done. What's that saying? The trash takes itself out? Her true colors will show, babe. Just give her the time to show them."

"To who? Because Nana's obviously blind to those true colors if she's considering giving it to her."

I hug her a little tighter. "Or maybe she already knows it's you, and she's just giving Amelia the chance to try to step up and do the right thing."

She sighs, and I feel her relax a little into my arms. "I hope you're right."

I kiss the top of her head, and then I let her go so she can dish out the eggs as I pour us each a cup of coffee.

I hope I'm right, too.

The doorbell rings shortly before I'm about to head over for another day of analyzing financial reports with Steve, and I spot a huge vase of flowers sitting on the porch. I pick it up and bring it inside, and Grace is just finishing up the dishes.

"Oh, Spencer," she says, wiping her hands on a towel. "How sweet!"

"These aren't from me," I admit, though I'm sort of kicking myself for not thinking of sending my wife flowers.

She looks confused as I set them on the table. "Not from you? Then…who?"

I finger the card on the stick that says *Grace*, and I pull it off and hand it to her.

She pulls the card out and reads it aloud. "Grace, I heard you got married in Vegas, and it made me realize all I've lost. If it isn't real, give me a call. I've been thinking about us nonstop. Love, Patrick." She glances up at me.

"Patrick? Who's Patrick?" I ask.

"My ex," she says, rolling her eyes. "It's been years, but nobody knows better than my family how devastated I was when it ended. I'm over it now, for the record, and this is clearly Amelia already starting with games."

I see it the moment it happens. A fire lights up her eyes as she shakes her head. "She thinks she can win with stupid tricks like this, but she won't."

I raise both brows. "I'm right here beside you for whatever you need." I have to admit, I'm sort of interested in what my wife is going to come up with to ensure she gets what's rightfully hers.

Chapter 38: Grace Nash

Separating Emotion from Decisions

A Week After the Wedding

"I have some ideas for things we can do, but a lot of it would fall under marketing," I tell my dad. I'm here interrupting his time with Spencer, but I've been brainstorming all morning, and this is what I've come up with.

I'm taking the high road where Amelia is concerned. I'm not going to try to sabotage her relationship. Instead, I'm going to prove how much this place needs me, and by the same token, I'm going to show how irrelevant Amelia is.

"Areas dip into each other all the time," my dad says. "Just because Amelia has the title of marketing director doesn't mean the hospitality manager can't create marketing events as well. What are you thinking?"

"I thought we could improve our reputation by doing some charitable events, maybe do some live BTS type things on our TikTok and Instagram accounts, and reach out to some influencers with private tours," I say, naming a few ideas from my earlier brainstorm off the top of my head.

"BTS?" my dad asks.

"Behind the scenes," I clarify.

"Oh, right. Yeah, those last two are definitely marketing, but since you used to do all the marketing here, I think it'd be fine. Maybe run it by Mom first," he suggests.

"What about the charitable events?" I ask.

"Like what?" He leans back in his chair.

"I was thinking maybe we could do a charity event in the Grand Hall," I say.

"I have a lot of contacts in Minneapolis if you're interested in inviting some influential people," Spencer offers.

"That would be incredible," I say. "And I was also thinking we could create a brand-new blend that would be totally for charity. We could use the ball to kick off the blend, and we could either create our own foundation or maybe choose one related to heart disease since that's what we lost Pop Pop to."

"Oh, Gigi," my dad says. "What a wonderful idea. A red, I think, since I've heard about links between red wine and lower risks for heart disease."

"Great idea," I say, nodding as I type that into my phone to do more research on it later. I glance up and spot my dad sort of studying me. "What?"

"I just have to say, Gracie, I'm so damn proud of you and the way you're going about this."

I give him a hug and head back to my office and get a start on planning for the charity event. I don't know what Spencer's schedule looks like, but I'd love to have him here for it. So I either have to rush it to get it in before training camp starts, or I have to wait a year. I can't wait a year because that'll be closer to the end of this whole thing. I need to start laying on thick the reasons why it should be me now.

That tells me I need to do this thing around the middle of July. It'll have to be on a Sunday since Saturday weddings are booked for the entire summer, and we keep the Grand Hall available on Friday evenings to allow for decorating and rehearsals.

As I think of ways to increase revenue, though, the Grand Hall sticks out.

Right now, we really only use it once a week. What if we allowed Friday and Sunday weddings as well? What if we allowed other events during the week? We'd have to work out rehearsal schedules and things like that, but we could make it work.

We could charge enough to cover the staff and cleaning crew, and it would be more and more chances to showcase our products. More people would be visiting, which means more profits at the bar, the restaurant, the tasting room, and the gift shop.

I decide I'll talk to Spencer about it later since he's more familiar with the financials, but I don't see any downside to it at all.

Later comes in the afternoon when he stops by my office to check in. "How's it going?" he asks.

I nod toward the chair. "Take a seat. I have some questions for you."

"Open or closed-door type questions?"

"Closed."

He wiggles his eyebrows.

"Get your mind out of the gutter."

"My mind seems to permanently reside in the gutter when you're around," he mutters as he gets up and shuts the door. When he sits back down, he asks, "What's going on?"

"You're more familiar with the financials than me, so I wanted to discuss the idea of opening the Grand Hall for additional events on other days aside from Saturday. We've always cited staffing as our reason not to, but with the popularity of the venue, we could easily raise prices *and* get a ton more visitors to the vineyard each week." I give him a hopeful look as I wait for his reply.

"It's brilliant, Grace. The Grand Hall brings in the biggest profit margin of all the events we host here, and I suggested to your dad that we focus on that as one of the areas for expansion. But he said one a week is just the way we've always done it."

"I hate that phrase," I say. While I'm a strategist who works hard to analyze the best path forward, my dad finds comfort and security in tradition. Don't get me wrong; I love a good tradition. But when that *tradition* stops us from trying new things, I'm going to put up a fight.

I dial up my dad's line from my office phone. "Hey, Gigi," he answers.

"I had this idea I wanted to run by Spencer, and he loved it. But then he told me you won't go for it because the way we do it is the way we've always done it, and I'm not okay with that."

Spencer looks like I just threw him under the bus, and my dad is silent on the other side of the line.

I plow forward. "I think we need to open up the Grand Hall to more events than just one wedding a week. I know we've traditionally done only one, but why are we limiting ourselves to one event a week if events are our biggest profit margin? And it doesn't have to be limited to weddings, Dad. We could do charity events, birthday parties, anniversary parties, retirement…you name it, if someone wants to pay our fee, we'll host it. And I also think we need to raise our rates. People will pay it. Trust me."

My dad remains quiet on the other side of the line, and eventually he sighs. "If *you're* the future of this place, then I trust you to do what you think is right."

"Can I ask why you're hesitant?"

"You can, and it's a fair question with a complicated answer. I like that our venue has the reputation it has. I like that it's hard to get in, and couples book out up to two years in advance. I like that it's exclusive and small. And I like that my own mother and father were married here, and all the couples who have been married here have had successful, happy marriages. I worry that expanding could kill that for us, and sometimes the hope of more success isn't worth the growing pains."

Oh.

I didn't realize it was an *emotional* reason. His parents were married there, and he thinks of it as a sacred place because of that. He wants to keep it in the same state it was in when they were married there.

But just because he has an emotional reason for it doesn't mean it should stop us.

"I think we have to separate emotion from these types of business decisions, Dad," I say quietly. Even as I say the words, I realize I'm not living up to them. This marriage between Spencer and me was only ever supposed to be a business decision, and here I am, fully emotionally invested. I clear my throat as I add, "We can still make it an exclusive venue even with an expansion."

"I know you're right. It's just...sometimes success can breed other challenges we weren't expecting."

I glance at Spencer, who presses his lips together and glances out the window. I get the impression that he gets that side of it, too. But I'm confident that we have the resources to take on new challenges—especially if Spencer is by my side.

"I get that, but with Spencer by my side, we'll face those challenges head-on," I say.

He tilts his head a little as his lips tip up, and his gaze returns to me. He nods resolutely, and I know I have an amazing ally in my corner.

"I believe you will, too," he says.

I guess that means it's time to get to work.

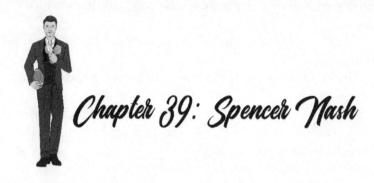

Chapter 39: Spencer Nash

Race You There

A Week After the Wedding

I t's rare to find Amelia in the tasting room, yet she's there when I walk by later in the afternoon.

"Do you have anything less…sweet?" the customer asks her, and she seems to glance around wildly before her eyes land on me.

"Oh, look! It's Spencer Nash, formerly of the Minnesota Vikings!" she tells the man and woman she's working with.

She knows I fucking hate when she does that, which is obviously why she chooses this moment to do it.

I offer a wave and a smile to the guests, and I step into the conversation because, as much as I want to see Amelia fail here, in particular in front of Maggie, who's talking to some guests on the other end of the counter, I don't want the *vineyard* to fail.

"We're huge fans," the man says to me. "Best of luck in San Diego. We're sad to see you go."

"I appreciate that," I say with a friendly nod. And then to get the heat off me, I switch back to the reason why these people are here. "The pinot noir here is my favorite." I walk behind the counter to grab the bottle from where I know it's kept.

Amelia does *not* know this fact, and if Grace hadn't just taken nearly a week away from this place, I know she'd be down here chatting with these customers. Instead, they got stuck with Amelia.

I get her trying to put in the effort, but even Maggie must see through it.

Except…it doesn't appear she actually does, which is a total mystery to me.

She doesn't see Amelia's near-flub. Instead, she walks over as Amelia is about to tip the pinot over the same glasses that still have a bit of moscato in them.

"New glasses," I mutter at her as I reach under the counter to produce those as well.

"Oh! Right." She tips the bottle over the new glasses.

"Didn't like the moscato?" Maggie asks the customers.

"It was lovely, just a little sweet for me," the woman says.

Maggie beams at Amelia. "I'm so glad my granddaughter set you up with the pinot, then."

"Oh, no. It was Spencer," the man says, and Maggie just smiles and nods.

But still, I mark a tick in the win column for Grace.

"What foods does this go best with?" the woman asks, glancing up at Amelia.

Both Maggie and I turn to Amelia, too.

"Oh, uh…" She trails off, clearly out of her element here.

"It pairs really well with beef or salmon," I say, swooping in. Everything I know about wine, I know because I've spent time here, and it's puzzling that Amelia hasn't picked up on any of it.

Most likely because she just doesn't care, and that's the worst part of it all. The *only* reason she's after this place is because she thinks it'll give her the money or the status she wants. It's a challenge to her. A way to beat her sister.

But no one will ever convince me that she deserves it as much as Grace does.

I return to Grace's place—the house to which I now know the code since my wife lives here—and when I check my email, I see a bunch of new correspondence from the Storm.

I have team activities starting in two weeks, which means I probably need to get my ass back to San Diego. I have two weeks to get in the kind of shape that won't make me look like I took the entire offseason, well, *off*.

It all kicks off with organized team activities, or OTAs, and we have two days of them in two weeks and three days of them in three weeks. They're usually voluntary, but since I'm new, I need to be there.

I don't know many guys on the team very well yet, and this is my chance to get to know them. I can hang with Clay, who's already introduced me to more of the receivers on the team, and I can get to know the rest of the offense before we head into camp in two months.

OTAs are sort of the unofficial start of the new season for players, and while at first I was upset about this change, I've shifted my mindset to try to look forward to it.

It just sucks that it means I'll have to leave Grace, and it's not like she's going to be able to come with me when she's here fighting for the vineyard.

I don't want to spend time apart from her—especially not now that I've started allowing myself to feel what I've always felt for her—but we don't have a choice. She has her job here, and I have my job there.

This would've been easier had I not been released, but it is what it is.

I don't have much here with me—just what I packed for Vegas, which I've washed to wear for this week. But I did pack my Nikes and running shorts in case I had time for the gym, so I decide to gear up for a run before dinner. The vineyard's walking paths are the perfect setting for a run, and in fact, I've done it many times.

I'm digging through my suitcase for the one dry-fit shirt I brought along when I hear the front door open and shut, followed by my name.

"Spencer?"

"In the bedroom!" I yell back, and Grace appears in the doorway a few seconds later.

"Well, well, well," she says, her eyes falling onto my abdomen. "What did I walk in on?"

I chuckle as I abandon my suitcase to turn fully toward my wife. "I'm getting ready for a run. Want to join me?"

She folds her arms across her chest and leans against the doorframe. "I only run if I'm being chased. By a bear."

"We should change that. Running can be quite fun, you know." I take a few steps toward her, and I press a kiss to her lips.

"Fun? Run? I don't think so." She purses her lips and shakes her head. "Now drop the shorts and take me to bed."

"What if I *don't* drop the shorts and instead we run to the barn, have wild sex in there, and then run back here?" I suggest, the idea out of my mouth before I can stop it.

"Like I'll be able to run back here after I'm all satisfied from what you do to me," she says sarcastically, and she probably has a point.

"Okay," I murmur, dragging my lips down her neck. "Then what if we run to the barn, fuck in there, and then walk back here once you can stand up straight again, and then we take a shower together?"

"Oh, God, Spencer. It's really not fair for you to suggest that when you're kissing my neck like that."

I laugh as I pull back. "Why do you think I did it?"

She glares at me, but she heads toward her dresser and pulls out a pair of shorts and a sports bra.

Oh, *hell* yes. Shorts and a sports bra are my kryptonite. Add in a messy ponytail, and I'm done for.

I slip a condom into the little pocket inside my shorts and find my shirt while she gets changed, and when she emerges from the bathroom, sure enough...messy ponytail.

"Do you have any idea how sexy you are?" I ask.

"Not sexy enough for you to bang me *before* the run, apparently," she mutters petulantly.

I grab her in my arms. "So sexy that I'm forcing myself to go on this run so I don't come the second I slide inside you."

She squeaks out some reply, and I can't help a laugh.

"Race you there," I say, and I take off for the front door.

"Hey, wait a second!" she protests. I stop and turn toward her, and she says, "What about water?"

"Oh, right," I say, and I detour toward the fridge to grab two bottles. As I do it, she darts out the front door.

"See ya, sucker!" she yells, and she takes off toward the barn.

I laugh as I shake my head, but I grab the bottles, head out the front door, and lock it behind me.

I'm a professional athlete. If an admitted non-runner needs a head start in a race against me, that's fine.

I start my jog down the path that snakes behind the tasting room out toward the lake, and I take a right toward the barn. I easily catch up with her even though I'm not going full speed, and it's clear she sprinted to this point before she lost steam.

I have a few tricks I can teach her, but hopefully the reward of what I plan to do to her in the barn will be enough to motivate her to go on another run with me in the future.

We lightly jog the rest of the way to the barn, which is just under a mile from Grace's bungalow, and Grace opens the gated door to let us both in.

She latches it shut from the inside behind us, and we both glance around. I set my hands on my hips, not winded in the slightest, and she doubles over, panting as she tries to catch her breath.

"You okay?" I ask.

She nods, and she paces around for a few seconds as she catches her breath.

The windows around the top of the barn are casting an evening glow, and the space is mostly cleared out because the tractors that are stored here in the winter are currently parked behind the barn. The maintenance workers will drive them in here via the back door to work on them in the spring and summer months out of the elements, but otherwise the barn is mostly used for storage.

And that gives me an idea.

"The plows and tractors are parked out back right now, right?"

Grace nods.

I glance around as I picture it. "What if we cleaned this place up a little, strung some lights around the top…and used it as a second event venue when the equipment is in use?"

She looks around, and her eyes start to light up as she envisions the potential this place has. It's bigger than the Grand Hall, which means our parties wouldn't necessarily have to be limited the way those are. There's plenty of parking between the parking lots and the long street we drive down to get to the barn.

"Oh! What if we built a shed over the spot where the equipment is currently parked?" she asks. "Then we could use the barn year-round for events!"

We both walk through the barn and open the garage door in the back.

"Shit," she says. "A shed would block this beautiful view."

We both look over the view of the fields the barn offers.

"And look at all this additional space we could use for outdoor seating," I point out. "But the tractors aren't behind the barn. They're parked behind the production facility. We could build a shed back there for the equipment and transform the barn into an incredible venue."

She tosses her arms around me, knocking me back a step. We both laugh.

"Spencer, that's genius!" she squeals.

It's her excitement over expanding this place that gets *me* feeling excited, too.

And horny.

Very horny.

Why is it that every time I'm around her, I lose all control?

I let her go and lower the garage door, sealing us back into privacy, and then I walk back over to her and take her in my arms.

I lower my lips to hers, and she kisses me back with that same level of excitement and enthusiasm. I walk us over toward one of the divider walls where the spare barrels are kept, and I lift her up and prop her onto one.

It's the perfect height for me to shove my hips against hers as I deepen the kiss, urgency rushing over me with the need to be inside her.

We have privacy here, and we'll hear if someone walks in. These are the things I think about—making sure she can keep her modesty, making sure nobody else gets to see what's mine now.

It's the first time that possessive thought has popped into my mind.

I have to admit, the flowers threw me.

In my mind, I know they were from Amelia, not Grace's ex as signed on the card. But the thought that someone from her past could walk in at any time is unnerving...especially combined with the way my relationship with Amelia came to an end.

It was over long before I knew she was cheating on me, but that doesn't make it any easier. It doesn't make me feel any better. Is there something intrinsic about me that makes women feel like they can cheat on me? I'm not a leader like Lincoln. I'm not gregarious and outgoing like Grayson. I'm not wild and spontaneous like Asher.

I'm just me. The borderline nerdy guy who likes numbers and businesses and finances, who prefers to build Lego sets during his downtime and also happens to play football professionally. I'd prefer my privacy out of the spotlight, but given my family history, paired with my profession, that's not always an option.

And it feels like Grace gets that. It feels like she even *wants* that. It's so far removed from the women of my past that sometimes it feels like a dream.

Something has to go wrong.

But for now, I plan to revel in everything that's right.

I pour that into my kiss, both of us panting as our hands explore haphazardly. We're newlyweds, and it sort of *feels* like it this time after our playful run here and the idea session we just shared and the future spanning out before us.

I could get used to that feeling. I could get used to having Grace in my life.

I don't want to pour too much of myself into her if she really intends for this to end in a year, but every day I spend with her, the hope is that she'll want to keep going once that year is over.

That thought spurs me to action. I reach up the leg of her shorts, push her panties to the side, and slide a finger into her.

"Oh!" she gasps, clinging onto me around my neck.

I hiss as I feel how wet she is. She's always so hot and ready for me, and this is no exception.

I keep kissing her as I bring her higher and higher, closer and closer to the edge, and even though this is still so new, I've gotten to know a few things about her body already.

Like the moment when we're about to hit the point of no return, that's the moment I slide my finger out of her, grab the condom out of my inner pocket, pull my cock out, and roll it on.

She shimmies out of her shorts to give me more room to work with, and I pull her tits up over her sports bra because I need a taste before I slide into her. She looks so gorgeous there in just her sports bra, perched on top of a barrel, her tits perky as she sits ready and waiting for me, her lips parted and her eyes hot on mine.

I suck her nipple into my mouth, and I love everything about how she tastes, how she moves, how she moans for more.

I suck harder, and she moans louder.

I move my mouth back to hers, and I hold my cock in a fist as I slide it through her before pushing into her. We both hiss at the feel of my entrance, and then I start to move.

She feels like sweet perfection as I pump into her, and I already know this won't last nearly long enough. One part of me feels like forever isn't long enough to spend right here in this place, while the other part of me needs the release like I need to fucking breathe.

Her moans goad me on to push harder, higher, faster, and we both grunt as pleasure starts to grip onto us both. I hammer into her, holding her around her back so she doesn't move around on the barrel, and her hands grip around my biceps as she lets me know how much she likes what I'm doing.

I can tell she likes it when she starts to get loud, and the crescendo is building. She lets out a squeal, and that's the thing about fucking her—she's quiet and understated in her day-to-day life, but when I get her going, she unleashes this sex goddess that resides inside her.

And I don't know if I've experienced anything hotter in my entire life.

"I'm coming!" she squeals. "I'm coming, oh, God, Spencer, you're making me come so hard!"

Jesus Christ.

"I fucking love watching you come," I growl.

Her words combined with the hot way her pussy pulses over and over around my cock are enough to spur me into my own release. It feels like I've left this world for another as my balls draw up and my body responds to her with spasms of its own as she convulses over and over around me, her nails digging into my biceps and her body gyrating in time with mine.

I grunt my way through my release, not wanting to drop out of her even when it's over. Instead, I stay exactly where I am, breathing her in as we both try to catch our breath after the run followed by that sexy workout.

I stay inside just a little longer, pulling her into me. She moves her hands from my biceps, lacing her arms around my waist.

And as we hold each other in the quiet afterglow of spontaneous sex in a barn after racing our way here, I can't help but think that *this* is what I want forever to look like.

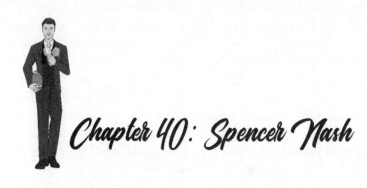

Chapter 40: Spencer Nash

She's Full of Surprises

Two and a Half Weeks After the Wedding

I stare in shock around the barn.

I legitimately thought I was coming here to have sex with my wife on my thirtieth birthday, and instead, the most important people in my life are standing here yelling *Surprise!*

I clutch my chest as the shock plows into me. My mom. My dad. All three of my brothers and both of my sisters-in-law.

Of all the things I thought might happen today…this wasn't it.

I've been facing the reality that I'm not just a year older but an entire decade older all day. I've been trying to sort through the feelings accompanying that. Many of my acquaintances who are thirty have been married for years now and have a kid or two, and that's not on my radar.

"Happy birthday," Grace says, a huge grin lighting up her face.

"You did this?" I ask.

She nods a little, and I just shake my head as I move toward her and lean down to kiss her. "I can't believe you not only arranged it but kept it a secret."

"I'm full of surprises," she says with a smirk.

If that isn't the understatement of the year.

Steve and Maggie are here, too, along with a handful of teammates I was close to in Minnesota. I make the rounds and greet everyone, and I can't help but be immensely impressed by the transformation inside this barn.

I thought she'd planned to use the charity event she's been planning as the kickoff to opening the new event space at the vineyard, but this small, intimate party is perfect here.

Complete with the lights strung along the pitched ceiling exactly as I imagined it when I mentioned that to her the night we fucked right over there on that barrel.

I glance at Asher. Sex on a barrel in a barn is probably more up his alley.

Grace asks if I'd like a drink, and I nod. "Whatever you're having." I nod toward her half-empty glass of red, and I know whatever it is, it's a Newlywed, and I'll love it.

Just like I love her.

It's getting stronger and stronger by the day, and as much as I'm excited to start another season with a new team...I'm dreading the moment I'm going to have to leave her.

We've grown close over the last few weeks, in part because of the amount of time we've been blessed with. That's inevitably going to change when we're away from each other for large portions of time. We're going to shift to long-distance, and given the inception of our marriage, I can't help but wonder what it's going to do to us.

I hope it brings us closer. I fear it'll push us apart.

I guess that's sort of what turning thirty is all about. New fears, new pressures, new anxieties. It's all about how I choose to deal with them.

Asher calls me an old man. Lincoln teases me even though he's approaching forty. Grayson says he doesn't feel a day over twenty-five.

My mom chats up Grace at the bar as she grabs me a glass of wine, and I notice Amelia is absent from this party. I'm curious what my family would've thought of her, though I know for sure they wouldn't love her the way they love Grace.

It's just the right fit.

She brings that glass of red and a wrapped box. "Open your present," she demands after she hands me both.

I set my glass on the table beside me after I take a sip. "You threw me this party, Gracie. You didn't have to get me anything."

"Open it," she goads.

"We didn't sing and eat cake yet," I protest.

"I'm too excited for you to see what I got you for all that."

I chuckle, curious enough to buck tradition to see what it is. And when I open it, I find a scrapbook inside with a printed page inserted in the front.

Spencer's 30 Adventures for His 30th Year.

My brows crinkle together as I open to the first page.

Cooking Lessons for Two at Crow San Diego. Beneath the words, I find two tickets to the lessons she's referring to.

I flip to the next page. *A Hike in the Mountains. Run a 5K. Go Camping. Go on a Road Trip. Build a Sandcastle. Have a Picnic. Learn a New Skill. Lego Master Builder Competition. Ride a Roller Coaster. Unplug for a Day. Volunteer. Plant a Garden.*

I glance through the pictures she chose to represent each new thing, which is always on the right side of the page, and the left side of the page is blank for us to add in our photos from whenever we complete each task.

"Grace, this is so thoughtful," I say as I continue flipping through each new thing.

And with every flip of the page, I can't help but think about how I want to do these things with her.

I'd love to head back toward Vegas and hike with just her. I'd love to keep running with her and eventually get to the point where we can run a 5K together. Camping? A road trip? Hell yeah. And the idea of a Lego competition against her is an actual turn-on.

She's grinning when I look up at her. "I can't wait to do each thing in there together."

I reach for her and hook my palm around her neck, pulling her closer to me. "Neither can I."

It's blissful as we both revel in these feelings. We laugh the night away with my family. We munch on flatbread, and we drink too much wine, and when the evening draws to a close and our final guests leave, I take my wife back to the bungalow that feels like home now and thank her in the only way I know how.

Naked.

And then she gives me another birthday treat.

Head.

This might just be the best birthday ever.

Which is why I feel awful that her birthday three days later turns out to be a total disaster.

Chapter 41: Grace Nash

Lego Closet Perfection

A Few Weeks After the Wedding

The plane touches down in San Diego on Sunday morning, and I'm excited that Spencer invited me here for my birthday—and not just because it means a couple more days away from Amelia, but because I can't wait to get a glimpse into my husband's apartment.

I'm not sure stranger words have ever been thought. Yep, I married someone whose apartment I've never stepped foot in.

My husband invited me over to his apartment.

Can't wait to see my husband's place!

The weather is perfect a couple weeks before the end of May, and Spencer navigates his car from the parking lot at the airport toward his apartment, which is situated a little closer to the beach than the stadium.

He parks in the garage, but he wants to show me the view of the water from downstairs before he takes me upstairs.

It's a mistake. When we reach the sidewalk, someone is poised near the parking garage entrance with a camera. He snaps our photos, and my brows knit together.

"Nash! Is it true you got married?" the man asks. "Is this your wife?"

Spencer holds up a hand and doesn't otherwise respond, and I'm not sure whether to feel relieved or insulted that he didn't respond.

I'm leaning toward relieved…but my heart can't help but feel like I'd love for him to answer that question.

I'd love for him to brag to whoever this man is that he's married now.

But he didn't.

When we get inside the building, I glance up at Spencer. "Who was that?"

"Paparazzi," he answers through gritted teeth.

Isn't that an even better reason to have given an answer? "Won't they just hound us until you answer?"

"In all honesty, they mostly left me alone in Minnesota, but this is a new place, and I need to find my footing. My agent always advises me to keep my mouth shut if I'm not sure how to respond." He shrugs as we step onto the elevator to take it up to his apartment on the top floor. "You okay?" he asks as we ascend.

"Yeah. I guess it just threw me."

"I can answer next time," he offers quietly. "If it'll make you feel better."

I shake my head. "No, no. I've just…I've only really dealt with the media that one time in Vegas with you. Otherwise, I'm used to my quiet little existence at the vineyard."

His lips tip up a little. "That quiet existence is one of the things I love about you." His eyes widen as he realizes the words he just said, and my heart trips a little over them. He lowers his voice to a rasp close to my ear. "And the fact that when you come, you're anything but quiet."

Heat rushes to my cheeks. "Oh my God, Spencer!"

"Yeah, baby. Just like that." He raises a brow, and all I can do is shake my head with a mortified laugh.

We exit on the thirty-fifth floor, and there are only two doors up on this level. He unlocks the door straight ahead of the elevators, and he stands aside to let me in first.

The first thing I see is the view.

I beeline for the windows, forgetting that I'm actually pretty curious about what secrets Spencer's home might hold about him.

The penthouse suite looks out over San Diego Bay. Coronado Island is a little to the left, and beyond that is the entire Pacific Ocean.

For a girl who's used to beautiful views out the window of some of those ten thousand lakes Minnesota is known for, paired with the vines and trees that represent my entire family…I'm stunned into silence.

Minnesota is pretty, sure. But it's not the beach, and there's something tranquil about looking out over land that isn't a part of my family history.

It's a completely different feeling than the one back home. This isn't home, but it's my husband's home, and I could get used to this life, too.

Just not at the expense of having to leave Minnesota. This is vacation…temporary. That is home…permanent.

Spencer walks up beside me. "The view is what sold me on the place. It's a little more than I wanted to spend for a rental, but it's worth it to come home and look out at that."

"I can imagine," I say. I turn toward him. "Show me around."

He nods. "Well, this is the view." He turns and sweeps his hands out. "And this is the place. Kitchen, building table…I mean *dinner table*." He points to the table as I chuckle. "Family room," he continues, pointing out the couch aimed at the television hung on the wall. I spot a few Lego sets here and there, and I follow him down a hallway next. "Lego room," he says, pointing into what I assume is one of the guest rooms. There's a project table in the middle, a television hanging on one wall, and shelves and shelves of completed sets all around the room. This view is out the other side of the building, boasting a city view that's not as pretty as the ocean side but is still incredibly interesting to look at.

I spot the Millennium Falcon in a place of honor on one of the largest shelves, and I walk over toward it. "The piece de résistance," I say formally, and he laughs as I inspect some of the other sets he's built in here. "Did you take them all apart when you moved here?" I ask.

He nods. "This is just what I've built since I moved in. And this is my Lego closet." He opens the walk-in closet, and Lego boxes are neatly stacked on shelving units spanning from the floor up to the ceiling, and they appear to be organized by branding. It's impressive, to say the least.

He is really the cutest.

And so, so perfect for me.

But it appears fate has other plans for us…ones we don't even see coming.

Chapter 42: Spencer Nash

Nash Is Trash

A Few Weeks After the Wedding

The Lego closet was a hit, and I showed her our bedroom last, where we ended up spending a little *quality* time enjoying the view out the window naked from the bed together before we decided to head out for a walk.

But the walk turns into a bit of a clusterfuck when that same dude who was on the sidewalk when we walked in earlier stands there when we leave. It's as if he's been waiting this entire time for us.

"I heard your marriage is fake. Is that true?" he demands as we walk out of the building and take a left toward the bay.

"No," I tell him. "Please leave us alone."

He doesn't follow us, but as we walk toward the stoplight to cross at the crosswalk, we find more cameras poised at us.

I think back to her words about her quiet existence. I get it. It's all I want for myself, too.

I brought her here for a taste of my life, and this ain't it.

The paparazzi weren't hounding me when I moved here. They barely acknowledged my existence, to be honest.

Is this what marriage does? Puts celebrities and athletes into the spotlight? I think about former teammates of mine who got married. As I recall, it wasn't even a blip on the radar of these gossip mongers.

But those guys didn't hail from football royalty the way I do. Those guys didn't have a family of brothers who also play in the league.

I guess that makes my stake worth something more.

But I don't like it.

"Do you still want to walk?" I ask her quietly as I try to ignore the three men now tailing us down the sidewalk and across the street.

"Not with them following us," she says.

I nod, and we duck into the nearest restaurant, an upscale fine dining establishment that we're likely underdressed for, but the paparazzi won't follow us in here.

"Is this your life?" Grace asks as we approach the host stand. She looks shell-shocked.

The hostess glances up at us, her eyes falling onto the jeans we're both wearing with a bit of disdain before returning to me. I spot the recognition in her eyes. "Mr. Nash, welcome. I heard you moved in locally."

I nod. "Thank you. My wife and I were being hounded by the paparazzi outside, so we ducked in here. While we're here, we'd love to check out a menu and maybe have a drink or two." I ignore the way she definitely twitches at the *my wife* line.

I don't, however, ignore the way my wife *also* twitches beside me at those same words. I snake an arm around her waist and pull her a little closer, and she leans into me.

"Of course. Would you like a table or a seat at our bar?" she asks.

"A private, quiet table would be great," I say.

My first thought isn't because a private, quiet table could lead to private, quiet activities, but when she shows us to a table in a quiet corner in the back, the thought certainly crosses my mind.

We each glance through the menu, and we decide on some sushi since we're here and we're both hungry. I pair mine with a Sapporo, while Grace opts for a Reisling.

We've just placed our orders and I'm debating when to start getting handsy under the table when her phone dings with a text

246

message. "Oh, sorry. Excuse me. I just want to make sure nothing's wrong at the vineyard." She pulls her phone out of her pocket, and her brows knit together before the color drops completely from her face. "No," she whispers, drawing out the word.

"What's wrong?" I ask.

She sets her phone on the table and scrolls through what looks to be a ton of photos of *me*. Only, I'm not alone. There's Amelia, there's a couple other women who are part of my history, and there are some photos that I don't even recall ever taking, which tells me they have to be photoshopped.

Each photo is accompanied by a caption telling the people viewing it when and where the photo was taken, and there are enough that could be corroborated in there that it makes the ones that *can't* be look realistic.

And the worst part of all of it is that each photo already has thousands of likes on it.

"What the hell is this?" I ask.

"I got a message from Jolene asking if we'd seen this," she says. "It's an Instagram account called *NashIsTrash17*."

Seventeen for my number.

Who the fuck would make—

I interrupt my own train of thought.

Who's the one person who not only has access to these types of photos but is good with Photoshop to create the rest?

"Amelia," we both hiss at the same time.

"Why, though?" I ask. "Why would she do this?"

"Because she wants to win." She purses her lips.

"How was I ever with her?" I mutter. I don't ask my next question aloud, but I can't help wonder all the same. How will this help her win?

I try not to live my life with regrets, but being with someone as awful and manipulative as Amelia would top the list.

Grace doesn't say anything, but the way her face falls makes my chest feel heavy. I can't help but wonder at what point she'll start to feel like being with me isn't what she really wants at all.

We finish our sushi and drinks, the heaviness surrounding us at the table, and instead of walking by the bay like we'd planned, we head straight back home, followed by the paparazzi the entire way.

And every time we leave the apartment complex, we're greeted with the exact same treatment. I wouldn't put it past Amelia to have arranged this as well. If she put half as much effort into the vineyard as she does into making my life hell, she'd have no problems running the place.

We spend a quiet morning in, checking off *Lego Build Battle* from my thirty things list as we drink coffee and pretend like everything's fine.

Our cooking lesson is fun, but when we go out to dinner afterward, we're bombarded by still more photographers than before.

And then they start in on the thing that presses on my last nerve.

"We've all seen the Vegas wedding photos. Exactly how drunk were you to marry this chick?" The snide way he says it as if there's something wrong with her is vile.

The photographer beside him agrees. "Yeah, man. Those chicks you're being photographed with are way hotter."

I walk over toward him and get in his face without touching him—never touching him since I know better than that. I'm not about to risk getting in trouble, but that doesn't mean I can't scare this fucker. "What the fuck did you just say to me?"

"Spencer, don't. He's not worth it," Grace begs behind me.

I turn toward her. "He's not, but you are."

I tower over this little piece of shit, and I move in close to his face again. "Get the fuck out of my face, and don't you dare disrespect my wife. Ever." I'm about to shove him when I think better of it, and as I turn and walk away, I'm grateful for that little voice of logic in the back of my head—even though I very nearly ignored it in favor of fucking that guy up.

He had it coming.

And what the fuck does he mean, the other women I've been photographed with? That stupid fake account Amelia is running?

Something tells me there's more.

Far more.

And I intend to get to the bottom of it.

But first…we're celebrating Grace's birthday, and I'm sick to my stomach that she was just insulted the way she was. Whoever I've been pictured with doesn't matter. Whoever it is doesn't hold a fucking candle to Grace.

And that's the sign that tells me I'm not just falling. I'm fucking there. All the way.

I just hope whatever Amelia is planning isn't going to be the very thing that tears us apart.

Chapter 43: Grace Nash

Moved Meetings

A Few Weeks After the Wedding

I don't want to go home.

I don't want to have to face my sister when she's the one causing all this pressure surrounding us...and I especially don't want to face her alone.

But I do need to get back to the vineyard, so he drives me to the airport on Tuesday morning then heads toward the training facility to start working out with his teammates after a tearful goodbye. Tearful for me, anyway.

It feels like I'm saying more than just goodbye for now. There's this tension between us that wasn't there before our two days together in San Diego, and it's absolutely and totally created by my sister.

I hate that he nearly got into an altercation with someone because he was trying to defend me. I hate how that man's words made me feel like I'm not adequate to be with someone like Spencer.

I hate that I feel Amelia slipping right in between us when I had such high hopes as we started growing closer and closer. It felt like we were in a bubble when we were at the vineyard—like nothing could get to us. Maybe it was because we were so close to the enemy threat that we could manage it more easily.

She picked her moment. She waited until we were away and not paying attention, and she pounced.

All it does is make me hate her more. I thought I was at my limit, and then she started up an account called Nash is Trash. What the hell is wrong with her?

She's trying to sabotage us, and it's working.

I spend my flight home thinking about how I want to manage this. I refuse to play a game where I'm hurting the vineyard at the expense of hurting her, so it's not like I can sabotage her work materials because I'd only be hurting Newlywed in the end.

I could make her look bad in front of Nana and others on the staff, but she's pretty good at doing that all on her own.

I could call meetings and invite her via the calendar invite function, which she always ignores, so she doesn't show up and looks unprofessional.

And that gets me thinking about more ways to make her look unprofessional.

When she took over as the marketing manager, Nana asked her to put together one marketing event each quarter— something that used to fall under my responsibilities. I know enough of the vendors that I can get them to donate bigger and better things to my charity event in July so she's left looking unprepared for the third quarter event.

None of these ideas attack her the way she attacked Spencer and me, but they should be enough to show Nana that Amelia is the wrong choice.

As I pull into the space behind my bungalow, I draw in a deep breath. I can't push her out of my mind since I live and work with her, but I can try to focus on something else for a while...like, for example, work.

I carry my suitcase inside before I head over to the office. It's quiet as I walk in and turn my computer on, and it's only when I log into my email that I see *why* it's so quiet in the office.

There's a major meeting happening over in the production facility with our bottle and cork suppliers, and I'm missing it.

Because it was moved.

It was supposed to be tomorrow.

It's today.

When I check the calendar to see who made the edit...yep. "Amelia," I hiss.

I haul ass over toward the production facility, but I'm too late. Two trucks are pulling away from the parking lot, and the others are all moving in opposite directions as the facility comes into my view in the distance.

Nana is heading toward the estate, my dad is heading back toward his office, and Amelia is heading in my direction, arm-in-arm with Drew.

A smile tips her lips once she spots me. "You missed an important meeting. Guess you should've been here rather than gallivanting around California with Spencer."

"You changed it," I say, not trying to keep the accusation out of my tone.

"Mr. Jackson called asking if it could be rescheduled, and I saw that we had room to handle it today." She offers a fake smile.

"You did it to make sure I would look like I was ducking out on my responsibilities." I point a finger at her.

"Don't point at me," she says as she rolls her eyes. "If you feel that way, it's probably your guilty conscience. Hope you had a great birthday with my ex." With those words, she yanks on Drew's arm and pulls him away.

"You won't get away with this," I call after her.

"I already did," she yells without turning around.

I hold in a frustrated scream. I will *not* let her see me sweat.

I'm busy calling vendors for Corks for a Cause, and I call up the vendors who attended our last event in February. All five were my vendors first, and they agree to give bigger support to our huge charity event on July fourteenth and offer a smaller donation to the Sips and Swirls ice cream and wine event Amelia is planning for the first weekend in August—something that was my idea, and she's taking all the credit.

And since it's *her* event now, *she* can figure out how to get vendors.

I head down to the tasting room before it closes toward the end of the day. I've put in a full day of organizing July's event, and I'm excited about the things I have in store.

Amelia is in there with Nana and Delilah, and she's watching Delilah as she talks to some customers. It's as if she's studying her every move so she can imitate her later.

"Wait a minute," the woman whose name escapes me at the moment says when her eyes fall on me. "Is it true that you married Spencer Nash?"

My cheeks flush. "Yes."

"Is it true about the other women?" Amelia asks.

I turn toward her with a glare. "No. It's false, in fact." She seems surprised I know what she's talking about. "Someone probably desperate for my husband's attention started some fake social media accounts about him."

"Too bad about the Vikings losing him," the man says.

"I was sad to see him go, too," I admit. "But I spent the weekend at his penthouse in San Diego overlooking the bay, and I think he'll be doing just fine out there." I wink, and the couple laughs.

"As long as his wife pays him visits," the woman says, and I laugh along with her.

Amelia stomps off as the couple finds me more interesting than her, and I wish I could rub it in her face that Spencer does, too.

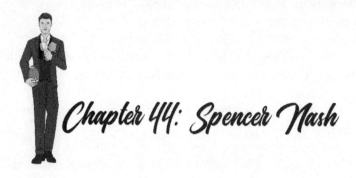

Chapter 44: Spencer Nash

Does Fiona Heat Have Single Friends

A Month After the Wedding

Tomorrow is one month since we were married, and I can't celebrate it with my wife.

I haven't seen her since her birthday nine days ago, and the time apart is slowly killing me. I miss her, and for once, it's not about the sex—though don't get me wrong, I miss that too.

I miss the easy way we have together. I miss falling asleep with her beside me. I miss waking up with her next to me. I miss breakfast together. I miss laughing with her. I miss her smile. I miss the heat in her eyes when she looks at me. I miss that feeling like this isn't a marriage in name only so she can get her hands on something that is rightfully hers anyway.

I miss *us*. We were forming an *us* at a rapid pace, and now we're stuck somewhere in neutral since we can't progress forward when we're apart.

If anything, it feels like we're falling backward, and I don't like it.

Someone continues posting photos of me. Someone seems to know my every move and has alerted the paparazzi to my calendar so I'm never alone.

And meanwhile, I'm trying to fit in on a new team while I'm asserting my place, and it's all change and upheaval while I fight off overwhelm without Grace by my side. It's a lot for a guy who thrives on routine and organization.

We talk daily. We text hourly when we can. But her voice and her words aren't a replacement for the physical person, and she can't leave the vineyard for fear that Amelia will do something underhanded while she's away.

It puts *us* on hold, and maybe that was Amelia's intent from the start.

Whatever her intent was…it seems to be working.

When I walk into the locker room on Wednesday morning for OTAs, Clayton Mack is sitting on the bench inside his sports locker, which happens to be situated directly beside mine.

I glance at the nameplate in my locker. I'm still number seventeen, the same number I've worn my entire career—including college, high school, junior high, and all the way back to peewee league. I chose it because my birthday is the seventeenth, and I never had to change it.

I can't help but wonder if this is the last locker room I'll play professionally in.

Maybe only a few months have passed since I signed on the line, but turning thirty feels suddenly heavy. I'm not at the start of my career anymore. Any injury at all at this point could easily mean I'll never stand on the line as the ball is snapped again.

And that's why I'm here this week. OTAs may be voluntary, but I've never missed them. These are the first moments where I can bond with the other receivers, get back into season shape, work on conditioning to avoid those terrifying injuries that could be career-ending, and start building chemistry with my teammates.

So I'm here.

She's there.

And we're stuck like this for a few more days.

I have a flight back to Minnesota booked for late Friday after OTAs, and I'm hoping I'm not as sore as I was last week so I can unleash the need I've had racing through me since the last time I was lucky enough to share a bed with my wife.

My wife.

The realization that I'm married now is on constant replay in my brain, and it's becoming less surreal now that it's been an entire month. What's surreal to me now, though, is the fact that every decision I make seems to be made with *us* in mind. It's no longer just *me*.

I'm not sure I ever got to that point with Amelia even though I'd asked her to marry me. I still can't imagine what drove me to do that. Between her conniving and my own need to categorize what we had, I acted spontaneously. It makes me realize that marrying Grace wasn't so out of character after all.

"Does Fiona Heat have any single friends?" Clay asks me. "Or hell, if she doesn't mind sharing…"

I turn toward him and pause for a few beats as I try to process the question. "Fiona Heat?"

His brows draw together as he clarifies his question. "The porn star."

To be honest, it's not much of a clarification. I have no idea who he's talking about. "How the hell would I know?"

He picks his phone up off the bench where it's perched beside him and scrolls a little. "Don't you know her?" He flashes his screen at me, and sure enough, it's me kissing some blonde woman's cheek. Her chest is most definitely naked and also most definitely blurred in the photo.

"Are you fucking kidding me?" I breathe, taking the phone from his hand to study it.

I zoom in—not for a better view of the tits, but for a better view of the photo. I try to piece together how there can be a photo that is *so* realistic that even *I* believe it when I know it never happened.

"My ex is apparently a Photoshop whiz, and she's trying to ruin my life. I've never met Fiona Heat before in my life," I admit. I hand the phone back to him.

"Jesus," he mutters. "That's…really something. She's got it out for you?"

"She's my wife's sister."

He bursts into laughter. "Your ex is your wife's sister?"

I nod, not joining in his laughter at all. "It's a long story, but yeah. I was actually once engaged to my sister-in-law."

"I take it she's out for revenge since you married her sister?" he asks.

"Something like that," I say dryly. I think about confessing the whole truth about the winery, but I also realize that the more people who know, the more likely it'll get blown out of proportion.

"I need a wild one like that," he mutters.

"Trust me. You don't want anything to do with her. I thought she was *just* a wild one, but as it turns out, she's pretty much a complete sociopath." I shrug.

"Well, best of luck with that, man." His tone is both teasing and joyous, but I can't muster up anything resembling joy over Amelia Newman.

I sink down onto the bench in my locker. "It's not the worst thing that I was called to a new city after the break-up."

"Well, we're happy to have you here."

"Even you?" I ask.

He nods. "Especially me. I already know it'll be you and me starting, and I also know you'll push me to a new level. I needed a challenge, if I'm being honest. It's the only way to improve."

"The other wide receivers are challenging," I point out, and I think through the roster. Apart from the two of us, we have Zach Moore, Sam Collins, Trey Clark, and DJ Evans. Of those four, Trey had the most receiving yards on the Storm last year after Clay. DJ was just drafted last month, so he hasn't had a chance to show who he is yet, and Zach was traded from Houston, so, like me, he's new, too.

It's a season of rebuilding—a nice way to say that the leaders decided it was time for a complete overhaul—but that also means OTAs and camps are the time where I can show what I'm made of. It's my opportunity to prove to the Storm why they're lucky to have me…and also to prove to the Vikings that it was a huge mistake to release me.

We start the day with a team meeting for those who showed up, and then we split off for different tasks. The defensive line heads outside for drills, and the offense heads to the weight room for conditioning.

We switch an hour later, and then we're given a working lunch as we sit through more team meetings.

So far, I'm impressed with how things work here. It's not so different from how it was in Minnesota, really, but I like how Coach puts his own spin on things. He's engaging when he's talking, and I can see how motivating he is to this team.

I'm excited to work with him, and instead of dreading the change, I'm working on a mindset shift to allow me to be eager to get to work.

I put all my focus into learning and growing when I'm at the training facility, but as I walk into my empty apartment, I see Grace everywhere she was when she was here with me.

I give her a call, but she doesn't answer.

I get a text from her a few minutes later.

Grace: *Sorry, just finishing up on a conference call, and then I have a few other things I need to take care of. I'll call before bed, okay?*

I glance at the clock. It's already after eight in Minnesota, and she's still hard at work. I love her work ethic. I love her dedication. I love that she wants the winery.

I just wish her fight for it didn't have to come *right now* when I want her to be fighting for the two of us to make this work. I want to fight *with* her for us.

I'm a pretty forgiving guy. I'd have to be to have been with Amelia as long as I was.

But if it's going to continually come down to me feeling like I'm taking second place to something else, I'm not sure we'll have it in us to be able to make the shift from fake to real.

And the more time we spend apart, the more I'm starting to think she doesn't want to make that shift after all.

Chapter 45: Grace Nash

Lady Boners

A Month After the Wedding

It feels like I'm being pulled in ten different directions all at the same time, but when I spot movement out my office window behind my bungalow, I glance over.

I see Spencer step out of the rental car that he drove here, and I leap up from my desk and race over toward him. I practically topple him over in my excitement to see him here.

"God, you're gorgeous," he says in my move to get to him.

"I missed you," I say, pressing my lips to his.

"Happy anniversary—a day late," he says, and he leans down to nuzzle my neck, pulling me into a tight embrace. "This feels so good. I missed you, too."

"Happy anniversary," I say, holding onto him tightly, too. It feels like more than eleven days have passed since we last saw each other, and at the same time, we seem to pick back up right where we left off.

I realize I left my office door open, and my laptop on, and anyone could go in there to access my files—which, of course, I don't want.

But the last thing I want to do is go back to my office when Spencer just got here.

I need some alone time with my husband, and all that tells me is that this is even more real than I thought it was.

Absence makes the heart grow fonder, and I'm fond as fuck right now after being away from him for far too long.

I grab his hand and pull him into my bungalow, and I kiss him again. "Let's make a pact that we're never apart longer than a week," I beg.

"Deal," he says, tucking some hair behind my ear before he moves in and *really* kisses me. It's urgent and deep, and I feel his neediness after being apart for too many days.

It won't be easy. We both have jobs that we need to be present for—albeit for very different reasons, but still valid reasons each in their own way.

But he's worth the effort, and his single word of agreement tells me that to him, I'm worth it, too.

His neediness scales up a level as his hands move along my body, and it's as if he can't help himself. He reaches for the bottom of my shirt to pull it over my head, and he tosses it on the floor. I do the same to his shirt, and then I move down to his belt buckle. I trail my hand down to cup his hard cock in my palm, and I'm not sure why it comes as a surprise every single time, but it does.

He's huge.

He's hard.

He's ready.

If lady boners were a thing, mine would be pointed straight up at the ceiling. Or at his chin, as the case may be.

He shoves his hips against my hand, and it's hot as *hell* to feel what I do to him. He growls then bats my hand out of the way as he takes over the belt duty, and he drops his jeans down with his boxers a moment later, kicking his shoes off in the process and working the pencil skirt I wore to work. He gets the zipper down and pulls my panties off with it. I kick off my heels, and voila, we're both naked.

He grabs me up into his arms as if I weigh nothing, and he deposits me onto my couch. He's on top of me a second later, no words exchanged between us as he fists his cock and swipes it through me.

WEDDING THE *Wide Receiver*

"Can I go in?" he asks, and the motivation behind his question is clear. He needs to know whether it's safe to fuck me without a condom.

We're both highly responsible adults, despite what the rings on our fingers might say, yet we haven't had a discussion about children or sexually transmitted infections.

"If you're fine with it, I'm fine with it."

My meaning is clear, too.

No further words are exchanged as he slides into me, and my eyes roll back as I grip onto his shoulders.

Holy. Shit.

Spencer Nash's cock is pure gold as it moves inside me with nothing between us.

"Open your eyes," he says, and even though it's a command, somehow it comes out tender and sweet.

I do, and all I see is him as our souls connect.

I've never had sex without a condom.

I've never been this head over heels in love with someone when I was having sex, either.

I've never felt *anything* like this before.

And as he pumps into me, pleasure and love and adoration written in his eyes, I feel myself start to go to a new plane I've never visited before.

Sex with Spencer is always incredible. But sex with Spencer without a condom is something for the books.

Those hot and spicy books, anyway.

He shoves into me, and I wrap my arms around him as he drops his lips to mine. He kisses me softly, a heady contrast to the way his body slams into mine over and over.

He takes me to the brink, and then he slows it back down. He takes me one step closer before he slows it down again.

He's playing a game that neither of us wants to win because if we win, then this is over, and we have to wait until we can be like this again.

He starts to slow his thrusts, lingering deeply before pulling out again, and it's those slow, luxurious thrusts that have my pussy tightening over him.

I cry out his name, and he growls mine back at me. The sound of my name coming out of his mouth in a growl that pushes me straight over the edge into the abyss of pleasure below.

"I'm coming!" I shriek as the tight spring of my body hits its climax. I start to pulse over and over around him as I grip onto him, my nails digging into his flesh as wave after wave of pleasure rolls through me.

"You're going to make me come," he grunts. "Inside or no?"

"Give it all to me," I cry, my pussy still clenching around him. "Give me all your come."

"Fuck, Grace," he mutters, and then he pushes up harder into me and holds still a beat as he spills into me. The jets of hot come stream inside me, prolonging my orgasm in a hot and unexpected way as I watch the pleasure on his face.

He follows directions, giving it all to me, and when both our bodies start to come down from the epic high, we both sigh. He leans down to kiss me tenderly, and eventually he pulls out of me.

I feel his hot come as it drips out of me, and he reaches down to catch some of it, spreading it up and around my clit. My body is still coming down from the orgasm he caused from hitting the right spot inside me, but as he rubs the hot semen around my clit, I feel another one starting to form.

My legs clamp around his hips since they're still spread, and he's still hovering over me, but I can't help it. My body is reacting purely on instinct now as I come again, and I'm thrashing beneath him as I fight my way through the intense pleasure.

He only stops touching me when I start to giggle and twist my way out of his hold, a sure sign the orgasm has ended, and now my body is overly sensitive to the touch.

He settles in beside me and kisses my cheek before he tosses an arm over my stomach, snuggling into my neck. "Jesus, you're hot when you come."

"Right back at you," I say, feeling suddenly shy after the double orgasm.

That has never happened before. Not once in my entire life.

And I'm freaking dead after that. I'm exhausted. Physically, mentally, emotionally…just done.

In the back of my mind, I know I still need to eat dinner. I still have things to finish up at the office. I still have responsibilities. But I'm having such a hard time caring about any of that when I'm this…*satisfied.*

And it's all thanks to Spencer Sex God Nash.

When we're together, life feels pretty damn perfect.

But it's when we're apart that Amelia works overtime to ensure we're *not* okay.

She sends photos of me to Spencer, and she's careful to make it look incriminating when it's nothing of the sort—like the time I hugged Pete when he told me his uncle had died, or the time I was standing close to Anthony in the fields as we inspected some of the vines as small, green grapes started to emerge after the winter months. Or even when I was working with the construction crew as they built the shed.

All these instances were innocent, but she insinuated they were not.

How do I know this?

He sent me screenshots of her texts.

Did you know she was cheating on you with Pete?

Looks like your "wife" has feelings for our construction worker.

But Spencer knows me, and he trusts me. She can send all the photos she wants. She can even manipulate however she wants. We're not going to let it break us.

When the second week of June hits, I haven't seen him in two weeks—since our anniversary weekend. We already broke our *not-longer-than-a-week* promise.

He has mandatory minicamp, which means intense days with his entire team. It's also the height of our busy season as summer gets underway and the people traveling the lakes of Minnesota stop at our little vineyard to give Newlywed a try.

It doesn't hurt that a Marriott resort is under ten miles away, and a huge Embassy Suites was built a few miles away from us four years ago.

It's great for traffic here, but it also means I can't get away to go visit Spencer—not even when Heidi's here to help me out on the weekends.

And it doesn't help when Amelia is flaunting her marriage in my face.

"It's so nice having my husband around all the time. He knows this place so well."

"Spencer and I never went more than three days without seeing each other."

Three days? How is that even possible?

Oh, right—because Amelia used to live in the city where Spencer played.

And also…it's a lie. When it got toward the end, I know they went more than three days without seeing each other.

I tell myself that over and over on repeat, but it doesn't change the fact that she's playing on my insecurities, and it feels an awful lot like she's starting to win.

Chapter 46: Grace Nash

Don't Let Your Guard Down

Two and a Half Months After the Wedding

I cut the ribbon hanging across the front, and I draw in a deep breath as I officially open the doors to the barn.

"Welcome!" I say gleefully.

The carefully planned speech has been executed, and the night can officially begin.

It's only been a little over two months since the idea for this event came to me, and here we are.

My dream is to turn this into an annual event, and it's comforting to know that next time, I'll have an entire year to plan for it versus pulling it together in just a couple months. But regardless of the timeline, I couldn't be happier with how things have turned out.

As I glance around, it feels like this barn has totally been transformed from a space of storage and maintenance to a beautiful venue fitting for tonight's formal affair.

Spencer moves in beside me, his hand at my hip as his lips glide across my cheek. "What a passionate speech," he says, and he glances in front of us at the people who are making their way inside now. "Look at what you've done. I'm so damn proud of you."

I lean in for a quick kiss. "Thank you. For everything—your help, your support..." I trail off. I almost said *your love*.

I don't want them to be words we just casually toss about. I want them to hold meaning, and I want to say them to each other when the moment is right since we still haven't said them.

This feels like it could be one of those moments, but then my dad walks up and slings an arm around me from the other side.

"You did good, Gigi," he says.

I give him a hug next. "Thanks, Dad."

My mom is right behind him with a hug, too.

Guests start to mingle as the band quietly plays instrumental music in the background. The silent auction tables are open, waiters walk around with trays of appetizers, and the buffet table with additional snacks and desserts is set up and ready for guests.

I can't believe all the auction items we received, and between the hotels nearby offering a weekend package and the goodies Spencer procured for us, we'll be able to cut a sizeable check to the American Heart Association.

I walk by the auction tables that are filled with guests waiting to check out the goods, and I see that one of the items I expected to get the highest bid already has a thousand dollars on it: two tickets to Spencer's suite at a San Diego Storm game. Little does whoever wins it know that they might be sitting in the same suite as MFB.

I'm too nervous to eat, so I pass up most of the food. The bar, however, is open for business, and it's serving exclusively our wines. I grab my favorite, the malbec, and Spencer gets one for himself as well.

We make a loop of the barn as we check out our guests having an amazing evening. Aside from the silent auction and the food tables, we also have raffle baskets, a photo booth encouraging guests to share their photos on social media, and, of course, a tasting area showcasing Newlywed wines. Some guests are dancing on the special dance floor we had installed for the event space, and others are sitting at the tables as they network, chat, or laugh with other guests—including the entire Nash clan who made it out for this event.

When I first spotted them outside before we opened the doors, I have to admit, I started to tear up. Spencer didn't tell me they were coming. He squeezed my hand and helped me hold it together during my speech as we introduced the grand opening of our new event space, but having Missy Nash out in the crowd cheering me on gave me a special warmth in my chest. And seeing Ava clapping for me after I wore her dress made me feel like I'm really a part of the family now, and the mistakes of the past are firmly left behind us.

"I made sure the drunken shrimp doesn't have any mustard in the sauce if you'd like some," I tell him, and he laughs.

"Maybe after I dance with my wife." He raises his brows suggestively.

"Only if you promise we can dance naked later," I murmur.

"You've got yourself a deal."

I giggle, and we set our glasses down as we step out onto the dance floor. He holds me close as we sway to the live music, and a sense of peaceful happiness engulfs me.

This is it. The planning is over, the night is half-over, and everything has gone off without a hitch.

And it's always in those peaceful moments where we let our guard down that something goes wrong.

"Do you want to get something to eat?" Spencer asks after we've been dancing for a while.

"Yes, let's get something." We head over toward the buffet table, and I fill a plate with all the goodies I handpicked to have at this event. I want to try one of everything, so I really load up my plate.

We find a table, and I set my plate down then excuse myself to the restroom. I'm gone far longer than I planned to be since I'm stopped periodically by guests telling me what an amazing event this is, and when I return, a fresh glass of wine awaits beside my plate.

"You're the best," I say, leaning in toward Spencer for a kiss.

He gives me the kind of smile that tells me he's feeling the same sort of way I'm feeling.

And that's pretty damn exciting.

I take a bite of mini quiche, and it's so good that I pop the rest of it in my mouth. I hadn't realized how starving I actually was until I ate the first bite of food. I eat a puff pastry next, and then some cheese, and then another quiche, and then...

"Oh shit," I mutter as I start to scratch my arm.

Spencer looks alarmed as he glances down at his quiche. "I just ate one, and I'm fine," he says.

I scratch my arm a little more, and as I lean in to inspect his plate versus mine, I see it.

Yellow powder that looks like it was sprinkled on my food. She was quick, but not very neat about it. I never once thought to actually inspect my plate before eating.

I glance across the room, and my eyes meet Amelia's. She's watching us intently...as if she's waiting for my reaction.

She must've done it when Spencer went to get us fresh drinks.

I look at Spencer, who isn't having a reaction at all. "I think Amelia might've put ground mustard on my food."

"Shit. The powder is stronger than actual mustard." His eyes widen as he studies me. "Your face looks like it's starting to swell."

If my face is swelling, it's a severe reaction. It also means I don't have time to wait for Benadryl to kick in. "I don't have an EpiPen with me."

"I can drive you over to the bungalow. I'm right out front."

I nod, and we bolt out of the room. He races through the parking lot and down the street, and we're back at my place thirty seconds later. I rush inside and grab my EpiPen from the cabinet, and I stab it into my leg.

Spencer stays right beside me, and if anyone can understand what I'm going through, it's him.

I take some Benadryl, too, just to ensure I won't have any further symptoms, further ensuring my night is as good as over.

Between the stress of the event and now this allergic reaction, I feel physically exhausted.

And then, to make matters even worse, I start to cry.

I'm going to miss the end of my event, and all because of my stupid sister.

I fucking hate her.

"I can't go back," I cry to Spencer. "But you can. Will you make sure Nana knows what happened?"

He nods resolutely, but he won't leave my side until I convince him that he can't let her win.

And then I'm left alone in my bungalow while my event continues on…without me.

Chapter 47: Spencer Nash

Watch Me

Two and a Half Months After the Wedding

Grace is adamant that she's fine. She asks me to get back over to the event to make sure Amelia isn't finding more ways to ruin it.

Who the hell does Amelia think she is? She essentially poisoned Grace, and knowing her, she will show exactly zero remorse for it.

And when I walk back into the barn, my fears are confirmed.

She's up on the stage, microphone in hand, in the middle of the speech Grace had planned to give toward the end of the evening.

Her eyes find me when I walk in, but she doesn't flinch.

"So once again, thank you for supporting my vineyard and the amazing cause we chose for tonight's event. Thank you for showing your support to the entire Newlywed team. We look forward to hosting you here again, and those auction items are only open another half hour, so be sure to head over with a generous spirit and grab that item you've been hoping for all night! Thank you!"

My vineyard? *We* chose?

She didn't have anything to do with the planning for tonight's event, and she's clearly taking credit. And that's when I spot the camera toward the front of the stage. It's the media here to report on tonight's charity event, and it'll show Amelia taking credit for Grace's hard work.

It's evidently why she figured out a way to get rid of her sister.

She exits the stage before I get the chance to publicly call her out on her behavior—not that I would, especially not in front of the media. I'm not like her, and I wouldn't ruin this event or my reputation, even at the expense of making her pay.

"Where's Grace?" a voice beside me asks, and I glance over to find her mom, Hillary. I don't know her as well as I know Steve since she doesn't spend as much time around here, but I'm sure she'd want to know what just happened.

"She had an allergic reaction, and I took her back to her bungalow. She's okay and resting now," I say.

"Oh, goodness. I'll head over and check on her."

I nod politely, and I weave through the crowd toward Maggie.

Before I get to her, though, Amelia stops me. "Where do you think you're going?" She folds her arms snidely across her chest.

"None of your business," I hiss at her. "I know what you did."

"Oh, like you'll make a scene here? Fat chance, good boy." She rolls her eyes, and then she smiles and waves to someone across the room. "Excuse me," she says.

I grab onto her bicep just hard enough to stop her without making the scene she said I wouldn't make, because she's right. She knows me decently well, and she knows I'd never ruin an event. She knows I would never draw attention to myself unintentionally.

"You're not going to get away with this," I mutter.

"Watch me," she hisses back. She yanks her arm from my grasp and walks away, and I feel like I should know what I'm up against with her, but I don't.

I don't know if I ever really knew anything about her at all.

I spot Steve across the room, and I beeline in that direction.

I'm stopped by Lincoln, who's ready to call it a night since he and Jolene brought both his stepson and their daughter tonight. Grayson and Ava are next, and then my mom. Asher and my dad seem intent on hanging around a while longer—probably because Asher bid on several auction items and wants to see if he won, though my dad wouldn't have bid on anything unless someone else was funding it for him, the cheap bastard.

Steve is no longer in the direction I was headed, but I do spot Maggie, so I head toward her.

"Last call for auction items! The auction ends in sixty seconds!" Amelia says over the microphone, and Maggie starts heading toward the auction table to help shut things down. I follow her over there, and when she spots me, she asks, "Where's Gracie?"

I lean in toward her and lower my voice so only she can hear me. "She had an allergic reaction and had to go home. She's okay now, but you should know that—" I say the words, but the roar of the crowd drowns out my voice.

"Time's up! Drop your pens! Nana, would you collect the clipboards and bring them over so I can announce the winners?" Amelia says into the microphone.

I help her gather up the clipboards, and as we carry them together toward the stage, she looks over at me. "What were you saying?"

All eyes are on us, so I hold it in.

For now.

Amelia reads off each item and the winner, and we're stuck on stage behind her, so I'm not able to tell Maggie what happened.

The raffle winners are chosen, too, and once the announcements are over, people start to leave in earnest.

All in all, it was a successful night for the vineyard...and for Amelia. Five hundred tickets were sold to this event, and it was incredibly well attended. I can't wait to see what the total raised tonight was.

But come morning, Grace will only feel like she lost.

And that's why I have to make sure Maggie knows what Amelia did.

Once the guests have all exited the barn, a cleaning crew ascends. I grab the items I'm certain Grace will want to keep, and that's when I spot Maggie talking to the head of the cleaning crew. Amelia, however, is nowhere to be found, and honestly, it wouldn't shock me if she ducked out early so she didn't have to help clean.

I wait until Maggie is done, and then I walk over to her. I get the words out before I can stop them. "I'm pretty sure Amelia sprinkled ground mustard on Grace's food tonight."

Her eyes widen, and she sits in the chair closest to her—one of the few that hasn't been taken down by the cleaning crew yet. "What?" she breathes.

I nod, and I kneel down beside her as I take her hand in mine. "I thought it was important for you to know. Didn't you see how Amelia stepped in and claimed all the credit for this thing that Gracie poured her heart into? That's how it always is with the two of them, Maggie. Gracie works her tail off for this place, and Amelia gets to shine as if she had anything to do with it. Maybe the concept of marriage isn't the thing that should determine who gets this place as much as work ethic and actual love for the vineyard." I press my lips together, hoping she can see the sincerity behind my words.

She clasps the top of my hand with her other hand. "Thank you, sweet Spencer. I hope you trust that even though I'm an old woman, I know what I'm doing."

My heart falls a little at the thought that maybe she doesn't think I know that. "You're not that old, Maggie. And of course, I know you do. I love you and this vineyard, and I hope you know that."

She pats my hand. "I do know that. Thank you."

"Where'd Gracie run off to?" Steve asks, sauntering up behind us. "Too much to drink or what? I thought she could hold her liquor better than that."

I lift to a stand as he moves in beside me. "Someone dusted mustard powder on her food, and she had a terrible reaction. She's okay, but she had to leave early to get her EpiPen. Hillary is with her now." I'm not sure why I don't tell him who did it. I'm guessing he can put that together on his own.

276

"Oh no. I'll go check on her," he says.

"I'll just help wrap things up here, and then I'll be over, too," I say.

He reaches over to shake my hand. "Thanks, Spencer. For all your work to make tonight a success."

"I was happy to help, but the credit goes to Grace," I say, and it's true. I'm glad this event was a success. I'm glad she took the idea to put landscape lights around the top of the barn on the inside, giving a glowing effect around the entire place. I'm glad we brainstormed ways to transform this place and ideas for the event.

I love being a part of this place.

I love being married to Grace.

I love the possibility that someday when I'm done playing, this will be my future.

But there's one thing I don't love, and I'm reminded what that is as I walk out the back doors of the barn for a quick, quiet moment on the back patio. I'm quietly wandering around the barn when I hear a voice. It's a whisper, but it's still loud all the same, and in the quiet of night, over the clanging of dishes just inside the barn, I can hear the entire conversation.

"She thinks it was *you*, not me."

I'm not sure whose voice that is, but I hear the response that's definitely Amelia. "Well, it *was* my idea. But I was smarter than to be the one who executed it."

A couple of snickers, and I can't help but wonder who Amelia's talking to.

It's a male voice, I think, though it's hard to tell since it's a whisper. Drew, maybe?

"Does Drew know?" the first voice asks.

"No," Amelia says.

"Does he know about us?"

"No," Amelia says again, this time with a giggle.

And then I hear…kissing? Smacking of lips, maybe. Possibly a moan.

Or maybe I'm dreaming all this up.

I don't move a muscle until I hear the crunching of gravel moving the other way.

I duck back inside the barn, and I run toward the front of it. The doors are wide open, and that's when I see Pete, the chef from the restaurant, walk around the side of the barn.

Jesus.

So Amelia is fucking around with Pete behind Drew's back?

And *Pete* is running around poisoning people on her behalf?

I thought Pete was a stand-up kind of dude. I'm honestly a little shocked right now that he turned on Grace. I can't help but wonder what Amelia promised him—apart from sexual favors, obviously.

What's next?

Earlier, she said, *watch me.*

Oh, I'll be watching, all right. I'm not going to take any action just yet until I gather enough evidence to make my case.

But I'll *definitely* be watching her, and I'll be doing whatever it takes with this information when the time is right.

Chapter 48: Grace Nash

Sometimes Good Girls Do Bad Things

Two and a Half Months After the Wedding

I'm feeling much better after last night's fiasco, though Spencer leaves this afternoon and I've been in bed all morning.

Lucky for me, he caters to my every need.

He makes me chicken noodle soup—mustard-free, guaranteed. He calls my doctor to let her know what happened, refills my EpiPen prescription, and runs into town to pick it up along with some groceries and goodies—including ice cream. He makes sure my dad sits with me when he has to leave, so I'm never home alone.

He's sweet and attentive, and he lays with me in bed while we watch comedies and laugh together.

But I feel the divide encroaching on us. I feel it coming.

Once he heads back tonight, I'm not sure when I'll see him again. Training camp will start, and since he's with a new team, that means an intense, rigorous month where he proves his place on the team. And once that ends, the regular season begins. He'll have Tuesdays off, but that's it—and he's not going to want to fly to Minnesota for twenty-four hours only to turn around and rinse, repeat another week of practice and another game.

I could go see him, and I definitely want to watch him play from his private suite, but weekends are our busiest time here. I'm going to try to get to as many games as I can, but it's hard to fight for my place at the vineyard when I'm not here to do it.

I'm scared of what the season will look like for us, but it's a large part of what I got into when I asked him to marry me.

I still can't believe he did.

"I don't want to leave," he admits.

"Then don't." I shrug.

He chuckles as he stops what he's doing to come over and press a soft kiss to my mouth. "I have to. I have an event tonight in San Diego with Clay."

I wrap my arms around his neck and pull him down for a few beats, and I kiss him again. "I'll miss you."

"I'll miss you, too."

I begrudgingly say my goodbyes, and I try not to be dramatic. I hold in my tears so he doesn't have to see them since he needs to leave.

But once his car pulls away, I let myself have a little breakdown.

And then I shower, pull myself together, and head toward my office to get some work done.

Two weeks later, I've done my best to avoid Amelia. Spencer and I text as much as we can, and we make sure to talk at least once a day. His first week of training camp for rookies and new players just ended, and it was intense as he had workouts and meetings and time to study the playbook.

The rest of the team will be joining the rookies on Monday, and he's looking forward to practicing with the other wide receivers. So far, he seems to like the coaching staff and his new place on the team, but I can hear the fatigue in his voice each night when we're able to touch base.

Next weekend is the Sips and Swirls event, and I've been trying to find the right time to execute my revenge plan. I think of something that would be an annoying nuisance but would only affect her.

She keeps complaining that it's time to get a new phone. What if I steal the SIM card out of her phone so she's without communication? Most phones are eSIM now, but her model still came with a physical SIM card—something I discovered when my own card was having issues, and I had to go to the store so they could activate eSIM for me. She probably doesn't even know her phone has one since I didn't.

I've been carefully watching Amelia's schedule, and she heads to the bathroom at almost ten in the morning every day. The problem is that she usually takes her phone, though every once in a while, she leaves it on her desk. She also heads to the restaurant at twelve-fifteen each day to grab lunch—and again, she usually brings her phone. But she's usually gone at least thirty minutes when she gets lunch, probably because she stops by the tasting room to put in an appearance with Nana and fake her way through knowledge about this place when she doesn't really know a thing.

I check every day leading up to the event, and so far, she's been meticulous about bringing it with her.

I think about giving up, but then I see additional appointments moved around on my calendar. The reason I know is that I started keeping a backup on my phone, and that's the one I rely on now. I'm certain it's Amelia at work, but once again, she works in an underhanded enough way that she knows how not to get caught.

It happens the day before the Sips and Swirls event. She takes her phone with her to the bathroom, but when she leaves to go to lunch, I see the back pocket she usually slips her phone into is empty.

I log into the software with the cameras so I don't get caught, disable the ones in this building, and rush into her office with a paperclip. I pull off her case, push the paperclip into the tiny hole to eject the tiny SIM card, and voila. It pops open. I grab the card, push the tray back into place, put the case back on, and rush back to my office. I reactivate the cameras, drop the SIM card into my desk drawer, and get back to work.

Or…I *try* to get back to work. My heart is pounding, and guilt washes over me.

The whole thing took less than sixty seconds.

I remind myself that she poisoned me. She has this act of revenge coming.

I still feel guilty. I hate that my responsibility is pulsing at me. I hate that I can't execute a silly prank without feeling bad about it. This isn't putting someone's life in jeopardy, and she sure as hell didn't feel guilty about that.

The entire thirty-two minutes she's gone today, I wait anxiously for her to return. I think about putting it back. I think about what Spencer will say when I tell him what I did. I think about what my parents would think about me sneaking into her office to do this. I think about what Nana would think about it.

The thought strikes me that I shouldn't mess with karma. I should let it do its thing. She'll get hers in the end. I shouldn't stoop to her level.

I grab the card out of my desk drawer, and I push to a stand to return it. This whole thing is dumb. It's a stupid plan that isn't going to teach her a damn thing anyway.

And just as I take the first step to exit my office, I hear her footsteps approaching.

I back up and plop back into my chair. I drop the SIM card back into my desk drawer and wait for the fireworks.

They come three seconds after she sits at her desk. "What the fuck?" she mutters loudly enough for me to hear from my own office. And then a loud, frustrated, "Ugh!"

She taps loudly at her keyboard as she likely looks up *why is my phone in SOS mode*, and then she grunts out more frustrated noises as she whines, "Why today of all days?"

She won't dare ask for my help, but I know she'll need it. She can't leave the vineyard right now since she has the crew setting up for tomorrow's event, which is taking place in our west parking lot. And by the time they're done, she'll still have to make the hourlong trip to Minneapolis where the phone store is located, and they'll likely be closed by that point.

The guilt is still there, but this silly little act of revenge actually sort of feels good. It's giving me a bit of a high that I can be a bad girl, too.

She appears in my office doorway. "Something's wrong with my phone."

I choose the path of not arguing with her and get to the point. "What do you want from me?"

"Ugh! Never mind." She bolts from my office doorway.

I give it some time. I finish the email I'm sending before I head down to the tasting room, staying in line with my normal routine. Delilah is in there, but Nana is missing.

"Where's Nana?" I ask her when she has a break for a moment.

"She's out with the crew for Amelia's event tomorrow."

I hate for Nana to have extra work, of course—but I don't so much hate that it's to save Amelia's ass, and now I get the opportunity to swoop in and look like the hero.

Sort of like *she* did at *my* event.

I head outside and see Nana talking to Eli, one of our maintenance workers, and I walk up to the two of them. "What can I do to help?"

Nana looks gratefully over at me. "Do you have this covered? I need to go sit a while."

"Of course," I say with a nod. I squeeze her around her shoulders. "Go sit."

"You're a lifesaver," she says, and she heads back into the tasting room. She's a firecracker, but she's not a spring chicken anymore in her mid-eighties.

Guilt racks me as she ambles away. Maybe I'm more of a good girl than I ever realized because I'm not cut out for being a bad girl.

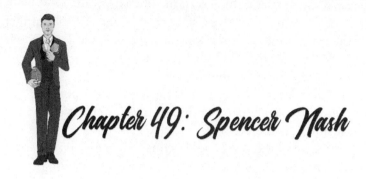

Chapter 49: Spencer Nash

Feeling the Crack

Four Months After the Wedding

"You *what?*" I ask.

It's the Friday night of my first full week at training camp with all of my teammates, some of whom *won't* make the fifty-three-man roster, and I'm exhausted. It's possible I'm mishearing things.

"I stole the SIM card out of her phone, and she had to go into town. Nana needed help, and I was there." She says the words again, and nope…I heard right the first time.

I draw in a deep breath. This isn't my problem to figure out, yet I'm so tangled in it that it feels like it is. "Grace, this isn't you. Revenge? Stooping to her level?"

She's quiet on the other side of the line, and I can't help the thought that the manipulations and lies were what spelled the end for Amelia and me in the first place.

"What were you thinking?" I ask, filling the silence between us.

"I was thinking I'm tired of getting played by Amelia. I was thinking I'm tired of losing to her. First you, next the vineyard."

"You didn't lose me to her," I point out. "I married *you,* didn't I?"

"Yeah, because we were drunk and high on allergy medicine!" she protests. "Not because you're in love with me and asked me to spend the rest of my life with you!"

She has a point...but I've also been thinking a lot about that over the last couple of weeks we've been apart, and I *am* in love with her. I *do* want to spend my life with her.

I just haven't told her that yet.

And now that she's stooping to the level of the person I broke up with in large part because of the way she lived her life, I'm not sure I *can* tell her that.

She'll be here next weekend. It's our first game, a preseason game where I'll only play a few snaps, and it'll be my first chance to pick my wife out of the crowd.

I blow out a breath. "What if I'm getting there?" I finally ask.

"Huh? Getting where?"

"To the point where I want to spend my life with you."

"Oh," she murmurs. "I, uh..."

"But I have to be honest with you, Grace," I add, too tired to sugarcoat it. "I don't want to be with someone who's like Amelia. I ended things with her for a reason, and this is something she would do."

"She intentionally hurts people, Spencer," she says quietly. "This was just a silly prank."

"That's how it starts. What's next? Look, I don't really want to get into this with you. I need to go take a shower and get ready for tomorrow, but just...take a step back and look at what you're doing. You'll get the vineyard on your merits, not because she had to go into town for a phone emergency. I gotta go."

"Okay. Goodnight." The two words sound so sad, but before I can backtrack and apologize, she ends the call.

I head to the shower with thoughts of her heavy in my mind, but I force myself to wash them away and focus instead on the strategy meeting with the wide receiver coaches today.

The playbook is vastly different from what I was used to in Minnesota. The Storm focuses much more on man-to-man offense versus zone. I was used to finding an open spot in my zone and running to it to make a play, but now I have to memorize all these plays on top of different strategies for breaking away from the defender covering me to execute the play. Neither is easier or more difficult—it's just a lot of change all at once to contend with on top of the typical physical aspects of training camp.

Coaches are constantly watching players to see where their strengths lie and how they'll best serve the team in the upcoming season, so players are forced to leave it all out on the field. We push ourselves to our very limits, and I'm feeling every second of that tonight.

I text Grace in the morning before I head to the practice facility where our training camp is taking place.

Me: *Sorry if I was cranky last night. Camp is intense. I hope you have a great day today.*

Her response comes just after I park my car.

Grace: *You were right. I don't want to stoop to her level, and I needed your honesty. You have a great day too.*

I can't help but smile down at my phone as I appreciate the open communication we have. It's what a marriage *should* have, and it's another sign that I'm with the right person.

But the signs against us are adding up…starting with the second I get out of my car.

There are only three of them, but it feels like a hundred as they hammer me with questions on the walk from my car to the front door with their cameras in my face, recording my every move.

"Spencer, is it true you and your wife were drunk in Vegas when you got married?"

"Mr. Nash, who is the blonde in the photos all over social media this morning?"

"Spencer, tell us how camp is going and how all these women play into your time off the field."

I debate what to do. I have two options: ignore them or answer them. Neither feels like the thing I *want* to do, which is rearranging all three of their faces, but violence has never been my default.

I turn to look at them as I set my hand on the handle to open the door. "I have no comments at this time." I open the door and head inside, knowing full well they won't follow me in.

It feels like a bit of a relief to have them off my back as my day gets started, but the jokes start up in the locker room as soon as I walk in with Jensen Bybee, a defensive end, trailing in right behind me.

"The paparazzi is out in full force this morning for Mr. Spencer Nash, everybody," Jensen announces when he walks in.

I lift a shoulder. "Just one of the many perks of being part of the Nash family."

"They sure as fuck weren't here for me," Jensen says. "But hey, can you hook me up with some of that blonde pussy you're getting?"

"I'm married," I say flatly.

"So?" Jensen asks.

And that's sort of the problem here. We're in a locker room, and men talk. Very few players I know were raised with the values I was. I was raised to respect women, and I'd never step out on someone I'm in a relationship with.

I guess I'd just marry her sister. Is that really any better?

What the fuck have these Newman sisters done to me?

Six days later, I'm pulling into the pickup area at the airport, and Grace stands with a suitcase, watching for my car. She smiles when I pull up right next to her, and I hop out of the driver's seat to help her with her suitcase.

But first...

I pull her into my arms and press my lips to hers.

"What was that pact about never more than a week apart?" I ask softly.

She chuckles. "We really need to be better about that."

"Agree." I grab her suitcase and toss it into my trunk as she slides into the passenger seat, and when I join her as I slip into the driver's seat, she reaches over and grabs my hand.

"I'm so excited to watch you play."

"I'm so excited to have you here," I admit. "But you've seen me play before."

"Yeah, but before when I saw you play, you weren't my husband."

"Fair point." I merge into traffic as we head toward my place.

The paparazzi are out again, firing questions at us. We continue to ignore them, but I can't pretend like it's easy.

I can't pretend like I don't feel the way it's creating more cracks between us. I can't pretend like I don't see her flinch every damn time. She hates it, but it's going to be a reality of life with me.

Maybe it wouldn't be if Amelia weren't somehow tracking our every move and tipping these assholes off. It *has* to be her doing it.

But it doesn't really matter why it's happening. The fact of the matter is that this is what my life looks like right now, and it's the ugly side of reality.

It's the side I wish I could hide from her to make her want to hang onto this thing with me, but I'm not sure it's what she really does want after all.

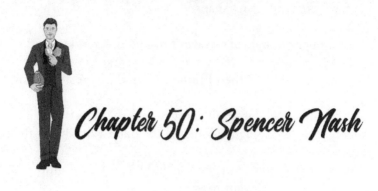

Chapter 50: Spencer Nash

There's My Wife

Four Months After the Wedding

The sex on Friday night was slow and steady—and amazing. We had light practice yesterday ahead of today's game, so I was able to give her a little more action last night, and hopefully tonight after a win, I'll be ready to celebrate.

Preseason games don't *really* matter, but we're competitors at heart. I don't want to fuck up my debut on a new team, so I'm laser-focused on playing today. And Grace seemed to understand that.

I gave her the rundown of when to take the Uber from my place and where to go once she gets to the stadium. She said she's too nervous to watch from my private suite, potentially with members of her favorite band, so she bought her own ticket to the game.

She gave me her section and row number, and I can't wait to look for her in the stands.

In fact, as soon as I get out onto the field for warm-ups, I take a lap around the field and look for the section Grace is sitting in.

And I spot her immediately.

She's wearing a black jersey with a silver number seventeen on it.

It feels like something snaps inside me.

That's my wife.

The thought immediately races through my mind when I spot her. She's grinning and waving wildly, and I raise a hand to wave back to her. And then I bring my hand to a rest over my heart.

It's my silent way of sending love up to the stands, and it suddenly feels like tonight should be the night I finally say the words.

Except...she leaves tonight. She has to get back to the vineyard, and I don't want her to go.

I want her to stay here with me.

I force my focus back to the game, something I'm admittedly pretty good at doing. I focus on each stretch as I warm up, and before I know it, the game is starting.

I play for almost the entire first quarter, and the defender covering me isn't letting up. I try out all my new moves to get away from him, but it's tight coverage. I'm able to break away for one good catch toward the end of the quarter, and Coach pulls me out when the second quarter begins.

The good news is it means he wants to keep me healthy to start me during the season. The bad news is it also means I don't get to play for the rest of the game.

Grace is waiting for me in the family area outside our locker room after my first victory with my new team. I'm freshly showered and ready to take her back to my place for a couple hours before she catches the last flight out tonight, and the moment I spot her, my heart warms in my chest.

She's smiling as I stride across the room toward her. "I'm so proud of you. You were amazing!" she says, and I drop my lips to hers.

"I love you," I say.

She gasps as she pulls back and looks into my eyes. She searches them for a beat, and when she seems to find what she's looking for, she says, "I love you, too. This whole thing...I don't think it was ever fake for me, Spencer."

Hearing those words out of her mouth does something to me. She's not *just* my wife in name only anymore.

Those words signify that she's mine.

And I plan to take care of what's mine…starting with giving her the kind of pleasure she's never felt before the second I get her home.

We walk hand-in-hand out to my car, and there aren't any paparazzi down in the player parking lot because they aren't allowed down here. There aren't any in my parking garage at the apartment complex, either, and we take the elevator up to my penthouse without anyone shoving any cameras in our faces or asking misleading questions to plant doubt in the other's mind.

The second the front door shuts behind me, I lock it, and then I'm on her. My mouth slams down to hers, and she reacts with a surprised gasp as the urgency I feel wraps around her, too. I shove my hips against hers, and as I kiss her, I walk her backwards toward the guest room.

I'd take her to my room, but I have a king-size bed in there, and my plan requires the smaller queen with the four posts in the corners. I brought my supplies over a few nights ago as I anticipated what I wanted to do with her in all the rooms of my apartment this weekend, and since I didn't have a hard practice today and didn't play much of the game, my body is recovered enough to have the kind of sex I've been craving with her.

The slow and steady kind is fantastic…but I want something that's going to blow us both away.

And tonight is the night for that.

I back her into the room, and only then do I pull back. "Strip," I demand.

She looks caught off guard. "What?"

"You heard me." There's a sitting chair in the corner of the room, and I walk over to it. I sit, hit play on my *music and chill* playlist, which is obviously code for sex music, and set my phone on the side table as the perfect Doja Cat song fills the room.

She looks like she has absolutely no idea what to do, and my lips turn up in a bit of a smile as I wait for her.

"Take off your clothes," I say gently, rather than the single-word demand of a moment ago. Maybe nobody has ever worshiped her body the way I'm about to, which is a damn shame. She deserves the fucking world, and I'm going to be the man who does everything he can to make sure she gets it.

And, if nothing else, she'll have the kind of orgasm that will live rent-free in her mind for the rest of time.

She kicks off her shoes and rolls her socks off, and then she takes a tentative step toward me. "I, um...I don't really know—"

I hold up a hand since she's fumbling here. "Don't be shy with me, Grace. It's just you and me, okay? You're my wife, and I want to watch my wife take off her clothes for me."

"Can I have a shot of something first?" she asks.

I chuckle. "Of course." I get up, shift my rock-hard cock, and head toward the kitchen for a bottle of tequila. Memories of the night we got married wash over me since that was probably the last time I drank tequila.

I bring the bottle back and hand it over, and she unscrews the cap and takes a swig before handing it to me. I take a swig, too, and I set the bottle and the cap on the table beside me.

She nods a little, snagging her bottom lip between her teeth. She really has no idea how goddamn sexy she is.

She's timid as she unbuttons her jeans and starts to push them down her legs.

"Yes, baby," I murmur my approval. "Just like that."

My words seem to give her a tiny confidence boost. She starts moving in time to the music without realizing it, and she gently sways as she reaches for the bottom of the jersey bearing my last name and the number I've worn for over two decades.

I almost want her to leave the jersey on. I want to fuck her in it. But I'll save that for another time. Tonight, it's all about *her* pleasure—even if she doesn't feel that way right now since she started out intimidated to do this little striptease for me. She seems less timid, though—maybe from the shot of tequila, which is starting to do its work, or maybe from my words of encouragement.

She pulls the jersey off and tosses it on the floor beside her.

"Fuck yes," I murmur. "Look at that gorgeous body."

She walks toward me and grabs the bottle for a second shot, and then she does a little twirl in front of me in her bra and panties after she slams the bottle back on the side table.

My dick is painfully hard as I force myself to maintain some semblance of control. I grip the arms of the chair, my knuckles turning white as I watch her dance in front of me. She straddles one of my legs, and I feel the heat of her pussy through her panties as she rubs it on my leg.

She reaches up with her hands and palms the sides of her tits, pushing them together for me to make a line of cleavage that I want to dip my face into.

God, I love her. I fucking love everything about her, from her quiet demeanor to her intelligent mind to her kind heart to her beautiful face to the perfect body that she's currently using to turn me all the way on.

She pulls back off me and sways to the beat of Doja Cat as she hooks a finger into the side of her panties. She's teasing me now, pretending she's going to pull them off, and I love the change in her confidence. I want her to be able to do this without the tequila, but since we have it here, it gives me another idea anyway.

She moves her finger from her panties and instead teases me with her bra as she lowers one of the straps. She doesn't take it off, instead sliding her palms up to cup her tits on the sides again, and then she slowly trails her hands down to her hips.

Fuck.

I can't take it anymore. I need to be inside her, but I have plans. I don't know how much longer I can last. She's driving me absolutely to the brink of need.

I dart up from my chair and reach around her with one hand, easily unclasping her bra. I slide it down her other arm until her tits are exposed to me, and rather than throwing it on the floor, I leave it there so she's slightly bound by it. I run my palms up her back as I pull her closer to me, and she lets out a small gasp when she feels my cock brush against her leg.

Fuck, I need relief. I move my hips against her leg, dying for some friction, but it's not enough.

I look down at her, and she's looking up at me, and Jesus, that look in her eyes is enough to fucking kill a man. Her eyes are full of need, desire…*love*, and I feel it too. All of it. It's heated and sensual as we prepare to share something new together for the first time—sex after the words that seal in a commitment to one another.

I let go of her only to grab her into my arms and toss her roughly on the bed. She squeaks out a moan, and I use her bra that's already around one of her arms and twist it to securely tie it around one of the bedposts. I make quick work with a silk tie, tying her other wrist to the other bedpost before she even knows what I'm doing. Her arms are spread out for me, and I work on her legs next.

"What are you doing?" she asks quietly.

"Tying you up so I can fuck you until you can't see straight," I say as I get her second leg tied to the bottom bedpost. "Is that okay with you?"

"Oh, God, yes," she moans, closing her eyes as I brush a thumb across one of her nipples. "But I want to touch you."

"Oh, you will," I say. "Later. First, we do you."

"Mm," is her only reply as I suck her nipple into my mouth.

I reach down toward her pussy spread out for me, sliding a finger into her without preamble. She cries out, shifting her arms up instinctively to try to wrap them around me, the ties preventing her from being able to move.

"Ugh!" she cries out in a bit of frustration, but it's a hot, needy sort of frustration, and I can tell she likes this already from how fucking wet that cunt is for me.

As painful as it is, I draw it out. I take my time with each of her tits, sucking on her nipples until they've formed tight peaks for me, and I slowly move my finger in and out of her, careful to avoid her clit since I know how sensitive she is right now and I don't want her to come yet.

Her hips start to sway, and her knees bend a bit, but she's too spread out and tied up to move into whatever position she's trying to get into. "God, Spencer, please," she whines.

"Please what?" I ask. My voice is raspy and filled with need.

"Fuck me. Please fuck me." Her voice is a breathless plea, and I don't know if I've ever heard anything hotter in my entire life.

"I will," I murmur.

I move my finger out of her, and I stand. She opens her eyes to watch me slide into her, but it's not my plan. Yet.

Instead, I walk over toward the side table by the chair and grab the bottle of tequila. I take another swig, and I walk over to her. I pour a shot into her mouth, and she swallows with a loud gulp.

I pour a trail of the liquid from her sternum all the way down to her pubic bone. I'm still fully clothed, so I slip quickly out of my clothes before I move over her backward, straddling her face as I push my cock between her lips. She moans as she sucks on me, and I lick my way down the tequila trail from her tits to her pussy. I carefully push my hips toward her mouth and pull back out. She can't move to fist me while she sucks on me, and her mouth is pure magic all by itself.

I'm not going to last long, and I'm not here for a blow job, anyway. I push in a few more times, fucking her mouth until I'm far too close to coming, and then I pull out. I'm not ready to end this pleasure just yet, and half the fun of it is the anticipation of release.

I flip back around until I'm centered between her legs, and I lick through her sweet pussy. She lets out a low moan followed by, "Yes, yes, yes."

I lick her clit before moving my tongue down to dip inside her, and her moans get louder and louder as she moves closer and closer to her orgasm. I replace my tongue with a finger as I move my mouth back up to focus on her clit, and she starts to cry out. "I'm going to come! Oh, God, Spencer! I'm coming!"

She screams, and I know she wants to dig her fingers into my hair and clamp her knees against my ears, but the ties prevent it. Her body reacts violently as she pulls against her restraints, but the ties do their job of holding her down—even the unconventional tie with her bra.

Her hips twist and shift as her body contracts over and over, and I hold on tight to ride out the wave with her, my tongue continuing to assault her sensitive clit. She starts to come down, and that's when I move quickly off her and slide my cock into her warm, waiting cunt.

I let out a low growl at how tight she feels after that first orgasm. Fuck, this isn't going to last long.

"Oh, God!" she screams, tossing her head back. "I'm not ready!"

"Open your eyes," I demand, stilling inside her. She seems to force them open to focus on me. "You feel so goddamn good, baby," I murmur. "You're ready. You can take it."

"Mm, yes," she says as I pull back, giving us both a little of the friction we need. "Give it to me."

I sway my hips slowly into her, letting her adjust after her first orgasm. "You have no idea how much I needed to be inside you. Fuck, that striptease, the way you look all tied up, the way you obey. The way you come. It's incredible. *You* are incredible."

"I love you, Spencer. I love you so much," she cries, and tears start to fall from her eyes.

I'm afraid I've hurt her, so I slow my movements.

"Fuck me!" she demands, practically screaming at me.

"God, I love you, too, Grace," I rasp, and then I start to hammer into her as the sacred words fill the air between us.

Her tits shake back and forth between us as she rolls her neck back. I drop my lips there, kissing her neck as I push in, thrust after glorious thrust.

Her moans start to ascend into louder, needier shrieks as she moves toward her second orgasm, and I feel my balls tighten as the need echoes through my veins.

"Yes, Spencer! Yes, right there!"

The words send me into my own release as the pleasure rockets through me. My cock pulses, each pulse sending another jet of come into her sweet pussy as it starts contracting over me, milking every pulse from my body.

I give her every last drop as she fights her way through the wave, and then together, we seem to float back down to Earth, both of us breathless as we try to regain our breath back here in reality.

I stay inside her for a few beats, and when I pull out, I make quick work of untying her. Her arms are immediately around my neck as she starts to cry in earnest, and guilt immediately rockets through me.

"What's wrong?" I ask softly as I cradle her against me.

She tries to draw in a shaky breath, but she can't seem to catch it to answer me. I just hold her to me, afraid I've done everything wrong tonight, afraid I stepped over some line or hurt her in some way.

"Are you okay?" I ask, my voice full of desperation.

"Yes," she pants through her tears. Eventually the tears subside, and she swallows hard as she's finally able to speak. "I'm sorry. That was…whoa. It was just emotional. I've never felt like that."

"So…it's good tears?"

She shrugs and sniffles. "I think so. It was just so much pleasure hitting me at once combined with so much love that I don't think my mind knew how to react."

I hold her tightly in my arms as that feeling like I never want to let her go washes over me.

I do have to let her go, though.

I have to take her to the airport in another hour, and I have to say goodbye. Again.

There's no way around it. With her life in Minnesota and mine here—for now, at least—we'll be apart for large chunks of time. It's just our reality.

And we could probably deal with it just fine if we didn't have someone actively working against us and trying to break us up.

But the more shots she takes at us, the more and more worried I become about the future of this marriage. The more and more worried I become that Amelia's going to win after all.

Especially with the shot that's waiting for me when I wake up in the morning.

Chapter 51: Grace Nash

I Hope It's Broken

Four Months After the Wedding

A sense of sadness pervades me as the plane touches down. It's a little after midnight, and I hate that we're apart again—especially after a weekend where we both said the words that have been building between us for months now.

It's after two in the morning by the time I get home, and I head straight to bed, knowing it'll be an early morning tomorrow after missing yet another weekend here at the vineyard.

I toss and turn all night. To be honest, I slept much better in Spencer's arms.

I glance out the front window a little after seven as I'm brewing my coffee when I see movement out front, and I spot Drew as he drives over toward the production facility to start his day there.

I head over to the office a little before eight since I'm up and ready…and exhausted. It's the kind of bone-tired exhaustion that even caffeine can't quite touch. I turn my computer on and run through my task list for the day.

I'm meeting with one of our distributors later this week who has big plans for getting our wines into some local restaurants, and if I can close this deal, it'll be a huge win for me. Nana once shared that she has visions of our wines being sold in grocery stores across the country, and this is a big stepping stone for turning that vision into a reality.

But as I look at my calendar for Wednesday's meeting, it's not there.

My heart sinks as I look a week ahead, thinking maybe I'm just off a week, but it's not there either.

I have a feeling I know exactly what happened, and I'm going to fucking kill her.

I storm into Amelia's office, but she isn't in yet—of course. Why would she be early for once in her life?

So I storm over to her bungalow and start banging on her front door.

It takes her a few beats before she answers the door, and when she does, she looks...disheveled. She's dressed for the day, but she looks like she's been working out or something, and she's acting a little strange, not opening her door to let me in.

There's no time to focus on that when I'm here on a mission. "What the hell did you do with my distributor meeting?"

"I have no idea what you're talking about. Maybe you need to keep better track of your own schedule." She folds her arms but keeps her foot on the back of the door to not let me see in.

"Did you delete it from my calendar to mess with me? I know when my meetings are, Amelia. This isn't going to work."

She rolls her eyes. "No, I didn't delete it to mess with you. I deleted it because it already took place."

Ice runs through my veins. "What did you just say?"

"We had the meeting on Friday. Shawna was all too happy to chat with me a few days earlier than expected." She smiles sweetly and moves to slam the door in my face, but I shove on it until it opens, and I push my way inside.

"Are you kidding me?"

"No. I would never joke about something as important to me as our family vineyard." She holds a hand over her heart as she fakes earnestness. "Now get the hell out of my house."

302

I rush toward her and push her, knocking her a little off-balance.

"What is wrong with you?" I yell at her. "Why do you hate me so much?"

"Are you kidding me? My entire life, you've been a splinter in my heel, and then you have the fucking *nerve* to marry the man I loved? The man who asked me to marry him first! There's no way in *hell* you're getting this place!" She's screaming at me now, so I scream back.

"You were cheating on him! You never loved him!"

"You don't know a goddamn thing about me, Grace!" she says, poking a finger into my chest. "You never bothered!"

Is she right?

No. I know for damn sure this whole feud between us started the second I slipped out of the womb.

I slap her hand out of the way, and I move toward her, anger filling me.

I had such a wonderful, peaceful weekend with the man I've fallen head over heels for, and *this* is what I have to return to.

I can't do it. I can't be at the same vineyard as this vile person who so badly wants me to fail.

And so I will do whatever it takes to take her out of the equation.

Not in a sinister sense. I'm not going to *kill* her or anything—at least not the way she tried to do to me with that mustard prank.

But I'm going to win this place if it's the last goddamn thing I do.

"I hate you," I hiss, and I rush toward her and push her with all my might.

She grabs hold of my hair, twisting it as my head yanks to the side. "Are you really going to stand here thinking you're stronger than me?" Her tone is full of scorn, and unfortunately, she's probably right. She's got four or five inches on me, and she's always been strong.

The pain from where she's pulling my hair nearly makes me fall, but I take a jab at her anyway, trying to punch her in the stomach from my angle but not hitting her nearly as hard as I mean to. "Maybe you're physically stronger, but I'd like to remind you that you tried to convince my husband to marry you for two years. It took me all of two seconds."

"You bitch!" she screams, and she lets go of my hair and slaps me across the face.

I reach up to touch the spot where it's stinging, a little shocked that she'd actually *slap* me. I glare at her as tears fill my eyes, and I take a menacing step toward her. She flinches for a beat, and I'm glad I can pulse even the tiniest bit of fear in her.

"You're going to regret that," I hiss.

She reaches her hand up to do it again, balking at my threat, and I grab her wrist and start to twist it as hard as I can.

"Ow! Fuck! Let go!" she screeches at me, trying to get out of my grasp, but I don't let go. I keep twisting. "Stop! Fuck! Stop!"

She's still screaming at me when I spot a movement out of the corner of my eye, followed by a man's voice.

"Stop!"

"Pete?" I ask, letting go of her wrist.

Her disheveled appearance. Her attempt to get rid of me.

It all comes together.

"Are you two…" I trail off as I look between the two of them. I shake my head as I try to puzzle this out in my own mind, but I'm coming up short because I can only focus on one thought that hits me like a ton of bricks.

Pete the chef.

The ground mustard.

Oh my God, the ground mustard. I thought Pete was my *friend*, but this is how she poisoned me. She slept with Pete and had him sprinkle it on my food.

She's cheating on Drew just like she cheated on Spencer, and she's going to end up with the vineyard because no matter what, she always wins. No matter the cost.

No matter the casualties.

She looks almost guilty as she cradles her twisted wrist in her other hand, and good. I hope I broke it.

I shake my head as I look between the two of them, and then I storm out of her bungalow, set to wreak havoc.

The only problem? She beats me to the punch.

Chapter 52: Spencer Nash

She Brings Out the Worst, but You Bring Out the Best

Four Months After the Wedding

The blood drains from my face and I feel lightheaded as I stare at the photograph.

It's the two of us at that Italian restaurant we ate dinner at after our wedding in Vegas. We're very obviously drunk, and it's the first time I've seen this particular photo.

I read the headline again just to be sure I read it right the first time, and yep…it hasn't changed.

San Diego Storm's Spencer Nash Exposed

The article doesn't just paint me as a liar. It paints me as someone easily manipulated. It's damaging to both my reputation and Grace's.

Normally I don't let shit like this bother me, but some of it errs too close to the truth, which is a little terrifying. And it's not just that.

Amelia is quoted in the article, which means this was her doing.

She's out to get her sister—and me, apparently.

I read it from the top again.

The Nash family was once known for their abilities on the field, but it's what's been happening off the field over the last few years that's garnering interest from fans everywhere. The latest scandal involves thirty-year-old brother, Spencer Nash. Previously known for his ability to run routes that would lead the Vikings into the red zone, Nash's latest venture is in wedded bliss.

Or is it?

Nash was quietly engaged to Amelia Newman of Newlywed Vineyard in Cedar Creek, Minnesota, but he recently tied the knot with her little sister, Grace Newman. He's been playing off the marriage as real when, in truth, it's as fake as it gets.

According to the elder Newman daughter, "Grace found out about a clause in my grandmother's will that gives the vineyard to whichever of her granddaughters is married for a year first. She flew to Vegas, got my ex drunk, proposed, and forced him to marry her. They're not in love, and I intend to prove that my sister doesn't deserve the land she's faking an entire marriage for."

Our investigative team is digging further into this developing story.

Fuck.

Fuck!

They're digging further, which means it won't be long before the photos from the chapel are all over the internet. People will make assumptions and speculations about our true intentions when it's none of their goddamn business.

We may have expressed our commitment with those three heavy words over the weekend, but I can't help but feel the hope drain out of me that love will be enough. How long can I put up with being married to someone whose sister's main goal in life is to tear us apart?

How many more shots can I take to my own reputation when this started as a lie anyway?

When I was on the same team for eight years, I couldn't have cared less what the media was saying about me or what my reputation was. I was respected in the locker room because I'd proven myself on the field, and my teammates knew that about me. They knew about my work ethic and my dedication. They knew *me*.

But my new teammates are still getting to know me, and this is the impression they'll have of me. The guy who was coerced into a drunken marriage. The guy who was proposed to by the woman who flew out to see him. The guy taken advantage of by a pair of sisters. Locker rooms have enough misogynistic chatter in them. I don't need articles like this fueling the flames.

I wonder if she's seen the article. I wonder how her day is going.

I wonder what mine will look like now that this is a part of it. I'm glad I have today off from the locker room, but I can't imagine going in there tomorrow will feel comfortable when the headline of the article brings up the fact that I'm on this team and the content of the article calls my very manhood into question.

I can't believe Amelia would stoop so low.

I text Grace.

Me: *Are you awake?*

She calls me in return.

"Hey," I answer.

"Hi."

We're both quiet, and I physically feel the distance spanning between us.

I wonder if I'd be able to handle this differently if she was here with me. I wonder if I'd be so fucking angry about it if we could talk it out.

But we can't.

"Did you see the article?" I ask, the emotion gone from my voice.

"Article? What article?"

I'll take that as a no. "There's a photo of us from the restaurant where we ate after we got married. The article quotes your sister and paints me to look like I let you walk all over me and forced me to marry you so you could get your vineyard."

"I'll fucking kill her," she hisses.

"Probably not the best option, but I'm not taking it off the table." I sigh.

"She moved up a meeting with an important distributor while I was out of town. I confronted her about an hour ago, and we got into a physical fight. She keeps doing this to me, changing things on my calendar and running important meetings, and I can't take it anymore."

"Jesus Christ, Grace," I mutter. "Are you okay?"

"Yeah. I'm fine. She's not, though. She left right after with Drew, presumably to get her wrist checked out since I twisted the hell out of it. Oh! And get this. Pete was there at her place."

"Pete?" I echo, the night of the charity event plowing back into me.

"Yeah. The guy who makes the best flatbread in all of Minnesota is apparently sleeping with my sister," she says dryly. "Oh, and this is fresh. I think he might be the one who poisoned me at Corks for a Cause."

"Do you have proof?"

"Proof he poisoned me?" she asks.

"Proof of any of it," I say, not sure whether I should mention the conversation I overheard. "That he's the one who sprinkled the mustard, that he's sleeping with your sister…"

"No. But you can bet I'll be on the lookout for some now."

"They'll be careful now that they know you know. Can we circle back to this physical altercation? Grace, this isn't you." My voice is calm, but my chest is anything but.

"She brings out the worst in me."

"Then get away from her." I'm not sure why my tone sounds like I'm begging, but I have the sudden fear that between this goddamn article and her fighting with Amelia, being apart right now is the *worst* thing for both of us.

"I can't leave the vineyard. It would be handing it over to her."

"Then maybe it's time to let it go." The words are out before I can stop them, but they're the first words that come to my logical mind. I blow out a long, frustrated breath as I wait for an answer, but she's silent on the other end.

To her, it must feel like I'm telling her to choose between me and her dream.

I can't do that to her. I love her, and maybe that means I'm going to have to let her go. It's too much all at once—the article, starting over in a new city, pure exhaustion, missing her, falling for her, wanting to be with her…and we can't.

Falling for her has been something out of this world. But maybe love just isn't enough.

A physical altercation? I can't picture my sweet Grace getting into a physical fight with Amelia, and yet…she just admitted that she did.

I finally break that silence. "I'm sorry. I shouldn't have said that. I just…I don't know how to deal with any of this."

"I don't either," she admits. "But for as much as she brings out the worst in me, *you* bring out the best."

It's my turn to be silent for a beat, and when the words come, they might be even worse than telling her to let go of her fight for the vineyard. "I'm not sure I can be that balancing act for you."

I hear Maggie calling her name in the background.

"I have to go." She hangs up before I can tell her I'm sorry, before I can tell her that maybe I can't be that balance, but I want to try anyway.

Before I can tell her I love her. Before I can tell her I want to fight for her.

Maybe it's for the best. I need to focus on football, anyway. My workouts. This season.

Fighting for my reputation.

And so I place my focus where it should be, and sure enough, those thoughts about what I should have said start to fade the moment the phone disconnects.

Chapter 53: Grace Nash

An Awful Lot to Lose

Four Months After the Wedding

I'm careful to keep my eyes focused on my screen as Amelia loudly walks by, but I catch it out of the corner of my eye anyway.

She's wearing an elastic compression bandage around her wrist as she cradles it. She probably sprained it—or, rather, *I* probably sprained it.

Would that be considered assault? I guess if she wanted to press charges, she could. But it's not like she's innocent. I have a laundry list of things she's done to me, too, but we've always managed to handle things privately. I really don't see her calling the cops on me when I could press charges for attempted murder just as easily. I'm sure someone somewhere has a picture catching her or Pete sprinkling mustard on my dinner.

I hear her in her office, and I stand to close my own door so I can concentrate when my dad stops in my doorframe.

"Can we talk, Gigi?"

I sit back down and nod, and he shuts the door behind him as he walks fully into my office and takes a seat across from me.

He runs a hand along his jaw, and then he levels his gaze at me. "What happened?"

I bit my top lip between my teeth before I answer. "She moved a big meeting while I was out of town so she could take the credit for it, and I confronted her about it."

"And sprained her wrist?" he asks.

"You want the truth? She slapped me across the face, and when she went to do it again, I grabbed her wrist and twisted it." So I leave out the part about me shoving her first. It was self-defense.

He blows out a breath.

I've always been a little closer to my dad than my mom, and the opposite is true for Amelia. I think it's part of why she went off to be a teacher for a few years, honestly. She was closer to Mom in the city, and I grew even closer to Dad.

But that doesn't mean he'll take my side in this. She's the one milking a sprain, while I'm the one who looks like the monster.

"Be that as it may, I can't have you two fighting like this. I can't have you hurting each other on purpose," he says.

"She keeps moving appointments and meetings around to try to make herself look better. I feel like I can't leave town to watch my own husband play in his games because I'm terrified about what she's going to do while I'm gone. What do you propose we do?"

"I don't know, but I have to be honest here." He stands and paces my office for a beat. "I'm at my wits end with you two, and I'm not sure either one of you deserves this place when you're acting the way you are."

It feels like yet another physical blow even though this one is strictly emotional.

"Are you kidding me?" I practically gasp at him. "I've worked so hard my entire life to show how much I love the vineyard. You know what she loves?" I ask, jabbing my thumb toward the wall we share. "She loves money. She loves status."

"She loves Drew," he says softly.

"Then why is she sleeping with Pete?" I hiss, and I slap a hand over my mouth as soon as the words are out.

His eyes widen. "What?"

"He was there this morning when I confronted her about moving my meeting," I say flatly.

"Do you have proof they're…you know?" he asks, getting a little awkward at the end as he addresses the fact that his daughter is sleeping around with the vineyard staff.

"Not photographic, but the insinuation was there, and nobody tried to deny it. He was hiding and only came out when we, uh…got into our little altercation." I raise my brows pointedly at the end. If they had nothing to hide, then he wouldn't have been hiding.

He shakes his head with a bit of disgust. "I'm sorry I asked."

"I'm pretty sure he's who sprinkled the mustard on my food, too."

"Do you have proof of that?" he asks.

"No." I shake my head. "But maybe we're even now. She tried to kill me, I sprained her wrist. Eye for an eye."

He purses his lips and tilts his head as he narrows his eyes at me. "You really think that's what she was trying to do?"

"It's what she almost did. Nobody seems to think it was all that serious since I was able to get my EpiPen right away, but what if I didn't have one at my place? What if someone had to drive me a half hour to the hospital?" I shrug. "She took a risky shot there."

"Yeah," he murmurs. "I guess whatever the case, whichever one of you Mom chooses…the other should pack it up and move out. Or maybe she won't pick either of you."

My brows dip in alarm. "Did she say that?"

"No. But she sees everything, and I don't see her saying she's okay with the way either one of you is acting."

I press my lips together. I know he's right, and I have the very strong inclination that Nana is going to try to find a way to get Amelia and I to work together.

I already know how that's going to go.

Either way…it looks like I have an awful lot to lose.

Chapter 54: Spencer Nash

Nothing Left to Say

Five Months After the Wedding

"There's Mr. Newman," Jensen says when I walk into the locker room.

"Ha-ha," I mutter, not really finding it very funny after an entire month of being teased by this asshole.

Ever since that article broke, the jokes have been relentless. I'm either Mr. Newman or Mrs. Nash, depending on the day. It doesn't matter that I proved myself in training camp or in the first three exhibition games. It doesn't matter that he can't stay on top of me during practice when he's guarding me. All that matters is one stupid fucking article that came out that insinuated that my wife goaded me into marriage, and that's what this prick likes to hang onto.

I ignore it for the most part, but today's game day. It's our opening game of this season, and I'm working my hardest to stay focused.

It's why I told Grace I couldn't spend time with her this weekend. I felt like a real dick about it, but I needed some space…which seems strange given the fact that all I have is space.

I haven't seen her since that first preseason game last month. It's been almost an entire month since our pact that we'd only let a week go by without seeing each other.

A few days after the first article broke, another one came out with photos of us at our wedding. Someone—Amelia, probably—got to the Now or Never Vegas Chapel, and they provided the photos.

All of them.

Even the unedited ones that weren't sent to us as part of our package.

Including one where we both look pretty fucking wasted, only proving all the rumors true.

I haven't made a statement. I don't want to. It's nobody's business, and instead, I'm choosing to leave it all out on the field.

But as much as I'm trying to focus...I can't. The distractions are everywhere, including inside the locker room—the one place that should be sacred from the outside noise. And it was safe from all that back in Minnesota. Here, I'm the new guy, so I'm open to whatever they want to fire at me.

It doesn't help that the ringleader is the guy who guards me in practice. He says whatever shit he can to try to get to me—to try to make himself look better. To take me out of the right mindset so he can look like he's keeping up with me when the truth is...he isn't.

I ignore his jab when I walk in, but without her here for the last four weeks, it's getting harder and harder to remember that feeling of love I felt so strongly when we were together.

I think we may have jumped the gun with those words. Maybe I fell in love with the idea of her. I wanted things to work out so badly that I convinced myself it was true.

The more time we spend apart, the easier it is to push those feelings aside, and the easier it is to convince myself that she loves the vineyard far more than she ever could love me. And that's fine. This started as a business arrangement, and feelings got involved along the way.

But I'm not sure I can continue to really give this a try when I know I'll always come in second.

It's a depressing thought to have immediately before a game, and the thought reflects on my ability to keep my focus on the field. I miss what should be an easy catch. I drop the ball when it hits me square in the palms. I fumble on another play.

It's three mistakes—three more than my usual average per game.

And it's because I'm distracted. If I don't pull my shit together, I'll lose everything I've worked for my entire career.

We lose our first game of the regular season. It's a deep, dark sort of disappointment after we were so goddamn excited to take what we worked on in the offseason onto the field.

He was only good in Minnesota.

He should never have left.

He should have just retired.

I hear the murmurs when people think I can't. I see the headlines.

It's pushing me further into a place I don't want to go, and it comes to a head when Grace calls me shortly after I arrive back home.

I'm sipping a glass of straight bourbon. It tastes like shit, but it's taking the edge off as I answer with a grunt. "Hey."

"You okay?" she asks. It's nice to hear her voice. Relaxing. Comforting.

Which is why I hate the words I know I have to say. "No."

"Talk to me."

"I played like shit today, and we lost because of it."

"It's a team effort." She's spouting the same shit people who don't get it always spout when they're trying to make a person feel better.

"I can't do this, Grace." My voice is strained and barely above a whisper because I can't seem to make it work.

"I get it. Get some rest, and we'll talk tomorrow, okay?"

"No, I don't mean today. I don't mean the game." I pause, and I draw in a fortifying breath. "I mean us."

I'm met with silence.

"I'll stay married to you for a year so you can get your vineyard, but for me...I think this has to be the end of the road."

317

More silence.

I think about filling that silence, but the words weigh heavy. There's nothing left to say anyway.

"Oh," she finally says. "Okay. I guess I'll go then."

That's it. There's no fight. No protest. Nothing except a beep followed by the dead air of an ended call. A closed line. A closed chapter.

I hold my phone to my ear another minute even though the call is over, and the grief seems to slowly roll down over me from my head to my heart down into my stomach, which knots and twists violently.

I slowly lower the phone, and then I let it fall loose in my hand. It drops to the floor with a clatter.

I stare out the window into the darkness of night for a beat, and then I turn around and look at my empty apartment in a town where I still don't feel at home.

And it's because *she* is home.

But *her* home isn't me.

Loneliness engulfs me.

"Goddammit!" I yell, and I throw my glass across the room. It bounces off the wall and lands on the tile floor, proceeding to shatter everywhere.

I'm not a violent man, but this need for destruction surges through me.

I walk into my Lego room, grab the Millennium Falcon off the shelf, and stare at it for a few beats.

I toss it to the floor like I'm spiking a football, bricks flying off in every direction, probably getting lost in the carpet or sliding under the chair or maybe even breaking in the process.

I walk out of the room, not feeling any better even after leaving destruction in my wake.

In the morning, I walk into the locker room before team meetings to go over the many mistakes I made. I stop Jensen before he can start up with me.

"It's over with my wife, so if you could just lay off me, that'd be great."

His face falls a bit. "It's...over?"

I press my lips together, and he claps me on the shoulder.

"Dude, you okay? The teasing was all in good fun. I didn't realize—"

"That's sort of the problem with constantly teasing someone, isn't it?" I ask, interrupting him. "You don't take the time to realize."

He clearly feels like an asshole, which is an accurate representation of who he is. I hope he learned something.

I hope he lays off me.

But most of all, I hope this searing ache in my chest subsides soon. I have a feeling it won't.

Chapter 55: Grace Nash

The Agenda

Five Months After the Wedding

I stare at the blank phone in my hand as tears fall down my face. They land somewhere on my shirt, but they're coming too fast for me to keep up with them.

How the hell did we get here?

It wasn't so long ago he was telling me that he loved me after a game...and now it's over?

I knew the season would be hard on us, but I thought we had a *little* more time. He's been preoccupied with practice and meetings and games, so I threw myself into my own thing. I thought it was a *good* thing for us to have separate interests. I thought I was respecting his boundaries when he told me he needed to focus. It was all working out—his focus shifted to the game, and mine to the vineyard.

I've been trying to find something, anything, to use against her in this whole vineyard fight, but I keep coming up blank. It feels like she's winning the vineyard, and all I had left was Spencer.

But now he's walking away, too. Another blindside.

What does that leave me with?

Nothing. The answer is *nothing*.

And I have no idea what to do to fight for him. His voice made it sound like he didn't *want* a fight. He's just done. It's over for him. There's nothing left to fight for.

It makes me wonder if he ever really meant those words when he said he loved me. What would make him just end it out of the blue? We didn't have a fight. There wasn't even enough time that passed for us to really grow apart.

The tears start to dry as anger steps into their place. Why is he just giving up? Something must have happened, and he's not letting me in.

I want to talk this out with somebody, but I realize once again…I don't *have* anyone.

I don't know if I've ever felt so alone.

It doesn't get any better as the end of the day Monday rolls around. I pick up my phone no less than ten times as I think about texting or calling my husband.

He's still my husband. He still cares enough to stay married to me for the rest of the year. That has to mean something, doesn't it?

I wonder what he's doing. It's only three o'clock there, and surely he's at practice or in meetings. He told me if they lose, they don't get Mondays off, but Tuesdays are always their day off.

Maybe I should fly out to see him tonight. I take a quick look at flights. There's one out of here in a little over two hours. If I hurry and carry my bag onto the plane with me, I can make it.

I glance at my calendar to see what's on the agenda for tomorrow.

It shouldn't matter, but it does.

I have meetings booked for most of the day. I'm scheduled to meet with Nana about some ideas we had for the tasting room in the morning, and then I'm touching base with my dad about the cellar workers and their change in schedule for the fall months. Then I have a Zoom call with Heidi regarding this weekend's wedding, plus we have a retirement party on Friday night that Heidi can't make, so it'll be on me to get the barn ready for that.

It's too many things to juggle, too many things to cancel, to just abandon this place to fly out to see him.

Still, I text Heidi and ask if we can Zoom today instead of tomorrow.

She replies with a video call.

"What's wrong, Grace?" she asks as soon as she sees my face.

"Is it that obvious?"

She ducks her head a little, but then she nods. "Yeah."

I blow out a breath. "The physical distance between Spencer and me is starting to get to us, that's all." I don't get into the nuts and bolts of it. She doesn't need to know, and I don't need to be talking about it in an office where my sister could put a glass up to the wall to overhear every single word.

"Then call him, silly. Go see him. We can handle the vineyard." She purses her lips and raises her brows meaningfully at me.

"I know. It's just…" I trail off, but she finishes for me.

"Just Amelia. I know. We won't let her steal it out from under you while you're gone."

"She's tried every time I've left. I'm terrified to leave now," I admit quietly.

"Listen, Maggie knows all you do. We all know it, Gracie. This place is as good as yours, and you know I'm fighting for you to have it over her. I can't imagine her being my boss." She strains her face into an exaggerated grimace. "Now go get your man before it's too late."

She's right.

I need to go talk to him in person. I need to fight for him. I need to fight for *us*.

I nod resolutely, and then I scramble up from my seat. "I gotta go."

I rush toward my office door, ready to run to my bungalow, throw some stuff in an overnight bag, and race to the airport.

Just as I'm about to clear the doorframe, I see my dad as he rushes down the hallway toward me. He's pale, his eyes are wide, and he looks like he's seen a ghost.

"What's wrong?" I ask.

"It's Nana. I…I think she's having a stroke."

* * *

It's interesting how you can waffle back and forth over a decision, but when an emergency situation arises, the decision is made for you.

All my meetings are canceled for tomorrow. The thought of flying to San Diego is stripped from my mind.

She has to be okay. Please let her be okay.

I'm sitting in a waiting room at an emergency department thirty minutes from home, and I'm holding my dad's hand as we pray silently and wait for the doctor to come in and tell us what's going on.

A woman in scrubs walks in. "The family of Margaret Newman?"

The four of us—my dad, Uncle Jimmy, Amelia, and me—all push to a stand at the same time. I'm still holding my dad's hand, and I feel like a little girl again.

"The good news is that Margaret didn't have a stroke. She had what we call a transient ischemic attack, which can mimic the signs of a stroke. It's a temporary block of blood flow to the brain that can serve as a warning sign, and because of her age, we're going to admit her so we can have our neurologist run some more tests and assess her risk."

I let out a breath. It wasn't a stroke, but it was still *something*.

I'm not ready to lose her. Nana is one of the most important people in my life, and I can't imagine a world that exists without her in it.

My immediate thought upon hearing she's okay is that I want to call Spencer. He loves her, too. He should know.

"Visiting hours are over for the night, and we'll be transferring her to a floor bed," the doctor continues. "She can have visitors in the morning starting at eight, so feel free to go home and get some rest. She'll need you at your best tomorrow."

"Can I just get in to say goodnight?" Dad asks, and Uncle Jimmy nods beside him.

She flattens her lips, but then she nods. "Quickly, please."

They both nod, and Amelia and I are left alone in the waiting room.

"Thank God she's going to be okay," Amelia says once Dad and Uncle Jimmy follow the doctor out of the waiting room.

I press my lips together and nod, and then I start to cry.

"Hey," she says softly. This isn't the Amelia I'm used to, but I'm not used to facing an emergency medical situation for a close family member either. "She's going to be okay."

"I was just holding it together for Dad," I admit as I swipe away the tears.

"Me too," she says, and her voice cracks.

It's the most tender moment we've ever shared, I think, and it feels...strange.

Here's this strong, independent, sometimes wild, sometimes wonderful woman, and I can't help but think what a team we'd make if we could just find ourselves landing on the same side of things.

We haven't eaten, so once Dad and Uncle Jimmy return from seeing Nana, Dad offers to take us all out to dinner. Uncle Jimmy rode in the ambulance here with Nana after she'd been confused and her face was starting to droop, and he sits in front of Dad's car while I sit in back with Amelia.

There's a bit of awkwardness in the air between us, but I also can't help but wonder what's going through Nana's mind right now.

The most important thing is that we get her healthy and back home with us.

I wish I could talk to Spencer. I wish I could tell him what's going on.

And I try to. The moment I walk in through the front door of my bungalow, I collapse on my couch and dial his number.

It goes straight to voicemail.

I tried. He didn't answer.

I'm reminded once again how very well and truly alone I really am.

Chapter 56: Spencer Nash

I Think My Clock is Broken

Five Months After the Wedding

My phone was blowing up, so I turned it off. Jensen must've talked to somebody connected to the media about me because he's the only person I told that my marriage was over, yet it's all over social media. It's vague comments from unnamed sources, and it hurts that maybe *she* will see it. I should have warned her, but I got an assignment from Coach Clark, the wide receiver coach, to review my footage from yesterday's game.

So in order to focus, I turned my phone to Do Not Disturb, and then, since I rarely use that feature, I pretty much immediately forget that I turned it on.

Since it's my one day off this week, I think I just want a day off from, well…everything.

I leave my phone at home, slather on sunscreen, throw on my swim trunks and a baseball cap, and I head down to the beach. I take my slides off and leave them in the sand.

And then I start running.

I run until my lungs burn, and I keep going. I run until my legs burn, and I keep going. I'm sprinting through the surf on an empty beach on a warm Tuesday morning in September, and I want it to feel better than it does.

This is all new. It's fresh. I haven't even had a chance to talk to her in person.

It's better this way.

This way, I don't have to see the disappointment in her eyes. Or maybe I'm making it even harder by picturing what that looks like. Maybe the reality isn't as bad. Maybe this was only ever a marriage of convenience to her—a way for her to get her vineyard, and then she'd be done with me after a year.

I don't believe that for a second.

Still, the words in my head are my soundtrack today. The only sounds in my periphery are the water as it rushes and retreats from the shore, my feet slapping on the wet sand, and the birds as they call just before they dive toward the water.

Eventually I stop my sprint and slow to a jog, and then I slow to a walk.

And then I stop.

I sink down onto the sand, my knees perched up and my feet flat, and I wrap my arms around my knees as I stare out at the water.

It's only been two days.

I'm the one who left.

It'll get easier. Time heals all wounds. I can hear the sage advice from my brothers and my mother now. My dad would have something to say, too, I'm sure, but it's not anything that would comfort or heal me in this moment.

But if time heals all wounds, I think my clock might be broken.

In the last two days, it hasn't. It's only gotten harder.

I force myself up after my ass starts to fall asleep from the hard sand, and I walk slowly the rest of the way back toward my slides. I rinse my feet and head home.

I finally check my phone. I see a missed call from her from last night, but no voicemail. I also have an email from her father that was sent late last night.

Spencer:

Can you review the document attached? I don't know what to do with my two girls, and you're probably the wrong person to ask since you're involved, but I just want to try to settle this thing between them. I hate when they're constantly fighting. I'll eventually have my lawyer look at it, too, but I trust your sense for these things and your duty to responsibility. And I figured you'll get back to me faster than my lawyer will anyway. It's all a bunch of legal mumbo jumbo to me and I can't stand even thinking about what my mother's intentions are with this place in the event of her death. I know you're busy, but I'm hoping I caught you at a good time.

Thanks,

Steve

I download the document he attached, and as it turns out…it's Maggie's will.

I scroll through it until I find the clause regarding the vineyard.

Newlywed Vineyard of Cedar Creek, Minnesota, including land, buildings, equipment, and all subsidiaries, are hereby bequeathed to whichever of my granddaughters [Amelia Newman or Grace Newman] first maintains a successful marriage free from infidelity for a minimum period of one year. If neither granddaughter is married upon my passing, I hereby bequeath the vineyard to my sons, Steven and James Newman, at fifty percent each.

It is my intention that whoever is bequeathed the vineyard:

Preserves the title "Newlywed Vineyard" for the life of the vineyard.

Continues to operate the vineyard for the commercial production of wine.

Agrees to bequeath the vineyard to a blood relative in the event of her death *or* in the event that she no longer is willing or able to manage the vineyard.

Additionally, the Newman Winery of Temecula, California, currently under the management of Theodore Monroe, is bequeathed to whichever granddaughter maintains a successful marriage free from infidelity for five years, *or* whichever granddaughter produces the first grandchild within a faithful marriage, *or* whichever granddaughter is willing to move to Temecula to manage the vineyard there, whichever event comes first. In the event that neither Amelia nor Grace meet these conditions within the first ten years upon my death, the vineyard is hereby bequeathed to Theodore Monroe. The same intentions labeled 1-3 above apply, with the exception to the title being preserved as either "Newman" as it currently stands or being changed to the "Newlywed" brand, whichever the new owner prefers.

I glance up into space for a beat, questions swirling around my mind...starting with the first one. Who in the hell is Theodore Monroe?

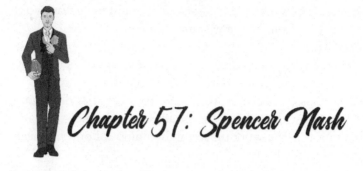

Chapter 57: Spencer Nash

What the Fuck is in Temecula

Five Months After the Wedding

I replied to him right away that I'd take a look, but then it took me almost a week to get back to Steve—mostly because I had other shit to take care of. I had a charity event in the evening, and then it was back to practice and preparing for our next opponent as we traveled to Miami.

The first and most obvious solution here is for someone to catch Amelia in the act of cheating. The clause in the will is very clear on that point, and I'm not sure how much of this I'm supposed to know—or how much of it he wants Grace to know. It feels like a heavy responsibility he laid on me, but he said he trusts me. And I take that to heart.

Which is why I've carefully avoided Grace.

I don't want to talk to her and slip what I know, but I also told her it was over the last time I spoke with her.

I still stand by that. I still want her to have her vineyard. She deserves it, and we've been faithful to each other despite how I ended things personally between us last week.

I wonder how she's doing. I think about calling her. I think about texting her. I think about *her*.

But she hasn't reached out to me, social media rumors or not, and so I think maybe it's just better this way.

A win against the Dolphins at their home stadium feels good—and even better since I actually caught a pass or two this time, one that I ran all the way into the end zone for a touchdown.

I'm getting my head back in the game because it's the only place it *can* be right now. After the rumors hit social media about my possible divorce, the locker room chatter died out.

The other wide receivers have rallied around me, and having their support as we work on strengthening our bond has been everything I need.

But as the plane touches down on Sunday evening after our game and I make my way back to my empty apartment, that same sense of loneliness hits me again.

I can do this for three years. It'll be fine. It'll be good.

But then what?

Then I'm thirty-three and alone.

I thought my life would look different by now than it does.

I stand near my windows with a glass of bourbon again, and this time I don't slam it against the wall to shatter it. I contemplate what I want to do, and I finally decide that if I want to help Steve get the answers he needs, I should head up to Temecula tomorrow and find out what's going on. It's only about an hour from where I live, and I'd like to check out this place my *wife* has no idea about.

I have this strange feeling like I don't want to go alone, but I have no idea who to ask.

I could ask one of my teammates. Clay, maybe. But I'm not close enough to him to admit what I'm going through.

I think of one of the few people who is impulsive enough to be game to go with me, and at the same time, would drop anything and show up at my door if I asked, and I text him.

Me: *You got any plans tomorrow?*

Asher: *Just a workout in the morning. Why?*

Me: *I need to take a trip to Temecula. Want to go?*

Asher: *Temecula? What the fuck is in Temecula?*

I laugh out loud, and it feels good to laugh with one of my brothers after the heaviness that's been swirling around me the last few days.

Me: *Just have something I need to do and don't want to do alone.*

Asher: *I'll be there. Name the time.*

Me: *My place at eleven?*

Asher: *I'll be there.*

When morning comes, Asher shows up at my place a little after ten thirty.

He's wearing jeans paired with a button-down, collared shirt that has neon geometric shapes. It reminds me of something out of the nineties.

I've said it plenty of times before. I try to go for the quiet elegance of looking put together without really trying all that hard, while my brother here is all about statement pieces.

This *Saved by the Bell* shirt is better than the purple velour tracksuit, I guess.

"Brochacho!" I yell after I take in his clothes.

"Broski!" he yells back, and our hands meet in the middle before we share a quick bro-hug complete with a slap on the back.

"You're early," I say as I let him into my apartment.

He glances around. "I'm at the mercy of the airline."

"Did you bring a bag?"

He shakes his head. "Just my phone and AirPods. By the way, I'll need to charge this in your car." He holds up his phone, and I can't help a laugh.

We head to the parking garage, and he slips into the passenger seat of my car.

"So what's all this about?" he asks.

"Buckle up," I say, and I'm not sure if I'm telling him to physically buckle his seatbelt or figuratively prepare for my story. Both, I guess.

I draw in a deep breath, set my GPS, and start from the beginning with the night I met the Newman sisters. He knew about the wedding in Vegas, but he wasn't as clear on the fact that I actually did fall in love with Grace somewhere in the middle of all of it.

By the time I get to the end of the story, we're only ten minutes from the vineyard. "And now I need to find out who this Theodore Monroe guy is so I can help Grace get both the Cedar Creek and the Temecula vineyards."

"Can't you just set a trap to catch Amelia?" he asks.

I shrug. "I'm not there. It's not that simple, you know? I've got practice and workouts and meetings. Events and endorsements. You know how it goes, and I'm not sure how to present all this to Grace. I want her to have her vineyard, but I feel like it's sort of at the expense of whatever this is between the two of us."

"I do know how it goes," he says with a nod. "And when something feels important enough, I make the time." He waves a hand between us. "Like this. You never call me out of the blue like this, so I knew something was up. And you know what, Spencer? For being the smart one, you're sure being a dumbass."

"Excuse me?"

"You heard me," he mutters.

"How am I being a dumbass?"

"You're trying to deal with this whole thing like you deal with everything. You're letting logic lead the way, but if I've learned anything from Gray and Linc…well, it's that love isn't always very logical. My man Grayson ended up with his best friend's little sister. Old Bro Lincoln waited around twenty fucking years for his woman. And hearing what you have to say…what you have with Grace is most definitely love, my friend."

"How am I leading with logic?" I ask, ignoring the rest of everything he just said.

"Jesus, you're even dumber than I first thought. You really don't see this?" He leans back in his seat and folds his arms across his chest.

I shake my head.

He sighs. "Dude, you're protecting yourself. You're putting a stop to things before you're even giving it a chance to work, and I think it's because of Mom and Dad."

"Because of Mom and Dad?" I ask, not sure where that came from.

"It affected all of us in different ways. Their divorce, I mean." He shrugs. "For me, it made me not want commitment. For you, you're scared because you jumped too fast into a commitment, and now you're backing slowly away."

When the fuck did Asher get a psychology degree?

"I get it," he says, holding up both hands before I can ask that question. "You don't want to be with Amelia, and Grace did a few things that reminded you of Amelia. But guess the fuck what? You proposed to Amelia, too, so there was something about her that you loved. But then you married her sister. Not very logical for my man of logic, is it? As an outsider, here's what I can gather. You chose the wrong sister first. You've been in love with Grace since the night you met her, and it was inevitable you'd end up with her, but there's something in your brain telling you that you can't be with her. So fix whatever that is and stop stepping in your own goddamn way so you can wear that same sloppy, drunk in love, dumbass smile Grayson and Lincoln have."

I can't help but burst out laughing at the end of his tirade. "What about you?"

"What about me?" he asks.

"You don't want commitment because Mom and Dad got divorced?"

He shakes his head. "Not really. Gray said Mom told him she wouldn't trade in the years she had with Dad, but dude, I *live* with Dad. He's a handful, man. I don't know that I could've put in forty years or whatever she did with him, and I can't see myself ever finding someone I want to spend that much time around."

I think about Grace and how it feels like total devastation when she's not around.

Is my dumbass brother right?

Am I trying too hard to be logical about all this when there's absolutely no logic when it comes to love?

We can't help the way we feel, and sometimes we can't just categorize that into a neat little box. Asher's words actually make me wonder, for the first time ever, if I've really been in love with Grace since the night I met her. Or maybe I *could* have been if her sister would've given her the chance to shine.

And now she's trying to take more away from Grace, who never deserved to lose any of this.

We pull into the parking lot of Newman Winery, and I wonder why it has a different name than Newlywed. It's one of the many things I intend to find out.

But I also want to find out without being recognized. If this Theodore person has some connection to Maggie, he might know that I married her granddaughter. It's too late now to disguise myself, so my brother and I head inside as I hope for the best.

Chapter 58: Grace Nash

Give it to Amelia

Five Months After the Wedding

"It's so good to see you back in here, Nana," I say as I walk into the tasting room.

It's been a week since her health scare, and she's supposed to be taking it easy—which she is. Dad brought her recliner in so she has somewhere to rest back behind the counter, and her feet are up as she reads a magazine when I spot her.

We don't have any guests in yet, but it's early. They'll come.

"Where's Spencer?" she asks. "Haven't seen that cutie pie around here in weeks."

"He's in season, Nana. Remember?" I say it gently, and it worries me that she's confused again.

"Oh, right. Silly me. But I remember him coming by when he was in season to visit your sister." She says the words pointedly, as if she's pointing out the fact that her memory is just fine. "As I recall, he usually had Monday and Tuesday off, and he'd come by."

"He's in San Diego now. It's not quite so easy to get here."

She raises her brows. "Then why are *you* here?"

"Excuse me?"

LISA SUZANNE

"Honey, I've been around the block once or twice. I know how these things work. You're here, he's there, something's wrong. He played in Miami this past weekend, fine. But why weren't you at his first game of the season the week before that?"

I sigh. I didn't want to get into this—especially not with her—but maybe it's time she knew the truth. "I'm afraid to leave. I'm afraid Amelia will do something that will give her an edge when I'm working so hard to prove that it should be mine."

"Sounds to me like you're putting the vineyard first." She presses her lips together.

"Is...isn't that what you want for this place?"

She shakes her head, puts the recliner down, and pushes to a stand. She's a little unsteady on her feet, but overall, she's making great progress. "No, honey," she says, and she stops in front of me. She rests her hand on my forearm. "I want someone who has a real, true partner that can help manage everything that comes with a winery. I want someone who can raise a family here and see a future here. What I don't want is someone who's willing to sacrifice all that for this place. This?" She holds a hand up. "It's just a place. It's important, and it's a legacy, but it's not everything. And I'm afraid I've sent you the completely wrong message if that's what you took out of it."

Her words pulse a new thought in me.

Am I throwing everything away for this vineyard?

I may have inadvertently pushed him away when I was trying harder to hold onto the vineyard than I was to him.

But what good is the vineyard if I don't have him?

I've been so busy with the fight here that I've neglected other areas of my life—the most important area, if I'm being honest.

And I realize only after hearing her words that every time I think of the future of this place, I picture *him* as part of it.

I don't want to inherit Newlywed if I don't get to stand on my back deck watching my children in the old tire swing while my husband presses a glass of malbec into my palm.

Tears spring behind my eyes as I realize what I've done.

338

"You're right," I finally say, and I pull her into my arms and squeeze her tightly. "I've been trying so hard to beat Amelia so you would see I'm the obvious choice to inherit this wonderful land that I forgot that it isn't worth inheriting if I don't have Spencer." I pull back and shake my head as her eyes meet mine.

I realize something else, too.

If I walk away, Amelia will stop. She'll stop feeding details to the media. She'll stop having paparazzi follow Spencer everywhere. She'll stop making our lives miserable.

She'll stop coming between us.

All I want is to have a future with Spencer. The love we share is way more important than the dream I once had to run the vineyard, and all it took was one conversation with Nana to realize it.

"You should give the vineyard to Amelia. I have to go."

Her eyes twinkle as she nods. She squeezes me once more, and then I race over to my bungalow. I check flights to San Diego, and there's one that leaves in ninety minutes—just enough time to get to the airport, park, and make it onto the plane.

I book the ticket.

I toss some clothes into my backpack along with my toothbrush and a few essentials, and then I hop in my car and rush toward the airport. It's a race against the clock as I hit some traffic. The minutes seem to tick by more quickly than their usual sixty seconds, and I pull into the parking garage that lets me know it'll cost me thirty bucks a day.

Fine. Worth it.

I find a space and race toward the terminal.

Why security has a line at one-thirty in the afternoon on a Monday is beyond me, but here we are.

I tap my foot as I wait, wishing I would've been smart enough to book an appointment to get my TSA pre-check done so I didn't have to wait in this line.

It's a five-minute wait that feels like freaking *forever*, and then I'm *randomly* selected for the Explosive Trace Detection test. The agent selected to swab my hands certainly isn't in the same rush I happen to be in, but I force myself to smile and bear it as nerves race through my spine that I'm not going to make it.

I run through the airport to my gate, which naturally is all the way at the end of my terminal, and my flight is still boarding.

Thank God.

I'm panting from my sprint across the airport as I get in line. I blow out a huge breath as I try to calm down, but my heart is racing and I'm nervous and excited all at the same time.

Did I really just do that?

Did I just tell Nana to give the vineyard to Amelia?

I did.

I don't want it if it's at the expense of my relationship with Spencer, and I feel positively sure in that decision, even if it's the most terrifying thing I've ever done.

I take my seat, and that's when my mind starts to race with all the thoughts I didn't give myself the time to consider.

What if I get there and he doesn't want me?

What if I just told Nana to give the vineyard to Amelia, only to lose both my dream and my husband on the same day?

If that's what happens, so be it. I refuse to live my life with regrets, and the biggest regret of all would be throwing away the beautiful thing Spencer and I have built.

We have challenges in front of us, and we have hills to climb. But if we can do that hand-in-hand, then we can overcome all of it.

I hold onto that optimism with everything inside me.

I keep it close to my heart for the entire flight and the Lyft ride over to Spencer's complex.

I hold it tight as I flash my ID at the front desk, as they check for my name on Spencer's list of approved guests, and as I wait for the elevator up to his penthouse.

But when I knock on the door and he doesn't answer…I feel it starting to slip away.

I shouldn't have assumed he'd be home without calling first. He's a busy man, and he has a lot going on. But I thought maybe he'd be at home doing Lego sets on his day off.

Instead, I can't help but think he's out trying to find some way to move on from what we had.

I can't help but think he's *already* moved on. It felt like everything was falling into place, like he'd *have* to be here waiting for me to arrive after I made this realization and somehow managed to make my flight and ended up right here.

But he's not, and somehow that feels significant and awful.

I lean against the door and slide down it until I'm sitting on the floor, and I let that bubble of optimism shatter into a million pieces all around me.

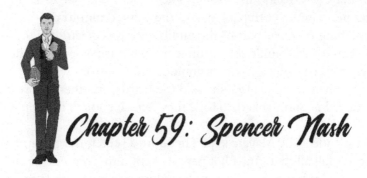

Chapter 59: Spencer Nash

Intricately Woven into the Thread

Five Months After the Wedding

Holy shit.
Holy shit.
We pull away from the vineyard, and it's all so clear to me now—the reason why Maggie wants to keep Newlywed in the family. The reason why Maggie wants to pass down her vineyard to a married couple. The reason why *no infidelity* is an actual part of her conditions for handing it down.

Theodore Monroe isn't just some random dude running Newman Winery in Temecula.

Theodore Monroe is Maggie's younger half-brother, the product of an affair between her mother and another man.

I have about a million questions, but this was all information I gleaned from Sylvia, the manager of the tasting room. She had no idea who I was, and I was careful with the questions I asked.

She had a way of running her mouth, as if she told this story all the time. Sometimes tasting room workers love to chat about the lore of the place—as if that'll give people something to talk about. And an affair might be considered one of those juicy details that would help people remember a place, I suppose.

"Oh, yeah, the man who runs this place does it for his half-sister. She's a sweet little old lady who owns both this one and another vineyard in Minnesota. I guess she found out about him after her parents both passed, and she wanted him to run something that was part of the family. She was devastated to learn about the family secrets after her parents passed, and she decided she's willing it to her granddaughters, from what I hear." She shrugged after she said the words, and then she sort of leaned in and winked. "Hope they're nice enough to keep me on."

I wonder why Maggie kept Theodore a secret, but the apple doesn't fall all that far. If her parents kept him a secret from her, she must've had her reasons to keep him a secret from everyone else in her family. The fidelity clause makes a lot more sense now, and knowing what I know now tells me she must've clung to the vineyard after her parents were gone as a way to hold onto them in the way *she* knew them rather than in the way they were exposed after they died.

I bought a case of cabernet sauvignon and walked out once I had the information I needed, but I didn't get the chance to meet Theodore, who was over at the production facility.

Not only does Grace have a relative she doesn't know about, but she could potentially inherit a vineyard that's less than an hour from where I live and work right now…and she doesn't even know?

I need to tell her, but I also need to tell Steve.

But I probably shouldn't tell Steve without talking to Maggie first.

And…when the hell did I get so intricately woven into the thread of this family?

I quietly told my wife we could stay married so she could get her vineyard, but I'm out. And the fact that I come in second with her still remains true. As much as my mind is blown after visiting the vineyard, I can't help but remember why I felt like I needed to end things.

I thought those words would give me the sense of relief I was seeking. It's only been a week, but it's been one of the goddamn worst weeks of my life. Not because of anything in particular that happened to make it bad, but because there's a hole in my chest where my heart used to reside, and I fucking miss Grace.

I love her.

I miss talking to her every day. I miss her random texts and cat memes.

I don't want to be without her, but I also know I can't stay married forever to someone who doesn't count her husband on her list of priorities.

Asher is quiet beside me—for now. He's letting me process, and I appreciate the hell out of him for that.

Or maybe there's more to it. Maybe he has something of his own going on, something he wants to talk about but can't because I've filled the space with my own issues.

Why else would he have dropped everything to come be with me when I never even said what the fuck I was doing?

"You okay, man?" I finally ask.

"I could ask the same of you."

"No," I answer truthfully. "I ended things with Grace a week ago because I couldn't keep coming in second to her vineyard, and I think it might've been a mistake."

He sits up a little straighter. "Because I made you realize it?"

I grunt. "No. Because I realized it all on my own."

He rolls his eyes as he sinks back into the seat. "Whatever."

"Maybe a little because of your help. But can I ask you a question?"

"What?"

"Why'd you come out without an explanation?" I ask.

"You sounded like you needed me, and I'm nothing if not loyal to my brothers." He lifts a shoulder.

"Something's going on with you," I accuse. "The talk about commitment. How love isn't logical. All of it. What's up with you?"

He blows out a breath. "I met someone. We only had one night together, and we didn't exchange anything more than first names and bodily fluids, and now I can't stop thinking about her."

My jaw slackens. "You *met* someone?"

"You heard me," he mutters, and he turns his gaze out the window.

I blow out a low whistle. "Women." I shake my head at the single word that pretty much sums it all up. We drive the rest of the way back lost in thought about our own situations, I suppose, but it's nice having my brother here with me in the silence anyway.

It makes me feel like I'm not really alone.

He fiddles with his phone as we approach my apartment complex.

When I pull into a space, and before I get out of the car, I glance over at him and ask, "So what are you going to do?"

"Checking flights back to Vegas now that your mission is complete."

"I meant about the someone you exchanged bodily fluids with," I say dryly.

"Oh," he says. He clicks his phone off and sets it in his lap, and he stares out the windshield. "I don't know. She was just in town for a weekend, and I'll probably never see her again." He shrugs, but I sense the sadness in his tone.

"There's no way to get in touch with her?"

He shakes his head. "All I've got is the memory and a first name."

"Do you *want* to do something about it?"

"I'm in season. I need to put my focus there." He says the words, but I sense something else in there. There must be *something* he could do—go to the place he met her and ask for footage or receipts. But he doesn't seem to want to talk about it, so I back slowly away.

"I get it. I've been trying to do that, too, but I haven't been successful in getting her out of my head."

"Neither have I," he admits.

"Want to come up for a drink before you head out?"

He nods. We get out of my car and head toward the building, and I hit the button for the penthouse. I wrestle with what to do with this new information, and I think before I say anything to anyone, I need to touch base with Maggie. It's the right thing to do. She kept all this a secret from her family for her own reasons, and it's not my place to expose any of it.

The elevator doors slide open, and my eyes are on my keys in my hand as I flip through them to find the one that opens my door.

When I glance up, I spot the woman sitting on the floor leaning against my door, and all the air is squeezed out of my lungs as a warmth fills my chest.

She's here.

Chapter 60: Grace Nash

A Chance to Make This Right

Five Months After the Wedding

"What are you doing here?" His voice is cautious as those five words fall from his mouth in the form of a question.

I glance at Asher beside him, and the moment he spots me, he takes a step backward onto the elevator. He waves at me, but he doesn't otherwise say a word—not even goodbye to his own brother—as the doors slide shut and the elevator carries him down.

Spencer holds out a hand and helps me rise to a stand.

"Can we talk?" I ask. I slip my arms around him for a hug, and my *God*, does it feel good here. It feels *right*. It feels like I'm home again after far too long away.

He holds me tightly against him, and I hope against hope that it's because he's feeling the same things I am. I spent the entire trip here praying that this will be enough. That *I* will be enough.

He is *everything* to me, and I hate that I let my competition with my sister come before that.

He finally draws in a deep breath then lets me go. He unlocks his front door, and he holds it open for me to walk in first, ever the gentleman.

He leans against it after he shuts it, and I turn to face him. He looks nervous. Wary. Unsure.

But I've never been more sure about anything in my life.

"I love you, Spencer. I want to be with you. I realized something today when I was talking with Nana, and the second I realized it, I rushed to the airport and got on a plane to talk to you in person. And then I got here, and you weren't here…" Tears start to fall as that same feeling of devastation rolls through me again.

But he's here now. He's here, and I have a chance to make this right.

I suck in a shaky breath as I try to get through this. "Let me back up. Nana had a mini stroke last week, and she—"

"Oh, shit," he interrupts. "Is she okay?"

I nod. "She's okay. She's getting stronger each day, and we're all keeping a close eye on her. I tried to call you, but you didn't answer, and then we were taking care of her, and you had a game and—"

"Fuck, Grace," he says, and he rushes over to grab me in his arms. "I'm so sorry you went through all that alone. I should have been there with you and your dad. For Maggie."

"It's okay. You didn't know." I rest my cheek on his chest, and I breathe him in. It's his familiar, clean, soapy scent that just smells like home. It *feels* like home right here. I always thought the vineyard was home, and it is. But nothing beats the feeling of being in the arms of the man I love.

He clears his throat and pulls back, letting me out of his grasp. "You said you realized something."

I nod, and I pull it together to get this out. "Right. I realized the vineyard has been my top priority my entire life."

His face falls a little as he takes a step back, putting a bit of distance between us, and that's the moment I know Nana hit the nail on the head. He didn't tell me he wanted out because he doesn't love me. It was because he needed to feel like I love *him*. And the fact that he doesn't know that breaks my heart.

"But then I met you. We became friends first when you walked down the wrong path, but I fell in love with you anyway, even when I shouldn't have. But then we got married, and it was rushed, and it happened for all the wrong reasons, but it was also *right*. And I realized today that I don't want the vineyard at the expense of our marriage. That place is meaningless to me if I can't have it with *you*. And so I told Nana to give it to Amelia, and then I hopped on a plane and came here to tell you that I love you. I love *us*. I want to make this work with you more than anything."

He stares at me, his jaw working back and forth in that sexy way men have as he contemplates my words.

I add more. "Besides, if I let Amelia win, maybe she'll stop trying to come between us. She'll stop with the paparazzi and the fake social media accounts and the constant manipulations, and we can focus on *us* and building this life together instead of on fighting her."

He's quiet as he stares at me for a few beats, and the very real fear that I got it all wrong plows into me.

"You gave up the vineyard? For me?"

I nod slowly, pressing my lips together as I wait for his reaction.

He shakes his head a little with wonder, and then he glances out the windows behind me before his eyes return to me.

"For us," I say.

He takes a tentative step toward me, and then another, and then he reaches forward to grasp my upper arms as he pulls me toward him. And then his lips crash down to mine.

It's like I'm home again.

This kiss is aggressive and urgent, needy and full of lust as it seals in the unspoken promise between us.

I slide my arms around his neck and cling to him as he lets his grasp on my biceps go to wrap his arms around me. His tongue glides against mine, and his hips shift as I feel the firmness of his erection against my stomach.

I gasp when I feel it, and a warmth spreads through my chest that this is it. It's real. It's right. It's all I've ever wanted with him, and finally, *finally* all the obstacles are out of our way so we can walk this journey forward together rather than apart.

It feels like a weight has lifted off me. I thought letting go of the vineyard would be the worst thing for me, but as it turns out, maybe it's the best.

It's what led me back to Spencer. It's what led to this moment.

He doesn't move his lips from mine as he starts to guide me backward through the house. We devour each other through our mouths, and it feels like we were apart for years rather than weeks. The time doesn't matter. The fact is, if we make another pact about time apart, this time we're sticking to it.

This time it's real.

This time it's forever.

I feel the kitchen counter behind me, and he lifts me and perches me on it. I wrap my legs around his waist as he moves in closer, his fingertips moving beneath my shirt and brushing the skin of my back. His hands, his fingers, his mouth…it all feels so *good*.

He pulls back and leans his forehead against mine. "I missed you, Gracie." His voice is a low rasp, and it sends a thrill up my spine. "Every fucking second of every fucking day."

I wrap my arms around his broad shoulders then pepper kisses along his jawline. "I missed you, too. I promise I'll never let a week go by without you again."

He doesn't respond with words, instead sealing our promise by lifting me off the counter. I link my legs around his waist as he carries me over toward the couch. He tosses me down and dives on top of me, not wasting a minute as he starts to slam his hips to mine. I gasp as I feel him against me, and I need to be naked. I need him inside me like I need to breathe right now.

"Fuck me, Spencer," I beg as his lips dip down toward my cleavage.

He pulls back and tears my shirt over my head, tossing it on the floor. He works my bra next and tosses it on top of my shirt, and his hands move down to squeeze my breasts. "Fuck, I missed this body." His mouth goes straight to my nipple, and when he sucks, a searing ache darts between my thighs.

I need relief. I need release. It's been far too long without him, without *this*.

I thrust my hips as I try to find some relief, but he backs away, teasing me. He pulls off me completely then, and he reaches for the button of my jeans. He pushes them along with my panties down, and I kick off my shoes and jeans so I'm laying naked on his couch.

He pulls his shirt over his head and gets naked next, and I don't know if I've ever seen anyone move as quickly as he's moving now. We're both desperate to get to this sacred reunion, and as he climbs on top of me, he hovers for a few beats. His eyes meet mine, and this erotic intimacy passes between us. It's a new feeling, heightened in a way I've never felt before.

I think it's because it *finally* feels like forever.

His lips drop to mine as he reaches down to grip his cock before he slides it into me, and if the intimacy of a moment ago was erotic, the feeling of him moving inside me as he kisses me is on another level. Our souls are connecting here as our bodies do the work, and as his deep, slow thrusts start to quicken, his mouth moves from mine. He presses hot kisses to my jaw, my neck, and my chest as I moan at the feel of his drives into me.

"You feel so good," he says, his breath hot against my ear. "Even better than I remember. Your pussy is so tight, like it was just made for me."

"God, you feel good too," I moan.

"Tell me how much you love when I fuck you." He slams his hips against mine.

"I love it. I love it so much. I love *you* so much," I say, my voice gaining in volume with each choppy, moaned sentence.

"Fuck yes, baby," he growls as he picks up the speed even more.

"I'm close. I'm so close," I cry.

"I want to hear you scream my name while I make you come."

His hot words throw me headfirst into my climax. "Oh God, yes, Spencer!" I scream.

My body jolts with pleasure as I writhe beneath him.

"That's it. Come for me," he says, his voice firm, and then he lets out a low growl as he starts to come, too. "Fuck, Grace," he groans as he thrusts up hard a few more times, seeing us both through wave after wave of intense and all-consuming pleasure.

When it's over, he relaxes on top of me for a few beats, still inside me. I feel his cock twitch and his body tremble, and I wrap my arms around him to hold him tightly to me.

This is it. This is us. This is forever.

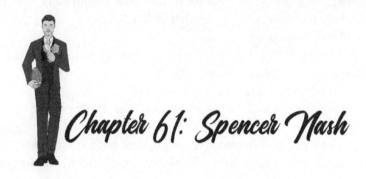

Chapter 61: Spencer Nash

Brace Yourself

Five Months After the Wedding

I don't want to move. I don't want to pull out of her and lose this connection. I didn't want to come, either, but I didn't have a choice. I wanted it to last longer—all night wouldn't be long enough.

I can't believe she's really here. I can't believe she really gave it all up. For me. For us.

Nobody I've been with has ever done anything like that before, and to know that I come first in her world means everything to me.

It means forever. It means the sort of future I wasn't sure I would ever really have.

Eventually, though, I have to move. We may be back on the same page, but we have some things to talk about. Important things—things about our future together and how we're going to fit all the pieces into place.

I pull out of her, and I pad over to the bathroom to clean myself up as I think about what just went down.

With Amelia, it was constantly pushing things back, and in the recesses of my mind, I know now that it was because it wasn't right.

With Grace, though, I want to rush forward with her hand in mine toward a shared future. I want to put a baby in her and watch her body grow because of our love. I want to raise kids and stare out over the fields that belong to us.

I just hope it isn't too late.

I return with a washcloth to clean her up, too, and then I slowly start to put my clothes back on.

She makes a face, and I chuckle.

"Just let me look at the abs a little longer, okay?" she requests, and I pull my jeans on but leave my shirt off.

"You can feel free to stay naked, too, but I need to eat something." I glance at the clock. It's nearly three, and I never ate lunch. "Are you hungry?"

She nods as she stands and starts picking up her clothes. "I could eat."

There's a restaurant in my apartment complex, so I call down and place an order. A half hour later, we're eating on my balcony as we look out over the bay, and I can't help but think about how I want to fuck her over the balcony as we look out at the bay. I want to fuck her on my bed. My kitchen counter. In my backseat. In my front seat. On vacation. In the locker room.

Okay, fine. I pretty much just want to fuck her everywhere I possibly can, and it finally feels like we have forever to do that.

As we dig into our late lunch—or early dinner in her time zone—I contemplate what to say. Ultimately, this is a partnership. She deserves to know what I know.

"I have some, uh...information I'd like to share with you."

Her brows dip as her eyes lift to mine. "Everything okay?"

I nod. "Yeah, it's just...it's a lot, so I want you to brace yourself."

"It's a lot for me?"

"It might be."

She sets her fork down and takes a gulp of water. "Okay. Hit me with it."

"Your dad sent me Maggie's will last week. He asked me if I could review it because he didn't like the idea of reading about his mom's final plans, but he was fed up with you two and your fight over the vineyard."

"Well, that fight's over, so I guess he can rest easy now." She picks up her fork to keep eating as if that's the end of my story. She spears some of her chicken with her fork, and then she glances up at me. "Is that it?"

I shake my head. "That's the beginning."

"Oh." She sets her fork back down. "Okay. Go ahead."

"There were several clauses regarding the vineyard, one being that whichever of her granddaughters is married for a year and free from infidelity will inherit the vineyard."

"Free from infidelity?" she echoes. "So…Amelia's out?"

I lift a shoulder. "There's more." I draw in a breath. "It also says the vineyard must continue to operate, so even if she *does* somehow get it because you withdrew your name, she wouldn't be able to break it up and sell it off."

She gasps.

"Still more," I warn, and she sits back in her seat like I just physically struck her. "That clause about the vineyard in Temecula—it's not exactly what you think. There were a few clauses—yes, it could be whichever granddaughter produces the first grandchild, or it could go to whoever is married for five years first *or* to just whoever is willing to move to Temecula to manage the vineyard there. And if neither of you want it or meet those conditions, she wills it to the man currently managing it."

Her brows dip. "The land in Temecula is currently operating as a vineyard?"

I nod. "Newman Winery."

"Who's running it?"

"A man named Theodore Monroe."

She shakes her head. "Never heard of him. Why would Nana keep it a secret?"

"I wanted to know the answer to that, too, so I drove out there this morning." Was that really just this morning? It feels like weeks ago at this point after everything that's happened. "Asher came with me. And this is where things really get wild."

She sits forward as she waits for the bomb.

"Nana's mother had an affair that produced a younger half-brother," I say, and she gasps at the pronouncement. "She didn't find out about him until after both her parents passed, but she wanted him to feel like he was a part of the family. He's been managing the Temecula winery for the last two decades."

"Oh my God," she murmurs. "That's why fidelity is part of the clause. But it's also what's going to keep Amelia out of the running."

I nod. "We just need to prove she's sleeping with Pete, and *both* vineyards are yours. If you still want them."

She sinks back once again as she contemplates that heavy bombshell. She stares out over the bay, and then she glances at me. I can see her wheels turning as she thinks through everything I just laid on her.

She sucks in a breath, and then she asks maybe the one question I'm not expecting. "What do *you* see out of our future?"

One side of my mouth lifts in a smile as I shake my head. I feel like I've been in a daze since she showed up today, but this single question is all the proof I need that she really means it when she says she'll walk away from the vineyard.

I just told her she's on track to inherit two of them, but she's not clinging to either until she hears what I think.

And *that* is the true sort of partnership I always wanted out of life.

Who would've ever thought I'd find that partnership with my ex-fiancée's sister?

"I don't know. Ideally, I guess I'd see us here when I'm in season for the next three years, but after that…who knows? Maybe to Temecula because we put down roots here. Maybe back to Minnesota because we love it there too. Or maybe, in the best case, we split time between the two. As long as my hand is in yours and I don't have to go longer than seven days without holding you in my arms, it doesn't matter to me."

Her eyes get misty at that. She clears her throat. "Does Nana know what you learned?"

I shake my head. "Not yet. I was just on my way back from Temecula when I ran into you, so I haven't had a chance to talk to anyone yet."

"Then I think we need to make some calls."

"Starting with…?" I ask, trailing off to let her fill in the blank.

"Starting with letting Nana know what I want to do."

"And what's that?" I ask, a little nervous about what she's decided.

"I want to stay here with you. I want my dad to keep running the vineyard in Minnesota. You and I will check in when we can. But I want to get to know my uncle, and I want to get to know the land and the grapes here in between cheering you on at every single Storm game. I want to build a life wherever you are, and I want to take that life with us wherever we go. We don't have to decide right now."

I reach across the table and take her hand in mine. "And your sister?"

She twists her lips as a little sparkle twinkles in her eye. "She's fired." She laughs. "I'm kidding. The place will need a new hospitality manager, and she's worked hard to learn more about the vineyard since she's been trying to prove she deserves it."

"A promotion? That's awfully generous, don't you think?" I ask.

She sighs. "Someone has to be the bigger person."

"It was always destined to be you. Giving it all up for love? I think that will tell Maggie everything she needs to know about who deserves to raise a family there…someday."

Her eyes get a faraway look in them as she shifts her gaze back to the bay, and I can see her imagining that future now— just as she once described it to me.

Our kids playing out in the tire swing.

Her sitting on our patio, watching them after a long day of work.

Me meeting her out there with two freshly poured glasses of wine—one that I press into her hand, the other that I hold in my own. We toast to our love, our future, our family, our land, our many blessings.

And then we live happily ever after.

Epilogue: Grace Nash

The Best Drunken Mistake

Six Months After the Wedding

"I'm so glad you're home," Dad says to me, and I hug him tightly.

"This is Theo," I say, linking my arm through my great-uncle's.

My dad sticks out a hand for his uncle to shake, and Theo bats his hand out of the way as he pulls my dad into a hug.

"I knew I had nephews, but I never thought I'd actually get to meet them," he says. "And you must be Jimmy," he says to my great uncle, whom he hugs next. "Gracie has told me so much about both of you." He leans in as if he's telling a secret. "Once you get this one talking, it's hard to get her to stop."

I playfully jab him in the arm. He's only about ten years older than my dad, and somehow he was my great-grandparents' best-kept secret...which is a real shame because Uncle Theo is a freaking hoot.

He's like the male version of Nana.

The apple doesn't fall far from the tree, I guess.

It only took me a month to convince him to come out and meet the rest of the family. Once Spencer got the green light from Nana, we found a hole in the schedule that coincided with

Spencer's bye week, and here we are back in Minnesota so Theo can check out Newlywed Vineyard and take notes to bring back to Temecula.

Nana hasn't officially signed anything over to me yet, but the paperwork is in progress. For now, I'm just letting both vineyards run as they always have, and I'm taking a little time off as I get to know everyone in California. It's starting to feel like home, though most days I'm pretty sure I'm waking up in some sort of dream.

When Spencer goes to practice, I drive an hour to the vineyard that will be mine after all the proper paperwork is filed. I check in on the other vineyard that is set to be mine, too, and then I head back home, stare out over the bay, and wait for Spencer to join me for dinner.

Amelia steps tentatively out of her office when she hears voices. She's never been tentative a day in her life, and I can't help but wonder what's up with her.

"Theo, this is my sister, Amelia," I say.

He purses his lips and narrows his eyes. "I've heard about you, too," he says, and I'm certain he's teasing since I've reserved my gossip where she's concerned other than to tell him we don't always get along.

But I do feel like I have a sister I get along with now. Over the last month, I've grown closer to my sister-in-law, Ava...the one whose dress I wore to my own wedding.

She texted me when she heard from Grayson that Spencer and I were back together and I was moving to California, and she commiserates with me about what it's like being married to a football player when he's in season.

She's quickly become one of my best friends, and we're both looking forward to December when the Vegas Aces come out to San Diego to play the Storm—mostly so we can spend the weekend hanging out on the balcony and gossiping about the other football wives we've met.

I mean...sharing industry secrets.

Never gossiping.

"I'm just kidding," Theo says, and he hugs Amelia, too.

"Can I talk to you?" Amelia asks me quietly after Theo spots Nana and beelines for his half-sister.

I nod, and I squeeze Spencer's hand before I head into her office. She closes the door behind me.

"What's going on?" I ask.

"I, uh…just wanted to apologize to you. I know I've been an asshole to you your entire life, and you never deserved that."

She lifts a shoulder. "Well, you didn't *always* deserve that. Especially not the mustard thing. I just got so hellbent on *winning* that I stopped caring about who I'd hurt. But the truth is that you always deserved the vineyard."

"What's bringing this on?" I ask, not trusting that she's being genuine with me.

She blows out a breath. "I'm pregnant."

"You're…you're *what?*"

"Pregnant," she repeats.

"Drew's?" I ask.

She shrugs. "I'm not sure."

"Oh, Amelia," I say. "What are you going to do?"

She sighs. "I don't know."

"It's either Drew's or…?" I trail off to allow her to fill in the blank, and I hope it's only one.

"Pete."

I nod. "You know about the will, right?"

"Yeah. Dad told me when he walked in on Pete and me in the kitchen a few weeks ago." She cringes at the memory.

Sometimes I wonder how it's possible that we're related at all when we're so different from each other. The idea of being in a relationship and stepping outside of it would just never occur to me. Yeah, my own sister is cheating on her husband after she was cheating on *my* husband back when they were together. It hurts my heart to know that this is how she treats people, but it shouldn't be fully unexpected considering how she has treated me my entire life.

Still, this might be the first time I actually feel bad for her.

I was young when Mom and Dad split up, so I don't know all the reasons why their marriage didn't work. Given the fact that my mother remarried, and my father has remained single his entire life, I have a pretty strong inclination that she stepped outside. I'd venture to guess that he was so hurt by it that he never found it in himself to get into another relationship.

And if Amelia was old enough to witness that, I could see how it might affect her in a way that made her feel like that's what relationships are supposed to be, whereas I was oblivious to what was really going on. Instead, I sympathized with my dad, who I was closer to anyway.

I wish I could sit here and tell my sister that I'm here to help her or that I'll be with her through this as she navigates the difficult situations that will surely arise from being pregnant and not knowing who the father is.

But I can't be that person for her.

We're not close, we've never been close, and a single apology when someone is hit with the blunt force of her own actions would never be enough for me to get over the lifetime of hurt she's caused me.

Still, she's bringing a baby—my niece or nephew—into this world, and that precious child doesn't deserve to have its mother's terrible actions held against him or her.

"Have you told anyone?" I ask.

She shakes her head. "I didn't know who to turn to."

"So you turned to me?" I ask, holding a hand to my chest.

"I know I'm a dick, but I see the way you live your life, Gracie. You're doing things the right way, and I guess I've always been the screw-up. I took that out on you."

Wow. I guess pregnancy really fucks with a mother's brain.

I nod. "You did, and while I can forgive you, I won't forget. I don't know that I'll ever trust you, Amelia. One conversation doesn't change the twenty-five years of hell you put me through."

She lifts a shoulder. "Not the college years when I was gone. Oh, except when I hid all your socks when I was home for break. Okay, fine. Not the years I was a teacher and only came back once in a while."

I flatten my lips pointedly. She still managed to make my life hell even then by waltzing in and pulling Spencer right out from under me.

But I ended up where I was supposed to be. I'm twenty-five, and I own two wineries. I'm married to an NFL star who happens to be the absolute man of my dreams, and our entire future feels like it's right in front of us. The possibilities are endless.

It all worked out how it was supposed to. For me, anyway. I'm not so sure what Amelia's future holds.

And later, once Spencer and I have retired back to my bungalow and we're lying in bed after a particularly exhausting round of sex followed by a shower together, he asks the question he's been waiting to ask all day. "What did Amelia want to talk to you about?"

I pause for a beat as I draw little circles on that perfect abdomen of his. "She's pregnant."

"Oh, shit. Drew's?" he asks.

"She isn't sure."

"Damn."

"Yeah, you lucked out with the Newman sister you ended up with."

He chuckles and taps me on the nose. "I thank the stars every single night for that. And, you know, Elvis."

"You thank Elvis?"

He laughs. "When he said we 'Can't Help Falling in Love,' and that's what brought us to the chapel that night, I think he was right. He knew even before we did. So as long as you 'Don't be Cruel,' I promise I won't be a 'Hound Dog.'" He presses a kiss to my temple.

I giggle as I look up at him, and I see the love he has for me as he gazes down. I shift up to press a soft kiss to his lips.

Wedding the wide receiver turned out to be the best drunken mistake I've ever made.

Bonus Epilogue: Grace Nash

Benadryl, Tequila, and Elvis

One Year After the Wedding

"It's time. Are you nervous?" my dad asks me.

"You know, I was too drunk to be nervous the first time, and I'm too happy to be nervous the second time."

He chuckles. "That's my girl. You're stunning, by the way. Let's get you down the aisle toward your husband."

I glance over at my dad in his tux. I'm sad we missed out on all the pomp and circumstance of a wedding the first time, but we're doing it right this time. It's hard to believe a year ago we were in Vegas, and I was wearing Ava's dress as we drunkenly got married so he could get revenge on Amelia and I could get my vineyard.

How very much things have changed in the last year.

Amelia is nearly eight months pregnant—and huge. She's having a girl.

Pete was fired once he admitted he's the one who sprinkled the ground mustard on my food the night of Corks for a Cause. But as it turns out, the test she had done determined Pete wasn't the father.

It's Drew.

Their divorce has been final for two months now, but he's still our head cellar worker. Maybe he's overpaid, but he's good at what he does, and I wasn't about to get rid of a good employee because of my sister.

He wants to be involved in his baby's life, and it really does seem like Amelia is trying to turn over a new leaf. They are no longer together, but since they both live here at the vineyard, it's a best-case scenario for the baby to be around both of her parents.

My sister and I are still not close, but she has stepped up in my absence here—and for her baby. I'm proud of her for trying, but I've spent the majority of my time in San Diego, so we haven't had the chance to make amends for the past. I can't wait to meet my niece, though, and I just know that holding her in my arms is going to give me my own dose of baby fever.

My matron of honor today is Ava, and I happen to be wearing her dress—again. It's on loan for the occasion, and it was actually *her* idea for me to wear it.

I didn't tell Spencer, but I know he'll recognize it the second he sees me in it.

My dad drives us from my bungalow over toward the Grand Hall where our ceremony today is taking place, and I see the chairs set up outside on this perfect Wednesday at the end of April as we pull up. My dad pulls up behind the hedges where the bride always hides before making her grand entrance.

Ava hugs me before she walks down the aisle with Grayson, Spencer's best man. They're the only two standing up with us today, and somehow it felt right to have them here. Spencer's other two brothers served as ushers for our guests, and once they're seated and Ava walks down the aisle with Grayson, the music changes, and it's my turn.

I take my dad's offered elbow.

"Go get 'em, Gigi," he says, and then we start our walk down the aisle.

I spot the recognition in Spencer's eyes the minute he sees me as his eyes sweep down my dress. And I recognize what he's wearing, too—the tux Grayson wore when he married Ava. I can't help but think that this was her doing too, and there's something really sweet about that. It feels like they're on our side, even after everything that happened. And this feels like the start of something new.

It's our one-year anniversary, and it's a chance for us to renew our vows in front of our friends and family and then celebrate our union with them in a way we didn't get to do the first time.

As I walk down the aisle, my eyes connect with my husband's as he waits for me.

For just a brief moment, I break my gaze and allow myself to live in this moment. I look around at our guests. The Grand Hall is beyond and to the right of where Spencer is standing, but the backdrop to our wedding is the rolling hills and the lake below. Instead of having our reception in the Grand Hall, the barn has been transformed into a wedding wonderland.

I can't wait to party, but first we'll say our vows in front of the family and friends who are most important to us.

My entire family is here, including my great-uncle Theo. On the other side of the aisle is Spencer's family, including both of his parents. New and old teammates, and Heidi and Delilah and Sylvia and others who are like family to us are here, too. My old group of college girlfriends are here, along with new friends I've made in California.

I feel the love for us here today, both as individuals and as a couple.

When I first proposed this outrageous idea of marriage to him, in my wildest dreams, I couldn't have imagined that this is where we would end up just a year later—all thanks to Benadryl, tequila, and Elvis.

It's not Elvis this time but rather Nana, who hasn't had any further health scares, who is presiding over our ceremony today. She ended up signing both wineries over to me a few months ago. She wanted to do it while she was still here to watch it happen, and she tells me often how proud she is of me.

I'm proud of me, too.

I've kept my sister on despite the beef we often have with one another. You can't choose your family, and if I could have, I'm not sure I would've chosen her. But she's still family, and my dad and Nana are good at keeping her in line when I'm not in town.

Today is meant to remind us of our promises to one another. But this time, these promises are made in the sacred covenant of what a marriage is supposed to be, rather than the drunken haze of our first go at this.

This time we're both of fully sound mind, body, and spirit, and this time we're vowing forever with the intent for it to actually last forever.

"Welcome all to the blessed union of Spencer and Gracie," Nana begins. "I'm honored they chose me to preside today, and I want to start with a little story about these two. It was around January last year when I first took notice that something was wrong with my dear Spencer. His eyes were sad as he sat out back by the firepit, and it wasn't the twinkling of the fire that helped him roar back to life. As I stared outside from the tasting room at this boy I'd grown to love as much as my own grandchildren, I saw Gracie settle into the chair beside him. His eyes sparked with life, and later, when she confessed to me that she had feelings for Spencer, I had a feeling that someday we'd end up right where we are now. I'm pleased that everything worked out as it was supposed to, and I'm even more excited as I watch them talk animatedly about their plans for the wineries under their care. The couple has decided to exchange their own vows, and we'll begin with Spencer."

She nods at Spencer, who draws in a deep breath. He grabs a sheet of paper out of the pocket inside his lapel, glances at it, and then slides it back into his pocket.

He takes both my hands in his, and I see the love in his eyes as he starts to speak the vows he's making to me.

"Can you believe we've been doing this a whole year? In some ways, it was the hardest year of my life, but in other ways, it was the easiest. I love you, Grace Nash, and today I want to make you the promises that'll carry us through the rest of our lives. I promise to never go more than a week without being together. I promise to be your best friend. I promise to check your food for mustard." Our guests laugh at that, and they laugh even more at his next promise. "I promise to keep Benadryl handy, but also not to mix it with tequila unless it's on purpose. I promise to dance with you to Elvis songs. I promise to raise any children we may be blessed to have with patience and love. I promise lots of glasses of wine, firepits, and walks on the beach in between handling all the responsibilities together at the two vineyards we're lucky enough to be running. Most of all, I promise to laugh with you, love you with everything I am, choose you first always, and tackle this thing called life with you through every challenge and every joy that's put in our path. I love you."

His lips tip up at the end, and he reaches over to thumb at a tear as it tracks down my cheek. It's a physical example of the love he has for me, and I think he pretty much covered all the bases with those promises. He even told me he'd choose me first always—one of the most important parts of why we work so well now. Showing up for each other, choosing each other, and putting each other first.

I have no idea how to follow that up.

"And now for your vows, Grace," Nana says.

I look up into Spencer's eyes, and I see my home. I draw in a deep breath before I start speaking from the heart.

"I wasn't sure what to write. I'm never a last-minute person, which you all know about me." He chuckles, as does the group of our friends and family gathered here for us, before I continue. "But I knew when I got to this moment, my heart would tell me what to say. We're both logical and responsible, but something about our love story is neither of those things, and I think that's what makes it so special. You are my home. Whether it's here in Cedar Creek, in Temecula, at the apartment in San Diego, or even when we're traveling to Vegas or Mexico, if you're by my side, I'm home. I promise to be home for you, too, no matter where in the world we find ourselves. I promise to take on the challenges that face us with logic, but I promise to make decisions with love. I promise to keep you safe, whether it's from mustard or tequila or some combination thereof. I promise to love you, honor you, and remain faithful to only you always, and I promise that you and our life together will always top my priority list. I love you."

He leans in and presses a gentle, tender kiss to my lips, and Nana clicks her tongue behind us. "I haven't told you to kiss her yet," she scolds Spencer, drawing a huge laugh from our guests.

She finishes the ceremony, including the part where we exchange rings. He wanted to redesign mine, and as he slips it onto my finger, I see that he added three beautiful emerald-cut diamonds to my original band. I slip his original band on his finger, too, and when she pronounces our vows renewed, he dips me down and kisses me in a way that is neither gentle nor tender but is perfect for us.

We head to the barn to party with our loved ones and dance to a variety of songs—including a lot by Elvis, of course—and when the night is over and we've returned to the bungalow where we're still living when we're here for now, he unwraps me out of the gown that is part mine and part Ava's. He sets it gently over a chair, and he stares at me as I stand in front of him in my lacy white lingerie. He rushes over to me and pulls me against him, and the fabric of the tux he's wearing is heated against my skin.

"I love you, my wife," he says.

"I love you, too, hubby. Should we start making babies now?"

He laughs. "I'm ready when you are." He pulls back and spins me around. "Goddamn, I'm one lucky man. You want it slow and sweet tonight or down and dirty?"

I pretend to think for all of two seconds, but there's only one right answer here. "Down and dirty."

He raises a brow, and I think he might laugh, but his face is stone-cold serious.

"I want you to take control and make me come until I see stars."

And when we both finish and we're panting and breathless, our eyes connect in this sweet, intimate moment after the workout we just put the other through. It wasn't *down and dirty*, exactly, because every moment we're together like this has meaning and intimacy connected to it.

That closeness, that love, that tenderness, is what keeps me warm on the nights he has to travel for work or when we can't be together for some other reason.

But no matter what, marrying Spencer Nash one drunken night in Vegas turned out to be the best thing I've ever done, and it won't be long before that dream I had of my husband handing me a glass of wine while we watch our kids play in the backyard of our vineyard becomes reality.

THE END

Acknowledgments

Thank you first as always to my husband! Thanks for inventing hours for me to write, for supporting me, and for being the best dad to our sweet babies. I love having you as part of my team, and I love the family we've created together.

Thank you Valentine PR for your incredible work on the launch of this series and this book.

Thank you to Valentine Grinstead, Diane Holtry, Christine Yates, Billie DeSchalit, and Serena Cracchiolo for beta and proofreading. I value your insight and comments so much.

Thank you to Renee McCleary for all you do.

Thank you to my ARC Team for loving this sports world that is so real to us. Thank you to the members of the Vegas Aces Spoiler Room and Team LS, and all the influencers and bloggers for reading, reviewing, posting, and sharing.

And finally, thank YOU for reading. I can't wait to bring more football and more Nash family! I'm so excited for what's coming next!

Cheers until next season!

xoxo,

Lisa Suzanne

About the Author

Lisa Suzanne is an Amazon Top Ten Bestselling author of swoon-worthy superstar heroes, emotional roller coasters, and all the angst. She resides in Arizona with her husband and two kids. When she's not chasing her kids, she can be found working on her latest romance book or watching reruns of *Friends*.

Also by Lisa Suzanne

DATING THE DEFENSIVE BACK
(The Nash Brothers #1)

THE COACH
(A Vegas Aces Complete Series)

FIND MORE AT AUTHORLISASUZANNE.COM/BOOKS

Made in the USA
Coppell, TX
28 August 2024

36562372R00218